FINAL EXAM

FINAL EXAM

MAGGIE BARBIERI

THORNDIKE
CHIVERS

This Large Print edition is published by Thorndike Press, Waterville, Maine, USA and by BBC Audiobooks Ltd, Bath, England.

Thorndike Press, a part of Gale, Cengage Learning.

A Murder 101 Mystery.

The text of this Large Print edition is unabridged.

Other aspects of the book may vary from the original edition.

Set in 16 pt. Plantin.

Printed on permanent paper.

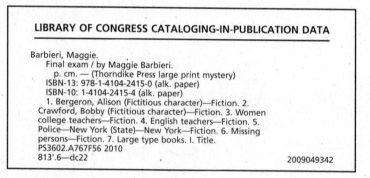

LIBRARY OF CONGRESS CATALOGING-IN-PUBLICATION DATA

Barbieri, Maggie.
  Final exam / by Maggie Barbieri.
    p. cm. — (Thorndike Press large print mystery)
  ISBN-13: 978-1-4104-2415-0 (alk. paper)
  ISBN-10: 1-4104-2415-4 (alk. paper)
    1. Bergeron, Alison (Fictitious character)—Fiction. 2. Crawford, Bobby (Fictitious character)—Fiction. 3. Women college teachers—Fiction. 4. English teachers—Fiction. 5. Police—New York (State)—New York—Fiction. 6. Missing persons—Fiction. 7. Large type books. I. Title.
  PS3602.A767F56 2010
  813'.6—dc22   2009049342

BRITISH LIBRARY CATALOGUING-IN-PUBLICATION DATA AVAILABLE

Published in 2010 in the U.S. by arrangement with St. Martin's Press, LLC.

Published in 2010 in the U.K. by arrangement with the author.

U.K. Hardcover: 978 1 408 47836 3 (Chivers Large Print)
U.K. Softcover: 978 1 408 47837 0 (Camden Large Print)

Printed in the United States of America
1 2 3 4 5 6 7 14 13 12 11 10

*To my parents, Peggy and Ken Scarry,
whose karaoke/book-signing parties
words cannot describe*

ACKNOWLEDGMENTS

Thank you never seems like enough, but it will have to do.

Thank you to Deborah Schneider, my agent and friend.

Thank you to Kelley Ragland, Matt Martz, and Sarah Melnyk at St. Martin's Press/Minotaur Books for your attention to detail and good humor while dealing with one not-so-detail-oriented author who looks and sounds suspiciously like me.

Thank you to my posse at NYU (in no particular order of importance; you can fight that one out among yourselves): Rosie Smith, Kathy Madden, Rajni Kannan, Caroline Sorlie, Crystal Jan, Joanne Staha (Nurse Joanne!), Norma Sparks, and Anna Pavlick. Wow — this bus ride is a long one and I can't believe how much I'm enjoying it!

Thank you to my extended family and to my wonderful husband, Jim, and to my children who are rapidly becoming too old to call "children," Dea and Patrick.

ONE

"I'm Mary Magdalene!"

Now that got my attention. I was leaning against a wall in one of the dorm's dining halls, scanning the crowd in a laconic fashion for anyone drinking an illegal substance and hoping I could get in on that action. We're a dry campus. And let me tell you, there are some people who teach here who just need to get lit.

I was bored silly. Until I saw one of my best friends in the world, Father Kevin McManus, school chaplain and all-around nice guy, cutting a rug to some Kanye West song with another chaperone, a member of the sociology department. Nancy Weineger was married, a mother of four, and about fifty years old. She favored the peasant-skirt-cum-clog look, and tonight she was also wearing a white cardigan sweater with, curiously, a lacy camisole underneath it. I had always thought of her as more of an

Elisabeth, the proud mother of John the Baptist. It never would have crossed my mind that she fancied herself Mary Magdalene, a woman of (ahem) bad character.

I don't read the Bible and I hardly ever go to church, but what seventeen-year-old, upon learning that the Bible boasted a prostitute, hasn't sat up and taken notice? I heard it lo those many years ago and it had stuck with me ever since. And oh yes, I had highlighted every passage devoted to her. Because if the Bible has a hooker, well, I'm in, even if it never actually calls her a hooker.

I stood up a little straighter as Kevin turned in mid-gyration and looked at me, his eyes wide behind his tortoise-framed eyeglasses. Nancy was doing some kind of cross between a clog dance and the chicken dance and getting progressively closer to Kevin as the song built to a rap-flavored crescendo. We were at a post–spring break faculty mixer that has a history of being the most boring event to be held anywhere. Ever. But it's a command performance and you can't just make a quick appearance and then duck out because the president, Mark Etheridge, thinks he's very clever and prepares awards for everyone, which he hands out only after the buffet dinner has been served. So, if you're not there to accept your "Worst Parallel Parker!" award, you'll hear about it. You can't get out of it by using an excuse — not even my old standby (diarrhea) because he's on to that one.

Nancy was working herself into a frenzy, so Kevin danced closer to me.

"Cut in," he said breathlessly.

I cupped a hand to my ear, faking deafness. "What?" I asked. "I can't hear you."

"Cut in," he said a little louder as Nancy grabbed his arm and dragged him back out into the middle of the floor.

I love to dance — in the privacy of my bedroom. There, I perform nightly. It's a one-woman show and the audience consists of my golden retriever, Trixie, and, I just learned, the prepubescent kid across the street. I caught him with binoculars the week before, peering through my second-story bedroom window. When confronted, he claimed to be concerned that I was having a seizure. But Kevin needed help, and being as he's the one who's usually bailing me out, I felt like I needed to repay the favor. I put down my glass of flat Diet Coke and disco-strutted onto the dance floor. I grabbed Kevin around the waist and spun him around because while he's quick and fit thanks to a childhood filled with Irish dancing and boxing lessons, he's also more of a flyweight to my bantamweight. And he's also a good three inches shorter than I am so that when we do dance together at school functions, I always lead. It's the curse of the tall girl. Or the bossy one. I can't decide which is more accurate.

As I prepared to get down to "Gold Digger," the mood, and song, changed abruptly and we found ourselves slow-dancing to "Wind Beneath My Wings," the top of Kevin's head grazing the bottom of my chin. He's one of my two best friends in this world, so nobody thought twice about seeing us in this terpsichorean clinch, yet I suddenly felt suitably uncomfortable and so we beat a hasty retreat from the dance floor — or middle of the dining hall, as the case may be — and into two open chairs at a small round table.

One of the reasons I love Kevin is because he's an inveterate gossip. The minute we sat down, he leaned in conspiratorially. "So, I guess you heard what happened to Wayne Brookwell?"

I shook my head. "Nope." Unless Kevin tells me, I have no idea what goes on on campus. I flagged down a passing student who was a server for the party and probably getting either community service hours or

12

work study credit for her time. I asked her for two Diet Cokes. "But before we get to that, what's with you and Nancy Weineger? Or should I say, 'Mary Magdalene'?"

Kevin shook his head, clearly embarrassed. "She's one of those wacky Catholics who fall in love with priests. I've seen it a thousand times."

He had? This was a new phenomenon to me. I'd heard of "Fr. What-a-Waste" — the handsome priest who devotes himself to Christ rather than a woman — but I didn't see Kevin in that role. My incredibly handsome boyfriend had once confessed to thinking about becoming a priest. Him? He would have been the ultimate Fr. What-a-Waste. Kevin? Not so much. "Explain."

"Nothing to explain," he said, taking a sip of the soda that had been delivered to our table. "The collar turns some people on." He was pretty matter-of-fact, confident that his collar was setting libidos ablaze, so I took him at his word.

"Interesting." I poked him in the ribs with my elbow. "Ever think of taking her up on it?" I asked, only half joking.

He gave me a horrified look. "No!" He smoothed down the front of his black clerical shirt. "I have to be careful with these kinds of situations. You know that."

"I do know that," I said. "Just joking, Kev."

"Besides," he said, "you know the archdiocese isn't my biggest fan."

I knew that, too. Kevin had been sent to St. Thomas after several complaints from parishioners at the church in which he had been installed prior to this job. Something about repeated sermons about the cardinal and his champagne tastes, which was fine, if said cardinal wasn't closing churches and parochial schools with wild abandon due to lack of funds. The archdiocese figured that sticking him at a Catholic college with a small enrollment and a host of blind and deaf nuns was better than having him preach the Gospel at a thriving parish. So far, Kevin had made it work. And he had made my teaching here that much more enjoyable through our delightful, yet unorthodox, friendship.

He looked around and leaned in again. "So, Wayne Brookwell?"

"Remind me who he is again?" I drank my second flat Diet Coke and made a face. "This would be much better with a shot of rum." Unless I broke into the nurse's office and got us all a shot of Robitussin, flat Diet Coke would have to do.

"He was the resident director over at

Siena Hall."

I filed through my brain, trying to remember him. "Tall? Gangly? Just misses at handsome?"

Kevin did a finger gun at me. "Bingo." He looked around again, obviously afraid of being overheard. But "Wind Beneath My Wings" was reaching its crescendo and I could barely hear him, never mind the people standing at least five feet behind us. "He's gone. His room's cleaned out, and he didn't let anyone know he was leaving. Dean Merrimack has no idea where he is or why he left."

Merrimack was the director of student housing and a general douche nozzle, a word I had heard one of my students using. I tried it out in my head and kind of liked the way it fit. "Well, I can't imagine that RD is that fulfilling of a job. Maybe he got something else," I said, not really caring what had happened to Wayne Brookwell or why he left so unceremoniously. "Maybe he got deployed?" I said. "Didn't I see him in a uniform?"

"Yes, as a limo driver," Kevin said. "He had a side job driving executives to the airport."

"Are you even allowed to do that?" Maybe moonlighting could solve my problem of funding a vacation to France. I mulled over a second career as a barista until Kevin brought me back to the conversation by waving his hand in front of my face. I refocused. "What are they going to do about another RD? Once spring break is over, there's only five weeks left for the semester."

Kevin shrugged. "I have no idea. I know that a couple of the guys who live in the dorm drive limos, too, to make extra money." He looked around the room, taking in the styles of our colleagues and commenting on their dance moves. "I think this whole thing with Wayne is extremely suspicious," he said pointedly after he had finished dance-hall reconnaissance, raising an eyebrow at me.

I stared back at him. "Oh, no you don't," I said, finally seeing where he was going with this conversation. "My sleuthing days are over."

"But where did he go? Aren't you the least bit interested?" he asked, working himself up to the point where he had to down his Diet Coke in one swallow to quench his thirst.

"Couldn't care less." The only reason I knew who Wayne Brookwell was that he bore a passing resemblance to my cousin Armand — quite the cheesemaker and

16

cocksman according to my very proud, and very late mother — from Baie Ste. Paul in Quebec. Other than that, I wouldn't have known him from Adam.

Something over my shoulder caught Kevin's eye and he sat up straight. "Pull yourself together. It's Etheridge."

Mark Etheridge, in addition to being the president of our college, is also not my biggest fan. He's *mezzo mezzo* on Kevin because of Kevin's lackadaisical attitude toward the pomp and circumstance of Catholicism but has a certain amount of respect for him because he's a priest. Me, I'm just a nontenured professor who's been involved in a few too many skirmishes with the law, mostly stemming from my being involved in a few too many murder investigations. See? Nothing serious. I felt Mark's presence behind me and my back straightened instinctively, too.

"Father. Dr. Bergeron," he said by way of a greeting.

I turned in my chair. "Hello, President Etheridge," I said, trying my best to hide my disdain. What president of a school with a mere twelve hundred students insists on being called "President"? Mark Etheridge, that's who. He and I have a tenuous relationship at best; at worst, we're archenemies, just like in a comic book. I'm "Big Tall Girl" and he's "Little Short Man" and we engage in mortal combat every so often. I still don't have tenure and I'm betting he's behind it because even though my direct boss, Sister Mary, isn't really crazy about my off-hours pursuits — basically, murder investigations — she thinks I'm a good teacher. And not for nothing, but my doctoral dissertation was a masterpiece, if I do say so myself. That should count for something. But Etheridge doesn't like the body count and I don't like that he's just not very nice to me. I remained seated so that I wouldn't tower over him.

"When you get a moment, Dr. Bergeron, I'd like to see you in my office," he said, turning on his heel and walking away.

I guessed that meant now.

Kevin watched in wide-eyed amazement. "Wow. That was rude, even for Etheridge." He pushed his chair back and stood. "You'd better go. Do you think this has to do with tenure?"

I took one last sip of liquid courage — flat Diet Coke — and stood. "I doubt it." I smoothed my skirt and headed across the dance floor. I called back to Kevin, "Wish me luck!"

He crossed his fingers and held them in

the air. "Good luck!"

I didn't realize just how badly I would need it.

TWO

I followed close on Etheridge's heels to his office in the Administration Building. When I got there, Sister Mary was there as was Dean Merrimack, for whom I had decided "douche nozzle" was way too kind a moniker. Etheridge waved generously toward the only open seat across from his desk. Sister Mary kept her eyes on her hands while Merrimack stared at me with his rat eyes as if I were a piece of cheese. I sat, placing myself as close as I could to the edge of the chair without falling off. This wasn't about tenure and that was painfully obvious.

"I guess you're wondering why I asked you here on a Friday evening," Etheridge said, his eyes glinting behind his Teddy Roosevelt–style horn rims. Out the window behind his head, I could see the bones of a new dorm taking shape.

I stared back at him until it became obvious that I was going to remain silent.

He harrumphed a bit and rearranged himself in his chair. "Well, as you may or may not know, Wayne Brookwell, the resident director at Siena dorm, has unceremoniously left his position."

I continued staring back at him, not sure why I was hearing about Wayne Brookwell not once, but twice, in the same evening. I could barely pick the guy out of a lineup but everyone seemed very concerned about his whereabouts. And I suspected that I should probably be more concerned about his disappearance, too.

"And that, Dr. Bergeron, is where you come in," Dean Merrimack said, close to orgasm in his chair.

"Oh, my sleuthing days are over," I said, as much to convince myself as to convince them.

Etheridge gave me a withering look. "We're not interested in your sleuthing skills, Alison."

I slid a little closer to the edge of my chair, close to tipping it over. "Then why am I here?"

Etheridge looked down at the desk calendar that took up most of his desk and counted the number of weeks left in the semester. "We have five weeks left in the semester, Alison, and we need someone to

21

take Resident Director Brookwell's place until school ends."

I looked over at Sister Mary, who continued to stare at her hands. Her complexion flushed pink all the way up to the hairline of her sensible, gray permanent. Panic was starting to take hold and I felt a little short of breath. "No, I can't . . . ," I said, my voice wavering.

"Yes you can. You must." Etheridge pushed back from his desk. "So, that's settled. Shall we go back to the party?"

"No, we should not go back to the party!" I exclaimed, jumping up from my chair, surprising everyone. The force of my ejection sent the chair flying backward and everyone in the room regarded it with horror. "I have a life. I have a dog. My best friend is going through a horrible separation from her husband and living with me. I have a boyfriend," I said, realizing too late how inane that sounded. "I cannot . . . ," I said, grabbing the edge of Etheridge's desk, "move into the Siena dorm."

Etheridge gave me a steely look. "You can. And you will." He came out from behind his desk and stood before his floor-to-ceiling bookcases. I had once made Kevin a bet that the bookcases only housed decorative spines, and not real books. I suddenly had an urge to race over and pull one of the books down just to check, but I suspected that action wouldn't be a big hit. "You can begin to move your things in this weekend."

"No, I can't," I said.

Etheridge moved closer to me and the air got uncomfortably warm in the dark-paneled room. I towered over him by a good four inches. "Dr. Bergeron, your tenure — or lack thereof — here has been marred by your 'sleuthing' as you call it," he said, finger-quoting, "and the people who love this university are not pleased." We were now just a few inches apart, close-talking to one another. "And by the university, I mean the board. And our donors. One dead body was one thing, but the untimely death of your former husband?" I heard Mary mutter a prayer under her breath for my murdered ex. "That was just too much, even though it had nothing to do with you. You spend too much time in pursuits other than those required of an academic. So being on campus full-time should allow you to focus entirely on St. Thomas, your courses, and your students."

"I love this university!" I protested. Just because a dead student had once been found in the trunk of my car and my ex-husband had been dismembered in my

23

kitchen didn't mean that I didn't love St. Thomas. After all, I had graduated from here years before. They could question my judgment, but they couldn't question my loyalty to the school. "And is anyone concerned about what happened to Wayne?" I asked, sounding way more familiar with him than I was.

"We're looking into his disappearance," Merrimack replied.

"I hope so," I said. Still, he didn't sound terribly concerned, which gave me pause. "Did you call the police?"

Etheridge and Merrimack exchanged a look that could only be described as "fraught," but with what, I had no idea.

Etheridge started for the door, not answering my question. "As for your *boyfriend?*" he said, with a sneer. "Detective Crawford, I presume?" His hand was on the knob and Merrimack was right behind him. "He'll just have to wait."

I ran over all of the options in my head and concluded that I didn't have any. I decided to go with the path of least resistance with one minor caveat. "Fine. But the dog's coming with me." I straightened my spine and attempted to sound unyielding. I really didn't have anything to bargain with but I hoped Etheridge had a heart.

Merrimack decided to exert his influence at that moment. "We don't allow animals on campus."

If that were the case, I thought, you'd be out of a job, Rat Boy. I wisely kept my mouth shut and appealed to Etheridge. "Listen, she's a wonderful animal and very docile. I can't leave her at the house."

Etheridge considered this and decided to confine his cruelty merely to making me move in. "The dog can come."

I heard Mary let out a sigh of relief, for what I wasn't sure. I hadn't pegged her as a dog lover, but you never know. I also knew that she wasn't mute, though she had done nothing to disprove that during this meeting.

Etheridge opened the door and gestured that I should leave. He smiled as I walked past him and into his secretary's area, vacant at this time of day. "I think this will work out very nicely. Consider it extra credit." He chuckled. "Dean Merrimack will give you the Code of Conduct folder and all of the other necessary information you'll need to execute your tasks. We'll expect you to be ensconced in your suite by Monday morning, latest."

"Code of Conduct?" I asked.

Merrimack rubbed his rat hands together.

"Yes. For instance, coeducational visitation ends at eleven P.M."

My heart sank. That was going to put a serious crimp in my relationship with Crawford.

"And we're, of course, a dry campus."

I already knew that, obviously, and I didn't want to hear anything else. I did know that I was going to go home and mainline Ketel One like an addict on their way to rehab. I looked impassively at Merrimack and held out my hands. "Keys, please?"

He dropped an ancient-looking set of keys into my palm. "The black key is the front door and the other key is to your suite. The one with the red dot on it is the school master key. It is imperative that you do not lose that one especially."

Got it, chief. Don't lose the master key. It was a wonder they paid me a salary, so handicapped did they consider me. I knew that "suite" was probably a very misleading term to describe my new accommodations, so I didn't get my hopes up. I had seen one of the resident director's quarters once, twenty years earlier when I was a student. I was sure things hadn't changed dramatically since that time.

I walked out into the hallway outside of

Etheridge's office cursing a blue streak in my head. I stopped by my office and picked up my bag, papers spilling out and reminding me that my spring break was supposed to have been spent grading. But now I was moving, and with the lack of grading I had done, I was up the creek.

Before I left my office, I clicked on the school intranet and looked up Wayne Brookwell. There was a picture and a bio. He was exactly who I thought he was — skinny, with a square jaw and eyes just a little too closely set. His mouth hung open slightly in the picture, giving me the impression that he was an habitual mouth breather. Just missed at being handsome, as I had reported to Kevin. He was the guy I would have dated in college, while Max, my best friend, would have dated his dumber, yet much better looking, roommate. I read his bio: "Wayne Brookwell graduated from Syracuse University with a degree in art history," I read. That degree made him perfectly suited to a life as a resident director because, God knows, without a master's degree, he wasn't getting a job anywhere outside of the souvenir shop at the Metropolitan Museum of Art. No offense to art history majors. The bio was brief, but to the point. It said that Wayne was twenty-six but didn't make any mention of his moonlighting career as a limousine driver. I stared at his picture. "We've never met, Mr. Brookwell, but you've ruined my life. I hope you're happy."

He stared back at me, in all of his slack-jawed awesomeness.

"Where did you go, Wayne?" I asked, staring at the picture for a few more minutes. When Wayne didn't answer, I printed out his picture and folded it up so that it would fit in the front of my briefcase. I turned off the computer and headed home to give the news to my new roommate, Max, that I was moving out for several weeks.

And to let my dog, Trixie, know that we had a new home.

And to let Crawford know that his level of sexual frustration — at a fever pitch since I had inherited Max as a roommate — was about to increase tenfold.

THREE

I was in a foul mood when I got home and even the sight of my gorgeous boyfriend — I had recently come to terms with using that word to describe him vis à vis our decidedly middle-aged romance — sitting in his sedate Volkswagen Passat station wagon at the curb did nothing to lift my spirits. I left my car in the driveway and stomped down to where he was parked; he was in a coma in the front seat, and when I jerked open the driver's side door, he sat up with a start, his hand going instinctively to the gun on his hip.

I held up my hands. "Don't shoot!" I hollered. "It's me." This night was off to a really bad start. I thought it couldn't get any worse, but ending up with a slug in the chest would really ruin things for good.

He put his hand over his heart. "Don't do that!" he said, relaxing only slightly when he realized who it was. He swung a long leg out of the car and took in my sour demeanor. He pulled on his tie and smoothed it down, something that he did when he was at a loss for words. I've seen him pull on so many ties that I'm surprised he had any left that weren't twice as long as they should be. "What's wrong with you?"

"What's wrong with me?" I asked. "What's wrong with me? I'll tell you what's wrong with me," but I wasn't able to get out a coherent explanation.

When I didn't respond, just continued to gesticulate wildly, he looked at me quizzically. "So, what's wrong?"

I burst into tears. "I have to move into a dorm on campus!"

He leaned against the car and folded his arms across his chest, taking in my shaking shoulders and tear-streaked face. I had cried most of the way home. "Is that bad?" he asked, genuinely interested.

"Yes! It's bad!" I wiped my nose on the sleeve of my sweater before he had a chance to pull out the fresh, pressed handkerchief I knew he kept in his blazer pocket.

"Start at the beginning."

I hiccupped and coughed my way through the story and was in full-blown hysteria by the time I finished. He looked at me calmly. "So you'll be out by the end of the semester?"

I rooted around in my messenger bag for a tissue and came up with a previously used one. I smoothed it out and blew my nose. "Looks that way."

"And that's only about five weeks from now?"

I nodded.

He chewed on that for a minute and then held his arms open. I fell into them and took a whiff of his clean laundry scent, hoping that would help me pull myself together. "We'll manage. It's not that long," he said.

"I don't understand why Etheridge hates me so much," I sniffled.

"I don't, either," Crawford agreed unconvincingly. He knew exactly why Etheridge hated me but was too much of a gentleman to list the reasons. He led me up the walk to the front door. We sat down on the stoop and he wrapped an arm around my shoulders. My life for the last year had been unpredictable, to say the least. I had gotten divorced, been involved in three murder investigations, seen my best friend's marriage fall apart, and embarked on a relationship with this wonderful man, whose single status hadn't been quite so clear-cut when we met. And just when things started to right themselves, I ended up with a roommate (Max) and a new living situation (the dorm).

Can't a girl catch a break?

We sat for a few more minutes, watching cars travel back and forth on my usually quiet street. Spring was coming early and I could see some buds on the trees that stood sentry between two-story suburban homes and tidy, swept sidewalks. I could hear Trixie scratching at the front door from inside the house; she sensed that I was home and wanted to see me. I'm her reason for being, and sometimes, she's mine. Crawford hooked a thumb toward the house. "What's going on in there?"

"Oh, that's a whole other story," I said. Max had been living with me for a couple of weeks, having broken up with her husband, to whom she had been betrothed less than six months. As luck would have it, her husband was Crawford's longtime partner, another detective named Fred Wyatt.

He knew what was going on — from Fred's perspective probably and from my updates — but I guess he was hoping that his visiting wouldn't be an issue. Max was still extremely angry — at Fred and at men in general. "How's she doing?"

I shrugged. "How would you be doing?" I asked, my mind still on my predicament.

"Do you still want to come in?"

He thought about it for a moment. "I guess so, unless it's going to upset her."

I put one hand on the doorknob and the other on his face to get his attention. "Here's what we're going to do. If she's playing the Linda Ronstadt version of 'You're No Good,' and singing along, she's angry. If she's got Crystal Gayle's 'Don't It Make My Brown Eyes Blue,' she's sad."

"She has green eyes."

"Yes, I know, Captain Literal," I continued. "But if it's Alanis Morrisette," I said, putting my key into the back door, "run."

"Run?" His eyes showed a little flash of fear. He knew Max well and knew that she was overly dramatic and more than a little hostile right now. She was tiny but could be deadly.

"Run," I repeated. "Very fast."

I opened the door and peered inside. "Max? Hi! It's me," I called in, "and Crawford. Crawford's here," I repeated. "I've got Crawford with me." The sound of the television in the background told me nothing; I had come home on more than one occasion to find her gone and every appliance running. I turned and looked at him. "All clear."

Trixie gave us her usual adoring welcome,

jumping up on Crawford for a love fest. He let her lick his face a few times before pushing her down.

Max — one hundred pounds soaking wet with the appetite of a fleet of sailors — was ensconced on my living room sofa, eating a giant bowl of what appeared to be linguine carbonara, the remote in her other hand, her feet on my coffee table. She was wearing the same yoga pants and sports bra that she had been wearing for the last two days and her hair had seen better days, both in terms of cleanliness and highlights. She looked up and took in the two of us, standing tentatively in the hallway adjacent to the living room, then looked back to the TV. "Hey."

My first thought was to tell her that if she got that carbonara on my sofa she was toast, but I refrained. "How was your day?"

"My day?" she asked, shoveling another forkful of carbonara into her mouth. "Same as it ever was," she said, quoting a Talking Heads song. She had reverted to quoting songs from our youth to describe her situation and I was finding it exceedingly tedious.

Crawford looked at me questioningly. He doesn't exactly have his finger on the pulse of pop culture. I told him it didn't matter if he didn't understand what she meant.

"We're going to go into the kitchen and have a glass of wine. Do you want one?" I asked.

She picked a bottle of beer out from between the sofa cushions and held it aloft, her eyes never leaving the television.

"I take that as 'no, thank you'?" I said, raising an eyebrow. Crawford took my elbow and steered me toward the kitchen, Trixie in tow. As bad as I felt about Max's situation, I was starting to lose patience. She had been with me since she had found out that her new husband had had an affair with the Bronx medical examiner. And the ME's sister. But it had been ten years ago, which to me was well outside the statute of limitations on infidelity. Max's issue was that he was now working closely with the ME — she had just been transferred from some office in the bowels of hell or something like that — and he had never told Max about the affair or his new working relationship with the ME.

To which I say, "So what?" But I kept that to myself.

I understood her initial consternation; nobody likes their spouse's former lovers working in close proximity to them. But that's life. And it's messy. And if anyone knows from messy, it's me. My husband had been a champion philanderer, yet I had still felt sadness when he had been murdered. Messy, indeed.

Methinks someone — namely, Max, the former consummate party girl who had married Fred mere months after meeting him — was looking for a "get out of marriage free" card. One had been presented to her and she had played it.

Crawford sat at the kitchen table and I got a couple of wineglasses out of the cupboard. "Red or white?" I asked.

He settled on a new merlot that I had opened the night before. I poured him a healthy glass and finished the bottle off in my glass. I leaned against the counter. "Can you help me move?"

He rolled his eyes toward the living room. "When are you going to tell her?" he whispered.

I shrugged. "No idea." I repeated my initial question, "Can you help me move?"

"Of course."

"And can you help me find Wayne Brookwell?"

He chuckled.

"I'm not kidding."

"You're going to try to find him?" he asked, incredulous.

"Uh, yes," I said, equally incredulous that

36

he didn't think that that was the first item on my to-do list. "Did I mention that St. Thomas is a dry campus with limited coeducational visitation?"

"No drinking, no sex?"

I put my index finger on my nose. "Bingo."

He looked up at the ceiling; that got him thinking. Specifically, the faster we found Wayne, the faster we could get back to our lives. I watched him work through the details of the situation. Finally, he looked at me. "You're going to look for him whether or not I help you, so let me know what you need." I could tell he was resigned — but not totally opposed — to my snooping around.

I put my wineglass down and walked over to him, sitting on his lap. I gave him a long kiss. "Thanks, Crawford. I knew I could count on you." I kissed him again. "How are you going to occupy yourself while I'm in hell?"

He looked up at the ceiling again and thought about his answer. "I guess I'll have to go back to fantasizing about Fred until we get back together."

I got off his lap. "Come on. Let's go make out in the garage before I start packing."

FOUR

Max took my departure as I expected she would: she was alternately half delighted to have the house to herself and half horrified that she would be living in the suburbs by herself.

"This is not what I signed up for," she said to me the next morning, standing before me in our now-shared bedroom. I had one guest room but it held the detritus of my childhood, along with several boxes my ex had never retrieved before his untimely demise.

"Not what *you* signed up for?" I asked. Last I checked, I was single and shared my home with a dog. I had a boyfriend who could come and go as he pleased and spend the night when the opportunity arose. If anyone had been inconvenienced by her abrupt departure from her two-thousand-square-foot condo in SoHo, it wasn't her. I went into my closet and took out a small suitcase from the upper shelf. I threw in some work clothes along with some T-shirts and jeans since it appeared that my weekends would be spent doing desk duty or being "on call" as the resident directors were required to be every third weekend.

I was going to miss my bedroom. It was a beautiful, soothing cream color with white trim on the ornate moldings that I had put in right after my husband had bid adieu to me and our marriage. After that and the installation of elaborate woodwork, I had taken over the rather substantial closet that ran the length of the wall by the door. My bedding had set me back a small fortune, with high-thread-count sheets, a duvet with a down comforter inside, and a quilt on top. It was like being in a bed-and-breakfast while never leaving home.

Max flopped onto the bed, facedown. "What am I going to do here without you?"

I folded a dress shirt carefully so I wouldn't have to iron it when I took it out of the suitcase at my new residence. "Well, you can have the bed all to yourself. And you can use the computer when you want."

"Good. I signed up for Match.com."

I didn't mean to grab my heart, but that was my first reaction. "What?"

She rolled over and considered her big

toe. "You heard me."

I finished folding the shirt in my hands mostly to buy some time to craft an appropriate response. I placed it on top of the other clothes in the suitcase. I started with the obvious. "You've been separated for two weeks. Don't you think that's kind of soon?"

"Nope."

I sat down next to her and took a look around my bedroom, which I was sure wouldn't look quite as neat and tidy when I finally did return from my dorm "suite." "Max." I was at a loss for words. "Max," I repeated, my tone conveying my disappointment.

She looked at me quizzically. "Alison," she replied, sounding as grave as I felt.

I took her hand. "It's too soon. You're not ready for an emotional, let alone sexual, relationship right now." I knew how quickly she worked so jumping into bed with one of her "matches" was not out of the question.

"Oh, don't go all *Vagina Monologues* on me," she said.

I didn't know what she thought *The Vagina Monologues* were about and I didn't have the energy to tell her they have absolutely nothing to do with online dating, but I let it go. "Don't do this. Don't give up on your marriage yet."

She jumped off the bed and headed for the door. "It's over. Over and out. Stick a fork in it. It's done." I heard her head down the stairs; for a little person, she's got a heavy footfall.

"Well, that went well," I murmured to myself. I had known Max for a long time — coming up on twenty years — and I knew her to be flaky, mercurial, and a host of other, not-so-flattering adjectives, but I also knew her to be loyal, devoted, and the best friend a girl could have. She was more like a sister to me than a friend. But ever since she had met and married Fred, she had morphed into someone I didn't recognize — first by getting married at all and second by moving out and past the marriage. I knew she was impulsive, but that? That was just plain crazy. And believe me, I know crazy. I stayed married to a man who cheated on me repeatedly out of some sense of honor and commitment.

I didn't want to leave her alone but a little part of me wondered if my moving out could be considered a small blessing for me. I immediately felt a little queasy at the traitorous thought.

I continued my packing, stopping periodically to bend over and pet and kiss Trixie, who knew something was afoot; I was leaving Trixie here overnight until I could figure out my situation on campus. She circled my bed, moaning and snuffling, trying to figure out what was happening. It was almost as if she were saying, "Don't leave me here with that other one." Many a day I had returned home in the past few weeks to find Trixie practically crossing her legs in discomfort and staring at an empty water dish. There was no point in upbraiding Max; she was in some kind of postmarital fugue state and my admonitions would be met with the blank stare of the terminally sad. I assured Trixie that she was coming with me in the end and that we would be very happy in our new, albeit temporary, home. She looked at me like she wasn't sure about that.

I was done in about an hour and carried two suitcases and a small duffel bag filled with toiletries out to the car. It was a gorgeous day, sunny and cool, with more than a hint of spring in the air. I took a look around my backyard and prayed that I would be back soon enough to enjoy the chaise lounge that Crawford — romantic devil that he was — had bought me. And I wondered if my "suite" had a balcony or patio; the school sits majestically astride the Hudson River and the views are spectacular. I expected the worst and hoped for the best as I slammed the trunk shut for the final time before departing.

I went back into the house to say goodbye to Max, who was in my spare bedroom, working furiously on the computer. "I'm leaving," I said, leaning casually against the door. "I'll be back tomorrow to get Trixie, though."

She looked at me, her fingers poised on top of the keyboard. "Call me when you're settled in," she said, surprising me. I thought she would have sent me off with a dismissive wave.

"Can I give you a hug?" I asked.

"I'd rather you didn't," she said, her back stiffening. Her eyes filled with tears before they focused on the computer monitor, her face pale and drawn.

"Are you surfing on Match.com?" I asked.

"Nope," she said, tapping away. "I'm putting my engagement ring on Craigslist."

I pursed my lips and thought about that. Maybe this was exactly the right time to leave.

Crawford was waiting for me when I got to school. I pulled into my usual parking space and hit the button that popped the trunk. Visitation hours were still in effect what with it being noon on a Saturday, but we still greeted each other with an ironic

43

handshake. "Thank you for coming," I said formally.

"My pleasure," he said. He peered into the trunk. "Not too much stuff to move," he said.

"I'm not staying long, remember?" I said, and hoisted out my toiletries bag. I dug the set of keys out of my pocket that Merrimack had given me and consulted the instructions for their use. I fiddled with the old black key to let myself into the dorm by the side entrance, and took a look around the first floor. There was a big desk in the main foyer where the resident assistants in the building sat in the evening to welcome guests, accept packages, and make sure that the building was locked up at the end of the evening. Beyond that were two common areas on either side of the hallway: one was a television room, the other a dining room, a vestige from the old days when the residents of the dorm ate together at an assigned time. Being as spring break had commenced the week before, the dorm was essentially a ghost town. That fact, coupled with the old architectural bones of the building, lent it a decidedly spooky vibe.

The newer-looking key opened up the first door on the right, which led to my new suite. Crawford followed closely behind me carrying my biggest suitcase; he let out a low, depressed-sounding whistle when I gave him a view of my new digs.

I leaned in and discovered my suite was basically a long, narrow room with hardwood floors and one window next to a twin-sized bed. The suite part, I surmised, was the small living area to the left of the bedroom that contained a desk, an old musty chair, and a bookshelf, and that was separated from the bedroom by rather nice French doors. A bathroom was next to the bedroom, and while I'm a fan of period detail, the subway tile that encased the shower looked like it hadn't been cleaned since it was installed in what I guessed was the 1940s. I looked at Crawford and said, "Get me some Comet."

"You're not even in the door," he said. "Let's go in and see what else you need before I go to the store."

"Besides a blowtorch to burn this place down?" I asked, sitting dejectedly on the bed. A puff of dust flew up around me and I shivered in revulsion.

"Is there a laundry area in this building?" he asked, pulling me up off the bed and placing me in the doorway between the bedroom and living room. He pulled the bedding off and threw it onto the floor. "I don't want you sleeping on Wayne Brook-well's dirty sheets," he said.

"That's Wayne Butthole, to you." I leaned on the doorjamb. "Forevermore, he's Wayne Butthole." I crossed my arms, and continued my visual reconnaissance of the area. "I hate him."

"Laundry?" Crawford repeated.

"No idea," I said. "I assume it's in the basement but I can't be sure." Although I had parked outside of this building for the better part of a decade, I had never been inside, save for the lobby. The building was five stories high, with men housed on all but one floor, a floor that had been reserved for the overflow of female students in any given year. But Siena was still known as the men's dorm and had been since I was a student here, years previous. It looked pretty much the same as I remembered it — ornate, varnished moldings; marble floors; heavy mahogany doors stained a dark, cherry brown. It smelled of Pledge and floor polish and decades' worth of smelly gym socks and young adult hormones.

Crawford picked up the pile of dirty bedding and started down the hall, his sneakers making a squish-squish noise as he proceeded. I went back into the bedroom and sat down on the denuded bed, surveying my surroundings. I couldn't imagine spending one night here, never mind five weeks, but that was my lot and I had to suck it up. I don't want to suck it up! I wanted to yell, but I made an attempt at maturity and swallowed what ever feelings I had. The one thing I couldn't ignore was my bladder, which obviously was past the point of no return. I got up and went into the bathroom, looking around as I did my business, taking in the rust stains in the porcelain pedestal sink, and the dirty ring around the tub. There were a few squares of toilet paper left on the roll and I made a mental note to tell Crawford to get toilet paper, too.

When I flushed the toilet, a torrent of water, toilet paper, and various other bits of flotsam and jetsam that had been residing in the toilet since the Mesozoic Age came spewing up at me from the filthy bowl, and I put my hands over my face to protect myself, a little too late. The front of my shirt and my jeans were instantly soaked, and water poured onto the tile floor and puddled around my feet. I spat a few times, wondering exactly what I had almost ingested. I grabbed a less-than-clean towel from the towel bar and wiped off my face and hands. I looked at the floating detritus on the floor and stifled a gag.

Crawford returned and knocked softly on the bathroom door. "Everything okay in there?"

"No!" I called back while attempting to open the door with the ancient doorknob. I finally got it open and gave him a view of what the bathroom looked like.

"What the hell happened?"

"What do you think happened?" I asked, and threw the soaked towel at him, catching him squarely in the solar plexus. "We are not off to a good start here."

He went into the bathroom and threw the towel on the floor, attempting to sop up the mess from the exploding toilet. I riffled through my suitcase, finding a clean pair of jeans and a T-shirt. I stripped off my clothes and put them in a pile by the door. Once I was redressed, I stopped by the bathroom. "I'm going to go down to the laundry room and throw these clothes in, too." I watched as Crawford raised the toilet seat and stared solemnly into the toilet. I had no idea whether or not he was handy and I wasn't sticking around to find out. "It's in the basement, right?"

He didn't turn around but put his hands on his hips, surveying the damage. "Right."

I padded down the hall toward the grand staircase, which led me to a laundry room that was much nicer than my new accommodations. Six new, state-of-the-art washers and companion dryers lined one wall; the other wall was lined with vending machines with soda, candy, and snacks. There was a change machine, and a machine to buy bleach and detergent. It was clean, well lit, and modern with signs advertising its Wi-Fi access. I looked around enviously. My basement was musty, dusty, and home to more than one mouse, I suspected. Okay, so things were looking up. A little bit.

I threw the dirty clothes into the wash that Crawford had started and returned to the lobby floor, which was still empty. I had forgotten to ask Merrimack if any students were staying on campus during spring break and made a mental note to send him an e-mail once I unearthed my computer from the mound of my possessions in the middle of the little patch of floor between my bed and the dresser.

"Do you want to get Chinese food, Crawford?" I asked, back upstairs and going through items in my open suitcase. He didn't answer. I guess I owed him an apology for biting his head off and throwing the dirty towel at him, but I didn't expect the silent treatment. "Crawford?" I went to the bathroom door and found him kneeling on the floor in his undershirt, the toilet off its seal, the top removed. A collection of rusty old tools, apparently gathered from the maintenance closet across the hall from my suite, were arranged around him. His shirt was draped over the side of the tub and he was dirty and wet, his dark hair flopping over his sweaty brow.

"Crawford?"

He leaned over and stretched out, ending up on his right side, his left arm disappearing into the gaping hole of the upended toilet. He came out with a Ziploc bag filled with something that I knew wasn't Mrs. Brookwell's famous home-grown tea.

He looked up at me. "Call Fred."

FIVE

"I don't do floaters and I don't do toilets."

I hadn't seen Fred since he and Max split and I saw that his mood hadn't improved during that time. I knew that he didn't do floaters; Crawford was quite verbal on that subject every time someone turned up in the river in their jurisdiction. Fred's mood seemed to have gotten worse in the past couple of weeks, which was completely understandable, given the situation. He stood next to the toilet, his ham-hock legs splayed and his hands on his hips, regarding the toilet with a mixture of revulsion and horror. Crawford still lay on the ground, a flashlight in his hand, peering into the waste hole on which the toilet had previously resided.

Things had escalated since Crawford had made his interesting discovery. As it turned out, had I not been so cranky and preoccupied by my new living situation, I would have seen that there was hardly any water in the toilet, but I had been pre-occupied with my full bladder. The heroin was in an airtight bag and had been jammed into the toilet, obstructing the flow of water into the waste pipe, which caused the explosion.

I had called Fred who, in turn, called the U.S. Cavalry, or so it seemed. Two police cars — "cruisers," as I like to erroneously refer to them — screeched to a halt outside the building, unloading a quartet of uniformed cops, three male and one female, young and old, big and bigger. Two detectives from the narcotics bureau also arrived, looking dazed and bedraggled, not unlike the people with whom they usually dealt. Crawford explained to me that the drug squad liked using guys who had a certain "grittiness" to them; if these two — Marcus and Lattanzi — were any indication, I'd say that the department had succeeded. I would have mistaken the two of them for junkies had I passed them on the street.

I was pushed out of the way and told to sit in my "living room" with my hands in my pockets so that I wouldn't touch anything. My "living room," I wanted to clarify, was in Dobbs Ferry, not in this two-hundred-year-old building that smelled like

Murphy's oil soap and sweat.

Lattanzi, compact and swarthy in jeans and a worn pair of cowboy boots, knelt in front of me, his pad resting on his knee. "Start at the beginning."

The beginning? Like how I was just minding my own business, drinking flat Diet Coke at a faculty mixer, and ended up living in an ancient building with cranky toilets? Or this beginning: I had had too much coffee before I left the house that day which facilitated my having to pee immediately upon entering my new digs? I looked at Lattanzi's black eyes and decided to go with the short and sweet version.

"I had to pee. I flushed. The toilet exploded."

"And this Brookwell guy? Ever met him?"

I flashed on Wayne Brookwell's face, his mouth hanging slightly agape in his official St. Thomas Web site photo. "Nope."

Lattanzi stood up. "Lucky for you your boyfriend can plumb."

"He can? He can plumb?" I asked, having no idea what he was talking about.

The detective rocked back on his cowboy boots. "Well, he can stick his hand down a toilet. That's more than I can say for his partner."

I heard Fred gag as Crawford came up

with something not, shall we say, germane to the case.

I went into the hallway and perched on the desk in the main part of the lobby. From what I was told, we were waiting for the Crime Scene people, who would dust the room and look for any additional evidence.

I thanked the stars above that spring break was still on and that no one would be back to the building until at least lunchtime the next day. Because if Etheridge, Merrimack, or anybody else in the administration saw what was going on, I was toast. I wouldn't put it past them to enter some trumped-up charge in my file to continue to withhold my tenure and get me off campus *tout de suite.* Even I had to admit: I was becoming a giant pain in the ass, even if the stuff in the toilet had no relation to me whatsoever.

The cops, Marcus and Lattanzi included, were congregated outside of the suite in the hallway, chatting amiably about a variety of topics. I got bored sitting in the empty lobby and came back to the room, not obeying the cops' command to stay out of the way. I stood on my tiptoes trying to observe what was going on in the bathroom over Fred's hulking frame.

"Find anything else?" I asked, watching Crawford hand Fred something wet and nasty, which Fred put in a Ziploc bag. He took a permanent marker and wrote something in his chicken scratch along the top. He added the bag to a couple of others that sat on the sink next to the toilet.

Crawford hoisted himself up from the floor, wetter and dirtier than he had been when he arrived to help me move. He wiped his hands on his pants. "That's it." He looked around the bathroom. "Is there somewhere else where I can clean up?"

I shrugged. "I have no idea. Let's take a look."

Crawford exchanged a few words with the cops in the hallway, one of whom was plastering the bathroom door with yellow crime-scene tape. I felt a little sick: the reason I was here was because the administration at the school thought I was trouble. And now? They had all the proof they needed. I had only been on campus in my new capacity for under an hour and already my door was lined with crime-scene tape. I wondered if I could keep this quiet and knew that the answer was a resounding "no."

Crawford and I wandered up to the second floor of the dormitory and found a communal bathroom for the male residents of that floor. It looked like it had been cleaned and disinfected during the break and that was a relief to both of us. Crawford washed his face and hands thoroughly and dried them with several rough paper towels that he took from a dispenser on the wall. I leaned against one of the sinks, watching him and thinking.

"What are you thinking, Crawford?" I asked.

"I'm thinking that some moo shu pork would go a long way toward making this day disappear," he said, looking in the mirror and wiping some grime off his temple.

"No, seriously."

He nodded. "I am serious. I'm done here and you can't go back in until Crime Scene finishes. I'll leave Fred. Because if he doesn't do toilets, he can wait around while they dust for prints. And he can also let the head of security know that he's got a problem in Siena Hall," he said rather testily, probably more so than he intended. It occurred to me that he might be losing patience with his partner as quickly as I was with my roommate. He looked pointedly at one of the urinals. "Meet you downstairs?"

I took the hint and straightened up. "Right. Sure."

"Better yet, meet me at my car."

We reconnected a few minutes later, after he had finished up with Fred and the uniformed cops. I didn't know what shape my room would be in when I got back, but from experience, I did know that every square inch of space would be covered with fingerprint powder. Crawford and I went over what we knew about the situation after we were seated at Hop Sing, our favorite Chinese restaurant in the neighborhood.

Crawford ordered a beer and I asked for a Blazing Dragon. He raised an eyebrow at me. "Blazing Dragon? I've never seen you order one of those before."

"It's rum, cranberry, coconut, lighter fluid, and rubbing alcohol," I said, dipping a cracker into duck sauce. "It comes in a fancy glass with an umbrella and it's just what the doctor ordered." I crammed a few more crackers into my mouth. I didn't realize how hungry I was until we sat down in the restaurant. Almost every table in the cramped space was filled and the din of hungry eaters made it so we had to yell across the table at each other. "I need you to find out if anyone put in a missing persons on Wayne Brookwell."

"Whoa!" Crawford called, a little too loudly even for the current noise conditions. A couple of diners looked over at him and he quickly composed himself. "Can you wait until I get my beer before you start hammering me?"

"Sorry."

He looked around and pulled at his collar; he wasn't wearing a tie so he didn't have his usual security blanket to tug on. "And I already did," he said, smiling slyly when he saw my surprised expression. "No missing persons. No forwarding address. No record of him at DMV, except that he's got a New York State license. The guy's gone and it's going to take a miracle for us to find him."

I watched as the waiter approached our table carrying a tray with Crawford's beer and my drink, which was delivered in a bright blue ceramic glass with a dragon's face protruding from it. I took a long swig; it tasted exactly like what I had described, with a lingering taste of lighter fluid remaining long after my first sip. "What about other Brookwells? Any Mama Brookwells? Daddy Brookwells? Brookwell sibs? Where's this guy from?"

Crawford drained almost half of his beer before he answered. "Scarsdale."

"Scarsdale? Like in not-quite-fifteen-miles-from-here Scarsdale?" I was surprised. I didn't expect the Brookwell family manse to be quite so close. That was convenient.

The waiter returned and we ordered enough food for four people; investigative toilet work apparently makes you hungry. "And another Blazing Dragon!" I called after the waiter, who gave me a knowing smile. The first few sips were deadly, but after that the drink went down rather smoothly. Our waiter seemed to know that.

"Take it easy," Crawford said. "You don't want to drink too much before going on a stakeout."

I clapped my hands together excitedly. "We're staking out? We're going on a stakeout?" I asked. I had never been on a stakeout and had been envious that Crawford got to do it on a regular basis. It never occurred to me that they were deadly boring and didn't come with portable johns.

"I figured we'd take a ride over to Wayne's family home to see what's what. I don't think we'll stay there all night but we could hang out for a few hours and see if anything comes up."

"Sounds like a plan," I said, finishing off my drink.

The waiter delivered a few plates of food and we dug in. Crawford speared a dumpling with his chopstick and pointed it at me. "Listen."

Whenever he starts a sentence like that, I'm going to get admonished. I made a face. "What?"

"I know you're going to ask around campus about this guy, but you need to be inconspicuous."

I nearly spat out my pork fried rice. "Inconspicuous?" I'm five feet ten in stocking feet with a mane of frizzy auburn hair. It's not like I can *blend*.

"Yes. Inconspicuous." He ate his dumpling. "You know, make it so you're not actually poking around when you really are."

I saluted him. "Got it, chief." I polished off the rice on my plate and helped myself to more. "What are you going to be doing while I'm inconspicuously poking around?"

"Nothing."

I raised an eyebrow.

"I've already done a little poking, but it's not our case. Narcotics will take over because of the heroin, obviously, but until we find a dead Wayne Brookwell," he said, "which I'm hoping we don't, I'm not involved. I got the address, reached out to DMV, but I'm done. There's nothing more that I can do."

"So you're prepared to lead the life of a celibate?" I asked, thinking ahead to my many months, and possibly years, of servitude as a dry, chaste resident director. Because if we didn't find Wayne Brookwell — and entice him to come back to his job

— I was stuck there for as long as Etheridge and Merrimack drew out the interviewing process. And with their energies focused on the construction of the new dorm across the campus from Siena, finding a new RD to replace me was not a top priority.

He looked at me as if to say, "What do you think?" "I told you that I would help you but I deal with dead bodies, not missing ones."

"So I'm on my own?"

"Yes and no."

The rest of our food arrived and I helped myself to some General Tso's chicken. "What does that mean?"

"You'll know if you need me. And I'll help you as long as it's legal," he said, giving my arm a little jab with his chopstick. He knew, from experience, that my definition of legal often didn't jibe with the standard one.

"Hey!" I said, rubbing my arm. "I get it." I forked some food into my mouth and chewed quickly, washing down the rest with my Blazing Dragon. "Okay," I said, wiping my mouth, "let's go to the Brookwells'."

He was still working on his plate of food and second beer. "I'm not done."

I was antsy. "I want to start the stakeout."

"Let me finish eating. Use the restroom before we go because I don't want you

61

complaining that you have to pee while we're sitting there."

"I'll just do what you do if I have to go."

"No," he said, getting up and taking me by the elbow, "you won't. Trust me." He pushed me in the direction of the restroom at the back of the restaurant.

I passed the kitchen and saw a group of white-uniformed cooks flinging ingredients around with abandon, some of them ending up in woks, the others on the floor. My cell phone, in my front jeans pocket, simultaneously trilled and vibrated, startling me. I let out a little cry, attracting the attention of some of the other diners. "Hello?"

It was Kevin. One advantage to being assigned to Siena dorm was that one of my dorm mates was also one of my best friends; Kevin lived on the top floor in a real suite with a living room, bedroom, and galley kitchen. "It's me. What's going on downstairs? I just got back from Jack's and saw a bunch of police cars."

Jack was Kevin's brother and a former paramour of mine. He was good-looking, smart, and gainfully employed, with the best-looking teeth I had ever seen. But alas, it wasn't meant to be, despite how hard Kevin had tried to keep the romance alive. "It's a long story. But suffice it to say, our friend Wayne Brookwell was moonlighting as more than a limousine driver." I filled Kevin in on the remaining details, such as they were.

He whistled his disbelief. "You're kidding."

"I wish, Kevin." I stood outside of the locked ladies' room and waited for the occupant to emerge, keeping an eye on the goings-on in the kitchen. I didn't know what I expected to see, but it was nice to know that one of my favorite restaurants adhered to at least some of the board of health codes. "Crawford and I are out but when I get back we need to talk about what you know about this guy. Maybe we can figure out where he went. And why."

"Okay, as long as it's before ten. I have six A.M. mass tomorrow morning."

I didn't know if I could accommodate Kevin's schedule but told him I would respect his bedtime. "If I don't talk to you tonight, let's get together tomorrow."

He sighed. "Tomorrow might be tough. The kids are coming back from spring break."

I heard the occupant of the ladies' room unlock the door. "Why would that make it tough?"

"Oh, you know. There's a lot of sinning

that goes on during spring break so I often have a lot of counseling to do." He paused. "You're the RD now. You should probably be around to help out, if necessary."

With sinners? Not exactly my bailiwick. I live vicariously through sinners, being a repressed, guilt-ridden lapsed Catholic. But I promised him I would be available and asked him to let me know when we could get together.

The door to the bathroom opened and I came face-to-face with my boss, Sister Mary, who was surrounded by her usual cloud of Jean Naté and hairspray scent.

"Dear!" she said, surprised to see me. Her angular Irish face was its usual ruddy hue. She was close enough for me to kiss her cheek but I didn't want to do that, for obvious reasons.

"Sister?"

"What are you doing here?" Her eyes narrowed behind her round glasses. "And were those police cars I saw in front of Siena Hall?"

I let out a strangled laugh. Busted. "Yes, they were."

"Visitors? Or trouble?"

Visitors? Would six cops be visiting me in my new home twenty minutes after I moved in? It seemed a little unorthodox but Mary was at a point, I was sure, where nothing I did would surprise her. Visitors or trouble? A little of both, I thought, but I went with the truth. I had worked for Mary for the last nine years, and she had been my professor when I was a student, but she still scared the bejesus out of me. "I found something in my room and —" I started, but stopped when I felt Crawford's strong arms around my shoulders, crushing me against his torso and indicating that I should shut up right this very second.

"Sister, hi!" he said brightly. We were jammed together in the narrow corridor leading to the restrooms, two laypeople and a suspicious nun. "Are you ready, hon?" he said. He never calls me "hon," so I knew this was a rescue mission. He was behind me and had me in what Mary would think was a romantic embrace but which I knew was one that was subliminally telling me to "be quiet."

"Yes, sweetheart."

Mary grabbed my arm. "Your room? What did you find? Was it something to do with Wayne?" I noticed that her Irish brogue got stronger the more excited she became; right now, I could barely understand her.

Crawford dragged me away from her and toward the front door. Our table was on the way, and I picked up my Blazing Dragon and drank the last of it as we exited the restaurant. I dropped it on the table where another couple was eating just before Crawford pulled me onto the sidewalk. I turned back toward the restaurant and saw Mary picking her white cardigan sweater from the back of her chair and grabbing her purse, purposeful in her actions. The other nun seated at the table seemed perplexed. "She's coming this way," I said.

Crawford perp-walked me to his Passat, his arm still around me. He beeped the car key and the doors unlocked. "Get in."

We were in the car and out of the spot in seconds. I turned around and saw Mary staring after the car, her face a mask of consternation. I turned back around and put on my seat belt. "That was a close one."

Crawford maneuvered through the traffic and onto the highway going north.

"To Scarsdale, James."

"Who's James?" he asked.

Literal as always. "Never mind. Just drive."

Six

"So what do you do when *you* have to pee during a stakeout?" I asked, squirming around in my seat, trying to get comfortable.

"I told you to go the bathroom before we left the restaurant," Crawford said.

That wasn't an answer.

Under normal circumstances, this would have been a very romantic scenario: a dusky sunset on a cool spring night, a handsome guy sitting next to me, a tree-lined street, no one else in sight. But my engorged bladder, protesting after two huge Blazing Dragons, and the fact that we were looking for a wayward resident director broke the mood. I shifted again, crossing one leg over the other. We had been sitting there for about an hour and hadn't observed anyone coming in or out of the Brookwell house.

"What do you usually do? Go in a bottle? An empty coffee cup?" I asked, knowing that neither of those options were available to me. I'm pretty limber, but not that much.

"You could go outside," he suggested. He reached into the glove compartment and handed me a stack of yellow napkins from Wendy's, the top one stained with burger grease.

"Gee, thanks." I looked around. We were on a pretty suburban street, big, old Tudor mansions on either side, some surrounded by stone walls. I didn't see a tree that afforded enough privacy to allow me to relieve myself and I couldn't envision myself hopping over one of the stone walls. Who knew what was on the other side? Might be rabid guard dogs, for all I knew. And with my luck, that was the best-case scenario.

The Brookwell house was one of the smaller houses on the street, and newer by about fifty years. It was a tidy, classic Colonial, white with black shutters, columns flanking the front door, and a long driveway running along the side to a detached garage. Very southern Westchester County, very old money. "I'll be right back," I said, hopping out of the car before Crawford could ask where I was going. The situation had become dire and I never would have considered this normally, but desperate times and all. I crossed the quiet street and walked up to the Brookwells' door, lifting the heavy knocker, a brass Claddagh ring. So, someone in there was Irish, apparently. I knocked a few times before I heard footsteps on the other side of the door.

An older gentleman, probably in his late sixties, answered the door. He was wearing khakis with a neat crease down the front, a blue oxford with some kind of insignia on the breast pocket, and penny loafers without socks. He was the epitome of Scarsdale preppy, right down to his round, tortoiseshell glasses, which perched on the end of his nose. "Can I help you?" he asked, more pleasantly than I would have if a strange woman appeared on my doorstep. But this being Scarsdale and all, good manners were de rigueur and who was I to complain?

"Oh, hi," I said, not realizing until that very moment that I had no idea what to say. I turned and looked at Crawford, who was slumped down in the front seat of the Passat, trying to become invisible. He was no help. I decided to put him in the role of directionally challenged spouse. "My husband and I are looking at houses in the area and we were driving around looking for the Coldwell Banker office and got turned around. Could you point me in the right direction?" I took a chance that there was a Coldwell Banker realty office in the area; my experience was that every Westchester town had one and I hoped that Scarsdale was typical in that regard.

He smiled. "Are you sure it's Coldwell?"

I laughed. "I thought it was . . ."

"Was it Houlihan-Lawrence, maybe?"

I hit my forehead with my palm. "Of course! Coldwell is the realtor selling *our* house," I said. "Can you tell me where Houlihan is?"

"Of course. It can get a little confusing around here," he said. He was so charming that I felt bad lying to him. Where's your kid? I wanted to ask him, but I refrained, watching while he stretched out his arm and made some gestures trying to describe exactly where I was supposed to go. I made some mouth noises that conveyed my understanding of where he was talking about, even though I was just as clueless as when I had begun this charade. "So, that's it," he said. "You're really close. No more than three minutes away."

"Great!" I said. "Now here's the really embarrassing part," I started, taking in his kind expression. I shifted from one foot to the other to demonstrate my discomfort.

He stepped aside, sweeping an arm into

the foyer. "No need to explain. Powder room is just beyond the staircase there, right before you get to the kitchen. On the right-hand side."

I turned and looked at Crawford, my eyebrows raised to convey my surprise at my quick entry. He slumped farther down in the seat, shielding the side of his face with his hand. I went into the house and ran down the hall to the well-appointed powder room, but took a minute to look at a few pictures that hung on the wall across from it. There were a few little Brookwells, it appeared: Wayne, an older sister, and two older boys. At one time, they had had a West Highland terrier, who posed with them in a few formal holiday pictures where the little Brookwell boys wore short pants and vests while the sister wore an explosion of organza that made it appear that she had no legs. I pulled my eyes away and went into the powder room where I took care of business, and helped myself to a little of the Jo Malone grapefruit hand lotion that was perched on the glass shelf over the sink. I smelled my hands and decided that I would definitely put this on my Christmas list. I heard voices outside of the bathroom, one of them female with an Irish brogue, the other belonging to Mr. Brookwell. Aha, I thought. The purveyor of all things Claddagh. She was probably wondering what the heck had led her husband to allow a stranger into their home. I dillydallied a few more seconds hoping that I wouldn't have to run the Mrs. Brookwell gauntlet just yet; I was enjoying Mr. Brookwell so much that I figured I could chat with him for a few more seconds, ostensibly about Scarsdale but mainly about his kids. Or, more specifically, one kid. Wayne. The butthole.

I pumped a little more lotion onto my hand and rubbed it in before opening the powder room door. I went back out into the hallway and saw Mr. Brookwell still standing by the open front door, waiting for me to return.

"I can't thank you enough," I said. "Nothing worse than being lost and not having access to . . . facilities," I said, choosing my words carefully in front of this lovely, well-mannered man.

He chuckled. "Not a problem, dear." He held out his hand and I took it in my well-moisturized one. "My name is Eben Brookwell."

I stopped for a moment, not realizing that I would need an alias. I quickly decided to go with the old "your first pet/your first street" rule of thumb. I forgot that that's what you were supposed to use for your stripper name — at least that's what Max had told me when we had played this ridiculous renaming game — but it worked in a pinch. The only problem was that I had grown up on a street named "New Broadway." Obviously, that wouldn't work. And my current street name was "Palisades," after a line of cliffs that ran along the Hudson River. I thought quickly, staring into Mr. Brookwell's handsome, older-gentleman face. "Coco. Coco," I repeated, flashing on my first dog, a teacup Yorkshire terrier. I searched my brain for an appropriate surname. "Coco Varick," I finally said, using Max's former street address in lower Manhattan.

"Well, Coco Varick, happy house hunting," he said. "And tell Mr. Varick that we'll get together for a drink when you do move to town. Look us up, will you?" He gave Crawford a little wave, which Crawford returned sheepishly.

"I definitely will, Mr. Brookwell."

"Eben."

"Eben," I said, my discomfort at the number of lies I had told growing by the second.

"What do you do, dear?"

"Do?" I asked.

"Yes. What's your profession?" He blushed a bit when he realized I might not have a job that required me to leave the house, like raising a small brood. "Or are you home with the little ones?"

"No. No little ones," I said, deciding to go for broke. What was one more lie to Coco Varick? "I'm a flight attendant."

"Ahhh," he said, some kind of look passing across his face. Lust for flight attendants of yore? Who knew. But he seemed impressed so I went with it.

"I fly for Air France."

"Très bien!" he said enthusiastically, the flush in his cheeks getting deeper. Yep, he likes the flight attendants. Especially the French ones.

"Do you have children, Mr. Brookwell?"

"Four," he said proudly, regaining his composure after his momentary flight of fancy, pun intended. "Twin boys, then a girl, and then a boy."

"How lovely."

"I'm a very proud dad," he said. "One of the twins is a lawyer in Boston, the other a doctor at NYU. My daughter is also a doctor in Miami. And my youngest is a resident director at St. Thomas University. Have you heard of it? It's local. Right over the border in the Bronx."

"Oh, yes," I said, exuding enthusiasm. "I have heard that it is quite an institution."

"It is," he said, and his face fell a little bit. "Our youngest — his name is Wayne — is at a bit of a crossroads. We're hoping that he doesn't spend his life living in a dorm."

"Not exactly the path you had mapped out for him?" I asked.

He shook his head but before he had a chance to elaborate, a woman emerged from the kitchen and came up behind him. She was tall and thin, her crisp white blouse open just enough so that I could see her Miraculous Medal of the Blessed Virgin glinting in the light coming from the overhead fixture in the foyer. Eben turned around.

"Dear," he said, gesturing toward his wife and putting an arm around her waist when she got close enough. "This is my new friend, Coco Varick. Coco, my wife, Geraldine."

I held out my hand and hoped that she would hold me up when I crumbled to the floor on my shaking legs.

Because I was looking into the face of Sister Mary.

Well, obviously it wasn't Sister Mary, but someone who looked exactly like her. The reason I knew it wasn't Mary is because she

75

was *nice.*

She held out her hand. "Nice to meet you, Ms. Varick."

"Oh, please call me Coco." I couldn't stop staring at her. She was Mary down to the sensible shoes and short haircut but definitely had more élan and flair than my stodgy boss. I pulled my eyes away from her when Eben started talking, my eyes coming to rest on a St. Thomas sweatshirt thrown casually over the banister of the staircase. It was hard to miss: St. Thomas's school colors are a bizarre combination of purple and yellow, which I'm sure had some deep religious meaning lost on me, the pagan. The sweatshirt material was the purple, and I could see some yellow lettering peeking out from under the wrinkled fabric. I was itching to ask them if their son was a drug dealer and if he had just quit his day job, but being as we had just met, I thought it might be a tad impolite.

"Coco and her husband . . . ," Eben started, looking at me questioningly.

"Chad," I said.

"Chad are looking for a house in the area. They got a little turned around and stopped to ask for directions."

"I'm glad you did!" she exclaimed. "Who's your agent?"

"My agent?"

"Yes, dear," she said, fingering her necklace. "Your real estate agent?"

Crawford tapped gently on the horn and we all looked over at him. "Chad seems to be in a hurry," I said apologetically, and started down the walk.

Eben followed me. "Please do look us up when you move in, Coco. We'd love to have you and Chad over for cocktails sometime."

I hurried down the walk and called over my shoulder, "We'd love to, too!" I put my thumb and pinkie to my ear. "We'll call you!"

"We're in the book!" he said. "And don't forget! A left at the Catholic church!"

"Got it!" I called back and gave him a thumbs-up. Of course it was a left at the Catholic church; I wondered if we could stop in for a little on-the-go confession. I jumped in the car and returned Eben's wave as we drove off.

Crawford looked at me when we got to a stop sign. "What the hell is wrong with you? I thought we were going to spend the night there, you were with him for so long."

"Before I forget, your name is Chad and mine is Coco and I'm a flight attendant for Air France."

"Of course it is. Of course you are." He

let out a little exasperated sigh. "What do *I* do?"

I put on my seat belt and adjusted my pocketbook between my feet. "I didn't get that far. Do you want to be a firefighter?"

"Do *you* want me to be a firefighter?"

New York City cops and firefighters have a not-always-amicable relationship with each other and are somewhat competitive when it comes to whose job is more important and who is braver. It's stupid civil servant man stuff, but I knew I had to choose my words carefully regardless of how ridiculous I thought the whole thing was. Crawford was already irked that I had gone into the Brookwells' so telling him I wished he was a firefighter would not help. "No. Of course not. Do you want to be a graphic designer?"

He started thinking and then realized that we were off topic. "Whatever. What did you find out?" he said, pulling into a parking spot in the middle of town.

I looked out the window and took in the row of quaint shops and restaurants. "Maybe we should look for a house here," I mused. Crawford cleared his throat and I realized I had to tell him about the Brookwells. "Very Junior League, country club, blue-bloody types." I held my hands out to

Crawford. "Smell my hands."

He did it instinctively before realizing he didn't actually have to.

"Smells good, right?" I asked, putting my hands back in my lap. "The hand lotion in the bathroom goes for around sixty bucks a pop."

"That's fascinating," he said. "What did you talk about?"

"Chad and Coco's house hunt, mainly," I said. "Wayne's a loser compared to the rest of the brood, but we could have guessed that."

"He's not a loser," Crawford protested. "He *is* gainfully employed."

I snorted. "Did you get a look at Mrs. Brookwell? Geraldine?"

Crawford shrugged. "Not really."

"She's the spitting image of Sister Mary." Crawford shuddered involuntarily. Mary scares him, too.

"I think Wayne Brookwell is Mary's nephew." I thought about that for a second while acknowledging the rumbling in my stomach. If it wasn't one bodily complaint, it was another. The Chinese food from two hours before was a distant memory and nature was calling again.

Crawford motioned that I should continue. "And . . ."

"And I don't know what that means. Could indicate why he got the job on campus. Could give me a clue as to why Mary didn't say a word during my interrogation and subsequent imprisonment by Etheridge and Merrimack. Could mean a lot of things." I looked out the window and spied a Thai restaurant; I knew where we'd be having dinner. I thought back to my encounter with Sister Mary outside the bathroom at Hop Sing. "Could be why she asked me about Wayne at the restaurant."

"Or it could mean nothing."

"Right," I agreed. "But you got to admit it's weird, right?"

"It's weird," he agreed, adjusting himself in his seat so that he could restart the car. "I called Fred while you were inside and he said they need another hour before you can come back. What do you want to do?"

I pointed to the Thai restaurant.

"But we just ate," he complained.

"That was two hours ago. And I didn't get to finish my . . ." I looked at him. "What was that anyway? It really wasn't lunch and it really wasn't dinner." I put my hands together, pleading. "Please, Crawford. Please?"

Five minutes later, we were seated in the Thai restaurant in the main village of Scarsdale, picking at some spring rolls.

"Did you see anything in the house to indicate that Wayne might be living there?" he asked, looking around the restaurant. I don't know what he hoped to see, but he was taking it all in, from the paper lanterns hanging from the ceiling, to the waitresses dressed in traditional Thai garb, to the guy cutting up sushi behind a long bar. Although it called itself "Thai," it seemed that the restaurant was going more with pan-Asian.

"I saw a St. Thomas sweatshirt hanging on the banister," I said with gravity.

"So what?" he asked. "If their kid worked there, I'm sure they have a ton of St. Thomas clothing."

"They don't strike me as St. Thomas clothing kind of people. He was wearing the old khaki-oxford-shirt-loafer combo and she was dressed to the nines, too. And it's a Saturday afternoon and they were hanging out at the house. I don't imagine Geraldine would be caught dead in a St. Thomas sweatshirt at the local Stop & Shop if she's not wearing it at home on a weekend."

Crawford stared at me for longer than I thought necessary. I snapped my fingers in front of his face. Finally, he spoke. "Wow. That was amazing." He put the rest of his spring roll in his mouth. "You've got this all figured out. I don't know whether to be amazed or frightened."

"Amazed. Go with amazed." I took the last spring roll from the plate and dunked it in a ramekin filled with sauce. "So, chances are, Wayne has been somewhere in the vicinity recently."

"You really think so." It was more of a statement than a question.

"I do." I handed the empty plate to our server, a gorgeous Asian woman with an elaborate bun and eye makeup. "So, Chad, I think we need to start looking for a house. The Brookwells have invited us for cocktails, too."

Crawford held up his hands in protest. "I'm out."

"You are not 'out,' " I said. "If you want me out of that dorm, you're very much 'in.' "

Crawford crossed his arms on the table and rested his head on them. "There's so much wrong with this plan that I can't even begin. And if Geraldine Brookwell is Sister Mary's sister, this is going to unravel so quickly your head will spin."

He had a point. But him having a point had never stopped me before. And it sure wasn't going to stop me now.

"That kid's obviously in a heap of trouble

so I hope, for everyone's sake, he's safely ensconced in Scarsdale. His parents seem like very nice people. I would hate to have to tell them their kid's a drug mule or a dealer or something of that ilk." I thought about them for a moment. "I really hope that he doesn't put them in any danger."

Crawford looked sad all of a sudden. I was sure it was the parental connection, being as he was the father of twin teenage girls. "Me, too." He leaned back in his chair, his long legs grazing mine under the table. "We need to find out if there's a missing persons on him in Scarsdale. Let me poke around." He closed his eyes, thinking, trying to work out that part of it. He opened them a few minutes later. "When's your next flight?" he asked, a twinkle in his eye.

"I'm on the New York to Paris flight at midnight," I said. "And I won't be back for two weeks."

"And I have a graphic design convention in Cleveland next week," he said. He waved to our server. "Check, please."

SEVEN

I was able to get back into my room around nine o'clock, where I fell into the bed that Crawford had made up again with fresh sheets after we had returned from the restaurant. I lay there, my arms behind my head, and thought about how the day, and even the whole week, hadn't turned out as planned. If it had been normal, I would be home, alone, petting my dog and watching a reality show on Bravo. I would have been less surprised if I had ended up on a space shuttle mission than where I was now. Never in my wildest dreams did sleeping on a thirty-year-old mattress on campus come into play.

But here I was. Crawford had bid me a chaste adieu in the dorm hallway, heading back to his apartment in Manhattan, because even though visitation was still in effect, I didn't want to look like a hussy my first week on the job. He was working the next day, and I wouldn't see him for a couple of days, which, in itself, was depressing enough. Now this. Living in a dorm room — there was no place on earth where this would be considered a "suite" — every surface covered with fingerprint dust, with hissing pipes overhead. I decided to make the best of it, and fell into a deep sleep, thinking that I would clean up the fingerprint powder in the morning.

I hadn't set my alarm; there was no reason. The only thing I had to do the next day was unpack and go back to Dobbs Ferry to get Trixie. It was going to be a tight squeeze with the two of us living here but we would manage. I got up around nine and used the communal bathroom on the second floor again, making a mental note to call maintenance before I left so that they could give me a new toilet. Because you know what? The cops had taken my toilet "as evidence." Yes. Just when I thought my life couldn't get any weirder or more embarrassing, the appliance upon which I had sat my ample behind was now in some evidence room at the Fiftieth Precinct.

I dressed and headed off to Dobbs Ferry, hoping that at the very least, Max was in a semigood mood and not in her usual fugue state.

I entered the house and was greeted by an overly enthusiastic Trixie, who pushed past me to go out into the backyard where she ran free for a few minutes before rooting for field mice in the giant pile of leaves that I had never bagged the autumn before. When she tired of that, she came back in and paid me the respect I deserved by jumping on me and slathering me with wet, dog-scented kisses. I pushed her down and called for Max, who didn't respond. A quick survey of the area told me that she wasn't home.

She really hadn't left the house for any significant length of time in the past two weeks, so I was surprised that she was gone. I scribbled a note with the phone number in my room on campus and put it next to a can of paint sitting on the counter.

I looked at Trixie. "Where did this come from?" I asked her. It is not unusual for me to ask her questions and even more common for my questions to be met with adoring silence. I looked at the top of the can and saw a little dab of paint on the label: Million Dollar Red. I had no idea where this had come from or what it was for, but I left it there, thinking that Max might have purchased it to redo a room in her own apartment once she revoked Fred's squatter's rights and she returned there. She had been talking about making a fresh start and I couldn't think of a fresher start than painting a room red.

I pulled together everything I needed: Trixie's food, bowls, leash, and chew toys. We got into the car and headed back to St. Thomas, never seeing Max.

The director of security, Jay Pinto, was waiting for me when I returned from my trip. He held the door to the dorm for me as I carted in a box with Trixie's supplies, her leash dangling off my wrist. We made our way down to my room, where I set the box on the ground and commanded Trixie to "sit." She responded by taking off down the hallway, skidding up and down on the marble floors, investigating her new environment.

I folded my arms over my chest, expecting the worst. "I guess you heard what happened."

Jay, shorter than me with a thick shock of black hair and a neatly trimmed mustache, looked up at me and nodded. A faithful practitioner of kickboxing — a fact I had learned during one of Etheridge's goofy awards ceremonies — he was in excellent shape for a man in his early fifties. "You know I'm retired from the Job?" he asked, using the term cops normally used to refer to their time on the NYPD. Obviously, it was important for him to establish that I knew that before we got down to the business at hand, namely my exploding toilet. "I really wished your boyfriend would have called me first. We could have kept the whole thing a lot quieter."

I hadn't known he had been a cop but it didn't surprise me. It also didn't surprise me that he knew about Crawford. "So you talked to Detective Lattanzi?"

"The other one. Marcus," he said. A couple of students, tanned from their spring break adventures, came through the side door near my room and scampered down the hallway, encountering Trixie on the way. She was thrilled to make new friends. Jay leaned in so that we wouldn't be overheard. "We're going to try to keep this quiet anyway. If we can."

I wasn't surprised to learn that, either. "I won't tell anyone."

"Really quiet," he said meaningfully. He raised an eyebrow. "Understand?"

I nodded slowly even though I didn't have a clue as to what he was talking about.

"Sit tight. Do your job. Keep your nose clean."

"That's my plan," I said. The presumption that I wouldn't do those three things irked me slightly. I wondered how many people had seen two police cars and two unmarked vehicles peel into campus yesterday, and I decided that whoever did was given the evil death glare — the same one I was getting at that moment — from Jay. I guess he was under the same strict orders as everyone else on the campus with the same mantra: "We're one big, happy family! Nothing bad ever happens here! It's heaven on earth!"

Except it wasn't. We now had exploding, drug-filled toilets to add to our roster of "bad things that happen at St. Thomas." As if murder hadn't been enough.

"So, we'll never speak of this again?" Jay asked pointedly.

"I can't guarantee that," I said, honest to a fault. Because I was going to find out where those drugs had come from, where Wayne Brookwell was, and how the drugs and Wayne were related. That meant I'd have to talk to someone, sometime, about this situation.

He glared at me some more. But coming from a five-foot-five grandfather, even if he was a champion kickboxer in his age bracket, it just wasn't that intimidating.

"Oh, okay," I relented. "We will never speak of this again," I repeated with tremendous gravitas. I crossed my fingers behind my back and said an Act of Contrition for the lie I just told.

He gave me one final glance before saying, "Good."

He started to walk away, whistling a Miles Davis tune. "Oh, and one more thing." He stopped a few feet from my room. "You'll need to move your car."

"That's my regular parking spot," I reminded him.

"That's your regular parking spot if you don't live on campus. The resident parking lot is up the hill past the auditorium." He seemed to derive great pleasure in passing this information on to me.

"That doesn't make any sense."

He put his hands up. "Not my rules. The school's. You'll have to move your car into the resident lot before the students start coming back."

I started to protest to his back as he continued down the hallway.

"Have a good day, Dr. Bergeron," he called back.

"You, too!" I said but I didn't mean it. I hoped he had a very bad day. Like the one I had had the day before. I called Trixie and she came running, sliding to a stop in front of me. I watched Jay turn the corner and go out the main entrance of the dorm. Was it me or was this place an insane asylum? "Want to see your new room?" I asked her.

Her enthusiastic tail-wagging suggested that she might. I opened the door and her tail became flaccid, eventually tucking between her legs. "It's not scary, Trix," I said, putting my fingers between her chain-link collar and the thick rug of fur around her neck. I dragged her into the room. "See? It's just like home," I said, but even the dog could tell I was full of it. She went into the shoebox-sized living room and, with a heavy sigh, fell into a heap on the floor, dust rising up around her from the Oriental carpet. She looked up at me, her doleful eyes watching my every move. I went to the bathroom door and pulled down the police tape.

"Wayne?"

I peeked my head around the doorjamb and saw a young woman, long curly, black hair hanging to her shoulders, her eyes behind a pair of glasses with black, Buddy Holly–esque frames. She was in jeans and a Princeton sweatshirt, her feet in a pair of pink flip-flops. She was going for the art-student vibe but even that couldn't hide how cute she was under the helmet of hair and the outdated glasses.

"Sorry. Wayne's not here," I said, holding out my hand. "I'm Alison Bergeron. I'm the temporary RD."

She took my hand. "Hi. I'm Amanda Reese. I'm the RA on the third floor. Where's Wayne?"

Where's Wayne? That was the sixty-four-thousand-dollar question. "Not sure. I think he took a short leave of absence," I said, trying not to arouse any suspicion, which made me ask myself why I felt compelled to cover for this guy.

I recognized Amanda from around campus but knew that I had never had her as a student. The look on her face, however, led me to believe that she knew exactly who I was: the same Alison Bergeron who owned the car in which a student's body had been found the previous year; the same Alison Bergeron whose ex-husband, the head of the biology department, had been found dead, missing his hands and feet, in her kitchen; the same Alison Bergeron who got herself involved in too many fracases to mention. I don't know if it was my presence or the fact that Wayne wasn't where he was supposed to be, but she seemed nervous.

"He didn't mention anything to me about a leave of absence," she said, her eyes narrowing behind her thick lenses, her flip-flopped foot tapping on the marble.

"It was sudden," I said. Trixie came out from the living room and introduced herself to Amanda. "This is Trixie." I looked at the dog. "Trixie, this is Amanda."

Trixie held up her paw and allowed Amanda to hold it.

"I didn't think they allowed animals in the dorms," she said, dropping the paw.

"Special dispensation from the pope," I said. She didn't get the joke. "Special circumstances, really. I live alone and I wouldn't have anybody to take care of my dog while I lived here." And no, I wasn't lying: living with Max these days was like living alone, and she certainly wasn't going to take care of Trixie while I was away. "Now, is there something I can help you with?" I steeled myself for some kind of spring break confession about irresponsible sex or a wet T-shirt contest but there was none forthcoming.

"Are we still having our house meeting tomorrow night?"

"House meeting?"

"Yes. When all of the RAs get together and discuss the upcoming events and any issues that exist in the dorm." She looked at me as if I were a moron. "House meeting," she repeated.

"Sure. We can have a house meeting," I said. I wondered if she'd like to hear about my "issues," namely, that I didn't have a toilet. "Where and when?"

"Seven o'clock in the TV room," she said, leaning in to get a better look at my accommodations. "All of Wayne's stuff is gone," she whispered to herself.

"Sure is." I looked around. I hoped it was. If I discovered anything like what I had found yesterday, I wasn't going to be happy. "So I'll get to meet the other RAs tomorrow?"

She nodded. "There are six of us. Me, and five guys." She stepped out of the room and back into the hallway. "There's only one floor of women here. You knew that, right?"

"I knew that," I confirmed. "Hey, were you close with Wayne?"

She flushed a pink that was close to the color of her flip-flops. "No. Why would you ask that?"

I shrugged. "I don't know. He lived here, you live here . . . just thought I'd ask. I thought maybe you knew where he went."

"Why would I know where he went?"

"Just thought I'd ask," I repeated. When she didn't move from her place in the hallway, I asked her, "So, tomorrow at seven? TV room?"

She nodded and took off down the hallway, her flip-flops slapping a guilty staccato on the marble floor. She knew more than she was giving up. Or she was madly in love with slack-jawed Wayne. Or both.

The next thought hit me like a ton of bricks.

Could he have been her dealer?

EIGHT

The next school day passed without incident and I managed to keep my nose clean for the entire day. I spoke with Crawford at lunchtime and he told me that he had found a woman in the squad who had a hook in Scarsdale. She had reached out to a detective there and found out that Wayne had not been reported as a missing person, at least not so far. But the detective promised to keep an eye out and an ear to the ground and to let Crawford know if anything turned up.

We were running out of metaphors so I hoped this wrapped up quickly.

I got back to the dorm just in time to pay the pizza guy, who was waiting for me at the front desk when I walked in. I skidded to the front desk in my high heels; my first duty as RD was going to be to have a conversation with the custodian about the high gloss on these floors. There was *clean* and then there was *dangerous.* We had entered into the latter category with Mr. Janitor's overzealous buffing.

I had called for a pizza before I left my office thinking that I would be back at the dorm in minutes; I had gotten waylaid by a student who was not guilty about spring break, but guilty about the D he was getting in my creative writing class. If he had channeled all of that guilt into his creative writing, he would have had something to work with, but instead, he was frozen. We worked through a few scenarios, with my mind on my impending pizza delivery, his on getting a grade higher than a D.

I took my pizza back to my room and opened the door. I spied Trixie sitting on the bed, dutifully awaiting my arrival. She jumped off and ran circles around me, nearly knocking me over. I knew what we had to do before we got to eat our pizza, so I put her on the leash, stuffed a *New York Times* delivery bag into the waistband of my skirt, and took her out the side door into the parking lot.

I was still wearing my heels, but the only place I could see to take her was the cemetery, directly across the parking lot from the dorm. It wasn't a straight shot, but up a little hill, which I reasoned I could scale in my black suede pumps. I started across the lot and up the hill, using my heels to dig into the soil. Going back to change my shoes wasn't an option; Trixie had to go and any time I wasted going back to my room to change my shoes was going to be time taken away from eating my pizza before the house meeting. Trixie scampered up the little incline, dragging me behind her.

I realized that walking my dog in a cemetery probably wasn't the most reverent or polite thing I could do, but the dog had been cooped up in my dorm room since lunchtime and needed to go out. I didn't have time to do a leisurely riverside walk like we had in the morning and at noon, so this was going to have to do.

After everything I'd done and the decisions I had made, I was going to hell anyway, so if my dog took a dump on a long-gone nun's grave, what was the harm? I led Trixie down one of the paths between the graves and as far away from a final resting place as I could and looked around as she paused, sniffed, ran in circles, and then got down to business. I said a silent apology to Sister Margaret Dolores Russell, born 1845, died 1941.

"Look, Trix," I said, wiping off Sister Margaret's grave marker, "she died on Pearl

Harbor day."

Trixie was not impressed.

I got up and continued walking. Off in the distance, I could see the Science Building, where my ex-husband had spent many a day teaching, hitting on colleagues and students alike, and being a general shithead. Next to that was the library, a building that was virtually unknown to most of my students. And beyond that was the dorm where I had lived for most of my time here, right next to the new dorm that was going up. From what I had read in the latest campus newspaper, the building was going to be state-of-the-art, with Wi-Fi, flat-screen televisions in every lounge, satellite cable service, popcorn machines, and rooms decorated by some fancy designer who got to put his name on every piece of furniture. I looked at my old dorm and sighed. I guess things had to change, but was the change for the better? My dorm had had Murphy beds that folded into the walls to make more room for the two girls per, laminate-topped desks bolted to the floors, and televisions with rabbit ears. And we had been very happy. At least I had. Max had always complained that living at St. Thomas wasn't any better than living at a women's reformatory.

Trixie was taking an inordinately long

time, peeing on every gravestone she encountered. We wended our way through the cemetery, where I read some of the grave markings; others were worn away from years of exposure. Most of the sisters buried there had lived long, long lives, and many had survived well into old age without Wi-Fi.

Trixie sniffed at the grass and squatted to pee again. "Oh, for God's sake, Trix. We'll be back. You can mark your territory later." I knelt down and petted her, accepting her kiss. To my right, I heard rustling and my back straightened. "Who's there?" The hair on Trixie's neck went up and she let out a low growl, straining at the leash. "Down, Trix," I whispered. I stayed in the crouch, listening for more rustling.

The next sound was far more menacing as a beer bottle sailed past my head and hit the gravestone next to me, that of one Sister Catherine Marie LaGrange. The bottle shattered, shards of it landing in my and Trixie's hair. Trixie let out a yelp of surprise and bolted, dragging me after her. I flew into the gravestone directly in front of me, the top of the stone hitting me squarely in the diaphragm. I sucked in one last gasp of air before the wind went completely out of me. I hit the ground, landing on my back, staring up at the last remaining slants of daylight in the clouds.

The rustling got louder and I heard the sound of footsteps. In between gasping for air and wondering if you could die from having the wind knocked out of you, I sat up and saw a figure running through the gravestones. I couldn't see the front, but from the back, the figure was tall, male, and thin.

And if I could have guessed, I would say slack-jawed.

I tried to speak but couldn't. Trixie was in hot pursuit, having freed herself from my hold on her leash, jumping over gravestones and weaving in and out of the rows of dead nuns. I finally took in some air and screamed his name.

"Wayne! Wayne Brookwell!"

But Wayne, or whoever it was, ran up the hill and out of sight. Trixie wasn't chasing him anymore, so when I was able to breathe again, I got up to find her.

She was crouched on the grave of Sister Mary Lawrence Cassidy, born 1893, died 1995. I got closer and saw that Trixie was eating the remains of a ham and swiss on rye. She looked up at me guiltily.

"You almost killed me, Trix," I said, clutching my midsection. The pain was intense and I realized I had tears streaming down my face. I wiped my cheeks with the arm of my sweater and pushed my hair back, looking around. Still not a soul in sight, the bottle thrower long gone. I grabbed Trixie's leash and hobbled back to the dorm.

NINE

I was still breathless from nearly being impaled on a gravestone. "I think I saw him," I said. I was back in my room, sitting on my twin bed, talking on my cell phone. Crawford was at his desk in the squad.

"You'll have to be more specific," Crawford said.

"Wayne. Wayne Brookwell."

That got his attention. "Where? When?"

"A few minutes ago." I explained how I had been walking Trixie in the cemetery and how I was about 99 percent positive that Wayne was only a few rows of graves away.

"So, he's alive."

"I think so," I said. "But not for long if I get my hands on him. Between having to live in this dump, and getting a beer bottle thrown at my head . . . and, oh, yeah . . . getting pulled over the top of a gravestone, I'm getting more and more ticked off by the minute at this guy." I took in another deep breath. Yep, still hurt. "Even if he has the loveliest parents in the world."

Crawford asked me to hold on; I could hear his muffled voice as he talked to someone in the precinct. "Radio car is on its way over."

I groaned. "Why?"

"Because anyone who throws a beer bottle at your head deserves a tune-up."

"A what?"

"A talking-to."

I didn't think that that's what it really meant, but I let it go. "How are you going to find him?"

"I told them to start with the cemetery and take it from there." He paused again. "Now I'm pissed."

"It's okay, Crawford," I said, knowing that him being angry at Wayne would not help the situation. "I'm fine."

"Are you really okay? Or are you just telling me that so I won't make a big deal out of this? Because if we find Wayne, he'll have bigger problems than a brick of heroin in his toilet."

I touched my midsection, and while it was sore, it wasn't excruciating. "I don't think I broke anything but I could be bleeding internally," I said, only half joking.

"Do you want me to come over?" he asked.

"Under normal circumstances, I would say 'yes,' but I have a meeting tonight with my resident assistants."

"That sounds like fun."

"And with the internal bleeding and all, I don't think you'd enjoy being around me."

"Right."

I thought of something else. "Hey, did Lattanzi or Marcus say anything about the stuff from the toilet?"

"Haven't seen them. But I'll hook up with one of them tomorrow and see if they found out anything. I haven't heard anything on the prints that were taken, either, but I'm guessing we're also not going to get anything back from those." He sighed. "Unless you can find Brookwell on your own, you're stuck there until the end of the semester, I'm afraid. First chance I get, I'm coming over to poke around with you."

"That sounds vaguely dirty."

He chuckled. I heard his radio crackle again in the background. "I've gotta go. Are you sure you're okay?"

"I'm fine. Thanks for listening."

The house meeting commenced right at seven o'clock, just like Amanda said it would. Internal bleeding probably would have been the only thing that could have kept me from attending, given Amanda's insistence the day before. She was as jittery that night as she was the first time we met and I watched as she took a seat on an upholstered ottoman directly across from me, her leg going up and down in a nervous rhythm. She was in the same getup as when I had first met her: pink flip-flops, jeans, the Princeton sweatshirt. Fortunately, the other RAs seemed like an amiable, if laconic, bunch. One, Bart Johannsen, had brought his lacrosse stick, which he twirled repeatedly during our meeting, making me dizzy. He was a giant kid whose Scandinavian genes had presented themselves in an impressive genetic specimen: Bart was well over six feet, built like a redwood, with a tanned face and a head of platinum-blond hair. Another, Michael Columbo, bounced a basketball. Michael was a boy in a man's body — giant feet that he didn't know quite how to maneuver yet, and long arms that swung at his sides when he walked. Yet another, one Spencer Williamson — a nebbishy-looking kid who looked like he was straight from central casting — I had had in class in an earlier year. He sat across from me, looking dolefully at the back of Amanda's head. Although these kids had gone through a rigorous interview process and were responsible for the students who lived on their respective floors, they didn't seem any different from their charges, so I wasn't sure what had set them apart from the other students who had interviewed for these coveted spots that afforded them free room and board for the duration of their tenure.

"So, what did Wayne usually talk about with all of you at these meetings?" I asked, perching gingerly on the edge of the credenza against the wall. I assumed that word of Wayne's unceremonious departure had swept the dorm and that we didn't need to cover that.

My question was met with a bunch of vacant stares, with the exception of Amanda, who looked up at the ceiling as if it held great interest.

"Any issues?"

Nothing.

"Any concerns?"

Michael Columbo spoke up. "Yeah. I need someone to cover the desk for me Wednesday night. I have to work." He dribbled his basketball a few times, deftly working it between his legs. He pretended to shoot at an imaginary basket.

Impressive, I thought, watching his basketball skill. I wondered about his "work." Wasn't being an RA a job? "Okay. Any takers?" I asked. There was murmuring and mumbling about plans made and studying to do but no commitments. I looked around. "Spencer? What about you?" He didn't look like the type who would have an impressive social calendar, but who was I to know, really? I took the chance that I was right.

He responded with a huge sigh and a shake of his blond, overgrown mop.

"Is that a 'no'?" I asked.

"I've got a Japanese anime convention in the city that night."

Of course you do. That was so weird that I knew he hadn't made it up. If you're going to lie, you usually use something a little less, well, specific. "What do you do if nobody can do it?" I had a feeling I knew the answer but I hoped against hope that I was wrong.

Amanda looked at me. "The RD has to do it."

Of course they do, I thought. I looked at her and smiled weakly. "Is that what Wayne used to do?"

They all nodded in unison.

"Wayne was the best," Amanda said, her eyes filling with tears.

"Well, he's not dead! We don't have to talk

about him in the past tense," I reminded her. "Why was he the best?" I asked. I looked around the room. "Anyone?" I felt like I was leading the "Wayne Brookwell Seminar" with a group of unwilling students.

Everyone was silent. Finally, Bart Johannsen stopped twirling his lacrosse stick long enough to proclaim, "Wayne was just really cool."

What a testament. "Anything else?"

"Really cool," an RA named Jamie chimed in. There was a collective murmur of "cool, really cool," uttered by the RAs.

"What made him cool?" I asked.

"He just *was*," Amanda said, wiping another tear from her eye. "You wouldn't understand."

Why? Because I'm old? Or because I hated him for putting me in this predicament? I obviously wasn't going to get anywhere tonight, so I called the meeting to an end at precisely seven oh seven and headed back to my room.

Crawford was leaning against the door to the janitor's closet, across from my room, talking on his cell phone. He smiled when he saw me coming down the hall.

"I love you, too," he said to the person on the other end of the conversation, and mouthed "Erin" to me. She was one of his twin seventeen-year-old daughters, and from what I had both gathered and observed, the needier of the two. "You, too, honey. Sleep well." He flipped his phone shut. "You can't joke to me that you're bleeding internally and not expect me to follow up." He gave me the once-over, holding me at arm's length. "You look pretty good."

"Pretty good?" I asked. "Pretty good?" I repeated, my voice rising. "I expect better than that."

"You look amazing," he revised. He gave me a hug and it didn't hurt, so that was a good sign.

"Did the guys in the radio car turn up anything?" I asked.

He shook his head. "Nothing. They went through the cemetery and all of the usual hiding places on campus, but nothing."

I hadn't expected that they would turn up anything, including Wayne, but it was worth a try, I guess. "I'd ask you to come in, but you know, I wouldn't want to look like a hussy," I reminded him, shrugging my shoulders apologetically.

He nodded. "I know. And I wish I could take you to dinner but I have to go back to work."

"I've got an entire cold pizza in there. Want to take a few slices back to the precinct?"

He mulled it over. "No. But thanks. I'll pick up a sandwich on my way back." He looked me over once again. "You sure you're okay?"

"I'm fine," I said. "Really. Go back to work."

"Stay out of the cemetery," he pleaded.

I hustled him toward the door. "I will. Promise." I crossed my fingers over my heart. Even in my heels, I was still not tall enough to reach him without standing on my tiptoes. I kissed him good night, my toes squishing into the front of my heels. "Now go. If you get found here after eleven, I'll have to write you up. And then I'll get written up, and suffice it to say, it will be a big giant mess."

"I wouldn't want that."

"No, you wouldn't," I said, and watched him as he went through the side door and back to his police-issue Crown Victoria. I gave him a little wave as he drove off.

"Good night, Crawford," I whispered, tracing a little heart on the glass on the door.

TEN

I got up at the crack of dawn the next day and walked down to the river with Trixie, who I have to say was really enjoying her new accommodations. I always looked at Trixie and thought that I should adopt her devil-may-care attitude; as far as she was concerned, as long as I was around, she was happy. It didn't matter where we were or what we were doing; I made her happier than anything, or anyone, else.

But she did love the water. My house in Dobbs Ferry is fairly close to the river, but not as close as my dorm room. Trixie and I wended our way along the path that led from the dorm all the way down to the water's edge, where I let her off the leash. She stopped short of going into the water, surprisingly; golden retrievers love to swim, but she seemed more interested in getting done what she had come out to do and digging a hole in the narrow shoreline. The sun rose behind us, its early morning rays warming my back as I watched her frolic in the soft sand.

I looked at my watch and saw that we had been walking for close to an hour. My thoughts had been focused on Wayne and where he was. If that had been him in the cemetery, that meant he was close by. And what role did Sister Mary play in all of this? Did she know that Wayne was in trouble and had she stashed him somewhere else on campus? I ran through a bunch of scenarios in my head but came to the conclusion that my primary goal — as it had always been — was to find Wayne Brookwell.

I had an eight o'clock class, which meant that Trixie and I had to hurry back up the hill to the dorm. I put the dog on the leash again and started walking briskly up the steep incline toward the dorm. I passed a couple of guys on their way up the hill, towels slung around their necks, fresh from a swim in the indoor pool. St. Thomas didn't have a swim team but it had renovated the pool building since I had been a student and now it was used more than when it was a green, murky mess in the bottom of the Student Union. I waved to one of the guys, the practitioner of anime — and apparently, swimmer — Spencer William-son.

"Hi, Spencer!" I called.

"What are you doing on campus so early, Dr. Bergeron?" he asked, peeling away from his group and coming over to give Trixie a quick hug. He took in my sweatpants and jeans jacket. We were midway up the steep hill to the men's dorm and I was grateful for the break.

"I live here, remember?"

He shook his wet mop and droplets of water sprayed everywhere. "Oh, right!" he said. He gave himself a knock to the head. "Can't believe I forgot that."

"It's okay," I said. I wasn't that memorable as a teacher, and now was nonexistent as a resident director.

"Nice dog. She yours?"

"She sure is," I said.

"How do you like living here?" he asked.

I was a little stunned. A student who cared about my comfort and well-being? That was unusual. "Well, I wish Wayne hadn't left campus but I'm making the best of it."

"Left campus? More like hightailed it out of here." He shifted from one foot to the other, a broad-shouldered man with a boy's face and demeanor.

"Did you see him leave?"

He looked at me, deciding how much he was going to tell me.

"Come on, Spencer," I said. "The longer he's missing, the longer I'm you're RD. And from what I gather, Wayne was a really cool guy," I added, even though I didn't believe it. There was no way that doofus was cool, even if all of the RAs said so. I took that to mean he was completely checked out and they didn't have to do their jobs with anything approaching competence.

He hemmed and hawed a few more minutes before giving it up. "I saw him leave the night spring break started. In his car. I was waiting for my father to pick me up to go home and I saw Wayne peel out of the parking lot."

I didn't know why he was reluctant to share that with me so I asked him.

"You're right. He was a cool guy. I just don't want him to get into trouble."

So he left of his own accord and with his own car. "What kind of car did he drive?" I knew from experience with male students that they couldn't remember to bring a pen to class but could recite make and model years of cars with alarming accuracy.

"A Prius. Black."

How sensible of young Wayne. Not very cool, but sensible. I thanked Spencer and started back up the hill. He called after me.

"You're not going to tell anyone, right?"

"Right," I lied. What was with everyone and their trying to extract promises of silence? I wasn't going to keep my trap shut and it was their fault for believing otherwise. The first thing I was going to do when I got back to my room was leave a message for Crawford.

Trixie pulled me along and I made it to the top of the hill, panting slightly. My midsection still hurt and I promised myself that first chance I got, I was going to kick Wayne Brookwell in the nuts as retribution. He wasn't directly responsible for my gravestone injury but he did play a major role in it.

I got back to my room and heard my cell phone ringing, deep in the bottom of my purse. I pulled it out and flipped it open. "Hello?"

"Me."

"Hi, Max. What's happening?" I sat on the bed and prepared myself for a long-drawn-out conversation about love and marriage.

"I'm going back to work today," she said dully.

"Good!" Max is the president and general manager of a very well-known and successful cable television station called Crime TV. I didn't know how she had stayed away from work for so long and still had kept her job and I was hoping that indeed she had a job to go back to.

"You think?" she asked, not sounding anything like the confident, carefree sprite that I knew her to be.

"I think it's great. You need to start getting back into your life, Max. Remember when I got divorced? What did you tell me?"

She repeated her own words back to me in a monotone. "The sooner you start living, the sooner you'll forget about that jackass."

That wasn't exactly how I remembered it, but that was the gist of her advice all those months before. Max had been no fan of Ray, my ex, but she had kept up an amazingly good front for the entire time I had been married to him. "I think you called him a much worse name but that's the basic idea." And I didn't think Fred was a jackass or otherwise, but I kept that to myself. "I think going back to work is a really great idea, Max."

"I'm so tired."

"I know. But getting into your regular routine will give you energy," I said, pulling off my gym socks. "Didn't you tell me that you've got a new reality show about Hooters' waitresses who are really private investigators that you're very excited about?"

"I guess so," she said flatly.

"Focus on that," I said.

"You're out of baked beans," she said. Losing track of the conversation was one of the hallmarks of my phone calls with Max.

"I'll bring some home when I visit on the weekend. Now what are you wearing for your first day back?"

"Well, right now I have on a black bra and tights."

She wasn't going to get very far in that getup. But she might be able to make a few dollars. "Put on that cute pencil skirt and the pink flowered blouse."

She snorted derisively into the phone. "That doesn't match!"

I knew it didn't and was hoping that I would get that reaction. By the time the phone call ended, she was sounding a little bit like her old self and I felt better. I smacked my head after I hung up. "I forgot to ask her about the paint!" I said to Trixie, who gave me a look that made it seem that she wasn't surprised. I was hoping that Max's going back to work would usher in a period of routine and order and, ultimately, reconciliation with her husband. Because after she went to work for a few days from my house to her job downtown, the commute, while not a terribly long ride, would definitely begin to wear on her. Max likes her world to be very small so that she can work as late as she likes yet still be home in fifteen minutes. Commuting on Metro North and being a slave to a train schedule was not in her plans; I was sure of that.

I left Crawford a message about my conversation with Spencer and updated him on the house meeting from the night before. "Apparently, Wayne was really *cool*," I said. "That's all I know. And that he drives a black Prius. They haven't been out that long, so I'm guessing it's pretty new. Let me know what you find out." I remembered that Crawford hadn't gotten any information from DMV on Wayne, so I guessed that the car might be registered to his parents. "Try the parents. It's not registered to him, but maybe to Eben or Geraldine?" If that didn't make him cool, I didn't know what would.

After showering, I gave Trixie some fresh water and a bowl of food and headed out to the parking lot, where I saw Joe, one of the older and more rotund security guards sliding a ticket under my windshield wiper.

"Joe!" I called. "What are you doing?"

He looked at me sadly. "Sorry, Doc. I have my orders."

"Orders?"

"You can't park here. Pinto said he told you."

I walked over to the golf cart that Joe drove and placed my heavy messenger's bag on the passenger seat. "You're kidding, right? He's got to be insane. I live here now."

Joe nodded. "And all residents need to park in the residents' lot, up the hill," he said, pointing east, a fat finger extended.

I knew where the lot was. "But I live here now," I repeated. Was Pinto really serious about enforcing that rule for me?

He shook his head. "Doesn't matter. All residents park in the residents' lot," he said. "That means you."

"That does not mean me!" I protested. "This has been my spot for nine years."

"But you weren't a resident for most of those nine years," Joe explained slowly, as if talking to someone of impaired intellect. "Now you are. And you —"

"Need to park in the residents' lot," we recited together.

I figured that fighting with him wouldn't get me anywhere, so I decided to exploit our long history together. "Come on, Joe. It's me. I'm only going to be here temporarily so what does it matter if I leave the car here?" I asked, my tone conciliatory.

"I have my orders." He let the windshield wiper, which had been projecting out from the glass, slap back down. "You'll have to move the car if you don't want to get another ticket." He got back into the golf cart and started to pull away. "Have a nice day."

I reached in and pulled out my messenger bag before he got too far. I saluted him. "You used to be one of the good guys, Joe!" I called after him but the whirr of the cart engine drowned out my voice. Or he chose not to acknowledge my last comment, because he didn't turn around to respond.

I was still muttering to myself as I let myself in the back door of the building where my office was and where I taught all of my classes. I saw that I had fifteen minutes before my first class so I bypassed my office and went straight to the commuter cafeteria where I could get a quick breakfast before my teaching day began. Fortunately, the friendly face of my old friend Marcus, the grill cook, was the first one I saw, down at the short end of the L-shaped food prep area.

"Marcus," I said, breathing a sigh of relief. "It is so good to see you."

He looked surprised at my overly enthusiastic greeting. "Good to see you, too," he said in his musical Jamaican lilt. "The usual?"

"If you mean two eggs and Canadian bacon on a roll, then yes," I said, walking over to the coffee machine at the end of the food line. I filled a large cup with coffee and added a splash of milk, which I drank while waiting for my breakfast to come off the griddle. I was starving. I hadn't given a lot of thought to what I would do for food, since I didn't have a kitchen. I couldn't afford to put on the "freshman fifteen" but was thinking that it would be extremely likely if every day held the promise of a bacon-and-egg sandwich for breakfast as well as a nightly pizza. I made a mental note to invite myself up to Kevin's that night for dinner so I could have a home-cooked meal.

I looked around the cafeteria, which was essentially empty at this time of day. Most students who had eight o'clock classes went straight to class, not leaving themselves enough time to grab even a cup of coffee before they did. I was startled when I saw the cafeteria door open and Sister Mary come in, her back straight, eyes darting around to see who else was in the room. I remained at the end of the food area and hid behind the huge coffee station, staying out of sight. Mary grabbed a bowl of fruit, which was covered with Saran Wrap, a muffin, and a container of milk, which she purchased and put into a paper bag. The whole transaction took about thirty seconds and she was on her way.

"Marcus, keep my sandwich warm. I'll be right back," I said, and hurried to the front of the room, watching Mary's progression down the hall through the round glass in the double doors. My hackles were raised: the nuns had their own dining room in the convent, which was attached to the main building that housed the professors' offices and the classrooms. I couldn't imagine why she would be getting a takeout breakfast from the commuter cafeteria. Mary didn't strike me as the type to sleep in and miss breakfast with the other sisters.

My conclusion? She was getting breakfast for Wayne.

Maybe it was a stretch, but I had to check it out nonetheless.

When she was a safe distance away, I stepped out into the hallway and walked on my tiptoes behind her, the toes of my shoes making virtually no noise on the floor. I watched her as she strode purposefully down the long hallway, never turning back, seemingly confident that nobody was behind her.

I passed the bookstore, closed until nine o'clock, when it would open and start buzzing with activity almost immediately. Mary halted momentarily and pulled her cardigan sweater tighter around her shoulders, for what reason I didn't know, but the gesture made me duck into the anteroom of the bookstore and pin myself against the wall.

I heard footsteps clacking along the floor and pressed myself farther back into the little chamber. Once they had passed, I ducked out into the hallway again and saw Mary almost reach her final destination: the stairway that led up to the convent residence.

"Alison! Hi!" I heard Kevin's voice behind me.

Mary turned, the twenty feet between us not able to disguise her surprise and suspicion at seeing me so close. Her brow wrinkled and she pursed her lips.

Kevin, not one to easily get the hint, stepped into the little space in which I had been hiding. "What were you doing in there?"

Mary gave me one last look and started up the stairs to the second floor of the convent, leaving me standing in the middle of the hallway looking as guilty as I felt.

Just a nun with her breakfast after hitting "snooze" too many times?

Or a protective aunt, harboring her sup-posedly missing nephew?

I was inclined toward the latter.

ELEVEN

I waited until I was seated at Kevin's small kitchen table later that evening before I gave him what for for blowing my cover.

"How was I supposed to know that you were stalking Sister Mary?" he asked, carrying in a bottle of wine from the galley kitchen and placing it in a chiller on the table. The spectacular view he had of the river from his sixth-floor residence had lulled me into a dream state and I sat up straight, surprised to hear his voice.

"Why else would I be pressed up against the doors of the bookstore?"

"Because you're not normal?"

I picked up the wine and poured us both a glass. "Very funny." I told him everything — from the exploding toilet, to meeting the Brookwells, to the cemetery encounter with someone who I thought was Wayne, to finding Mary buying breakfast.

"What's wrong with that?" he asked in

reference to Mary buying breakfast in the commuter cafeteria. "Maybe she overslept."

I raised an eyebrow. "Yeah. And maybe I'll find out that Wayne Brookwell is in the Peace Corps building latrines in Uganda and just forgot to tell everybody." I sipped my wine. "Ain't gonna happen, padre."

Kevin had prepared pasta with pesto, garlic bread, and some chicken cutlets, and we chowed down. I had brought Trixie up with me, and fed her some scraps from my plate which she gobbled up excitedly. After she had had her fill — or realized that there was no food left — she leaped up on Kevin's leather couch and fell into a deep, snore-filled sleep.

"Make yourself at home," Kevin called to her, but she was already out like a light. He turned back to me. "Did Maintenance replace your toilet?"

I shook my head. "Not yet. Any ideas on how to light a fire under them? No pun intended?"

Kevin thought for a moment. "I'll make a call in the morning. Nothing scares the maintenance staff like the threat of eternal damnation. If that doesn't get you a new toilet, nothing will."

"Thanks," I said. "Whatever you can do. I already have three messages in to them but not one has been returned. Nor do I have my own toilet on which to sit my butt cheeks." I'd been sneaking around, using the decrepit bathroom facilities in the laundry room when I needed to.

"Too much information," Kevin said.

I leaned back and smoothed down my blouse. "That was delicious, Kevin. Thank you. I hope you'll take pity on me and invite me back soon."

He started to answer but didn't get a chance; the phone began ringing in the living room. Trixie raised her head as if the thought crossed her mind to answer it; when she saw Kevin crossing from the eating area into the living room, she laid her head back down and resumed her nap.

I busied myself clearing the table, trying not to overhear who Kevin was talking to or what the subject of the call was. I ran the water in the sink and washed the dishes; although Kevin has a pretty nice apartment, it lacks some of the necessary amenities, like a dishwashwer. In the time it took him to finish his call, I had all of the dishes washed, dried, and put back into the cabinets.

He was a little pale when he came back to the dining room table. He sat down and finished off his glass of wine in one gulp.

128

"What's the matter?" I asked.

"That was the archdiocese. I have a meeting with the bishop tomorrow."

I knew that couldn't be good and I could see that fact reflected on Kevin's face. "Maybe you're getting a raise?" I asked hopefully, even though I knew that priests didn't get merit increases like members of the general population. I started to feel dread creeping up my spine; Kevin looked pretty distraught. My only thought was that he was getting transferred. If Kevin left here, I would be lost.

He shook his head. "I don't think so."

I sat back down at the table. "What else could it be?"

"I don't know," he said, none too convincingly. He averted his eyes and balled up his napkin. He stood suddenly. "Listen. I have to call it an early night. I'll have some materials to prepare for tomorrow."

If he didn't know why he was being called downtown, then what material would he have to prepare? But it was obvious that he didn't want to talk about it and I didn't want to pry, so I called Trixie and we went to the front door. "You'll call me the minute you're back?" I asked, taking his hand in mine.

"I will. Promise," he said, and gave me a

quick hug. He bent and petted Trixie who gave his hand a generous lick.

I stood in the hallway outside his room, my stomach in knots. Kevin's relationship with the powers that be wasn't that great to begin with; he was a flaming liberal in a very conservative institution. What could they possibly want with him at their headquarters? I started down the hallway, Trixie in tow, and hit the button for the elevator that would take us down to the ground level and my lovely suite. We piled into the small, ancient elevator, Trixie pressed up against me. I pulled the gate closed and the outer door shut automatically. I pressed the button for the first floor.

The elevator lurched as it began its descent and I leaned back against the cool steel of the interior. Trixie decided that our journey was going to take longer than expected and fell to the floor with a thud, her head resting on her paws.

Through the small round window, I saw the fifth floor pass by, then the fourth. The third, however, never materialized as the elevator stopped in a very matter-of-fact fashion way short of its mark. No sudden or abrupt interruption of service, just a slowing, a slight whine, and a cessation of movement. Trixie looked up at me from her spot on the floor as if to say "uh-oh."

I remained calm and pressed the button for the first floor. Nothing. After a few minutes, I frantically began pushing every button on the panel, finally resting my finger on the alarm button at the bottom. I checked my watch and saw that dinner service was nearing its end. I prayed that dinner had been terrible and that the students in the dorm had eaten hurriedly and raced back to their rooms to dine on the hidden stashes from the care packages their parents sent with regularity. Having stepped over piles of boxes in the mailroom, I knew that care package deliveries were frequent and that they got many college students through the dicey menu that the cafeteria offered.

I also knew, though, that one of the RAs was supposed to be manning the desk in the lobby. I wondered if whichever dedicated person it was would hear my cries from their area or even if the call box was wired into the computer that sat on the desk.

When nobody responded to the alarm, I started banging on the door. "Hello! Anybody out there!" I looked through the glass and could see the fourth floor about five feet above the elevator. "Hey! I'm in here!"

When nobody answered, I jumped up and

down on the elevator floor, hoping to get it moving again. When that didn't work, I tried to pry open the doors; I wasn't sure what good that would do but I was hoping any movement at all might jolt the mechanism that made the damn thing descend. Trixie started to whine when she sensed my rising anxiety.

I continued calling out to someone, anyone, in the dorm. It occurred to me that most of the lacrosse team lived on the fourth floor and that possibly they were at a game somewhere. I pressed the alarm button again, leaving my finger on it until it ached.

Finally, after about fifteen minutes, the speaker for the callbox crackled and I heard a female's voice. "Can I help you?"

"Hi!" I yelled, grateful for human contact. Fifteen minutes seemed like a day and a half, stuck in the cramped space with a dog with halitosis. "It's Dr. Bergeron and I'm stuck in the elevator."

"Oh, hi, Dr. Bergeron. It's Amanda."

"Hi, Amanda. I'm stuck," I repeated.

"Yeah, that happens," she said.

I waited for her to tell me what the usual protocol was for a stuck elevator but none was forthcoming. "What do you usually do?" I prodded. What had happened to the jittery, anxious, uptight student whom I had met two days before? She had been replaced by a dullard, it seemed. Maybe without Wayne, she was nothing.

"Well, there're a few things we can do."

I waited a few beats. "Like what!"

"Did you jump up and down?"

"Yes."

"Did you try to pry the door open?"

"Yes." I sat down on the floor next to Trixie. "Suffice it to say, Amanda, that I've tried everything possible to get the elevator to start moving again. Let's skip everything and go to Plan B. What do we do now?"

She was silent. "We'll call 911," she said finally.

I was hoping that that wasn't Plan B, because my main goal was not to call any more attention to myself. First the exploding toilet, then the graveyard incident, and now this. I'd be living on campus for the rest of my known days if this kept up. But I had to get out of here and I was resigned to the fact that the NYFD was going to be involved. "Okay. Go ahead. Call 911."

"Okay." I heard her muffled voice as she relayed the location of the emergency to the operator. She came back on the callbox. "Called them."

"Thank you."

"Hey," she said, apparently to pass the time while we were waiting for the fire department. "Have you found out anything about Wayne?"

Wayne, Wayne, Wayne. This girl was a one-note Johnny. "No. Have you?"

"Well, no," she said, indignant. As if she would tell me if she had.

The callbox being our version of the confessional screen, I decided to prod her for more information, thinking that not being able to look me in the eye might prompt her to give up more information than she normally would be willing to. "You really miss Wayne, huh, Amanda?" I asked gently.

"I do," she whispered.

"Was he your boyfriend?" I asked.

She didn't answer right away. "Not really."

I tried to remember the term. "Friends with advantages?" I asked.

"What?"

That wasn't right. What was the damn phrase? Was I running out of air? Was that why I couldn't come up with it? I ran through some phrases in my head. Friends who are advantageous? Friends who are beneficial? I thought about adjectives to "advantages." "Friends with benefits?" I asked, thinking that I had hit on the appropriate terminology.

"Something like that."

Well, it was either that or not that, so I took her answer as a "yes." "Was that all it was?"

She sniffled loudly into the box, making Trixie's ears prick up. "I really, really liked Wayne!" she cried. "He was so cool."

So I've heard. "Like loved him?"

She didn't answer but made a muffled noise that sounded like an affirmative. "It's kind of complicated. I'm engaged."

I couldn't help myself. "Engaged?" I exclaimed.

She sniffled some more. "To Brandon. He goes to Princeton. I love him and I love Wayne. I'm so confused," she said, sounding very dejected and extremely lovelorn.

"That is complicated," I agreed. "Does Brandon know about Wayne?"

"I think he has an idea that I might be —"

"Conflicted?"

"Yes. That's a good word. Conflicted."

"Does Wayne know about Brandon?"

"Yes. He doesn't care. He thinks that we're meant to be together."

Oh, one of those. I had an ex-husband who had played the same tune on his love guitar. Until he had lost complete interest in me, that is.

"When are you supposed to get married?"

The sound of crying came through loud and clear via the ancient elevator's squawk box. "This August. After I graduate."

I'd be crying, too, if I knew I had to marry a guy when I was also in love with somebody else. The whole situation was starting to depress me. I decided to change the subject.

"Amanda, do you have any idea where Wayne may have gone?" I asked. "Please. He might be in trouble and we need to find him."

"He might be in trouble?" She sounded truly frightened.

I had let on too much; that was clear. I looked down at Trixie. "Damn," I whispered. "Well, I don't know, Amanda, but don't you think it's weird how quickly he left?"

"He said he was going to Mexico for spring break but that he would be back Friday. When I saw you in his room, I knew that he hadn't come back." She paused. "Maybe he got delayed?" she asked hopefully. "Maybe his flight got canceled?"

I didn't answer because I was thinking about Mexico. And drugs. That was a start. I readjusted my position on the floor and Trixie took the opportunity to lay her head on my lap. As long as you're comfortable,

Trix, I thought to myself.

"Are you still here?" she asked.

"I'm still here." Where would I have gone? "Did the 911 operator say how long it would take for the fire department to come?"

I didn't hear whatever she answered because above me I heard a man's voice. Like God. "Alison?"

"Kevin?" Not God, but close enough.

"Are you stuck?" he asked.

"I'm not in here voluntarily," I said. I thought that was obvious.

"No need for sarcasm, honey. Press the 'four' and 'five' button at the same time," he called down. "I pried open the door on six but I'll close it now. See if that works."

I heard the door to six slam shut and I stood, doing as Kevin suggested. In an instant, the elevator heaved downward, slowly, and picked up a little speed as we descended but not so much as to throw us to the ground upon arrival on the first floor. I pulled the gate open and the door took a moment to open, but finally did. I was greeted by four firefighters, Amanda and her tearstained face, and the most welcome sight of all, Crawford.

Trixie and I stepped from the elevator. "Everything's fine," I said. "I'm sorry for bringing you out for a nonemergency."

The shortest and stockiest of the firefighters was wearing a coil of rope around his shoulder. Presumably he was the one who was going to haul himself into the elevator shaft and rescue the big, tall woman and her dog. "You okay, ma'am?"

"I'm fine," I assured him. "You can go. Really. But thanks for coming."

He turned to the other firefighters and waved them off. They looked like an eager bunch, ready for some action in the elevator shaft.

I turned to Crawford. "Hiya, Crawford. What are you doing here?"

"I thought we could catch a quick drink before I go home. But I didn't know that you were this lonely. You didn't have to call Hook and Ladder 13," he said, hooking a thumb toward the firefighters clustered in the hallway who were reassembling the gear that they had brought in with them. He smirked a little bit. "How did you get out?"

"Oh, Kevin gave me some cockamamie trick for getting out that required me to hold down two floor numbers at the same time." The firefighters left, en masse, and got into the fire truck, parked at an angle in the front parking lot. Amanda shut the door behind them and locked it. "Thanks for calling in for me, Amanda."

She was still sniffling. "You're welcome." She looked at Crawford. "Weekday visitation ends at eleven," she reminded me.

"I know," I said. "We'll take it outside." I watched as she settled in behind the big desk, her eyes going to the textbook on top of it. "Do you want Trixie to keep you company while you're on desk duty?" I knew that she would be there until eleven and figured she might want some company for the next four or so hours.

"Sure," she said, looking up briefly before turning her attention back to her textbook. Her hair, more unkempt than usual, fell in front of her thick-framed glasses, a curly halo.

I walked Trixie over to the desk and told her to keep Amanda company. She settled into the deep space under the desk and fell asleep. "She shouldn't have to go o-u-t," I whispered. Trixie had an uncanny ability to spell words that meant a lot to her including "food," "water," "ball," and "bone."

Amanda looked up at me. "Dogs can't spell."

"This one can," I said, and started off down the hall, Crawford in tow.

"What's her problem?" he asked. Having two teenage daughters made him acutely sensitive to their attitudes and problems.

"Besides being in love with Wayne?" I whispered when we were a safe distance away.

His eyes were wide. "Really?" We got to my room, continuing our whispered chat in the hallway. "How did you find that out?"

"Elevator confession," I said. "I have a couple of hours before I have to put this place on lockdown. Do you want to get a drink somewhere so I can tell you what else has been going on?"

His face lit up and that made any memory of being trapped in an elevator with Trixie and her fish breath melt away.

"I'll take that as a 'yes,' " I said, and opened the door to my room. I turned and looked at Crawford before kicking the door open with my foot. "Let me just get my bag and we'll go." I walked into the room and looked around. It still looked like it had when I left, but something felt different, off. I stood in the middle of the room, Crawford on the other side of the threshold, giving every surface the once-over.

"What's the matter?" he asked.

"I'm not sure," I said, and pulled down my shades. "I feel like someone's been in here."

Crawford stiffened. "Who has a key to the room?"

I looked at him. "Well, Wayne, for one."

"And we don't know where he is. Or even if he *is*."

"How Zen, Crawford," I remarked. I thought about who else might have a key. "Maintenance." I peeked into my bathroom. Still no toilet so they hadn't been here. "Housekeeping. But they don't clean until Friday. At least that's what Kevin told me." I put my hands on my hips and surveyed the area, still dusty, still littered with my personal belongings, most of which I hadn't had a chance to put away. I couldn't put my finger on it.

"Just doesn't feel right." I grabbed my bag and closed the door and then it hit me.

My pillows were gone.

Twelve

"Pillows."

I looked at Crawford. "Pillows."

"Why would anyone want your pillows?"

"I have no idea," I said. We were sitting in a bar on the avenue, me sipping a vodka martini that tasted like life itself, Crawford working on a cold beer from the tap. "But they're gone. First, the toilet. Now, the pillows. Is someone trying to make it so that I'm so uncomfortable I'll resign from the school?"

He shook his head. "No idea." He stretched his long legs out and crossed his arms. "You've been there what? Less than seventy-two hours? And already you've got a heroin-filled toilet and missing pillows? That's some kind of luck."

"I'll say."

The restaurant crowd was thinning out but the bar scene was just getting going. Crawford kept one eye on the Knicks game airing on the television behind my head. "I saw Lattanzi today," he said, fist pumping after the point guard scored a three-pointer. "He said that heroin is grade A, imported junk. That would have made Mr. Brookwell, or whoever stuffed it into the toilet, a boatload of money."

"Really?" I said, not surprised. "What else did he say?"

"Fingerprints haven't come back, but like I said, there are a hundred years of prints in that room." He made a face and I suspected the Knicks had just done something bad. "So we've got a huge bag of heroin, a missing person with no missing person report, and nothing else. It's a big zero."

"What about the Prius? Anything on that?"

"It's registered to Eben."

Just like I thought. "Where is it?"

"Don't know. But I've added it to the system, so if it turns up in the area, we'll know."

I told him about Sister Mary and the continental breakfast express.

"You think she's got Wayne in the convent?"

"Wouldn't be the first time the cloister had been breached," I said. He knew exactly what I was talking about: a few months earlier, I had stashed a friend in the convent who was on the run from a psychotic killer. The nuns had taken good care of my friend and had saved him from deportation — or worse.

Crawford was mesmerized by the game so I finished my drink in silence, looking at the bar denizens. I recognized one of the office staff from the admissions office who was lip-locking with one of the groundskeepers. Interesting, I thought. There were a thousand stories in the naked college, or so I paraphrased in my head.

"Can you send someone into the convent?" I asked.

"On what grounds? Suspicion of takeout breakfast?"

I faked a laugh. "Good one, Crawford." My drink was gone, so I motioned to the bartender for another one. "Extra olives!" I called as he walked away. There was no polite way to say "extra vodka" without sounding like a complete lush so I hoped the alcohol-soaked olives would suffice. "Oh, by the way, Kevin has a meeting with the archdiocese tomorrow."

Crawford grimaced; I wasn't sure if it was because of the Knick center's fourth foul or Kevin's situation. "That can't be good."

"I know." I leaned in and rested my head

against his chest, drinking in his clean laundry smell. "If Kevin goes, I'm sunk. This whole situation is a nightmare."

"You don't ride around with depressed Cro-Magnon man all day. *That's* a nightmare."

The bartender put my drink down on the mahogany bar and took some money from the stash of bills I had thrown down when we walked in. "Speaking of that, Max went back to work today."

"How did that go?"

"I don't know," I said. "I was going to call her but then the elevator thing happened. And my pillows are missing. Did I mention that?"

Crawford nodded. "I think so. I'm not sure. Should we cover it again?" He smiled. "Seriously, though, why don't you get Maintenance to change your locks after they install your new toilet?"

I picked up my drink and clinked it against his beer bottle. "Good idea."

"I'm full of them," he said.

"You're full of something, but I'm not sure it's good ideas," I said. I gave him a long kiss. "I've got to find this guy." I had an idea. "What say you and I head back to Scarsdale and take the Brookwells up on their invitation for cocktails?"

He was shaking his head before I had finished the sentence. "No, no, no, no . . ."

"Think about it."

"I've thought about it and the answer is no," he said. "Besides, I've got a graphic design convention in Tucson." He pulled away from me. "If you want to start somewhere, start with Mary." He shuddered involuntarily again, his usual response to thinking or talking about Mary. "See if you can find out something about her relationship to Wayne."

"I'm positive that Geraldine is her sister. And Wayne is her nephew."

"Yeah, but all you've got is a resemblance and that's not enough to go on."

"They have the same Miraculous Medal," I reminded him.

"And so does my mother and half of the Irish Catholic women in New York. We need specifics," he said, slapping the back of one hand into the palm of the other. "Haven't I taught you anything?"

I threw my drink back in one gulp. "No. But let's go back to your car and I'll teach you a few things."

He dropped me off right before eleven. We sat in the parking lot outside the dorm, getting in a few last gropes before I had to go in. He turned and looked out his window, his attention caught by something outside the car. "Did you know you've got a ticket on your windshield?"

"Oh, that." I explained the illogical rule regarding resident parking. "See you tomorrow?"

"I don't know. Fred's looking for overtime so that he can eventually move out and get back into his own place, so we may be pulling a double."

"Sounds horrendous."

"It is," he agreed. He leaned back against the headrest. "When you're not trying to figure out where Wayne Brookwell is, could you work on getting my partner and your best friend back together? He's a giant pain in the ass."

"I'll do my best."

"Should I walk you in?" he asked.

"Nah. Amanda has been at the desk all night and the door is locked. I'm sure it's fine," I said. "And she's got Trixie."

"Yes, the amazing watchdog. You'd be better off with a feral housecat than that lump of a dog."

I slapped him softly on the cheek. "Don't you dare disparage the Trix," I said, and then kissed him. "She's all I've got for company until I get out of here," I reminded him.

He held his hands up. "You're right. I'm sorry." He kissed me one last time before I opened the door. "I'd rather have you snuggling up to her than one of those firemen from earlier."

"They were kind of cute," I mused.

"Don't start," he said, and pushed me gently toward the door. "Get out. I have to go to work at seven tomorrow morning."

Amanda was still at the desk, her head resting on her textbook, sound asleep. Trixie was still under the desk, but when she sensed I was back she moved out from on top of Amanda's feet.

I bent and kissed my dog. "Hi, Trix." I walked over and touched Amanda's shoulder.

She bolted upright. "What?"

"You were asleep, honey. It's eleven. Time to go upstairs." I helped her gather her books and other belongings. "Everything okay here?"

"Everything's fine," she mumbled, straightening her glasses and pushing her hair off her face. "How long have I been asleep?" she asked.

Be damned if I knew. "Go to bed. I'll lock up," I said, and took a walk around the ground floor of the dorm. When I was sure that everything was locked up tight, I called

Security as my handbook advised the RAs to do before they left the desk, told the guard on duty that we were closed, and walked down to my room.

There was a package outside my room, propped up against the door. Trixie ran down to the package and knocked it over, sniffing at the contents. It was a giant plastic bag, and it had the ubiquitous and recognizable Target bull's-eye logo emblazoned on the front in the store's trademark red.

"What did you find, Trixie?" I asked, thinking that I should be concerned but then deciding that anything in a Target bag had to be innocuous.

If it hadn't been so weird, it would have been funny.

Because inside the bag were two brand-new, queen-sized down pillows.

THIRTEEN

Bringing Max up to speed on what was going on proved harder than I thought.

"Pillows?" she asked for the third time. "That's a new one."

"Yes. Pillows. First they were gone and then I had two new ones." I was walking toward my office and talking to her on my cell phone.

"You can't make this stuff up."

"You're right about that." I stepped gingerly on the unevenly spaced steps leading down to the back of the classroom building. "How was work yesterday?"

"Good," she said. "The Hooters PI series is going to keep me busy for the next few months so I'll have a distraction." She took a loud slurp of something. "Gotta go. Can I call you later?"

I reached the back door and put my hand on the knob. I had wanted to have a confab about her situation with Fred but it sounded like our conversation was over. "Can we have dinner?" I asked, but she had already hung up. I looked at my phone. "I guess that's a no?" I said to no one. I walked through the hallway and into the main office area. Dottie Cruz, the worst receptionist known to mankind, sat at her desk, surreptitiously reading a novel wedged under her inbox.

"Morning, Dottie," I said, and reached over her and into my mailbox. A few late papers, a few early ones, but nothing of note.

Dottie looked up at me and appeared to be trying to communicate with me telepathically. Her tattooed eyebrows went up and down in some kind of Morse code but I couldn't decipher the message. "Is there something you want to tell me?" I asked.

She tilted her head toward my office and I followed the angle to find Etheridge standing there, right outside my door. I hurried toward him, figuring it was better to get this over with rather than delay the inevitable. Which I was sure was a thorough interrogation over the toilet situation followed by all sorts of accusations and recriminations for my role in the sordid story of drugs, toilets, and pillows.

His hands were in his pockets and he was

rocking back and forth on the heels of his shiny brogues. "Dr. Bergeron."

"Good morning," I said, inserting the key into the lock of my office door with shaky fingers. "To what do I owe this honor?"

He waited until we were inside the office before answering. "Let's not do the witty repartee. Just give me the facts and we'll move on from there." He looked around my office; it was the first time he had ever set foot in it. "I've been away on a recruitment trip but Jay Pinto filled me in via a conference call."

I had been wondering why I hadn't heard from him sooner; that explained it.

The sun was streaming through the floor-to-ceiling windows that took up the back wall of my office and the room was warm. That didn't totally explain why I was dripping sweat in my lightweight sweater, though. I took a few deep breaths to slow my heartbeat. I could see students running down the back steps toward the rear entrance of the building; classes were starting in minutes but I didn't teach until next period, which I'm sure Etheridge had confirmed with his assistant, Fran. We had plenty of time to cover all of the goings-on in Siena dorm.

I closed the door and then sat behind my

desk. He took a seat in one of the guest chairs fronting the bookshelves across from my desk. "Why don't you tell me your version of events?"

"It's no different than Jay's," I said. "Exploding toilet, bag of heroin, police, crime-scene units, et cetera, et cetera." I hadn't meant to sound as sarcastic as I did, but something about his smug face, obviously pinning all of this inconvenience on me, made me angry.

He leaned back in the chair and folded his hands on his belly. "Have you gotten a new toilet yet?"

It was a strange question, coming from him. Never in my wildest dreams did I imagine that I would be talking to the college's head honcho about latrines, but here it was. I shook my head. "Not yet."

"I'll have Maintenance take care of it immediately."

I decided to go for broke. "Could I also get the locks changed?"

"Why is that necessary?"

"I just feel like I should have a new set of keys. It sounds like several people have keys, including Wayne, wherever he is," I said. "It just seems like a good idea."

He thought about that for a moment. "I think that can be arranged." He shifted in his chair. "We're going to keep this quiet, yes?"

"Of course," I said. Gee, anybody concerned about where the heroin came from? Where Wayne was? If Wayne *was*, as Crawford would say?

"I'll handle it with the police. Not a word, Dr. Bergeron. We don't want this getting out." He raised one eyebrow at me. "Not in light of everything else that has gone on here."

"Got it," I said. Please, please, please, I prayed in my head, do not go to the "remember when they found a body in the trunk of your car?" story. I was lucky; he changed his tune from the past to the present and we didn't have to go down memory lane.

"How are things going in Siena?" he asked, more out of curiosity for my charges' well-being than mine, I was sure.

"Things are fine. You have a top-notch group of RAs there so that makes my job easy," I lied. I couldn't pick most of them out of a lineup if they didn't have their sports equipment with them, but it sounded good. I had no idea how good, or not, they were at their jobs. I had only been in the building a few nights and it hadn't burned down, so I took that as a good sign, if not a ringing endorsement of their abilities to maintain the dorm.

He stood. "Remember. Not a word."

"I remember," I said. I'm clumsy, tactless, and a host of other things, but forgetful? No. I thought I could remember not to talk about a giant bag of heroin found in my toilet. "Have a nice day," I called after him as he ventured out into the main office area. I watched as Dottie tried to make herself disappear as he walked past, but he acknowledged her with a head nod and a mumbled greeting. I was positive that he didn't know her name, never mind her actual responsibilities.

She was in my office within seconds of his departure. "What did you do now?" she asked. Her ensemble today consisted of salmon-colored pedal pushers, three-inch wedge heels, and a tight yellow sweater. I guess spring had sprung in the Cruz household. Her peach-hued lipstick was a shade darker than her pants.

"I didn't do anything," I said. "Not that it's any of your business."

"I heard you're living at Siena," she said, fishing for information.

"My house is being renovated," I said by way of explanation. Wayne's disappearance wasn't a secret but I didn't feel like getting into it with Dottie. Was I being petulant? Probably. But I hated to give her any information regarding my living situation as it related to Wayne. I rooted around on my desk, collecting the papers I needed for class, hoping she would get the hint and leave.

"What are you having done?"

"This and that."

"Like what?"

I lost my patience. "Dottie, I don't have time right now to go through everything I'm having done. Suffice it to say that it's a big job and I needed to move onto campus for a while."

"I heard that Wayne Brookwell didn't come back from spring break." That was obviously her gossip trump card.

"Says who?"

She folded her arms across her chest and gave me a knowing look. "I have my sources."

I stared right back at her. "Well, tell your sources that they need to stop trafficking in idle gossip and get back to work."

She stomped off and returned to her desk; my hope was that she was so angered by my reaction that she wouldn't speak to me for the rest of the week. One can only hope.

I pulled my papers together and shoved

them into my bag. I had forty minutes before my first class started and I could either have breakfast or do the thing that I had conjured up while showering in the mold-filled stall in my bathroom. I really didn't have a plan but didn't think I needed a well-thought-out one, an assumption that would probably bite me in the ass later. But I took a chance and left my office, heading up to the administration-office floor one story above me.

Sister Mary's office was located between the dean of students and one of the reception rooms that when I was a student was called the "red room." It was now called the "DeGeorge Reception Room" after Sister Marguerite DeGeorge, one of the founders of the school and a revered figure here at St. Thomas. It should also be mentioned that the DeGeorge family was old St. Louis money and St. Thomas is nothing if not mercenary in getting funds out of alumni or even their rich families. Max can attest to that.

I didn't know what I hoped to find once I gained entry into Mary's office, a place where I had been only a handful of times. Mary usually visits me when we need to discuss something that can't be resolved on her favorite mode of communication, e-mail.

I crept down the hallway, passing the restroom, where I stopped in briefly. Not having a toilet made me acutely aware of every bathroom in the building and also spurred me to use every one I passed.

I was washing my hands when the smell of Jean Naté filled my nostrils and I turned slowly, only to see Mary coming through the door of the bathroom, as shocked to see me as I was to see her.

Startled by, first, seeing my very prim boss in a public restroom and, second, knowing that I had come up here to break into her office, I was startled. I flapped my hands in the sink, flinging water in every direction but mostly onto Mary. "Sister! Mary! Sister Mary!" I said. I grabbed a few paper towels from the dispenser and attempted to wipe off the water that I had flung onto the front of her starched white shirt.

"That won't be necessary, dear," she said coolly. She took the paper towels from my hands and sopped up the water soaking her shirt. She balled them up and threw them in the waste can. "This is an interesting place for you to be."

"I'll say," I agreed, sounding like a moron, my voice echoing in the tiled room.

The steady drip of the old, leaky faucet was the only sound as Mary stared at me, awaiting my explanation.

"I don't know if you've heard, but I'm without a toilet," I said. I made a face to illustrate just how inconvenient that was.

If looks could kill, I was dead meat.

"So, I've been making a grand tour of all the restrooms in the building. I realized I had never used the one up here." I pointed to the spot where I was standing in case she had forgotten where we were.

Mary's not stupid. And she clearly wasn't buying my ridiculous explanation. "Is there something you wanted to talk to me about, dear?"

Oh, where to begin? Having a conversation in the restroom wasn't ideal, but I decided to take a stab at it. "As a matter of fact, there is, Sister." I straightened up, prepared to find out the truth.

At that moment, the door opened, and Sister Louise, one of the nursing professors, busted into the room, her hands covered with blue ink. She rushed over to the sink and stuck her hands under the faucet. "Alison, be a dear and turn on the faucet for me? I'm covered in ink!" she said, the front of her wimple also stained.

I turned on the faucet.

"Thank you, dear." She washed her hands vigorously. "Oh, Mary, wasn't that a wonderful sermon by Fr. McManus this morning?"

Mary nodded. "Yes, it was, Sister."

"He is such a gifted speaker," Louise said, pushing in the handle of the soap dispenser and sudsing up. "And a delightful young man, to boot. We are very blessed to have him here."

Well, at least someone thinks so, I thought; I thought about Kevin heading downtown to the archdiocese's office and said a silent prayer for his well-being and return to the school. I excused myself, Mary giving me a look as I slid past her and into the hallway, making haste down the stairs and back to my office, where I hoped I would be safe for at least a little while longer.

If she had been trying to intimidate me into leaving things alone, she was having moderate success.

FOURTEEN

There was a new set of keys in my mailbox at the end of the school day, a welcome relief. I wondered how many people had copies of this set. Now if only there was a new toilet to go with my new keys, but I didn't hold out much hope. Progress is slow around these parts, something I had learned during my time here.

I was looking forward to getting back to my room and relaxing for a few hours before checking in with Kevin, but as I was walking up the steps toward the dorm, I realized I had promised — or more aptly, been coerced into — sitting desk for Michael Columbo. Because I was cool like Wayne! Or a giant patsy. So, I had one hour to freshen up, grab some kind of dinner, and get my behind into the chair behind the desk to monitor the comings and goings of both the students and any visitors they might have on this balmy Wednesday evening.

Since it had been two days since my Wayne sighting and I hadn't returned to the cemetery since, I decided to take Trixie back to the scene of the crime. Or the scene of the bottle throwing. I changed into jeans and a sweatshirt and leashed her up. We headed over to the cemetery and wandered around the gravestones, looking for evidence of Wayne's wanderings.

Trixie found a dead chipmunk, but other than that, we came up empty. By Trixie's reaction, we had found the pot of gold. She raced around the gravestones, the chipmunk hanging from her mouth, delighted with her find. I finally convinced her to drop it and dragged her back to another row of graves to get her as far away from it as possible.

After the dog was finished, we headed back to the dorm, where I loaded up on food from the vending machines in the laundry room. My dinner consisted of Oreos, pretzels, potato chips, Diet Coke, and a PowerBar, just to round out the cache. Two thousand calories and most of them junk. I felt like I had entered a time machine and gone back a decade and a half or so to my own college days. I didn't feel like pizza or Chinese and I didn't know if any of the other restaurants in the neighborhood delivered, so I made sure I stocked up so that I wouldn't starve to death. Not that there was much of a chance of that happening in a six-hour time span.

I relieved the day desk sitter and settled in, spreading my purchases around me. Trixie looked up at my hopefully. "Sorry, Trix, this is all for me," I said, opening the potato chips first. "And after where your mouth has been, I'm not coming anywhere near you."

She fell to the floor with a thud and a sigh, resting her head on my feet.

I looked around the desk to see what was what. I was still amazed that Merrimack and Etheridge had thrown me into this job without a lick of training. Either they thought that I was sufficiently intelligent and would figure it out or they didn't give a rat's ass about Siena dorm and hoped I would bring my Midas touch to the place — in which case, Siena dorm and its denizens were in huge trouble. There was a log-in pad to keep track of visitors (although this information should have been on a computer; St. Thomas is always two steps behind everyone else), a computer with some outdated word-processing programs and nothing else, a list of emergency numbers (which I didn't need — if there was an emergency, I was going straight to 911), a list of the RAs and their phone numbers, and a stack of takeout menus, all of which boasted delivery service.

Now we're talking, I thought, and perused the menus in the stack. I made a decision quickly and was on the phone to a local pub, ordering up a cheeseburger and fries, which they assured me would be delivered within the half hour.

I leaned back in my chair, happy that I wouldn't have to exist on vending-machine food, when my first visitor arrived, a stocky, bowlegged man in a polo shirt, slacks, and loafers, a heavy gold watch hanging from his meaty wrist. A diamond pinkie ring brought the whole look together. The whole look brought to mind a kind of Mediterranean, swarthier Neil Diamond. I sat up again, disturbing Trixie, who woofed her displeasure at me. "Can I help you?"

The man had one of those smiles that didn't go all the way up to his eyes, a half-smile that was supposed to lead me to believe that he was friendly when in fact he was just trying, but not successfully, to put me at ease. "Wayne Brookwell, please."

I stiffened a little bit. "I'm sorry. He's not available."

The smile left his face. The smell of his pungent cologne filled the small space between us. It reminded me of my late father and when he went through his Ralph Lauren Polo stage. I still had the lingering scent of Sister Mary's Jean Naté in my nose and now this. "When will he be available?"

I folded my hands on top of the log-in pad. "Not sure. He's on vacation," I lied. I didn't want to tell this man the truth although I wasn't sure why. "Can I leave him a message for when he returns?"

He regarded me with interest and I got another scent: the scent of menace. So did Trixie. She sat up and put her head on the desk, not exactly asserting her dominance, but letting the man know she was there and ready to rumble, if necessary. She was eighty pounds of unconditional love and affection, but he didn't need to know that. He stared at me for a few more seconds, seemingly deciding how far to take this. "No. No message," he said, and left as abruptly as he had come in.

Holding the door for him on the other side of the small entryway was Crawford, whom he brushed by without even a thank-you. Crawford looked after him, miffed, and came in, a bag of Dunkin' Donuts in hand. He was dressed for work in black pants, a nice blazer, white shirt, and tie. A little stubble on his chin told me that he had been at work for a while. But he was still hand-some Crawford, despite how tired and rumpled he looked. "Who was that?" he asked. Thankfully, Crawford didn't smell like anything except clean laundry and that was a good thing.

"Don't know. But you'll never guess who he was looking for."

"Mr. Goodbar?"

"Guess again."

"Carmen San Diego?"

"One more time."

"Wayne Brookwell?"

I put my finger to my nose. "Bingo. The plot thickens, eh?"

Crawford put the Dunkin' Donuts bag on the desk, ran out to the parking lot and stood there for a few moments, coming back in and reciting the words "roger, bert, eric, nine, two, five . . . roger, bert, eric, nine, two, five . . . roger . . ." He looked at me. "Write this down! Roger, bert, eric, nine, two, five."

I pulled out the log-in pad and wrote down the words he recited. I knew exactly what he was doing. "R-B-E-9-2-5." I ripped off the piece of paper and handed it to him. "New York plates?"

"Jersey." He pulled out his cell phone and made a quick phone call to the precinct. He recited the tag number while I checked in a female student going up to the fourth floor to see Michael Columbo, the kid I was sitting desk for. Wasn't he working? Isn't that why I was here? Why was she here? A booty call for when he arrived home? She was a lithesome young lady wearing a shirt that looked like underwear over her skintight jeans. She gave Crawford the once-over, along with a practiced come-hither look. Yep, he's a hottie, I wanted to say. And old enough to be your father. Crawford didn't notice, or was too much of a gentleman to acknowledge her in my presence.

"Name, please?" I asked.

She flipped her light-brown hair over her shoulder. "Mary Catherine Donnery."

I dutifully wrote her name down in the log-in pad. "Purpose for visit?" I told her that Michael was out of the building.

"I know," she answered. "I just have to pick up a book in his room." She turned and began to walk away but then came back. "Where's Wayne?"

Oh, for God's sake. Who cares anymore? I wanted to tell her that he was probably in the convent, having the dinner that his aunt procured from the cafeteria, but held back. "He's on vacation," I said for the second time that night. I hoped that if I said it enough it would actually start to sound true.

"Huh." She bit her glossed lip. "He was a cool guy."

"I know!" I said, a little too loudly. Crawford looked over at me and gave me a raised eyebrow. "I know," I said more softly, trying to look wistful at the thought of eternally cool Wayne on vacation somewhere.

"Amanda must be bummed," she said, almost to herself. She took another look at Crawford, looked back at me, and smiled.

"Why would Amanda be bummed?" I asked. I already knew that they had some kind of relationship but I thought this friends-with-benefits thing was a no-strings-attached arrangement. Her tears the day before would suggest otherwise.

"She was really into Wayne." She giggled. "But so were a lot of girls." She gave me a knowing look and flounced off, taking the stairs two at a time.

So, slack-jawed was in? Who knew?

Crawford finished his phone call and came back to the desk. He opened the bag and pulled out a cup of coffee out and handed it to me. "Dark and sweet, just like your men, right?"

"More like black and strong. We've been through this a thousand times, Crawford," I said, rolling my eyes in mock exasperation.

"I guess I forgot." He reached into the bag and pulled out another cup for himself and a chocolate glazed doughnut. He took a big bite and smiled, his teeth covered in chocolate.

"You're a walking cliché," I remarked, looking into the bag and pulling out a jelly doughnut, my favorite. I held my hands up at equal height. "Cops, doughnuts. Doughnuts, cops."

"How about 'thank you, Bobby, you're the best'?"

"Thank you, Bobby, you're the best," I recited dutifully. "Hey, did you see that girl?"

He shrugged. "Not really. What girl?"

"The one that I just signed in. She told me that a lot of girls had a thing for Wayne."

"So what? He was big man on campus?"

I walked Crawford through it slowly so that he would understand. "Well, if lots of girls on campus had a thing for him, and he in turn enjoyed this popularity, maybe the way to smoke him out is to use a pretty girl."

He considered that. "Another flawed plan but one I could get behind if you work out the details."

"Give me a couple of hours. I'm sure I'll come up with something." I took a sip of my coffee. "Now to what do I owe this honor?"

"I'm on my meal break," he said.

"Where's Unfrozen Caveman Homicide Detective?"

"Running errands."

"Is that code for 'doing surveillance on Max'?"

He shook his head. "No. Buying toilet paper at the Food Emporium. He's finally run out and realized that he needed that and a host of other items. And with Max not coming back anytime soon, it finally dawned on him that he has to do his own grocery shopping. He dropped me off here." He finished his doughnut and looked at his watch. "He'll be back in about ten minutes. Want to make out?"

I shook my head. "Can't. Sitting desk. I'm responsible for every person in this dorm until eleven."

"Damn."

I finished off my jelly doughnut. Crawford perched on the front of my desk and surveyed the tools of my night watch. "Very impressive," he said, taking in my log-in pad, computer, and master key.

"You have to be really organized to keep all of this stuff straight."

I saw Kevin coming in through the front door, Michael Columbo right behind him, dressed in a vaguely military uniform that I recognized as being the one Wayne wore when he was driving his limo. Crawford turned when he heard the outer door slam and Columbo gave me a quick hello, scurrying up the stairs either to get to his beautiful visitor — the one who was supposedly just picking up a book — as quickly as possible or to avoid a conversation with me. The look on Kevin's face was more dejected, more heartbroken than I had ever seen it, and I had seen Kevin during some pretty devastating situations. But those situations had everything to do with other people and his ability to shore them up; this seemed to be more personal. He came in, dressed as I hardly ever saw him in full black clerical garb: black shirt, white collar, black jacket. He stopped at my desk.

Crawford shook his hand. "Everything okay, Father?"

Kevin shook his head and I could see that he was fighting back tears. "It's worse than I imagined," he said, laughing ruefully. "I've really screwed things up this time."

Crawford, also used to helping people in emotional and dire situations, pulled a chair in from the TV room and told Kevin to sit down. He perched on my desk again and looked at my best friend — my priest —

and asked him what was wrong.

I had a very bad feeling.

Kevin uttered that nervous laugh again. "It seems that Mr. and Mrs. Wyatt — our friends Fred and Max — are not, nor were they ever, legally married."

Kevin looked at me, waiting for the outburst that never came. I was struck silent. "Their marriage is neither legal nor sanctioned by the Catholic Church," he said, which, while pretty straightforward, didn't make it any clearer to me.

I think I wanted to stay confused; if I began to understand this, even a little, I was going to go nuts.

Crawford stared at him for a long time. I think he got it sooner than I did. "The paperwork?"

Kevin looked up at Crawford, his eyes now wet behind his glasses. "Right."

Something passed between them, an understanding, and they both nodded.

I thought about it — the paperwork. I remember when I first met Fred — who is half West Indian, half Samoan — and him protesting that he had no religion, his parents were pagans or some such nonsense, his grandparents sent out on an ice floe when the villagers (he comes from Brooklyn, by the way) decided that their services were no longer needed. It was all part of the Fred mystique that he tried to create, and being as I was so gullible when we first met, it almost worked. But as the wedding day approached and the devoutly Catholic Rayfields pushed the church wedding thing, I remember Kevin casually mentioning that Fred had been baptized Catholic but had not received any other sacraments. And that he had "fudged" the paperwork to make it seem that he had so that Max could make her parents happy and have a church wedding without waiting for Fred to catch up on his rites of passage. "Fudged." His exact word. It now hit me like a ton of bricks.

"The *fudged* paperwork?" I asked, my dread growing in direct proportion to my anger. I found myself staring at him. "They're not married?" I stood. "They're not married!" I growled.

Crawford put his hand on my shoulder. "Let's get the whole story before we jump to conclusions."

"There aren't any conclusions to jump to!" I said. I thought about everything that Max had been through and the pain that she was in, thinking that her marriage was falling apart, even if she was the one that had precipitated it. Selfishly, I thought about how having her living with me, even if it had only been for a few weeks, had upended my carefully crafted solo existence. I thought about Kevin and how he had probably thought he was doing everyone a favor at the time. I looked around the desk and picked up the first thing I saw and threw it at Kevin. The log-in pad hit him squarely in the chest and the look of surprise on his face would have made me laugh if I hadn't been so irate. "They're not married?" I said for the third time. "What the hell is wrong with you?"

The outer door opened and I saw a group of students coming into the building, probably on their way back from the cafeteria. I was pretty confident that they were all residents and didn't need to be checked in, which would have been impossible given that the log-in pad was on the floor next to Crawford. I smoothed my hair down and took a deep breath, greeting the students when they entered the lobby area. Crawford handed me the pad and gave me a look that cautioned me to get a hold of myself.

After the students had started up the stairs and I was confident they were out of earshot, I asked Kevin to explain what had happened.

"The cardinal has it in for me!" he cried, running his hands through his blond mop.

"I've been under a microscope. You know that. And it's been a few years since my last wedding so they looked at Max and Fred's paperwork a little more closely." He slumped in his chair. "Seems the cardinal has a mole in Most Precious Blood. It wasn't hard to figure out."

Most Precious Blood was the local parish that sat just outside the gates of St. Thomas. "What does Most Precious Blood have to do with this?"

Kevin stared at his shoes. "In order to perform weddings on campus, I need to have delegation from the local parish. When Max and Fred got married, I didn't ask for delegation, so the wedding is invalid."

"What does that even mean?" I asked.

Kevin looked at me blankly.

"What's delegation, why do you need it, why didn't you ask for it, and how did Most Precious Blood find out?" I asked. Church law is extremely confusing but it didn't surprise me that there was an arcane rule on the books that governed who could get married — or who could marry — a couple in the college's chapel. "Answer those questions in the order in which I asked them, please," I said.

"First, delegation is permission. The college is governed by the local parish, technically. I need permission to perform weddings so that they are on the books at MPB." He crossed his arms over his chest in a defensive posture, sure that his next answer would warrant my throwing the telephone at him. "Let's just say I have a 'history' with the pastor at MPB and that's why I didn't ask for permission," he said.

I held up a hand. "I don't want to know."

Crawford sighed sadly.

"And one of our former students was at the wedding ceremony. She was looking at the St. Thomas chapel for her own upcoming wedding and wanted to see how things were done."

"And she's a parishioner at MPB," I stated, everything starting to come together for me. "That's how they found out. Through the quote mole."

"Exactly," Kevin said.

I glared at him. "So now what?"

"We have to tell them." Kevin looked at Crawford for support.

"We?" I asked. "We are not a team in this, Kevin. You are flying solo on this one. I'm not the one who has a 'history' with the pastor at Most Precious Blood."

Crawford, always sensible, chimed in after his extended silence. "Why don't we sit on this for a few days until *you*," he said, pointing at Kevin, "have a chance to digest this and figure out a way to make it right, and *you,*" he said, pointing at me, "aren't quite so emotional."

Another group of students walked in and I smiled, pretending that there was nothing wrong. Kevin greeted a few of them by name and chatted briefly with one kid I recognized from the house meeting. Behind them was the delivery guy with my dinner.

I peeled a couple of bills off the wad I had in my pocket and handed it to him. "Keep the change," I said, putting the bag with the food behind me on the computer desk.

Kevin looked at the bag wistfully. "That smells good." After what he had been through and what he had learned, I was surprised that he was able to eat.

I took the bag and pushed it at his chest. "Take it. I don't have an appetite." I turned and walked to the area behind the desk, stepping through a pair of French doors that led to a little patio area, where one of the students had left a plastic deck chair that had seen better days. I wiped off the dead leaves and layer of dirt and sat down, leaning my head on the stone railing. I had a bird's-eye view of the river and concentrated on that.

Trixie followed me out to the patio and

rested her head in my lap. Siena sits high on a hill on campus, and from this vantage point, one that I didn't know existed, I had a panoramic view of the campus. The stone was cool against my hot cheek and I turned so that I was looking north, up the river, as the expression goes. Crawford stayed inside, presumably still talking to Kevin.

I rubbed Trixie's head absentmindedly, thinking about the situation. Max was mad at Fred and had left him for a transgression that in my book would be considered minor. But let's not forget the lying, cheating fraud that my ex had been and consider where I was coming from; the lies had to be pretty bad in order for me to consider them divorceworthy. Fred wanted her back. Max had said the D-word once but I had made her promise that going ahead with any kind of legal action was a last resort. She had to try to work things out or at least hear Fred out.

But like I had thought more than a few times since this whole situation had begun, the simple truth was that Max wanted out. And fast. And using Fred's past dalliance with a woman he now worked with as an excuse was her way of making it happen.

So how would she feel when she found out that she wasn't really married? I had a feeling Fred would be devastated because he took the union very seriously. But Max? Would she be relieved once the truth was out?

I had no hope of answering these questions now because I had to return to the desk and finish up my tour of duty. I fixed my gaze on the gazebo that stood right next to the river in the middle of a copse of trees. Max and Fred had had a few wedding pictures taken there after their ceremony in the St. Thomas chapel. I saw a figure in the gazebo, which didn't surprise me, given the beautiful sunset and the mild temperature. It was obviously male.

And from where I sat, high above the rest of the campus, I could tell that it was Wayne.

I stood up so suddenly that the chair flew back and Trixie yelped in surprise. I ran into the lobby, past the desk, Trixie at my heels, barking madly. Crawford was lounging in the chair that had been vacated by Kevin, his head whipping around as I sailed past.

"It's Wayne!" I said, and hit the first door with the palm of my hand. "He's in the gazebo." I ran down around the back of the classroom building, past the convent, and continued toward the river. Trixie, delighted to be enjoying an evening run, was at my heels, her tongue hanging out, not as out of breath as I was.

God, I have got to get into shape, I thought as I rounded the corner, the gazebo no more than a hundred feet in front of me. "Wayne!" I screamed, my heavy clogs making my footfalls sound like cannonfire in my ears.

He was wearing a St. Thomas baseball hat tonight and I saw the top of it peek over the gazebo. As I got closer, he stood up straight and took off like a shot out of the gazebo.

I was officially out of breath. I bent over and started coughing violently. The last exercise I had gotten was when I had done the chicken dance, followed by the limbo, at Max's wedding and that had been six months ago. I took in a couple of deep breaths and took off again. But I was no match for slack-jawed Wayne's long legs and youthful speed; he was way ahead of me, winding his way through the trees, making his way down to the river. I tried to keep up, but eventually I lost him. Behind me, I heard Crawford, breathing heavily, bearing down on me.

Crawford caught up to me and stopped, his breath labored, but not as much as mine. "Was it him?"

"I think so," I said, panting. "I lost him. He's probably halfway to Spuyten Duyvil right now," I said, figuring he would make his way along the riverside train tracks to the next station stop. I put my hands on my hips and bent backward in an attempt to keep my muscles from seizing up.

We passed the gazebo, which was empty, and followed the road that led back up to the main part of the campus. On our way, Trixie following dutifully behind us, we ran into Amanda making her way down to the river.

She looked a little stunned when she realized the trio approaching her consisted of her RD, a cop, and a golden retriever. She stopped in her tracks, attempting to make it look like she was heading to the dorm she had just passed instead of on her way down to the river. She adjusted her glasses. "Is that you, Dr. Bergeron?" she asked innocently.

If she couldn't tell, she had bigger problems than a missing boyfriend. It meant she was going blind. "Yes, Amanda, it's me."

"Oh, hi," she said, and took in Crawford in all of his authoritative, coplike wonder. I could almost see the cold sweat break out on her.

"This is my friend Detective Crawford," I said. "Detective Crawford, Amanda Reese."

He held out his hand and shook her limp

hand. "It's a pleasure, Amanda." He smiled. "Where are you headed on this lovely evening?"

I was still out of breath and knew that I was going to awaken to sore muscles and leg cramps after my ill-conceived running plan. "Yeah, where *are* you going, Amanda?" Normally I would have let Crawford handle the questioning, but I was out of patience with everyone — Wayne, Kevin, Max, Amanda . . . and anybody else whose path crossed mine.

Crawford shot me the "shut up" look.

"I have to go pick up my econ notes," she said, and pointed. "Over there."

Crawford smiled again. "Come on, I'll walk with you. Alison, why don't you head back to Siena?" he suggested mildly.

But I got the hint; he wanted to talk to her and I was mucking up the works. I slapped my hip as I called Trixie and the two us headed back up the steep hill to Siena.

FIFTEEN

Crawford never came back; after he had dropped Amanda off at the dorm where she was ostensibly headed to get her econ notes, he had gotten a call from Fred that he was needed back at the squad. Fred had high-tailed it back from the grocery store and had picked Crawford up. He called me from the Crown Vic, the background noise and the bad connection making it virtually impossible to understand him.

"What? She said what?" I yelled into the phone. I was back at my desk in the lobby, surrounded by my tools: the pad, the computer, and the master keys. And of course my faithful pal, Trixie, who had gone back to sleep after our romp by the river. My next life? I'm coming back as a dog, preferably a golden retriever.

"She knows nothing about Wayne. She *promised*," he said. Even through the crackling of the cell phone, I could hear the sarcasm in his voice.

"So that's a dead end."

"For now!" he hollered, clearly hoping his voice was transmitting.

"Call me later!" I called back. I had heard all I needed to hear. Amanda was a liar. She had been heading down to see Wayne, plain and simple. She knew he was on campus. And if she knew he was somewhere on campus, chances were she knew where he was living. She was on to me, though, and she knew that I knew it. I'd have to play this very carefully.

Mary Catherine Donnery came skipping down the staircase into the lobby, her perky breasts jostling up and down under her flimsy camisole top. My boobs had never looked like that, and now, with them on the short side of forty, never would. "Bye!" she called breezily, a rosy red rising in her dewy cheeks. Something told me that she and Mr. Columbo weren't playing his preferred sport of basketball.

I looked at my watch and saw that it was a few minutes after curfew. "Hey, Mary!" I called. "I forgot to jot down your dorm and room number."

She stopped, obviously not in the mood to chat and knowing that there would be the possibility of repercussions for her tardiness. "DePaul, Room thirty-two."

I might need to locate her at a later date to talk about Wayne and fumbling around for her room number in the college intranet would be beyond my hacking abilities. I jotted it down on the pad, ripped off the piece of paper and shoved it into my pocket. She flounced out the door and into the night, her "picking up of the book" complete.

The night was progressing nicely with Kevin up in his room, probably licking his wounds, most of the students returning from wherever the night had taken them. Amanda had returned too, but had hurried up the stairs, leaving us without the chance to talk. At around eleven-thirty, I decided to take Trixie out for her final walk before putting the dorm on lockdown and calling it a night.

The night had gotten chillier, and I pulled the hood up on my sweatshirt in an effort to keep my neck warm. I crossed my arms and, like almost every other time I walked her at a late hour, implored Trixie to hurry up. Not that it made any difference. She was going to go when she was good and ready and that fact would never change. We were at the edge of the cemetery and I wasn't venturing in any farther; it was scary enough in the daylight so I couldn't imagine what it would be like at close to midnight. I had locked the front door before I left and I watched it so I could see any students approaching and needing entrance.

Trixie was remarkably cooperative and took care of business quickly, which I bagged and took back with me to the front door. I fumbled around in my jeans pocket for my keys, coming up with the slip of paper with Mary Catherine Donnery's information on it as well as the extra cash I had in there from dinner. I finally reached them and pulled them out, the old, black antique one getting stuck on a thread in my pocket.

I felt a hand on my shoulder and when I turned to see who it belonged to, I noticed a heavy gold bracelet hanging from the wrist to which it was attached. I turned slowly and came face-to-face with the man who had been looking for Wayne earlier.

"Hello," he said flatly.

I stared into his impassive black eyes. "Hi."

Trixie looked up at him as if he were the friendliest person she had ever met. Whatever menace he had suggested to her before had been erased, by what, I had no idea.

"Mr. Brookwell. I have some questions about him."

Me, too, I thought. "I haven't seen him," I

lied. "Nor will I." I ruminated momentarily on the fact that in spite of the suggested danger of the situation, my grammar was impeccable. If Sister Mary and I were speaking and not locked in a perpetual battle of wills, she would have been so proud.

"Oh, that's not true," he said, smiling slightly. "You've seen him, I bet, and you know where he is." His grip on my shoulder tightened. "So what do you have to say?"

"Please remove your hand from my shoulder," I said. "That's what I have to say."

In the distance, I saw a St. Thomas shuttle bus pull into the auditorium parking lot, just a few hundred feet from where I was standing. Relief flooded my body as I realized that it was delivering some sports team from some sporting event. I also knew that all of the guys on the various teams lived in my dorm. I relaxed slightly. They were on their way home and they had bats, sticks, balls, and various other types of equipment that could be used defensively, if necessary. "You're from Jersey, huh?"

"What?" he asked, confused. Having lost control of the situation and the hold on my fear, he wasn't quite sure how to respond.

"Jersey. Which exit?" I asked. "I have a cousin who lives in Parsippany."

"What the hell are you talking about, lady?"

I saw a group of male students disembark from the shuttle bus and collect their stuff from the equipment manager, who was pulling lacrosse sticks and pads out from the storage space under the seating area. I recognized Bart Johannsen and a couple of other guys from the dorm, two of whom made Crawford, a strapping six foot five, look like a ninety-eight-pound weakling. Their excited voices — they must have won — carried across the parking lot in the still night air.

The man turned and looked at the boymen walking toward us, twenty strong. He looked at me.

"Still want to do this?" I asked him. "Because, see those guys? They would just love to have an excuse to open your skull with one of their lacrosse sticks," I said, a little sick at the thought but happy to have that in my threat arsenal. "They get a little *Lord of the Flies* after a win." I let go of Trixie's leash and she ran toward the group, who were as excited to see her as she was to see them. It had only been a few days, but she had made a few friends.

He blanched a little bit and that's when I knew I had absolutely nothing to fear from this pinkie-ring-wearing, Neil Diamond doppelgänger. The man melted away into the night, as silent leaving as he was when he sneaked up on me outside the door to the dorm. I couldn't go to a rarely used public restroom in the main building without running into two nuns yet Wayne Brookwell was hiding in plain sight and Mr. Jersey was skulking around unnoticed, as well. I didn't see his car and didn't know how he was going to get where he was going — Jersey, I presume — but he hurried down the same hill that I had run earlier in the evening and disappeared.

The surge of adrenaline I had felt upon encountering him and then talking myself out of the situation left my body weak even though I now was pretty certain he wasn't a threat. The team members approached, Trixie in the middle of her new pack, and greeted me. I let them in, double-locked the door, rechecked every door on the first floor to make sure it was dead-bolted and went to my room.

I rested my head on one of my new pillows from Target and, despite my keyed-up state, fell into a deep sleep, Trixie by my side.

Sixteen

Etheridge had made good on his promise of a new toilet and I had one when I returned home the following evening. I didn't need to use it in the most literal sense, but I put the seat down and sat on it, just to get a feel for it. I had never been so happy to see a toilet in my entire life.

Max had called me earlier in the day and asked if she could come up to campus for dinner. "I'll bring Indian," she said. I told her that there really wasn't enough room in my dorm room to eat but that if she wanted to stay on campus, we'd have to eat in the TV room. "That's fine. I want to take a trip down memory lane. The present isn't turning out to be so great."

"And remember!" I called out before she hung up. "No booze."

"Just like old times," she said, sighing, but I didn't know what "old times" she was talking about. I didn't remember her ever being in a "no booze" state when she was a student here. I do, though, remember a keg in my closet when I returned from Christmas break and which I hadn't been too pleased to find out had a drippy spigot. I had at least half a keg drain into my snow boots so that whenever it snowed during the entire second semester, I walked around smelling like a bar wench, eau de Budweiser filling the air around me. Unfortunately, that winter had been particularly bad weatherwise.

Before she arrived, I stared at myself in the mirror and practiced the faces I would make to see if they looked guilty, indifferent, seminormal, or none of the above. I was carrying around the information about her marriage and I wasn't happy about it. Nor am I a very good actress, Coco Varick, Air France flight attendant, being the only exception. And I had been playing her a lot lately, at least in my head. I e-mailed Kevin and told him to stay clear of the TV room, the lobby, and anywhere else Max and I might be in the building from the hours of seven to ten, just to be on the safe side. I didn't want him seeing her, because as bad as I am at concealing the truth, I can only imagine how bad Father McGossippants is.

She looked much better than she had

when I had left her just a few days before. She received an appreciative glance from Tommy Moore, who was sitting desk when she arrived. I was already in the TV room, setting up the small card table for our dinner, but I could see out of the corner of my eye that he was sitting up straight and that his face was a little flushed. Max must be here, I thought. When I went out to greet her, she was signing the log-in pad, leaning over the desk, her ample bosom — usually rare for someone a hundred pounds dripping wet — peeking out of her V-necked top. She stood and I could see that her short hair had been colored, her eyebrows waxed, and her face the recent recipient of a facial.

It's amazing what a couple of days can do, especially when someone lives at hyperspeed like Max. Her recovery was like her metabolism — quick, efficient, and highly effective.

"You look so much better!" I said, and gave her a hug.

She broke away and picked up the bags of Indian takeout that she had left on the desk. "Going back to work was just what the doctor ordered."

Finally, someone had taken my advice, and finally, it had been right.

Over murgh tikka masala and Diet Cokes,

I gave her the details of my Wayne sighting, the man who approached me, and finally, because I had forgotten that part of it, the whole Sister Mary breakfast/bathroom sighting.

"So, old Mary uses the toilet, huh?" she asked. "Never would have thought she was human like the rest of us."

"I think she's got him in the convent," I said.

"Sounds like it."

The old Max would have immediately begun hatching a plan to get us into the convent, but this Max just sat silently eating her dinner. I asked her to tell me about work, figuring that might loosen her up a bit.

"The Hooters PI show is coming together nicely," she said, her mouth full. "Thank God I went back to work! My assistant program director was about this close to screwing the whole thing up," she said, holding her thumb and index fingers less than an inch apart.

I helped myself to some rice. "How's my house?"

She looked away quickly. "It's great!" she said with a little too much cheer.

"Great?" I put my fork down. "You sure?"

"Yes, great," she said, making a fast

recovery. "I'm keeping it clean."

"You'd better be. Remember, Magda comes every Friday to do a thorough cleaning."

"She does?" Although I reminded Max of this every week, she either chose to forget or didn't hear me at all.

"Yes," I said. "I told you that before I left. Remember?"

"Apparently not," she said. She pushed her plate away. "If I eat any more of this, I'm going to vomit."

Glad I had a new toilet. And if that was her way of changing the subject, she had succeeded.

"You know what would be nice?" she asked. "Some rum in this Coke." She got up and went into the lobby to talk to Tommy. "Hey, kid, got any booze in this place?"

I didn't hear Tommy's answer, but I hurried into the lobby to grab her before she did any more damage. I passed by the staircase and then the front door, where I spied Crawford's Crown Vic pulling into a visitor parking space in front of the dorm. I had to admit: living on campus had its advantages, particularly if Crawford was going to come by as often as he did; I was a lot closer to the precinct here than at my house. I stopped by the front door and watched as he maneuvered the car into the space.

He got out of the car and gave me a quick wave. And then the passenger side door opened and Fred emerged, his hulking shape unmistakable even in the fading light of day. The smile that was on my face left immediately like ice cream sliding off a cone. I returned Crawford's wave with a hand motion that I interpreted to mean "stop" but on which he apparently didn't get the memo. He waved again and pointed surreptitiously toward Fred who was lumbering behind him, his bald head catching the light from the one working streetlight in the little lot.

I turned to give Max the high sign but she was deep in conversation with Tommy, who apparently did know where there might be a stash of rum. He was on the phone as she sat on the edge of the desk, swinging her shapely legs back and forth, Tommy's eyes following every motion, mesmerized. He hung up and gave her a fist bump to indicate success.

Crawford came in the outer door and gave me a funny look, probably wondering why I was still pressed up against the glass of the inside door. As he put his hand on the doorknob, he looked over my head and caught sight of Max. Fred, right behind him, plowed into his back, flattening Crawford on the other side of the glass, creating a tempered-glass sandwich of me and Crawford.

Fred saw Max, too, because he shouted "Move!" at the two of us, and the sound carried through the thick layer of glass, across the lobby and to Max, who stopped swinging her legs and looked toward the door. Her face froze. Once happy about finding a rum dealer, she now looked a bit surprised, a bit angry. She jumped off the desk and stood in the lobby.

I backed away from the door because Fred, in a hurry to get to his woman, looked like the Incredible Hulk without the green body paint and torn pants. He pushed Crawford to the side of the little anteroom, pulled open the door, and walked into the lobby.

"Why won't you return my calls?" he demanded of her.

Tommy Moore stood up slowly and backed away from the desk, apparently thinking that Fred could read the impure thoughts he was having in his mind about Max. He picked up speed and hustled up the staircase to floors above, probably not stopping until he got to the roof.

"Why won't you get the hell out of my apartment?" she asked.

"*Our* apartment," he reminded her.

"Last time I checked," she said, throwing her hip out to the side and putting her hand on it, "my name was the only one on the deed."

Fred didn't have an answer to that. He's not the most talkative guy nor the quickest with a retort so it didn't surprise me that he had nothing to say. What was there to say, really, except for "Hey, guys, you're not really married so this is all a bit of a waste of energy." But I wasn't going to say that and neither was Crawford, who was rubbing his upper arm after being body-slammed into the door.

"Well, it was ours when we lived together," Fred said weakly.

"Yeah, until you made a mockery of our marriage," she said, but I could see that she was losing her strength on that one. It appeared that, exclusive of the apartment-ownership issue, Max's resolve was beginning to crumble slightly despite how hard she tried to hold fast to her stance.

He put his hands out in a conciliatory gesture.

"I wasn't married to you when that happened," he said.

I sat down on the stairs. This was going to take a while.

"Yeah, but you never told me. And that's what hurts."

"Have you told me everything about your life before?" he asked.

Good point. I knew she hadn't. Because if she had, they would still be undergoing a battery of blood tests.

She bit her lip. "Yes," she said, wavering.

I felt like this was a complete rehash of every other conversation they had had prior to splitting up and couldn't understand why we were going down this road again. I looked at Crawford, who was standing in a corner of the lobby, looking up at the ceiling, clearly wishing he were anywhere but here.

I encouraged the two of them to go into the TV room so that they could chat and have a little more privacy. I pulled the French doors closed behind me and asked Crawford if he wanted to come down to my room, visitation ordinances be damned. It was still early enough so that I wouldn't get in real trouble if he was discovered, but I hadn't signed him in and had no intention of doing so.

We went into the musty living room of the

suite and sat on the old Victorian sofa, which I was sure was an original.

"I think I've officially had it with this situation," he said, letting out an exasperated sigh.

"Which one?" I asked. "Because we've got so many 'situations,' I don't know where to begin."

A faint but persistent buzzing noise interrupted our ruminations.

"What the hell is that?" Crawford asked.

It took me a second to realize that someone was pressing the buzzer on the front door. Since Tommy Moore had taken off for parts unknown, no one was manning the desk and I was pretty sure that neither Max nor Fred would interrupt their conversation to let the person in.

"Stay here," I said, and started down the hallway. "Coming!" I called as I got closer to the front door. The buzzing continued. "Coming!" I yelled, louder this time.

I skidded to a stop at the front door and looked through the glass. I didn't think this day could get any worse, but it appeared it was about to. Because peering back at me through the two doors was Eben Brookwell. And behind him, the lovely Geraldine.

I hit the buzzer, unlocking the two doors. The Brookwells walked in.

Eben Brookwell couldn't contain his surprise or delight at seeing me. "Coco?"

Behind me I heard footsteps. Crawford had come out to investigate.

Eben smiled and held out his hand. "And you must be Chad."

Seventeen

"It is Coco, right?" Eben said, holding out his hand.

I had been stunned into silence. Crawford spoke first. "Yes, Mr. Brookwell. And I don't think we've met officially." The two men shook hands. I noticed that Crawford didn't perpetuate the lie by calling himself "Chad" but he was keeping up the charade nonetheless.

Geraldine gave me a quick hug. "What are you doing here, dear?" She looked at Eben. "This is so strange! Isn't this strange?"

"It's strange," he said. "But good strange." He was such a gentleman that I felt tremendous guilt over my subterfuge.

Crawford gave me a nudge in the back. "Tell them what we're doing here, honey."

I looked at him. "We're . . . ," I started, distracted by the sight of Mary Catherine Donnery bouncing up to the front door, probably for the booty call that was going to save my skin. "Here to see our daugh . . . niece!" I yelled and ran to the front door. I remembered telling Eben that Chad and I didn't have any children just in the nick of time. "And here she is!" I met Mary Catherine in the space between the outer and inner doors and pulled her close in an embrace. "My name is Coco Varick, and the big guy in there is Chad, and you're our niece."

She tried to pull away but I outweighed her by thirty pounds; I also had the Vulcan death grip on her arm. "What?"

"Just go along with it and I'll be sure to make it up to you." I continued to hug her. "Ready?"

She started toward the door and then stopped. "Wait. What's my name?"

"You can still be Mary Catherine. Just don't say too much and we'll be fine."

We walked in. "Look, Chad. It's Mary Catherine! Our niece has finally come home!" I said, probably too gaily, but fortunately the Brookwells didn't know me, didn't know that I wasn't a flight attendant, and probably thought my overly enthusiastic verbal stylings were a by-product of serving peanuts and martinis to strangers at thirty thousand feet.

Mary Catherine played her part perfectly, walking over to Crawford and giving him a big hug as well as a lingering kiss on the lips. Tonight's underwear-as-clothes ensemble consisted of tight jeans, a champagne-colored camisole, and high wedge sandals. A lacy thong peeked out from the back of her low-riding pants. "Uncle Chad," she said dreamily. It looked like she had been waiting to do that for a long time and I thought back to the undressing she had given him with her eyes when she had first seen him a few nights earlier. "I've missed you."

I was behind the Brookwells and pulled my flattened hand across my throat to get her to stop. "Okay, then," I said, clapping my hands together. "We're going to dinner. And we'll have to get going, Chad, if we're going to keep our reservation."

Crawford peeled Mary Catherine off him and took my hand. "It has been a pleasure, Mr. and Mrs. Brookwell." I could see a thin sheen of sweat on his forehead.

The murmured voices in the TV room were getting louder and I, too, felt the sweat starting at my hairline. Eben Brookwell looked at me quizzically. "Don't you want to know why we're here?"

"Right! Why are you here?" I asked, moving closer to the TV room.

"We're here to see our son Wayne," Geraldine said, beaming. "He's the resident director here. We wanted to surprise him and take him to dinner."

Not anymore, I thought. Then I thought about Trixie locked up in the suite and got a little sick. If the Brookwells went down to Wayne's room to knock on the door, she would bark, the jig would be up, and I would be out of a job in no time flat. I was sure of it.

Crawford was one step ahead of me. "Is that the nice young man that we just saw leaving?" he asked.

Mary Catherine proved to be a fine operative, as well. She made a sad sound and pulled her lips down in a beautifully executed expression of fake sadness. "I just saw him leaving campus. He was headed to the city to see a show," she said, her voice filled with regret. "You just missed him."

Geraldine looked crestfallen. "Oh, no!" She looked at Eben. "I told you we should have called first, but *you* wanted to surprise him."

The activity in the TV room was escalating and I heard a chair overturn. "We'd better be going, Chad," I said, and pulled him close.

Eben smiled. "Well, all's not lost. Geraldine's sister is a professor here and we'll take her to dinner instead. Maybe you know her. Sister Mary McLaughlin?"

I looked up, seemingly trying to remember if I knew her. I glanced over at Mary Catherine who was on the other side of Crawford. "Was that the fabulous professor you had for your Renaissance course last semester?"

Mary Catherine nodded enthusiastically. "It was, Aunt Coco. She's a great teacher," she said, looking at the Brookwells earnestly. She slipped her hand into Crawford's and he looked like he wanted the floor to swallow him up.

The Brookwells conferred for a few more minutes and then decided it was time to leave. "We just can't believe this coincidence," Eben said again, and gave me a warm hug.

"It's a small world," Crawford agreed.

"Shall we?" Eben said, suggesting we all leave together.

I gave Mary Catherine a look and sent her a telepathic message to delay. She picked up on it and ran with it. "Aunt Coco, I have to run upstairs and get my bag. Can you wait for me?"

"Sure, honey," I said, and she took off.

Crawford turned away so as not to have his eyes burned out by the sight of a twenty-year-old girl's ass in the tightest jeans I had ever seen running up the stairs. I knew what this meant: no sign-in meant nobody knew she was there. She was spending the night and there was really nothing I could do about it after bringing her into this nightmare of a one-act play.

We bid good night to the Brookwells, and when we were sure that they had gotten into their car and driven away, Crawford collapsed on the second to last step of the staircase, his head in his hands. "I feel like I'm going to throw up," he said.

"I guess you've never worked undercover?" I asked innocently.

"I'm a graphic designer!" he cried. "I'm not supposed to be undercover." He sat there for a few more minutes, his hands hanging down between his legs. "How old is that girl, by the way?"

"She's at least twenty," I said.

"Good," he said. His first guesstimate had probably been in the nonlegal area and that would have sent him off the deep end for sure. "How in the hell did we get into this situation?"

"I don't know," I said, and put my ear to the TV room door. It didn't sound like anything too exciting was happening and their voices were back to a normal timbre. "But what's interesting to me is that the Brookwells don't know that their son is missing. That is extremely disturbing."

Crawford stood. "Well, what do we do now?"

I thought for a moment. "I have to get into the convent."

EIGHTEEN

I finally kicked Max and Fred out of the dorm at ten-fifteen, a good forty-five minutes before I would have had to write them up and submit their transgression to the Student Judicial Council. Tommy Moore never returned to finish sitting desk, so I stayed put. Crawford and Fred were off duty when they arrived, so they hadn't broken any department rules when they dropped by and overstayed their welcome.

It seemed like détente had been reached, and while Fred and Max were amicable, they had come to no significant agreement, except that they were to see each other over the weekend to talk further. While they recounted this development to us, Crawford stood behind them, imploring me silently to tell them something, anything. But I couldn't. First of all, it wasn't really my place to tell them; that fell on their priest. And second, I was chicken.

I kissed Crawford good-bye outside the dorm. Fred and Max were talking quietly by the Crown Vic. "Good night, Chad."

"Listen, Coco," he said. "You'll have to have a talk with our niece. She can't wear underwear out in public."

"After my next trip overseas," I promised.

"As long as it's overseas and not into the convent," he cautioned. He didn't think my snooping around the convent to look for Wayne was such a great idea. I had to disagree. I thought it was an excellent idea. But I didn't tell him that.

After I bid him adieu, I went back into the dorm to call Tommy Moore. I hadn't seen Mary Catherine leave the building and probably wouldn't. I was sure her departure would be under cover of night or in the wee hours of the morning.

Tommy was in his room and answered the phone on the first ring. "Everyone's gone, Tommy. You can come back down," I said. He came down the stairs a few minutes later, looking around the banister before he reached the lobby, making sure that I was telling the truth. I waved him down. "They're gone."

He let out an audible sigh. "What was *that?*" he asked, referencing the event that had sent him scurrying a few hours before.

"That guy was pretty mad."

"Long story," I said. "Hey, are you going to finish out your shift? Because I have to go out for a half hour or so."

He took his place behind the desk and organized all of his supplies. "I'll be here."

"Good." I headed out of the dorm and down the side road toward the river. For some reason, the song "Cracklin' Rosie" by Neil Diamond popped into my head and I couldn't get it out. "Cracklin' Rose you're a store-bought woman"? I thought. What does that even mean? I hummed the song as I walked along in the dark, thoughts of Neil Diamond in his rhinestone-studded shirt keeping my mind off the fact that it was dark, damp, and downright spooky on campus after dark. The cemetery was to my right, the dark and uninhabited classroom building to my left, dark trees reaching over me and extending sinister limbs. But I had Neil Diamond to keep me company, at least in my head.

I turned the corner at the end of the road, the convent door in front of me, its big brass knocker shiny, even in the dark. The nuns have people for things like keeping the door knocker clean, the stairs swept, the smell of beeswax redolent in the air. I approached the door, not sure what I was going to do. I

was fairly certain that the door was locked
— it almost always was — but I flashed on
the keys in my pocket and Dean Merrimack's rat face.

"The one with the red dot is the master
key," he had said when he had handed them
over.

"Oh, yes it is," I whispered. I tried the
knob to see if the door was locked and it
was; I gingerly slipped the key into the lock.
The door opened silently and I stole in, trying to make as little noise as possible.

I've been in the convent a few times and
have always been amazed at how quiet it is.
I spend my day surrounded by students in
an area not too far from where I was now
but it might as well have been a world away;
at midday, the din in the halls is deafening.
I looked around, my eyes adjusting to the
dark. There were a few wall sconces casting
a warm glow in the foyer but no bright
lights; this place was closed for the night. I
stepped gingerly onto the stairs, so clean
that you could eat off them, and proceeded
up to the fifth floor.

A few months earlier, I had stowed my
friend Hernan here. At that time, I had been
informed by the lovely Sister Louise, she of
the ink-stained hands, that the fifth floor
was vacant, save for the presence of Sister

Catherine, who was legally blind. But from what I had gathered during my one trip to this residential floor, all of the sisters' rooms were now empty; Sister Catherine had been moved so that she could be closer to the other nuns. Hardly anyone joins the convent anymore, but at one time this place had been bustling. Empty rooms and only a handful of habited nuns was a testament to this fact of modern life. I made it up to the fifth floor undiscovered and stood on the top step wondering (a) what I was doing here and (b) what I was going to do now that I was here.

I didn't have to wait long to figure it out because while I was thinking, the door to the last room on the left opened up and a very relaxed-looking Wayne came out into the hallway, stretched, and padded down toward the bathroom, which was about four doors away from where I was standing. He didn't see me and walked down the hallway, mouth-breathing, a bath towel around his neck.

"Wayne!" I whispered. "Wayne Brookwell!" It didn't quite have the cadence of "Bond, James Bond," but I had found myself saying it more and more in the past week.

He stopped, looked at me, and went

white. And then he started running. Fast.

"Oh, jeez," I thought. "Here we go again." I took off down the hallway but that kid was speedy. And he obviously knew all of the nooks and crannies in the old building because he went through one door and was gone before I could even get my bearings.

I went through the door that he had entered and was submerged into pitch-blackness. I felt around the wall for a light switch but couldn't find it. "Wayne!" I whispered loudly. "Come out. I want to help you." I didn't actually want to help him but I at least wanted to tell him that we got the drugs out of his toilet and that he needed to answer for that one. "Wayne!" I had no idea what room I was in and what I would find once I did get the lights on, but it was dark. And smelled like feet. It had the smell of a young, slack-jawed man, living alone. It was the smell of Wayne.

I moved farther into the room and banged my shin on something hard and metal, hollering out in pain. But yelling a very foul expletive was the last thing I remember because someone came up behind me and, presumably, hit me over the head. Instead of thinking "lights out," because they really were, I just fell to the ground.

I woke up in the hallway; I'm not sure how

much time had passed. I had obviously been dragged out there because one of my shoes was abandoned by the door that I had entered. But the lights were on now, and Sister Catherine, she of the sketchy eyesight, was standing over me; obviously, old habits died hard and Catherine had returned to her old stomping grounds, for what reason, I'd never know. I sat up and took in her bonnet, long habit, and wimple. I rubbed the sore spot on the back of my head and winced.

"Hello, Sister," I said, struggling to get to my feet.

"Who's that?" she asked. Sitting up, I was almost as tall as she was. "Is that you, Sister Lawrence?" she asked. "Have you gotten into the chardonnay again?"

I stood, a little woozy. I grabbed on to her bony shoulder for support. I fetched my shoe and put it on. "No, Sister. It's Alison Bergeron. I'm sorry to disturb you."

"Alison? What are you doing here, dear?" she asked, staring up at me, her eyes huge behind thick glasses that probably did nothing to improve her sight. Her cataracts were visible behind the lenses.

"I got lost, Sister. I'm sorry to intrude," I said.

"Got lost?" she said, her voice thin and

reedy. "That must have been some cocktail hour down there in the faculty lounge."

I didn't disabuse of her of the notion that we had semiregular faculty cocktail parties and took off down the hall, my head throbbing in time to my footfalls on the worn wood floor.

I sneaked back down to the first floor and stole out of the front door without making too much noise. I gave myself a mental head slap for telling Sister Catherine who I was, but I comforted myself with the fact that she thought the professors were all drunks who had cocktail parties every week and couldn't find their way home afterward. That would go a long way toward explaining why I was on the nuns' turf after-hours if she chose to reveal my whereabouts.

I sat on the front steps of the convent and rubbed my head. I had a goose egg, but it wasn't too bad. I had had a concussion before and knew that this injury didn't approach it in severity, but I would have a mother of a headache in the morning, that I knew. I got up again and began my trek up to the dorm.

I almost had him and he got away. Again. I was going to have to go into training to get this guy. He was fast and I was not. Once my headache went away, I would start a full-blown exercise regimen, maybe even visiting the newly renovated St. Thomas gym to do all sorts of activities that would bring me closer to being able to run for more than fifteen seconds without breaking down.

Oh, who was I kidding? I wouldn't do any training. As it was, I wasn't having sex or drinking, so that qualified as hardcore discipline for me. Eventually, my body would catch up.

A figure emerged from the shadows, bowlegged but broad and solid. I slowed my walk to a near crawl and considered my options. Go back down toward the convent and the river? Or bid a quick "good evening" and continue up toward the dorm? I didn't have time to make a decision because the figure approached me and I saw it was Monsieur Pinkie Ring.

I didn't think it would be wise to greet him that way so I remained silent.

"Where's Wayne Brookwell?"

No hello? No nice to see you? Where did the love go? "I don't know," I lied. I didn't know if it was the head wound or that I was just completely exhausted by the Wayne Brookwell situation, but I no longer found this guy to be a problem. Or a threat. Or a combination of both.

He leaned in close and I got a new whiff of his cologne. Dear Lord; what a stench. "Do you know you're bleeding?" he asked, more out of curiosity than concern. He put the pinkie-ringed finger to my lip.

I followed suit and found that I had a bloody lip. "I must have bitten it," I said. And that was the truth. I must have bitten it when I had fallen. He took what looked like a used tissue out of his pocket and attempted to wipe my face. I put a hand up; although he had lost all menace, I still didn't want a perfect stranger touching my face not once, but twice. "I'll be fine." I rubbed at my lip vigorously, smearing blood onto the palm of my hand. I had a million questions to ask the guy, like who he was and why he was concerned with Wayne, but I was tired of investigating and started up the hill, hoping he would leave me alone.

"Hey, lady!" he called after me.

I turned.

"Tell that asshole that if I find him, he's dead meat."

"Why?" I asked. "Why is he dead meat?"

The man looked at me, apparently unable or unwilling to come up with an explanation. It was obvious that he never expected me to ask. He went with the ever-popular "none of your business" retort.

"You seem really interested in him," I remarked. "You've come all the way from Jersey, for God's sake."

"Would you get off the Jersey thing?" he asked, exasperated.

I shrugged. "I'm just saying. It's a long way."

"Not if you take the GW," he said, referring to the George Washington Bridge. "And then the Henry Hudson." It was a momentary lapse, this conversation about the best route from Jersey to New York, and he seemed to realize it quickly. "Anyway, just tell him, would you?" he said, trying to summon up some menace again. He pointed at me for emphasis.

I saluted him. "Will do." It was like playing a part in a bad mob movie, but being as I had some experience with the real mob, I knew that this guy was just a bit player if a player at all. A man who would hand a woman a used Kleenex to clean her bloody lip wasn't a killer, in my opinion.

But who he was, why he was here, and why we were having a conversation about alternate traffic routes were just a few pieces of the puzzle.

NINETEEN

Max called me the next morning, sounding more like her old self than she had in the past few weeks. "What's that fancy French word you use all the time?" she started.

I rolled over and turned off the alarm; I wouldn't be needing it this morning. It was seven o'clock and I had been awakened by the trill of my cell phone — a jaunty jingle from a popular television show about women on the prowl in New York City — next to my head on the nightstand. "You'll have to be more specific."

"You know," she said. "The one you used to use to describe your relationship with Ray?"

"*Insensé?*" I asked, not remembering when I had described my relationship with my ex-husband as "insane," but it was the only thing that made sense.

"No, that's not it. It was more like you weren't friends, but you weren't enemies, but you could be in the same room?"

I searched my cobwebbed brain. "Détente?"

"That's it!" she yelled into the phone.

I held the phone away from my ear and instinctively put my other hand to the lump on the back of my head.

"I think," she began solemnly, "that Fred and I have reached détente."

"Excellent," I said. "Does that mean you'll be moving back home?"

"Oh, no," she said, as if that were the silliest idea I had ever had. "I have a lot of work to do."

"What?" I asked. "What work?"

"On the marriage," she quickly amended, but I couldn't help thinking that she meant something else. What that was, I didn't know, but I knew Max well enough to know when she sounds like she's trying to put one over on me. She's a good liar but we had a lot of history on which to draw. Had I been more cogent, my Max radar would have been on full alert.

"So you'll be going to counseling?" I rolled over and took half of the covers with me.

"I don't think so," she said. Obviously, I had reached another silly conclusion in my sleepy state. "But I don't want to kill him.

That's progress, right?"

"Indeed." I sat up and attempted to wake up. The image of Kevin's stricken face relaying the news of Max and Fred's non-marriage entered my consciousness and jolted me fully awake; my mental to-do list now included tracking down Kevin and laying another beating on him for not resolving this situation. "Listen, it's early. Can we continue this later?" I was afraid I might reveal something in my addled state and wanted to end the conversation quickly.

"Sure," she said, and hung up.

I looked at the phone. She is always one for the precipitous good-bye but this was ridiculous. I looked over at Trixie, who was resting her head on my bed, looking at me in that sad way she has. "I think she just hung up on me."

Trixie raised one eyebrow as if to say, "Max always hangs up on you."

"No, really hung up on me," I explained. "Not like she usually does. I think I pissed her off." I stared at Trixie for a few seconds, contemplating how Max — who was still enjoying all the perks of living in my house, the lack of baked beans notwithstanding — could be mad at me. Once she talked to Kevin, hopefully all of her ire would be directed at him and I would be back in her good stead.

I rolled out of the bed and put my feet on the floor, still trying to shake myself awake. I felt the lump on the back of my head again and my ire toward Wayne Brookwell awakened in me like an agitated beast. I stood and was happy to find that I didn't have too bad of a headache, a state that I hoped continued the longer I was awake.

I headed outside to walk Trixie and took a look at the growing stack of parking tickets under the windshield wiper on my car. I was wondering how long this parking-space war was going to go on and decided that I, for one, was in it for the long haul. I wasn't moving and there was nothing that Jay Pinto and his merry band of potbellied security guards could do about it.

I took Trixie on a walk down by the river and returned to the dorm twenty minutes later to dress and get ready for the day. I was teaching three classes, one of my lighter loads this semester, and looked forward to the end of the day. I decided to call Crawford and see if he could get away for dinner.

"Hey, handsome," I said, sitting on the edge of my bed and pulling on a pair of black leather slingbacks. "Have dinner with me tonight?"

"If all goes well today, that is a distinct possibility," he said cryptically, and I guessed that he was sitting beside Fred. "Can we play it by ear?"

"Sure," I said, suddenly remembering something I wanted to ask him. "Hey, anything on that Jersey plate?"

"Yeah," he said. "But it's back on my desk. I'll bring it tonight. I can't remember what it is right now, but I know I wrote it down. All I remember is that it's a Greek name. Costas something or other."

"Okay, bring it later." I fiddled with the strap on my shoe. "I have a lot to tell you. I saw Wayne again."

"You did?"

"Yeah. The bastard hit me over the head."

"He what?" he called into the phone.

"You heard me. He hit me over the head." I put on my other shoe. "And he's in the convent."

"He is?"

"Yep. But I'm guessing that he won't be there for long now that I've smoked him out."

"I'll send another radio car down there." I could hear him telling Fred the basics of our conversation. "Are you okay?" he asked.

"Besides having a bump on my head and being incredibly pissed at Mr. Brookwell,

I'm fine," I said. "Oh, and I also had a chat with Mr. New Jersey."

"We've got a lot to talk about tonight," he said. "I'll definitely find a way to get over there later."

It took me several minutes to calm him down. He was more interested in finding Wayne and "tuning him up" than ever before, but I assured him that I was fine. We finally hung up and promised to talk after work. I headed off to class, crossing my fingers that I would see him later.

I entered the office area and was promptly ignored by Dottie; I assumed that we were still in a fight and that was fine by me. I reached around her and pulled a stack of papers out of my mailbox, the first paper being a pink-lined sheet from a message pad, which said in Dottie's scrawl, "Go directly to Sister Mary's office when you get in." I knew Dottie was looking at me for my reaction but I remained impassive. But I knew this couldn't be good. Mary generally leaves me alone, but my behavior of late, coupled with the fact that her sister and brother had come by campus the night before, could only indicate one thing: the jig was up.

I arrived at her office after doing a series of deep-breathing exercises as I traversed the stairs and the hallway one floor above. She was sitting at her desk, grading a paper for a student who obviously didn't have a handle on whatever it was they were trying to present. She drew a big red *X* through one entire page and grimaced. She looked up at me when I cleared my throat to announce my arrival.

She waved a hand toward the chair across from her desk.

"Good morning, Sister." My heart was beating so hard that I was sure she could see it through my blouse. I attempted to sit down gingerly, nearly missing the edge of it. I grabbed the arm and slid onto the wooden seat.

"Good morning, Alison." She folded her hands on her desk. "Or should I say 'Coco'?"

My heart went into my throat and I considered what to do. Deny? Too late for that. Call it a silly role-play that Crawford and I did to get in the mood? No, that wouldn't work; she was celibate and I didn't want to go there with her. I stared back at her, thoughts filing through my brain like a mental card catalog.

She stared back at me. "My sister, Geraldine, and her husband, Eben, took me to dinner last night and told me about a young woman, just shy of six feet with black hair and 'sparkling' blue eyes, whom they met recently. I think she was looking for a house in Scarsdale? And she's got a niece in the school?" she said, looking up at the ceiling as if looking for the answer. "Yes, that was it." She leaned back in her chair. "Apparently, she's got a fabulous job, too. She's a flight attendant for Air France."

"Sounds wonderful," I agreed. "She must have a lot of great stories to tell."

Mary was silent but her gaze said it all. The smile slid from my face. I cleared my throat again.

"I don't know what it is you're trying to do, Alison, but you'd be best advised to stop. Immediately." Her eyes went back to the paper she had been grading. "And now you may leave."

I stayed rooted to the chair for a moment before I realized that the conversation, all of thirty seconds long, was over. I jumped up, losing my footing and crashing into the front of her desk, knocking over her statue of Jesus praying on the Mount, her cup of tea, and a family photo. I attempted to straighten everything up, an ill-advised move if I ever saw one. Mary looked up again and picked Jesus up first, ignoring the cup of tea spreading across the desk and creating a mess of the research papers she had stacked neatly on one side. After she had deposited Jesus safely onto the radiator behind her to dry, she looked at me, the red in her face going from the skin above her starched white oxford to the part of steel-gray hair. "Out!" she commanded and pointed at the door.

I stopped cleaning up the desk and left, not stopping until I had almost reached my office. I came to a dead halt right outside my office door and stood for a minute, not sure what possessed me to do what I did next.

I marched back to Mary's office where it looked like the mayhem of the previous minutes had not transpired. She was exactly as she had been when I had first arrived, sitting at her desk grading the same paper. She was even putting a big red *X* through another page of the same kid's work. It was like I had stepped into some kind of time warp. I walked back into the office and went for broke. "Why are you hiding Wayne in the convent?" I asked, asking the first of the questions to which the answers eluded me.

She looked up again. "Did you say something?"

"Why are you hiding Wayne in the convent?" I asked again, determined not to let her intimidate me into leaving.

Now she was the one scrolling through possible answers in her head. I could see her mind working behind her dead blue eyes. "I don't know what you're talking about."

"You do. You know exactly what I'm talking about." I put my hands on the back of the chair on which I had sat minutes earlier, leaning forward and establishing my physical presence in the room. "I've seen him three times now, Sister, and last night, he even hit me over the head."

"He what?" she said, reacting before she had a chance to rein it in.

"I'd let you feel the back of my head but somehow I don't think you'd want to."

"You'd be right about that," she said, and quickly composed herself. "Alison, you need to leave this alone. For all we know, Wayne is on an extended leave of absence or a vacation."

"Does anyone else know that Wayne is your nephew?"

"Everyone knows," she said, unconvincingly.

"Then how come I didn't know? How come I had to figure it out on my own?"

"Get out," she said calmly.

"I'm not leaving. Tell me the truth." I went

228

for the family connection. "You owe it to your sister, Sister, to let the truth out." Had I not been trying so hard to appear strong, that last sentence would have made me burst out laughing. Sister, sister?

She stood, as tall as I was in her sensible loafers. It was the clash of the tall girls. "Do I have to call security?"

Although my first instinct was to laugh — an image of Joe, all three hundred pounds on his five-foot-five frame, ambling in to remove me — I thought about the implications of being removed from my boss's office by a member of the St. Thomas security staff. That would not be good. I took a step back from the chair that I was leaning on and gave her one last look. "I'll figure it out, Sister. You know I will. It's just a matter of time. And if Wayne needs help, you know that I can probably help him, too. Think about what's best here."

I didn't think she'd take me down in a wrestling move but what she did next surprised me about as much as if she had: she started crying. "Please leave," she pleaded. "Please. Just get out." Her voice cracked and a tear ran down her cheek and I immediately felt a deep shame, forgetting that it was her nephew who had gotten me a one-and-a-half-room *suite* on campus, had thrown a beer bottle at me, and had given me a near concussion. And that, ultimately, she was a big fat liar. But I'm a sucker for a crying nun, obviously.

"I'm sorry," I said, and fled, running down the hall toward the stairs that would bring me back down to my office floor. I got back to my office, breathing heavily as I made it to my office door. I could feel Dottie's eyes on my back and I took in one last gulp of air before going into my office. I had arrived just in the nick of time; my first class was starting in three minutes and it was clear on the other side of the building so I was going to have to hustle. Tomorrow, instead of slingbacks I was going back to clogs. Running around this campus in heels was ridiculous, but like many times before, I had opted for style over comfort. I grabbed my messenger bag, textbook, and a pen, and headed off, my face still red, my guilt complex in overdrive.

I got down to the first floor of the building, and seeing the hallways clogged with students in between classes, I decided to go outside to take a more direct route to my classroom. I hurried along the driveway that snaked in front of the building, slowed down by my slingbacks. I'm not that nimble in sneakers. In slingbacks? Catastrophe was right around the corner. I looked down at the river, hoping that it would bring me peace after my unfortunate encounter with Sister Mary. Instead, the sight of Amanda Reese in the parking lot between the building and the river, standing beside a late-model Lincoln Town Car, brought me to a complete halt. She was far enough away and distraught enough not to notice that I was standing about fifty feet from her, taking in her tearstained face. Her arms were crossed and she was talking to a young man in the driver's seat of the car.

I watched for a few minutes, knowing that it would make me late for class. St. Thomas has a rule in its college catalog that I'm not sure is enforced at other schools but that states if a professor is five minutes late for class, said class is canceled. I teach a bunch of kids who would never crack a textbook at gunpoint, yet know about this arcane and ridiculous rule. I looked at my watch and saw that I had less than two minutes to get to my classroom but I couldn't drag my eyes away from whatever drama was playing out in the parking lot. The man in the car got out and embraced Amanda, whose arms were crossed over her chest. I had been the recipient of a few of those hugs in my lifetime, mainly from my ex-husband. He would offer comfort and I would create a barrier between us. Amanda was doing the same thing. She continued sobbing while he held her, but she wasn't comforted at all by the embrace.

Things suddenly took a dramatic turn when the presumed boyfriend, who I concluded was the fiancé, Brandon, broke the embrace and grabbed Amanda by the arm. I surprised myself by taking a few steps toward them and screaming, "Unhand her!", which in my agitated state was the best I could come up with. The two of them looked at me but Brandon dropped his hand from her upper arm long enough for her to scurry away, up the hill, and past me, without ever looking at me or back at him. I called to her but she kept going, obviously not wanting to chat about this. I locked eyes with the boyfriend until he finally got in his car and drove off, leaving a cloud of exhaust in his wake.

This drama was far from over and was curious in nature; was Amanda ending her engagement to Brandon? I decided that I would delve into this later and headed off to my class, down the hall, around a corner, and in a dark section of the classroom building, where I saw a group of students clustered in the doorway.

"Sit down!" I called, skidding to a stop in front of the door, taking in their disappointed faces. I made it to my desk, where I put down my messenger bag and wiped my hand across my sweaty brow. "Essays, please," I said, and watched as they filed forward to drop their papers on my desk.

I gave my lecture but my mind was on Amanda Reese.

TWENTY

Crawford got away for dinner that night and that was the only thing that saved the day from being a total waste.

I had pissed off Max, made my boss cry, worn the wrong shoes (again!), and seen Amanda Reese in the grips of some kind of relationship drama. I had had enough for one day and was looking forward to seeing Detective Hot Pants, as Max refers to him, even if there wasn't a damn thing I could do to show him just how hot I thought he was.

I was sitting on the edge of the desk in the lobby of Siena when I saw his car pull up. It was time for Bart Johannsen to kiss his lacrosse stick good-bye and come down to do his weekly duty at the desk. That lacrosse stick had seen more action in the past week than I had seen in the last month. I looked at my watch. Bart was now five minutes late.

Before Crawford made it to the door,

Mary Catherine Donnery came bouncing up and pushed the buzzer. Crawford was right behind her and she turned, giving him a dazzling smile. I pushed the buzzer and watched as he held the door for her.

"Good evening," I said, and nodded to Mary Catherine, who bypassed the desk and started up the staircase without signing in. Crawford watched her as she made it to the landing and then looked at me. "Halt!" I called out.

She turned and gave me a look. She leaned over the staircase and Crawford turned bright red as we both got an eyeful of healthy young boob, a crested mountain of pink flesh, cascading out the front of her tank top. "Is there a problem?"

I held up the log-in pad. Besides the exposed boob? Yes. "You need to sign in."

"I do?" she asked. Crawford headed back toward the door so that he had no view of her at all. "Are you sure?" she asked sweetly.

"I'm sure."

"Really sure?"

"Mary Catherine, what's the issue? You know the rules," I said, and waved the pad in the air to remind her.

"Yes, but *Coco* . . . ," she started, and smiled again.

Oh, that. She wasn't going to blackmail

me with the Coco Varick cover story now that Sister Mary knew. "That's over, Mary Catherine, and we're back to house rules," I said.

"Are you sure?" she asked.

"Yes! I'm sure!" I said, my irritation getting the best of me. "Get down here and sign the flipping book!"

She flounced back down the stairs and peeked around the corner to smile at Crawford. "Okay. You don't have to get mad." She bent over to sign the pad while Crawford looked at the ceiling, assiduously avoiding seeing anything that he didn't want to. "There." She started back up the stairs and disappeared from our sight.

Crawford let out a sigh of relief. "And I thought it was bad when Erin wore her pajama pants to school every day."

"Yes, underwear on the outside is definitely far worse," I said, and got up from the desk. I gave him a kiss. "We have to wait a few minutes until Bart comes down to sit desk."

"What's she doing here every night anyway?" Crawford asked.

"My guess? Hot monkey sex with Michael Columbo."

Crawford put his hands over his ears. "Stop!"

I put my arms around his waist, slipping a hand into the back of his waistband, careful to avoid the firearm that remained on his hip even though his tour was over. "Remember hot monkey sex?" I whispered.

He shook his head. "Nope." He relaxed a little bit and let me kiss him. "Besides, I thought you had a hematoma?"

"It's not so bad," I said. "So, do you remember hot monkey sex?"

"No," he said weakly.

But something told me he did. I kissed his cheek, letting my lips linger on his earlobe. The sound of a lacrosse ball bouncing off the wall one floor above made the two of us separate abruptly, and Crawford headed down the hall toward my room and away from the impressionable young eyes of Mr. Johannsen, who I was sure had seen and participated in much more elaborate public displays of affection than what we had just done. I saw Crawford stopped in front of the bulletin board outside the janitor's closet, studying it with an intensity it didn't warrant.

Bart threw himself into the chair behind the desk and flew back a few feet on the wheeled chair, his lacrosse stick stopping his backward progression. "I'm here," he proclaimed, twirling the stick in the air.

"You know what to do, right?" I asked.

"I think so," he said, pulling up close to the desk. It looked like it was the first time he had ever seen some of the objects on the surface. He held up a stapler and examined it curiously.

"Are you sure?" I asked, suddenly afraid to leave him. I wondered if he was a special ed student.

"I'm just messing with you!" he said, laughing uproariously. He slapped his hand on the desk. "This is my second year, Dr. Bergeron. I taught those idiots up there," he said, using his lacrosse stick to point at the ceiling, "how to do this job."

"That makes me feel so much better," I said with just a trace of irony that I was sure was lost on him.

He finger-gunned me to indicate that he was on the job.

Crawford sauntered back down toward the lobby, looking more relaxed than before, and took a gander at Bart, who was happily twirling his stick and singing along to a song being piped into his ears through his tiny earphones. He bounced the lacrosse ball with his free hand in time to his song. We bid good night to him and went into the parking lot.

"Does St. Thomas have a special ed program?" Crawford asked, completely serious.

I laughed. "Uh, no."

"Because that kid . . ."

"I know. I know," I said, and took his hand. "Get used to it. That's the kind of boy one or both of your daughters is going to bring home after they start college."

He moaned. "That's what I'm afraid of," he said.

Once we were in the car, Crawford dug a piece of paper out of his pocket. "Here's the info on that plate number: Costas Grigoriadis, 17 Pine Terrace, Upper Saddle River, New Jersey."

I thought for a moment. "Never heard of him." I looked at Crawford, my face telling him exactly what I was thinking.

"We are not driving to New Jersey," he said emphatically.

I put my hands together. "Please, please, please, Crawford. We can get McDonald's and eat it in the car on the way. It will be like a road trip!" I said, trying to make my enthusiasm contagious.

He gripped the steering wheel, staring out at the encroaching dusk. It was mealtime on campus and students were starting to head to the cafeteria. He flexed his fingers and looked at me. "Why do you want to go there?"

He was cracking and I could tell. "I want to see *where* he lives and maybe figure out *who* he is."

"And then what?"

I was honest. "I'm not sure." I leaned in close and gave him a kiss. "How about it? A little road trip? We could be there and back in an hour and a half and still have time for dinner." I squeezed his thigh. "That's if you don't want to have McDonald's in the car."

"An hour and a half? That's a generous estimate," he said. He turned toward me, his hands still gripping the wheel. "Listen. There's no Coco, no Chad, no house hunting. Got it?" He thought of something else. "And no using the bathroom. That's what got us into this mess."

"Got it," I said solemnly.

"I could get in big trouble for this."

"For what?" I asked. "We haven't done anything wrong and we're not going to do anything wrong." I put on my seat belt. "And not for nothing, there's no problem with impersonating an Air France flight attendant or a graphic designer."

He banged his head on the steering wheel a few times. "There is if you're a police officer for the City of New York. Have I taught you nothing?" He sat up suddenly. "Oh, and how are we going to find Seventeen Pine

Terrace, by the way?"

I pulled off my seat belt. "Wait here." I jumped out of the car and ran a few feet to my car, ignoring the stack of tickets on the windshield. I reached into the glove compartment, retrieved my rarely-used GPS system and held it above my head victoriously. His face fell. He knew now that there was no way we weren't going to New Jersey.

He rolled down his window. "Where did you get that?" he asked.

"Max," I said. "Where do I get any purchases over a hundred bucks?" I asked, handing it to him. "I call her Lola. Make sure you follow her directions. She gets very cranky when you change direction."

Crawford made short work of setting Lola up on the dash and plugged in the directions to Costas's house. Lola told us that the ride was exactly thirty-seven miles and fifty minutes long. No give or take. That's what it was.

I looked out the window as we left campus, watching students walking around and enjoying the mild weather. We passed the library, where Amanda was walking down the steps, dressed in her usual uniform: jeans, flip-flops, and Princeton sweatshirt. Her hair hung down her back, a tangle of dark waves. I needed to get Max over here to give that girl a makeover. She would be a knockout with a trim and some decent clothes. She looked up just as we were driving by and raised her hand in a halfhearted wave.

Crawford slowed down to a crawl over the speed bumps. "Okay, grandma, speed it up," I said. "We don't have all night."

"I'd like to have some shocks left when I get off campus," he said, saluting the guard in the booth just as we exited onto the avenue.

Lola gave us our directions. "Go straight to Broadway."

"She's as bossy as you are," Crawford said, ignoring her directions.

"Recalculating," Lola said, and set about coming up with a different route for us to take.

Crawford ignored her and continued on his route. "So tell me about your evening with Wayne and Mr. New Jersey, who we can now call Costas or Mr. Grigoriadis."

"Wayne is a big, giant, scum-sucking piece of plankton, and I don't care how much trouble he's in or not but you don't go hitting a lady over the head," I said.

Crawford was silent for a moment. "But how do you *really* feel?"

"That's how I really feel." I gave him a

quick summary of my break-in at the convent.

"You broke into the convent." It was more a statement of fact than a question.

"I had to, Crawford," I said. "I just knew he was there and I wanted to prove it, once and for all."

"The uniforms went to the convent, searched the place, and came up with nothing," he reported. "Wayne's gone from there."

"They did?" I asked, feeling a little queasy all of a sudden. "Sister Mary's not going to be happy about that."

"Which part? The convent search or the missing nephew?" he asked.

"Both."

"The kid — her nephew — assaulted you, Alison. Of course I was going to send someone over to check it out."

"I guess I should have expected that," I said. I told him about my talk with Costas and how weird it was. I finished up with the Sister Mary debacle.

"And you made a nun cry?" This time he was genuinely surprised. "You made Sister Mary cry?"

"I know," I said as we merged onto the Saw Mill River Parkway. "That wasn't my best work."

He sighed. "I'll say." He looked into the rearview mirror and adjusted it slightly. "So Wayne was definitely living in the convent — which we already knew; we don't know why Mr. Grigoriadis keeps turning up; and Sister Mary isn't an automaton. Good work. We now know less than nothing." He smiled slightly to show me that he wasn't criticizing my sleuthing even though it sounded strangely like he was.

"Well, when you put it like that . . ." I looked out the window and then back at Lola's screen. "Follow her directions," I said.

"I know another way," he said.

"But she said to take the George Washington."

"Trust me," he said, and patted my thigh.

I watched as the various towns in southern Westchester passed by my window. We slowed down at the light that would take me to my house in Dobbs Ferry. I decided that now would not be a good time to mention that Max was embarking on an online dating adventure and wisely kept my mouth shut.

"What?" he said, seemingly reading my mind.

"Nothing," I said.

He pulled away slowly from the red light. "Liar."

I didn't dispute that and kept my mouth shut until we got onto the Tappan Zee Bridge. "Are you sure this is right?" I was a little nervous about going against Lola's advice.

"I go this way when I go down to the shore," he reminded me. "I know that it's easier at this time of night to go across the Tap than the GW."

I trusted him. Crawford has only given me one reason not to trust him — it involved an estranged wife that he had kept secret from me at the beginning of our relationship — but since that time he had reestablished himself as one of the good guys. I relaxed in my seat, enjoying the number of times Lola had to recalculate.

Once we had a general sense of where we were headed, I filled him in on what I had witnessed at school that day between Amanda and Brandon.

"*Unhand* her?" he asked. "You trying out for Shakespeare in the Park?"

"It was all that came out of my mouth," I said. "I was nervous that something was going to happen and I needed to get him to leave her alone."

"*Unhand* her?" he repeated.

"Yes," I said, annoyed. "So what do you think is going on?"

"No idea," he admitted. "Did it look violent? Abusive?"

I had to admit that it didn't. "But he clearly wasn't happy with her."

"If you should see Mr. Princeton Boyfriend put his hands on her again, get one of those senile guards to come down and get him off campus."

We were at the Grigoriadis house faster than the fifty minutes that Lola had predicted due solely to Crawford's sense of direction. He pulled onto Pine Terrace, an upscale street populated by large contemporary homes. He pulled up to one, an architectural marvel of planes and angles with floor-to-ceiling windows, and put the car in park.

"Swanky," I said.

"Mr. Grigoriadis does do well for himself," he said, leaning over me to get a good look at the house. It wasn't set too far in from the street, but had an impressive front yard with some extremely expensive landscaping. "So, what now?"

The house was dark — and with the plethora of windows that allowed you to look into the house, it was easy to tell that there was no one home — and there were

no cars in the driveway. Lucky. I looked at
the front door and noted that the mailbox
was full of mail, either from today or the
last few days; I didn't know how much mail
the Grigoriadises usually got, but if this was
one day's mail, they got a lot more than I
did on a daily basis. "Wait here," I said, and
opened the car door.

Although I had promised to be well behaved on this jaunt, my curiosity got the
better of me. Crawford barely had time to
protest and I didn't turn when I heard his
voice begging me to get back in the car. I
headed up to the front door as quickly as
possible and pulled the mail out of the box.
I riffled through the various bills, finding
nothing of interest except that Mrs. Grigoriadis — Victoria, by the way the bills were
addressed — had a lot of department store
credit cards. Lord and Taylor, Bloom-
ingdale's, Macy's . . . and wait . . . Target? I
guess even the rich liked a bargain. I put
the bills back in the box and pulled out a
couple of catalogs and stopped, finding
exactly what I was looking for.

The Delia's catalog? Addressed to
Amanda Reese.

TWENTY-ONE

While Crawford fumed, I programmed Lola to give us the name of an Italian restaurant in the area; I had a hankering for something parmigiana. I waited while she thought about it or whatever it is that computers do when humans request information.

"She says to go to Aldo's on Franklin Avenue."

"Franklin Turnpike?"

"No, Franklin Avenue."

"Well, I know Franklin Turnpike but I don't know Franklin Avenue."

Wow, he was pissy. "Well, she says to make a right . . . here!" I called out as the street we were supposed to turn on came up suddenly. "Okay. Stay on this for four point three miles." I put Lola back up on the dashboard. "I didn't take the catalog," I reminded him.

His face turned red with what I suspected was the effort he was exerting not to throttle

me. "Yes, Alison, but tampering with someone's mail — which includes going through
it to see who lives there — is a federal offense."

"Yeah, but nobody saw me," I reminded
him.

"I did!" he said. "I saw you. And I'm in
law enforcement." He continued on the
road, going faster than he should, breathing
heavily. "You promised me."

"I guess telling you you're gorgeous when
you're angry wouldn't be appropriate?" I
asked. His silence answered my question.
"Guess not."

We pulled up in front of Aldo's less than
ten minutes later and were seated in a red
velvet booth in the corner. "Do you want to
sit facing the door in case Michael Corle-
one comes in?" I joked as I opened the
menu. The waiter arrived and I ordered a
vodka martini. He looked at Crawford, who
was staring out the window and trying to
get his breathing back to normal. "He'll
have a glass of Chianti," I said.

The waiter, a little man in his fifties who
looked like he had been working at this
place a long time, scuttled off, terrified of
Crawford's dark mood. "Hey," I said, leaning over the round table. "Snap out of it."

He looked at me. "You have to promise

me you won't do something like that again."

I looked back at him, deciding whether or not that was a promise I could keep. "I promise," I said halfheartedly.

He studied my face. "You are the worst liar I've ever met, and I've met a few in my time."

"I bet you have," I said, and returned to the menu. "What looks good? How about the gnocchi?" I was dying to get his impression of this new development but I knew better than to push it. I was on thin ice as it was. Push too far and I would end up in icy waters. And I'm not that good a swimmer.

The waiter came back, delivered our drinks, and looked at us expectantly.

Crawford was still in a black place, so I ordered for both of us. "I'll have the salad *mista* to begin and the chicken parmigiana. My friend here will have the salad as well and the steak *pizzaiola*." I snapped my menu shut and smiled at the waiter.

"Excellent choices," he said, and disappeared again, taking a quick look back at our table; I was sure he was going to tell the chef to put a rush on it so he could get the lovely lady and her cranky date out of there as quickly as possible.

"That's not what I wanted," Crawford bellyached.

"Well, that's what you're getting." I pushed his wine closer to him. "Here. Drink."

I started in on my martini and had almost finished the whole thing before he started talking. "What else did you see in the mail?" he asked reluctantly in a low whisper. He didn't want to admit that we had found something out that was intriguing.

"Well, Mrs. Grigoriadis has a lot of department store credit cards. And they get a lot of catalogs."

"So do you. Doesn't prove anything."

I finished off my drink. I barely had to make eye contact with the waiter to have another one appear magically before me in record time. "I like it here," I remarked.

"Anything else?" He looked around as if to see if anyone could take him to task for allowing me to commit mail fraud, or mail tampering or whatever it was that I had done. "In the mail, I mean."

I shook my head. I took the spear of olives out of the drink and started on the first one. "So, what do you think? Amanda is a Grigoriadis through her mom's re-marriage?"

He nodded. "Seems like it."

She didn't bear any resemblance to the man who kept visiting campus but that didn't necessarily mean anything; not too many young girls, fortunately, looked like Neil Diamond. Something occurred to me. "Did you say anything to Lattanzi and Marcus about my seeing Wayne on campus?"

He looked at me as if to say, "what do you think?"

"Sorry I asked." A delicious smell wafted over to our table and I leaned out of the booth to see what it was. The couple next to me dug into a deep dish of clams with Italian bread and I immediately had order envy. "What are they going to do?"

"Lattanzi and Marcus have much bigger fish to fry," he said. "They're leaving it to the uniformed cops. And the one time they did go to the convent, they got the old freeze-out from the nuns." He chuckled, thinking back. "Lattanzi swears that some old nun gave him the evil eye and that he's cursed now."

He had already been cursed, barely breaking five foot four in his high-heeled cowboy boots, but I didn't acknowledge that. "And that's going to keep him from going back to find Wayne?" I asked, incredulous.

Crawford smirked. "Probably. But Marcus is an atheist, so he'll do follow-up, even with nuns, if he has to. Right now, they're working a big case and one bag of heroin isn't really going to occupy too much of their time."

Interesting. I wondered what it would feel like to be technically missing — on the run, even — and have nobody give a whit about where you were or why your toilet was filled with drugs. For one brief moment, I actually felt sorry for Wayne, and then I thought about my lumpy mattress, the bruise on my head, and the fact that I had almost been impaled by a beer bottle, and snapped back to reality. The waiter dropped off our salads and we ate them in silence.

Crawford finally spoke, his fork pointed at my face. "I can only do this with you if you follow the rules."

I shrugged. "Okay."

"I mean it."

"Me, too."

"I'm getting a little cranky," he admitted. "I want you back home." Even though our relationship was rock solid, he still wasn't so good at the heartfelt admissions; he blushed slightly.

That was interesting. He was the one who had been telling me it wasn't going to be too bad. Now he was cranky? "It's been less than a week, Crawford." I didn't want to tell him that I was actually starting to enjoy my new life. I was on campus and not commuting, I was away from Max, and someone came in and cleaned my room and changed my sheets every three days. Except for the expensive bra that had disappeared from the laundry room — and no, I didn't want to know where it had gone — and the fact that I was eating pretty poorly, I was relatively happy with the situation. Nothing a couple of Lean Cuisines and a daily delicate handwash couldn't cure.

I must have been staring at him because he snapped his fingers in front of my face. "You want to go home, too, right?"

I paused.

"You like it there, don't you?"

"I like not having to commute," I admitted. I filled my mouth with salad, hoping we didn't have to continue the conversation. I also liked getting up just a half hour before my first class, getting to take in the Hudson River views whenever I wanted, eating gigantic breakfasts in the commuter cafeteria, and having someone else clean my "suite" for me.

He continued looking at me. "You're not thinking of staying?"

I hadn't really thought about it very much but I had to admit that in the last few days, I had made a home for me and Trixie. It had gotten me out of my regular life, which these days consisted of miles logged on the Saw Mill River Parkway, Max, and Max's divorce. Crawford's work schedule was hectic and my being closer to the precinct had afforded us more time together. What could be bad about that? "No," I said in answer to his question, not entirely convinced.

"You are, aren't you?" he asked, amazed. He dropped his fork onto his salad plate and looked at a spot above my head.

I put my hand over his. "No," I said more definitively. I explained how I liked seeing him more, how being away from Max had been a good thing for me, and how I didn't want to go back to her any time soon. "Is that bad?" I asked, almost rhetorically. It didn't deserve an answer; I wanted to be away from my best friend in her time of need and that was just plain selfish. There was no other way around it. But two things were at work: one, she had split up with her husband for the flimsiest of reasons. And two, well, she wasn't really married. It was a mess and I didn't have the strength to sort it out right now. My chicken parmigiana arrived, a sweet respite from mental gymnastics, looking like heaven on a plate. I took a deep breath and inhaled the delicious garlic aroma.

Crawford eyed his steak.

"Do you want my chicken?" I asked, pushing my plate toward him.

"No, thanks," he said, about as unconvincingly as he could. I picked up his plate and exchanged it with mine. He smiled widely. "Thanks," he said, and dove into his plate of food.

I picked at my steak *pizzaiola,* not my first choice, but delicious nonetheless. I heard my cell phone ring in the bottom of my bag and I dug it out. It was a text message from Max. *"Call me immediately. It's an emergency."*

Crawford noticed my face go pale and put his fork and knife down on his plate. "What is it?"

I dialed Max's number. "It's Max," I said as the phone rang on the other end. She answered, out of breath. "Max, it's me," I said as quietly as I could so as not to disturb the other diners. "What is it?"

"Is it an emergency?" she called into the phone.

"What?"

"It is, isn't it?" she said, starting to cry. "Oh, God, I just knew it."

I had no idea what was going on and told her so.

"I knew I shouldn't have left Aunt Sheila

when she was so close to death. I'll be right there," she said, and the call went dead.

Moments later, I had another text message. *"Match.com sucks. I needed an out. I'll see you l8ter."*

When Crawford figured out that it wasn't a true emergency, he went back to eating. He had enough sense not to ask.

We capped our meal off with some coffee so that we could stay awake long enough to get back to campus. I also needed to sober up a bit, and still bought into the notion that a hot cup of coffee would do the trick. Crawford pulled into the parking lot of my building and right up to the front door, turning off the car.

"You know we can't make out here," I said. "Silly man."

"So how are we going to handle this?"

I was a little tipsy from my two martinis and one glass of wine and had no idea what he was talking about. "Handle what?"

He sighed, a little exasperated.

"Hey, it's way past my bedtime!" I protested, looking at the dash. It was — it was close to midnight. "I can't think past nine. And it's one hundred o'clock," I enunciated.

"How are you going to dig into the

Amanda Reese/Costas Grigoriadis connection?"

"Verrrry delicatelllly," I said, speaking slowly. I let out a loud giggle.

He unlocked my door with his key pad. "Okay. You're in no shape to discuss this. Just be discreet," he reminded me. He leaned over and gave me a long kiss. "Is there any chance you can come to my apartment this weekend?"

I leaned in and fell against his chest, something I hadn't been meaning to do but the momentum of the two martinis carried me. "Are you inviting me to a sleepover?"

"Yes."

I thought about it for a minute and then realized that I was on call for the weekend. "Can't. On call." I had another thought. "But I could sneak you in and you could hide out in my room!"

He patted my head. "I'm a little old for that. Let's talk tomorrow, okay?"

Party pooper, I thought. But he was probably right. I got out of the car and waved at him, watching him drive away. I turned and looked through the glass, where I spotted Bart Johanssen dead asleep at the desk, his head resting on the head of his lacrosse stick. That'll leave a mark, I thought, looking at his cheek deep in the crosshatched

basket. I rang the bell, but he didn't move. I started to rustle around in the bottom of my bag for my keys, unable to get purchase on the elusive set. I rang the bell again and watched as Bart raised his head, eyes closed, and then let it fall again. I dropped to a crouch and put my bag on the ground, opening it wide.

A hand over my mouth interrupted my cry of "Eureka" as I pulled the keys from the bag. I was dragged backward across the parking lot, my heels scraping along the macadam. I struggled to get up but being pulled backward in a semicrouch made it impossible. As a last resort, I threw the heavy key ring at the front door but missed by a mile. The keys fell with a clatter a few inches short of the glass.

I was thrown into the back seat of a two-door car, a feat that I marveled at later. The car was on, but silent.

Because it was a Toyota Prius, a car that makes no noise when idling.

TWENTY-TWO

Now I was sober.

Because believe it or not, this was not the first time I had been kidnapped. It seemed I was going for some kind of personal record.

But it was the first time I had been kidnapped while a little drunk, and the first time during which my kidnapper kept repeating, "I'm sorry, I'm sorry, I'm sorry, I'm sorry . . ." until I thought my head would explode.

I turned and looked at Amanda, who was in the back seat with me. "If you're so freaking sorry, then why did you kidnap me?" I asked. Wayne was in the driver's seat, driving like a bat out of hell off the campus and onto the main drag. Even in a sensible Prius, Wayne was making good time down the avenue.

Amanda pushed her hair away from her face and sighed loudly. She didn't have an answer for that one.

"Where are we going?" I asked, adjusting myself in the seat and putting on my seat belt.

"I don't know," she admitted. "Where are we going, Wayne?"

I watched the stores on the avenue whiz by as Wayne made every light, something I had never been able to do since I started commuting to St. Thomas; inevitably, I would hit one red light and have to wait. He headed down toward the highway but stopped short of Broadway, turning right instead into a small residential side street. He pulled over and stopped the car; we were about a mile from campus. He turned around and I got my first good look at Wayne Brookwell, former resident director, current bane of my existence.

His picture on the school intranet didn't do him justice. Yes, he was slack jawed, and yes, it didn't look like there was a whole hell of a lot going on upstairs, but there was a sweetness to his face that didn't show up in the photograph, a crinkling around his eyes that made me get why Amanda thought him the bee's knees or the cat's meow or whatever it was kids today called each other.

"I've got a lot to ask you, Wayne," I said. I rubbed the back of my neck, hyperextended during my drag across the parking lot.

"What the hell is going on?"

Wayne pointed out the window on his side of the car and I saw a playground. "Let's go over there."

We got out of the car and crossed the street to the small, deserted playground. A sign admonished YOU MUST HAVE A CHILD TO ENTER THIS PLAYGROUND. Well, I had two, so I guessed I was in the clear. There was one bench, suitable for two bodies, which Amanda and Wayne sat down on, leaving me to choose between a swing and one of those plastic character heads on a giant spring. I chose the swing. I put my hands on the chains that suspended it to steady myself. "Okay. Shoot."

Wayne bent over and put his elbows on his knees, his head into his hands. His shoulders shook slightly and I hoped to God he wasn't crying. I looked at the black sky, waiting for him to compose himself, and studied the only constellation that I knew, the Big Dipper, and counted the number of stars. Finally, Wayne looked up. "Those weren't my drugs," he pronounced.

I swung back and forth a little bit, my feet making divets in the soft sand. "Okay. Still doesn't explain why you disappeared, threw a beer bottle at my head, knocked me out . . ." I ticked off Wayne's offenses on my fingers. "Got anything you want to say?" I asked pointedly.

"Sorry?" he asked.

"That's it?"

"Sorry," he said more sincerely. He pulled his head out of his hands; Amanda rubbed his back.

"You've got a lot of explaining to do." The tranquil night, a slight breeze wafting through the air, did nothing to improve my mood. When I felt myself softening slightly toward the hapless Wayne, I touched the lump on my head to remind myself of my real feelings.

"Tell her, Wayne," Amanda said, dropping her hand from his back to his knee.

"It's kind of a long story," he said.

I didn't think this guy could get on my nerves any more than he was at that moment. I wanted to get off the swing and put my hands around his neck and choke him until he gave everything up. Every last detail. I gritted my teeth. "I've got time." I looked around the playground. "I'm certainly not walking home at midnight so unless you want to bring me back now, start talking."

Amanda looked at Wayne. "Let me. It's all my fault anyway."

This statement brought about all sorts of

"no, baby, it's not," and "yes it is," and "I love you," and kissing and hugging and forgiveness and such. I finally yelled into the night air, "Stop!"

They looked at me, two innocents caught in some kind of web of lies and deceit. Amanda took a deep breath and told me the tale. And it wasn't anything that I ever would have come up with, even in my very wild imagination.

"So, you're not her dealer?" I asked Wayne.

More vigorous head shaking.

I stopped swinging, bringing my feet to a stop. I continued to grip the chains on either side of the swing. "So, let me get this straight." I pointed at Amanda. "You are engaged to a senior at Princeton." Explained the ubiquitous sweatshirt but not the lack of an engagement ring. I pointed at Wayne. "And you're in love with her." I looked back at Amanda. "And you're in love with him," I said, pointing at Wayne. "And your current boyfriend and your stepfather — Costas — are after Wayne because your boyfriend is jealous and your stepfather wants you to marry him. And both of them want Wayne out of the picture." I took a deep breath. "That explains the man who keeps popping up on campus. But it doesn't explain everything." I kept my eyes on Wayne. "Where did the drugs come from?"

Wayne's eyes were wet and he looked like a little kid caught in a very bad situation; the truth wasn't too far from that. Except that he was a big kid — a twenty-six-year-old kid in big trouble. "I don't know!" he cried. "I was just about to leave for spring break and I came back to my room after a staff meeting. They were sitting on the floor of my bathroom. The only thing I can guess is that whoever put them there didn't think I was coming back to my room and that they could get me in trouble when house-keeping found them." He took a deep, shaky breath. "For all I know, they belong to that Williamson kid. He's a total stoner." He looked at Amanda pointedly.

"Spencer would never do anything like that," she protested.

"Okay, before we start making rash ac-cusations, tell me the rest of the story," I said.

Wayne looked at me. "Housekeeping cleans while we're out for the break. They would have found them, turned them in, and I would have been in huge trouble." He wiped his hand across his eyes. "I would have been fired. Or worse," he said, shud-dering at the thought of what might have happened.

"So you ran."

He nodded. "It was the only thing I could think of at the time."

I thought it would have made more sense to call the police but he obviously had a reason as to why that wasn't an option; I let that drop for the time being. "What did you tell Merrimack?"

"I left him a voice mail telling him that I wouldn't be coming back after the spring break."

"Right after you called your aunt, right?" I asked. It was starting to make sense.

He nodded. "Sister Mary is my god-mother. I couldn't think straight so I called her first." He wiped his nose on his shirt sleeve. "How much trouble am I in?"

I thought for a minute, looking up at the apartment building behind Wayne's head, lights twinkling in every unit. "I'm not sure, Wayne. But I sure wish you hadn't almost cracked my head open not once, but twice. That would have most certainly gotten you an assault charge."

"I panicked," he admitted. "You're mar-ried to that cop, right?"

"No, he's just my boy . . ." I was back to having trouble with this. The kids on cam-pus called each other "boyfriend" and "girlfriend" and I was decidedly older than all of them. What does one call their middle-aged companion? "He's my friend with benefits," I said, feeling sort of hip all of a sudden.

Amanda shook her head. "He's more than that. That would mean that you're just hooking up. He's your boyfriend."

"Fine. He's my boyfriend. But we're not married. And we don't just 'hook up,' " I said, using finger quotes. I shook my head to clear the cobwebs; talking to these two was bringing me down a conversational one-way street with nowhere to turn. "What does Crawford have to do with this?"

"I thought you would tell him everything and I'd end up in jail. I can't explain how those drugs got there. And there were a lot of them."

I knew that. "You're going to have to tell him now, Wayne. You can't keep living in the convent, mowing me down when you feel like it, and sneaking around campus like a modern-day hunchback. Time to come clean, mister."

He shook his head vigorously, something I couldn't do since he had smashed me over the head. "Can't do it."

"You're going to continue living with the nuns?"

"I'm not living with the nuns," he said. "But I'm going to stay missing until I figure this out," he said, nodding, a defiant tone creeping into his voice. He stuck out his jaw in an attempt to look confident, I guessed. "I want to figure out who's trying to frame me. And why."

"You've done an admirable job thus far, Wayne. By all means continue, Sherlock," I said, holding my hands out. "You're on your own." I got up from the swing. "I hope you enjoy Rikers. Because that's where you're going when I tell Crawford where you are and what you're doing." Something occurred to me. "Why did you steal my pillows?"

He looked dumbfounded, obviously shocked that I was able to figure out his deception so easily. "I didn't steal them. My aunt did."

"Why?"

"She wanted to make me more comfortable in the convent."

She makes my life a living hell and she's skulking around stealing pillows for her adult nephew? This woman was clearly an enigma wrapped in a conundrum.

I started walking away from the playground, listening to the mumbling and whispering going on behind my back. It was like they were my kids and I had told them that if they didn't leave the playground that very minute, I was going home without them. I walked slowly toward the chain-link gate and opened it up. "Okay! I'm leaving! See you later!" I let the gate clink noisily behind me and I continued down the dark street. Finally, Amanda called my name.

I turned; she was standing at the fence. "What should we do?"

I thought that was obvious. "I think you should go to the police. There are two very nice detectives working the drug investigation. Lattanzi and Marcus." Amanda was listening to me so intently that she didn't hear Wayne get up, hop the fence on the west side of the playground, and run toward the Prius. It took me by surprise as well; the kid was like a gazelle. He jumped into the car, and while it didn't exactly roar to life, it made a clicking noise as he put it in gear and drove away. Amanda looked at me helplessly.

"I don't think he wants to go to the police." She pushed her hair back and adjusted her glasses.

She was a regular Nancy Drew. "I got that impression, Amanda."

"Wayne doesn't do anything he doesn't want to do," she said, almost proud of him for what was, at this time, a serious character flaw.

"Then it sounds like your stepfather is going to kill him," I remarked offhandedly.

"But I love him," she protested. She sniffled and broke into a full-blown sob attack.

"I'm not the one you have to convince of that," I said, putting my arm around her shoulder. "You have to convince your stepfather, right after you break up with your boyfriend."

She gripped the fence and rocked back on her heels, thinking about what I had just said. "Do you think I should break up with Brandon?"

"How the heck should I know?" I asked, sounding far more exasperated than I intended. After having been married to a serial philanderer, I hardly qualified as someone who should be dispensing love advice. My mind flicked over an image of Max — someone else in need of counsel in this area — and I shuddered. I still had that situation on my to-do list — I wasn't going to leave Kevin hanging out by himself on that one as mad as I was at him — and didn't relish the conversation that revealed to Max that she wasn't legally married.

"What?" Amanda asked.

"Nothing," I said, shaking it off. "One question."

She looked at me, her eyes wide behind her Buddy Holly glasses.

"Did you know that he didn't go to Mexico?" In other words, did you lie to me? I wanted to ask, but she got the drift.

For some reason, I could tell that she was telling the truth. I don't know how, but I just could. "I didn't know that he was on campus until the other night." When she realized I needed clarification, she looked down. "The night at the gazebo." The night she lied about going to get her econ notes at the dorm down by the river.

"Oh," I said. "You were going to meet him."

She nodded. "I'm sorry," she said. "I thought I'd just make sure he was okay but when I saw you, I panicked. And lied."

"It's okay," I said. "Did you know your stepfather's been coming around campus?"

"No," she said. "But it doesn't surprise me. He knows something's going on between me and Wayne. I tried to talk to him and my mother about it over spring break. He's furious."

I raised my eyebrows questioningly.

"He wants me to marry Brandon. He loves Brandon. I'm not Greek, but my stepfather is. He wants me to marry a Greek man."

"And Brandon's Greek?"

"One hundred percent." She pulled her hair back and held it in a loose ponytail. "And his dad and my stepfather are in business together so our future is set. Brandon will inherit the business."

Interesting. I thought for a moment. "What do you want to do?"

She was less emotional about the situation than she had been before. "I don't know." She gave me a weak smile. "I'm hoping I can figure that out." She opened the gate to the playground. "What do you think I should do?"

I reminded myself that I shouldn't be, and didn't want to be, dispensing romantic advice, but I couldn't help myself. "Marry the one you love," I said definitively.

She studied my face carefully. "You think that's the best thing to do?"

"It's the only thing to do." I followed her out of the playground. "Want to start back to campus?"

When we got back to campus, my keys were on the ground next to the front door, right where they had landed less than an hour earlier. I let us both in and said good night to Amanda.

TWENTY-THREE

I had been living on campus less than a week and had been interrogated by a mad, Greek stepfather; had made my boss cry; had spotted Wayne several times and indeed been kidnapped by the erstwhile resident director; and had been knocked unconscious. All in all, a very exciting stay.

Not that I'm complaining; as I said before, I was enjoying rolling out of bed and into my office to start my day. And I was enjoying seeing Crawford as often as I was, although not on any overnights, which was not enjoyable. He had left a message on my cell phone asking if I was available for a quick dinner that night when he took his meal, but I had more pressing matters on my schedule, namely, getting Max and Kevin together to discuss the situation regarding her illegal marriage. I couldn't avoid it any longer. Crawford was disappointed but didn't want any part of that discussion so he bowed out gracefully, promising to call me later that night when he got off work for good. I gave him a quick update on my time in the park with Amanda and Wayne; he wasn't surprised to hear that Wayne was still lurking around, but he promised to pass the information on to the detectives on the case.

I sat on my bed and texted Max, knowing that this was the surest way to get a response: *"want to have dinner 2nite?"* I had finally figured out how to punctuate properly and was happy to find the question mark pretty quickly. I had barely sent it when I received her exuberant reply: *"SURE! Your place or mine?"*

"Mine," I wrote back. I didn't want to remind her that "her place" was really "my place" anyway and hoped that she understood that she was supposed to come to campus. I dialed Kevin and petted Trixie absentmindedly while I waited for him to pick up.

"Father McManus."

"Hi, Kev, it's me."

He didn't respond immediately. He had been avoiding me since his revelation, and I got the sense that if he never saw me again, that would be fine. Finally, he gave me a tentative, "How are you?"

"I'm fine," I said and cut to the chase. "Listen. We have to resolve this Max thing and I think the sooner, the better. She's coming for dinner tonight." He started to hem and haw, but I cut him off. "Tonight, Kevin. We're going to do it tonight."

He sputtered a little bit. "Well, all right."

"The faster we rip this Band-Aid off, the easier it will be."

"If you say so." He sniffled a little bit, and although it sounded like he was crying, I didn't want to imagine that. "Come here?"

"You know, I'm not sure what's better. It might be better to be in public so that she won't make a complete scene."

"I'll leave that up to you. Whatever you think is best."

I hung up and looked at Trixie. "What do you think, Trix? Kevin's apartment or the Steakhouse?" Her eyes lit up at the thought of steak, not that she would be having any, but my decision was made. The Steakhouse it was. I wasn't sure if this was the best plan in the world — taking her out to dinner — but I couldn't even begin to imagine the histrionics that would take place if we stayed up in Kevin's apartment. My head still hurt from where Wayne had clobbered me and I just didn't have as much mental stamina for a Max meltdown.

Selfish? Maybe.

More like self-preservation, I convinced myself.

Friday is an unusually busy day for me. Whereas most of my colleagues teach one or two classes and hit the road, I teach a record four. One is a class that only meets once a week, but it spans two class periods, making my day more hectic than a Friday has any right being. I finished up around four, after having organized a bunch of papers and assignments on my desk into neat little piles. They should have been put into my messenger bag and taken back to my dorm room, but I wanted a weekend without correcting, and if I needed them, I could always venture down the hill and pick them up.

I headed back up to the dorm, the sun warm on my face, the beautiful campus belying the feeling I had of doom and gloom. I passed a couple of students, joyful at the coming weekend. I could hear music coming from the campus bar — once a place to get beer, now dry since the drinking age had turned twenty-one — probably from a local band hired to play happy hour. I was surprised to see Max leaning against her car in the parking lot when I rounded the corner.

Her long legs were sticking out from a tailored black pencil skirt, her feet in improbably high black pumps with vivid red soles. By now, I knew that they were Louboutin and very pricey. She had a whole selection of them in my bedroom. She straightened up and I took in her soft suede coat, another item that I would never be able to afford on my teacher's salary. She looked better than when I had left earlier in the week and was back to her usual sprightly, well-groomed, gorgeous self. She smiled wide when I saw her and the transformation from depressed single to the old Max was complete.

"How come you never have your cell on when I call you?"

I was confused. "It's on." I pulled it out of my bag and looked at the screen. "Well, it was on. It's dead."

She approached me and gave me a hug. "How are you?"

"Good," I said warily. I hadn't expected her to arrive so early and I wasn't prepared. "You?"

"Great!" she said. "Guess who I talked to today?"

I looked at her, fearing the answer.

"Fred!" she said, and smiled even wider. "I think we're making progress."

"Oh, good!" I said, trying not to grimace. "So no more Match.com?"

She waved her hand dismissively. "No," she said, as if she had finally realized that there was no worse idea than her foray into online dating. "I met one guy and he was wearing his high-school ring and smelled like formaldehyde." She took her thumb and index finger and made an *L* on her forehead. "Loser."

"Be nice, Max," I said as we approached the dorm. Poor guy probably didn't know what he had gotten himself into with her and was probably hiding under his bed somewhere. After he dismembered the bodies in his bedroom and soaked them in formaldehyde.

Max cocked her head and listened to the music coming up from the bar. "Is that coming from Dunleavey?" she asked, referencing the campus bar.

"Yep," I said, continuing to walk.

"Remember when I made out with Jimmy Commiskey down there? And we accidentally knocked over that angel statue in front of the building?"

"No," I said, my step quickening. I knew where this was leading, and going down to Dunleavey to listen to a Genesis cover band wasn't on my to-do list. Telling Max that she wasn't really married was.

"Oh, sure you do," she said, her high heels clacking a staccato rhythm on the pavement. "You were working the door that night. And we had to find Krazy Glue so I could glue the angel's head back on?"

"I don't remember," I said as we reached the door.

She smacked me with her purse. "Hey! Focus! Jimmy Commiskey! Cute guy, looked like a young Johnny Depp. Johnny Depp from *21 Jump Street,* not Johnny Depp from *Sweeney Todd.* And the angel? You helped me glue its head back on?" she said.

I got inside the vestibule and fumbled around for the second key. "Maybe," I said.

She lost her train of thought, a result of my apathy toward the more dramatic details of the story. "Let's go down to Dunleavey before dinner!" she exclaimed, as if the idea had just occurred to her.

I shook my head. "No. We can't."

"Why not?" she asked. She looked at her watch. "It's four-thirty. We're not eating dinner yet, are we?"

"That reminds me," I said, unlocking the inner door. "What are you doing here so early?" We entered the marble foyer, still cool even though the temperature was steadily rising as spring progressed. We started down the hallway toward my room.

"I decided to cut out early. My boss still thinks I'm not up to a full day so I'm going to milk that for all it's worth," she said.

"I thought you were the boss?"

She chuckled. "Oh, that's right. I *am*." She put her briefcase down on the floor while I fiddled with the lock. "I mean the head of the station. The big cheese — Randolph," she said, referring to the mogul who had bought the station a few years back. He loved Max and would do anything to keep her happy. I suspected that his love for her knew no bounds but she managed to take it all in stride, chalking it up to him being an oversexed Australian. "Can we please, please, please go to Dunleavey for a soda?"

I greeted Trixie, whom I had locked in the bathroom after I had walked her at lunchtime. Pinto had called me and let me know that Trixie barked during the day and that there had been some complaints, hence her imprisonment in the bathroom. She ran out into the hallway to circle me, letting me know that she needed to go out. Now. When I thought about Max's proposition, I came to the conclusion that there was no reason why we couldn't go down to the bar for a soft drink; I wasn't going to convince Max to eat dinner at five in the afternoon and

Kevin wasn't meeting us for another hour so I thought it was as good a way to kill time as any. "Fine. But I have to walk Trixie first. Can you stay out of trouble if I leave you here alone?" I asked from the hallway. I leaned in and grabbed the leash off the hook right inside the door.

She looked around the room apparently assessing whether or not she could stay trouble free; she opened the French doors between the parlor and the bedroom. I had started keeping them closed because that room was so musty that I was convinced black mold was growing in there and killing me slowly.

"I guess so." She poked her head into the bathroom. "I think I had sex in this room."

I rolled my eyes. "Of course you did. Listen, just sit here and don't touch anything?"

She perched on the edge of the bed. "Oh, like your fabulous discount shoe collection? Or your drugstore lipstick? Or your fancy underwear from Target? I think I'll manage to keep my hands to myself."

"Nice," I said. Max had been in such a sorry state for the past few weeks that I had almost forgotten about snarky Max. Even though she was insulting me and my frugal side — underwear from Target? Hell, yeah

— I was happy that she was back.

Trixie and I wandered out to the parking lot and decided to head up to the cemetery for our nightly walk. I let Trixie off the leash and rested my backside on a tombstone, stretching my legs out as she romped through the small cemetery, stopping to leave her mark on the graves of nuns long gone. I looked up at the waning sun and warmed my face, still hearing the strains of the band playing at Dunleavey. Trixie came back a few minutes later and let me know that she was done; I went searching for whatever it was that she had left behind, hoping the whole time that she hadn't sandblasted the front of some old nun's eternal home with the remnants of her fiber-rich lunch. I cleaned up and the two of us headed back to the dorm.

Max was standing out in the hallway when I returned. "I couldn't take the smell in there," she said, pointing to my room.

"What smell?" I asked.

"I don't know, but if that's you, you need to see a doctor. Immediately." She made a face. "You've got some serious internal problems. Do you have irritable bowel syndrome?"

"No," I said, getting mildly concerned about the smell emanating from the parlor.

"Crohn's disease?"

"No!"

"Ulcerative colitis?"

"I have no bowel issues, Max," I assured her. I wondered how she had become so acquainted with diseases of the bowel but decided that was a conversation for another time. I lifted my arm and sniffed at my blouse. "I don't smell bad."

"Well, your room does, sister, so you'd better have a CT scan or an MRI or have them turn you inside out and figure it out because it smells really bad in there."

I was a cross between indignant and fearful, wondering what could possibly smell in my room. From the hallway, Max pointed to the small parlor. "It's mostly in there."

I entered the room tentatively. Frankly, the whole building was so old that it freaked me out, and I didn't even want to think about what could possibly be in the closet in the parlor to cause the smell that, yes, I was starting to discern. Trixie charged past me and headed toward the small linen closet in the parlor and began to bark wildly, scratching at the door.

This wasn't going to be good.

I turned and looked at Max, whose eyes were wide over the hand covering her nose and mouth. Out of the corner of my eye, I could see that the window in the parlor, open to let the musty smell out, was missing its screen so that it was open to the parking lot; the car right outside the window was so close I could touch it.

I walked over to the closet and opened the door.

The only thing I saw was the word "Princeton," black letters emblazoned on an orange sweatshirt, coming toward me.

TWENTY-FOUR

Max began screaming and ran down the hallway, Trixie nipping at her heels.

Me? I was lying on the floor of the parlor, a hopefully not dead Amanda Reese on top of me.

I lay for a few seconds, not sure what to do and terrified beyond belief. The smell of vomit filled the room, Amanda's open mouth inches from mine and expelling the same odor. Her glasses were still on but broken, both lenses shattered in a spider's web of disrepair.

Adrenaline finally forced me to move and I wiggled out from under her, lowering her gingerly to the floor. I watched as a puff of dust flew up around her. I heard a noise like a dog whimpering and realized that it was me; I tried to get a hold of myself as I knelt beside Amanda, who I wasn't sure was still alive.

I was pleading with her, with God, with

someone, that she wasn't dead. "Please, please, please, please, please," I repeated as I looked at her face, sideways on the rug.

I finally rolled her over gently and pulled her eyelid open; her eye rolled back. I laid my head on her chest and thought that I could hear a heartbeat but then realized it might just be the thudding in my ear from the blood flowing to my head. "Max!" I called but she didn't answer. I had no idea where she had gone or why she wasn't helping me but I needed her. "Max!" I screamed, my voice sounding unfamiliar to me, choked with hysteria and the sobs that were escaping. "Anyone!" I finally screamed, hoping that someone, anyone, was in the building, despite the band playing at Dunleavey, and the dinner service commencing across the campus at the dining hall. Even though it was only a week after spring break, a lot of students still went home for weekends, so I was guessing that the dorm was sparsely populated.

"Max! Anyone!" I called, hoping to get the attention of the person sitting desk. But as the seconds ticked by, it was clear that Max wasn't coming back and there was no one at the desk, something that was going to be brought up at the next dorm meeting if I had anything to do about it. I scrambled over Amanda to the phone on the dusty coffee table and dialed 911. After I explained Amanda's situation to them, I hung up and dialed Crawford.

When he answered, I burst into tears. "Crawford, get over here right away!"

I could tell that he was running to his car as I explained what was going on: Amanda was unconscious, her sweatshirt was covered with vomit, and her breathing was shallow. I put a hand on her chest and felt it rise and lower under my palm. I sat back on my heels, keeping my hand there.

I didn't see any blood on her but I didn't want to disturb her too much; falling out of the closet and on top of me was trauma enough for both of us. Her hands were tied behind her back and I undid the knots, rubbing her wrists to bring the blood back to them. I worked on the ropes around her ankles next. I wondered why her mouth wasn't taped shut and decided that she must have been unconscious when she had been stuffed in the closet and not a threat to scream. Someone wanted to scare her, not kill her, I surmised. I was glad that they hadn't covered her mouth; with the amount of vomit that was soaking the front of her sweatshirt, it was obvious that she would have choked to death if her mouth had been taped shut. I sat next to her with my hand on her forehead, waiting for the sound of sirens in the distance, which didn't take too long to start. Amanda moved her head from side to side, and threw up again onto the decades-old carpet, an action I took as a good sign; it meant she was alive and hopefully coming back to life. I lifted the back of her head so that she wouldn't choke.

She started to come to, her eyes opening slightly. She struggled to sit up but I held her down. "Stay down, Amanda."

I heard the sound of the sirens getting closer as they made their way down the hill toward the dorm and I started to breathe normally again. In moments, a team of paramedics broke through the side door with a stretcher and entered my small set of rooms. I got up and quickly moved to the side as they went to work on her.

One of the paramedics, a short stocky woman, asked me a series of questions, only a few of which I could answer. I didn't know how long Amanda had been in the closet, I didn't know how long she had been unconscious. I had no idea whether or not she had an ingested any substances. But I did know that she was twenty or twenty-one, and that she lived in New Jersey. I even had her home address. That much I knew.

When the paramedic was done with me, she went back to her partner and spent some time on Amanda, asking her a few questions. But Amanda was still not fully conscious and was clearly disoriented. I wrapped my arms around myself as I watched what was going on, standing close to the open window trying to get some air. I kept my arms close to my body so that I wouldn't be tempted to touch anything; the room was now a crime scene and I had been involved in enough crimes of late that I was starting to know exactly how to behave. I looked out the window and scanned the parking lot for a sign of Crawford, and I didn't have to wait too long before his puke-brown Crown Victoria skidded to a stop on the far side of the parking lot by the cemetery.

The paramedics loaded Amanda onto a stretcher, an IV having been started in her arm, an oxygen mask on her face. Her eyes were now open wide and she looked scared to death. I held her hand and assured her that someone would call her parents and that I would meet her at the hospital as soon as I talked to the police, a group of whom had congregated in the hallway waiting for the stretcher to pass.

Crawford entered through the side door

with Fred in tow. I ran to him and threw my arms around him. He held me at arm's length. "You okay?" he asked.

"I'm fine," I said, wiping my eyes on my sleeve. "I have to get to the hospital to be with her. Will you take me over there?"

Nobody had been murdered, so the case wouldn't be his. He spoke briefly with one of the patrol officers who had shown up and gave him a few instructions. "Where did they take her?" he asked the cop.

"Mercy," the cop said, and went into the room, his hands already gloved for the investigation.

I looked at Fred, standing by the janitor's closet, and remembered Max. A quick survey of the area revealed that she was nowhere to be found.

"Max!" I hollered, startling the cops who were clustered in and around the parlor. She didn't respond. "Max!" I called again. I had no idea where she had gone but figured she couldn't be far. I started down the marble hallway, the sound of my voice reverberating off the tiled ceiling. "Max!"

I heard the sound of her heels hitting the marble risers as she slowly made her way down the staircase in the lobby. She stopped at the bottom of the stairs and peeked around, looking to see who was there. "Is the coast clear?" she asked.

I marched toward her, my blood boiling. "You are completely useless, you know that?" I could hear Crawford call my name but the sound of my own pulse in my ears nearly drowned every sound out.

"What's that supposed to mean?" she asked, rooting through her pocketbook, not really paying attention to me.

"It means that you are completely useless!" I grabbed her pocketbook and threw it to the ground to get her attention. "I had a body fall on top of me. The body of one of my students. Who you didn't know whether or not was still alive."

"I got scared," she protested, and bent down to pick up the contents of her purse. Her indignant attitude toward what I considered a very serious situation made me irate.

"Well, what about me?" I asked, kicking a tube of lipstick out of her reach; it ricocheted off the wall by the unmanned desk and skidded to a stop by the TV room, where just a few days ago she had tried to sort out her feelings about her husband. Who wasn't really her husband. They hadn't been together long enough to even qualify as common-law spouses. I jabbed her in the chest with my index finger. "What about

291

Amanda? What if we needed help?"

She was finally starting to realize the depth of my ire and her green eyes filled with tears. "I'm sorry."

"Sorry? You're sorry? How about thinking about someone other than yourself every now and again?"

Crawford arrived at my side and took my elbow. "Let's go," he whispered.

I shook it off. "No, I have some things I want to say."

"You're very upset," he said, grabbing my elbow a little more tightly this time. "Let's go," he repeated forcefully.

I continued crying, more upset by Amanda's condition than Max's reaction to the situation. I spied Fred out of the corner of my eye and he wisely chose to keep his mouth shut and not use the opportunity to profess his love for Max or to make some sarcastic comment to me.

Max's expression turned sad. "That wasn't a very nice thing to say."

"You need to understand something," I said. "Sometimes you need to do the complete opposite of what your brain is telling you to do." I pointed at my own head and took a deep breath so that I could continue my rant. "That means that if your brain tells you to run, you stay put. That tells you that if you want to break up with your husband for some ridiculous reason, you stay put. That means that you do what's logical, not what I would consider completely illogical."

I heard Fred harrumph and give me an "amen, sister."

Max gripped her pocketbook a little closer to her chest; her lip quivered. I noticed that a group of students were now congregating in the lobby, watching this scene play out. If I hadn't been so upset, I would have taken this conversation to the TV room, but I was on a roll.

"Do you understand what I'm saying?" I asked. I don't know what possessed me at this particular moment to unleash nearly twenty years of anger toward this woman whom I considered the closest thing to a sister but it all came out in an ugly torrent; it wasn't unlike the one time my family's septic system had overflowed and befouled the backyard, not to mention the entire neighborhood. I was befouling the closest female relationship I had and I didn't know if someone with rubber boots and a wet/dry vacuum would be able to bail me out this time. "Sometimes, if you think that you can't handle something, you have to find a way. Because people might be depending on you." I stared at her, my anger increasing with every second I looked at her puzzled visage. "Did that ever occur to you?"

Behind me, I heard footsteps on the stairs and Kevin appeared at the bottom of the staircase. "Alison? What's going on?"

I turned and let out a long and shaky sigh. "Kevin . . ."

"Did you tell her?" he asked. If I had been thinking more clearly and not been so upset, I probably would have heard the relief in his voice. He was off the hook; someone else had done the dirty work.

I almost started in on him but Max looked at me, less sad now and more puzzled. "Tell me what?" She looked at Kevin, who turned crimson.

I threw up my hands. "Oh, you're not married. We might as well just go for broke tonight." I started walking down the hallway. "You're selfish, but you're not married. Kevin screwed up the paperwork. The archdiocese found out. You're not married. You never were. There. It's all out now."

TWENTY-FIVE

I woke up in Crawford's bed, his eyes trained on me. I sat up, startled. "Have you been staring at me the whole night?"

He stretched out. "Not the whole night."

"Okay, that's creepy," I said and sat up. I was really cranky. "You know who stare at people when they sleep? Serial killers, that's who. Crazy people. Dogs. Dogs stare at people when they sleep."

"Are you having some kind of breakdown?" he asked, completely serious. He looked at me with concern.

"No, I'm not having a breakdown." I put my feet on the floor and dropped my head into my hands. "This has been a terrible week."

"I thought you told me that you were enjoying the whole campus thing." Crawford is extremely literal and doesn't shift gears easily.

I stood. "Well, I was until an innocent,

lovelorn girl got mixed up in something she has no business being involved in."

Crawford adjusted his pillows so that he was half sitting up. "I noticed that we didn't hear any mention of the boyfriend at the hospital last night, but we did hear her ask for Wayne several hundred times."

"Yeah, and did you notice how the dad got angry every time she brought him up?"

Crawford nodded. "He's not a big fan of Wayne's." He knew he was stating the obvious. "By the way, who was the stoned-looking kid with the blond hair?"

"Spencer Williamson. Methinks that he, too, carries a torch for dear Amanda."

"Really?"

I yawned. "Really. It's nice to know that men can see past the outdated glasses and the Princeton sweatshirt to the beauty that resides underneath." I stretched my arms up and changed the subject. "How mad do you think Max is at me?" I asked.

Crawford's look said it all.

"Kevin?"

"I think you're in better stead with Fr. McManus."

"Fred?"

"I only know when Fred's hungry or tired. We don't delve into our emotions very often," he said.

"But he must have said something to you."

"The only thing he asked me is if killing Fr. McManus would be considered justifiable homicide." Crawford rolled out of bed and stretched; if I had to guess, I'd say his arm span was longer than his entire body. "I'm guessing you'll want to get back to campus soon."

He guessed wrong. I never wanted to go back there, but I had to at some point, at least to retrieve Trixie from Kevin. I figured it was the least he could do: he could watch my dog while I went to the hospital to see one of my charges. He had looked like he wanted to object to the request, but when he saw the expression on my face, he relented and took the dog up to his apartment on the top floor, my admonition to walk her before bedtime reverberating in the stairwell.

Crawford and I had spent a couple of hours at the hospital, and when it was clear that Amanda was in good hands and that her parents were there, we had left, stopping on the way home to have a drink at a little local bar in his neighborhood to take the edge off the evening. While we sipped our drinks, Crawford had told me what he had learned: Amanda said she had been picked up after her babysitting job by two men in a black car, driven down to a remote spot by the river and questioned about the whereabouts of the heroin. When she professed her ignorance about its origins or where it had gone in the meantime, they roughed her up, but not seriously. It seemed that they were hell-bent on scaring the bejesus out of her and had succeeded. When they determined that she didn't have anything to contribute, they had bound her, broken into my room, and stuffed her into my closet. Why in my room was anyone's guess. She had been in there for a few hours, scared out of her wits, vomiting intermittently from shock.

And not one person on campus, a security guard, the person who was supposed to be at the desk — one Michael Columbo — or a passing student had seen anything. That part of it frightened me more than anything. I would have to speak to Merrimack about that because if the last few years were any indication of the level of safety on the beautiful, bucolic campus, enrollments were going to drop dramatically.

"I want to go home," I said to Crawford. He made a sad face like I had just admitted that I was longing for home. "I need to pick up a few things." I wasn't having a Dorothy in Oz moment; I needed to find my black bra just in case I needed it for the week.

"I have to get the girls," he said.

I knew that. That was the Saturday drill: drive to Connecticut, pick up the twins, bring them back to the city, drive them back to Connecticut the next day, go to work on Monday. It was the rare emergency that disrupted the plan.

"Can I get you back into bed for fifteen minutes?" he asked.

"You need fifteen minutes?" I asked, incredulous.

He shook his head and smiled. "No. But you do," he said, and pulled me back under the comforter.

Fourteen minutes and thirty-eight seconds later, I was out of bed and in the shower. Crawford, exhausted from his week — or from the last fourteen minutes and thirty-eight seconds — was sitting on the bed trying to figure out the best way to handle our travel arrangements, what with me needing to go northwest and him needing to go northeast.

"I'll drop you off," he said after a few minutes.

"It's out of your way," I protested, even though dropping me off at school was a heck of lot easier than dropping me off at home.

"I'll drop you off," he repeated in a way that told me that the discussion was over.

So, he dropped me off. Who was I to argue? My goal was to get into my car and out of there as quickly as possible so that I wouldn't have to answer any questions about what had happened to Amanda; I needed a day away to get an idea of how I was going to explain to the kids in the dorm what had happened to her. I also didn't want to have to do due diligence with anyone in the St. Thomas administration just yet. I turned to Crawford and gave him a quick peck, and ran over to my car, which was parked in the space next to where he had pulled in. The coast was clear for the moment and I wanted to make my getaway without being accosted by any nosy students or even nosier administrators. I got into the car and started it, throwing it into reverse. The car didn't move.

Crawford was still in his car in the parking lot and looked over at me. Although I had my foot on the accelerator and was attempting to back out of the spot, the car was not in motion, instead making a grinding noise accompanied by a whining of the engine. Crawford jumped out of his car and put his hand up, giving me the signal to stop accelerating. I took my foot off the gas. I watched as he walked around the car and looked down at the front passenger side tire. He looked up at me and I knew that there was a problem.

The windows were closed. He mouthed the word "boot."

"Boot?" I repeated to myself. It took a minute for the realization to dawn on me. "Boot?" I said again, this time much angrier. "Those bastards," I muttered, and got out of the car to see for myself. Indeed, there was a boot on the front tire of my car that was going to prohibit my going anywhere for a while. I put my hands on my hips and looked at Crawford and told him the whole story of how because I now lived on campus, I was supposed to park a half mile away. I looked at him pleadingly, hoping he would take pity on me and either help me figure out a way to get the boot off or drive me all the way home. I knew neither was an option, given his schedule for the day.

"I'm late," he said regretfully, knowing that driving me the fifteen miles north to Dobbs Ferry was out of the question. "Can I drop you at the train?" he asked. He took my hand and led me back to his car. Once we were inside and on our way off campus, I let loose with a torrent of curse words I didn't even know I knew. I gave the finger to Joe, who was sitting the guard booth, but my hand was below the window and he wouldn't be able to see it. But I knew that I had done it and that was all that mattered.

"Did you just give your stomach the finger?" Crawford asked.

I didn't answer, still incapable of uttering a sentence that didn't have at least one or two multihyphenated curses in it.

"I promise you that as soon as I get back to work on Monday, I'll help you get that boot off the car." He turned onto the avenue. "A guy in Transit owes me and I'll give him a call."

"Those dirty bastards," I said. I sat in silence all the way to the station, at a loss for words.

Crawford pulled up close to the platform. "What time is the train?"

"I don't know!" I said, frustrated by the whole situation. Saturday trains ran infrequently so I could be sitting there for the better part of an hour if I had just missed the last local train.

"Do you want me to wait with you?" he asked, hoping against hope that I would say no.

I knew how much his weekly visits with the girls meant for him and wouldn't cut into his time. I took a deep breath to calm down. "No," I said. I leaned in and gave him a kiss. "Thanks. Have a good afternoon."

He promised to call me after dinner and gave me a final wave before driving off. I walked up to the platform and sat on the cement bench, staring out at the river and considering what had occurred over the past week and what, exactly, I knew.

The drugs weren't Wayne's.

And they weren't Amanda's.

But they were someone's and that someone was either the two goons or someone who had sent the two goons and who wanted to scare Amanda enough to have her tell them where they went, a fact that she didn't know.

I thought about the Wayne-Amanda-Brandon love triangle. I could understand why Brandon, her fiancé from Princeton, wanted to kill Wayne, but Costas? What was his stake in this? Did he see Brandon as more of a "catch" because of the Greek thing and the fact that Brandon stood to inherit the family business? Was that enough to try and kill someone? Or was it something else? Next time I saw Amanda, I wanted a little bit more information on Mr. Princeton and what his relation to her father was, if any. That whole part of the story confused me more than anything.

I rubbed my temples, trying to force myself to think more clearly. I thought about Max and realized that I had been very hard on her. One side of my brain screamed, "She always abandons you when the going gets rough and you have every right to be mad!" while the other cautioned, "She's going through a very difficult time." Both sides were right but it didn't excuse my behavior. I had been exceedingly hard on her and I had to make amends. Right after I went home and collected my black bra.

I didn't have to wait too long for the train; it arrived within fifteen minutes of Crawford dropping me off. I got off at the Dobbs Ferry station — another fifteen minutes down the train line — and began my trek up the hill toward my street. While I was walking, I left Kevin a message to keep Trixie for another couple of hours and to make sure she got water, she got walked, and that he gave her ample love. I was ready to make things better with Max, but when it came to Kevin, I was still incensed. I used to love Kevin's flouting of church rules — it assuaged some of my lapsed-Catholic guilt — but now that his lack of respect for the rules and regulations was affecting me personally — albeit tangentially — I was ready to flog him. I was glad that he didn't answer the phone when I left him my message because I was more incensed with him than I think I had ever been at one person and I needed what Crawford referred to as a "cooling-off period."

Smart man, that Detective Hot Pants.

I approached the house and despite the grass needing to be cut — a chore that I had hired out to the kid across the street — everything looked like it had when I left the weekend before. The block was quiet so I got up the front walk without running into anyone — my neighbor Jane appeared to be out, and she was really the only person I wanted to see. Being a single woman with no children left me out of many personal interactions in my neighborhood.

Max wasn't home, either, and I was instantly relieved. It seemed like she had left every single window in the house open but even the cool air wafting in and out, rustling the curtains, couldn't mask the smell of paint that assaulted my nasal passages as I entered the downstairs hallway. I sniffed suspiciously, looking around. The living room looked the same and the dining room, having been painted just a few short weeks earlier, was still the same color. A trip to the kitchen confirmed that it was still the outdated robin's-egg blue that it had been when I left.

I ran up the stairs to the second floor of the house. The hallway was the same fingerprint-stained beige. Curiously, my bedroom door was closed when I reached the top of the stairs and as I stopped on the landing, trying to catch my breath and prepare myself for what awaited me on the other side, my mind flashed back to the can of paint that had been sitting on my counter the previous weekend.

Million Dollar Red.

I grabbed my stomach and bent in two, breathing deeply, muttering, "Max, what have you done?" to myself.

I opened the bedroom door, my fears confirmed.

My bedroom, once a soothing ecru color with white trim was now Million Dollar Red. Floor to ceiling. With black trim. It was an assault to the senses and I knew at once that I would never be able to sleep in a color so jarring, so bright, so . . . tacky. My room looked like a New Orleans bordello and I wasn't going to be happy until it was back to the way it was.

Which, obviously, would take two coats of primer followed by three coats of paint.

Any goodwill I had toward Max evaporated. If I had felt guilty about being angry at her before, I now wanted to kill her with my bare hands.

TWENTY-SIX

I was still seething that evening, safely ensconced in my room and lying on my bed, when Crawford called. I had picked Trixie up from Kevin, neither I nor my once-favorite priest exchanging a word during the handoff.

I was losing best friends faster than someone losing weight on the Atkins diet.

"We picked up one of the guys who roughed up Amanda," he said. I knew that by "we," he didn't mean himself or Fred personally, but rather someone in the extended NYPD family.

I sat up. "You did?" My tale of woe would have to wait.

"Yep. Some two-bit idiot from the Newark area. Amanda, amazingly, got a look at the plate of the car and gave us a partial. The Newark cops got a tip, too. It all went very quickly and smoothly."

"That's great," I said, although it was the

kind of good news that comes with strings attached. Good news that they caught one of the guys; bad news because of the nature of his deeds. I was sorry we were having this conversation at all.

Trixie could tell something important was happening and came from her usual sleeping area in the little parlor room to the edge of the bed, resting her head on the mattress near my feet.

"He's not giving anything up, though," he said. "But he'll crack. They always do."

And not without a little help, I thought. But I didn't care. They could treat him like a suspected terrorist at Guantánamo Bay, if they wanted. I wanted him to tell the cops what he knew, who was involved, and why they had taken their aggression out on an innocent girl who suffered from the familiar and common problem of having bad taste in men. "Well, let me know if you find out anything," I said.

"You sound down."

I thought about going into detail on the whole painted-bedroom story but decided against it. In the grand scheme of things, it wasn't such a big deal. It just happened to be the icing on the cake for one of the most interesting and annoying weeks of my life. And I still had a healthy dose of guilt from my outburst at Max that was managing to creep in and add to my depression. "No," I said. "I'm fine." I attempted to shake off my mood and sound upbeat.

"You want me to come get you?" he asked. "The girls and I need dinner and we could just as easily eat in your neighborhood as mine."

He was being kind. Coming back up to St. Thomas and having dinner with me in my present mood was not going to be enjoyable for anyone. And it wasn't as easy as it sounded with the New York City traffic getting started at this hour. "No, Crawford, I'm fine," I reassured him. "Call me tomorrow."

I resumed my prone position, staring up at the cracked ceiling, moody and sullen. Finally, I decided that I had had enough and put Trixie on her leash, taking her outside for an early evening walk.

We headed down to the river where I took her off her leash and let her frolic in the sand and the little whitecaps that floated to shore, the foam dripping off her face after a few moments. I sat on a rock and watched her, wiping her chin off with my sleeve when she came over to give me a kiss. Whatever problem I was having, being with my dog made it all go away. I kissed Trixie on the nose and rubbed her belly.

We lasted until the sun had set and dusk had fallen on campus. I put her on the leash and walked back up to the main part of campus, the buildings silhouetted against the darkening sky.

I went to the parking lot of Siena and stood by my car, ruminating on the boot on the passenger's side tire. The parking lot was quiet and I was surprised when a car pulled up beside me, the Reese/Grigoriadis family revealed to be behind its tinted windows.

Costas got out of the car and came around to open the back door on my side, giving me a curt nod as a greeting. Amanda slid out of the back seat, her face still bruised, but otherwise looking the same as she always did — a little unkempt but adorable nonetheless. She had on what looked to be replacement glasses — these were more fashionable with a small tortoiseshell frame that didn't dwarf her face. She looked at me and then surprised me by coming over and throwing her arms around me. In the little space of light afforded by the open back door, I could see the back of a perfectly coiffed head, black hair pulled back into a sleek ponytail secured by a jeweled barrette.

"Say good-bye to your mother," Costas

said to Amanda.

Amanda pulled away from me and leaned into the car, putting her hand on her mother's shoulder. Her mother turned and kissed Amanda's hand, and I caught a glimpse of her blotchy, tearstained face.

"You'd better take care of my daughter." Amanda's father shook his finger in my direction. "If it were up to me, I'd pack up her room and get her out of this place." He looked over at the Siena dorm in disgust. "Her mother is beside herself."

I looked at Amanda who was studying the pavement during her father's minitirade.

"I'll do my best, Mr. Grigoriadis." I put my arm around Amanda's shoulder and led her toward the side door.

"You'd better do better than your best," he sputtered, and went back around to the front of the car.

I wasn't sure that was possible but I didn't want to get into a semantics discussion with him. Amanda and I went in through the side door and stood in front of the door to my room. "Amanda, what can I do to help you?"

She burst out crying. "I'm not sure. I'm so confused!" she wailed.

I leaned against the doorjamb. "Do you want to come in?"

"I just want to go back to my room and go to sleep and forget this ever happened," she said. She closed her eyes and shuddered.

"Detective Crawford told me that they got one of the suspects," I said, thinking that I probably shouldn't have shared that after I blurted it out.

"Really?"

"Yes. Hopefully, he'll point them in the right direction." I opened the door to my room. "Sure you don't want to come in?"

She shook her head. "No. I'm just going to go back to my room. Brandon wanted me to call him the minute I got back."

Something about that statement riled me a bit. The minute she got back? Was it a trust issue or was he that concerned? After seeing his behavior in the parking lot a few days back and knowing that Costas preferred him to Wayne, I got to thinking that young Princetonian Brandon may have had the Costas possessiveness gene. I thought about giving Amanda some advice along the lines of "ditch the guy," but I decided to keep my mouth shut. For one thing, I knew nothing about Brandon — or Costas, for that matter.

And for another, she was no longer standing in front of me in the hallway, having started down the hall, stopping briefly to chat with Spencer Williamson.

"Thanks for coming to the hospital last night," I heard her say.

I watched his cheeks flush red and thought, There's a boy with a serious crush. Miss Amanda Reese certainly attracted all kinds: Princeton boy, slack-jawed Wayne, and now, anime-producing Spencer Williamson. Looked to me like she had herself a nice love quadrangle in the works.

I went into my room and returned to my prone position on the bed after retrieving my cell phone from my messenger bag. I dialed Max's number; instead of hearing her greeting, I was put straight to voice mail. I didn't bother leaving a message because, wisely, I realized that that would just exacerbate things. Oh, so that's how we're going to play it, I thought. You think *you're* mad? I only called you selfish. I didn't paint your bedroom bordello red.

I decided to make one more call. The phone was picked up on the sixth ring, just as I was about to give up. The voice had its usual terse timbre.

"Hi, Mary. Listen, you're either with me or against me on this one, so what's it going to be?" I was emboldened by crankiness and nothing more.

"I don't know what you're talking about, dear."

"I think you do. Do you want to help me find who put that nephew of yours in this precarious situation or not? Because, frankly, I'm getting sick of living in this hellhole, in spite of its proximity to my office." I took a deep breath. "So what's it going to be?"

"It's not going to be anything, dear."

I sat and stared at the ceiling, waiting for her to continue. When she did, she stated something that I already knew.

"I'm afraid Wayne has left campus and I don't know where he's gone."

"That's obvious, Mary. Where did he go?"

"If I knew, would I be this upset?" she asked, a catch in her throat.

Probably not. "Where did he go?" I asked, not responding to her question. "His parents' house? Somewhere else?"

"I don't know," she said. "And I've been keeping the fact that he's in trouble from my sister and her husband."

"They still don't know what's going on?"

She got defensive. "Wayne asked me not to tell them and I'm going to respect his wishes."

I decided not to go any further with the conversation because Mary was stonewall-

ing and I didn't have the energy. I bid her a
good night and hung up, thinking about
how I was going to spin this whole thing to
Etheridge and Merrimack, who I was convinced had a dart board with my picture on
it.

TWENTY-SEVEN

Sunday passed without incident, and I caught up on some much-needed rest and overdue schoolwork. Crawford stopped by on his way to work on Monday morning to supervise the removal of the boot from my car. Visitation didn't start until three o'clock, so I dragged him into the janitor's closet across from my room so that we could have a discussion in private. He got the wrong idea.

I pulled his hand out from under my blouse as I avoided a dirty mop head that I had dislodged from its spot on my way into the closet. "Stop, Crawford. This is important."

He leaned in, his lips grazing my neck, and I lost my train of thought, going with the flow for a few minutes. But the sound of students passing by on the other side of the closed door brought me back to earth. I pushed his head up by applying the palm of my hand to his forehead.

"You are such a killjoy," he said. "Did you know that?"

I put a finger on his lips. "Shhh. If I get nabbed with a big hunk of cop in the janitor's closet, it's curtains for me. Hear me? Curtains!"

"You need to read other things besides Wonder Woman comic books," he said. "You're starting to talk like a superhero."

I pulled him in close by his collar to get his attention. "Pinto is coming by here in a few minutes to talk to me about what happened, so I'm glad you're here. He called me at six o'clock this morning and said that he's saving me a face-to-face with Etheridge so I had better give him all the details."

"Pinto is a cream puff. What are you worried about?"

"He's not a cream puff. He's a kickboxer. And I'm worried I'm going to get my ass kickboxed right out of a job if I don't tell them everything's that's going on."

"So you want me to be your wingman?"

I didn't even know what that meant, but I agreed nonetheless. "Make sure I give it to him straight."

He saluted me, giggling a little bit.

"What's wrong with you?" I asked.

"I haven't had a full night's sleep in days,"

he said, rubbing his eyes. "I think I'm getting punchy."

"I would have to agree," I said, and opened the door to the closet; the smell of cleaning supplies was starting to make me punchy, too. I peered out and saw Jay Pinto standing in front of the door to my room. I quickly ducked back into the closet and pinned myself against the wall. I motioned to Crawford to be quiet. "It's Pinto," I mouthed.

We stood in the closet, staring at one another, Crawford trying not to laugh. The mop, which was balanced precariously against the wall, slid down and made a racket as it clattered to the floor. In order to avoid getting hit on the head with it, I stepped out of the way and knocked into a semifull bucket of soapy, gray water, which sloshed out over the side and onto my shoes. The bucket scraped a few inches across the floor, adding to the cacophony coming from the presumably empty janitor's closet. I looked at Crawford, wide-eyed, as I heard Pinto's footsteps approaching the door of the closet.

He knocked. "Who's in there?"

I decided that the best defense was a good offense. I opened the door and exposed myself and Crawford. "Just us, Jay." I smoothed down the front of my skirt and adjusted my blouse, thinking as I did that the best time to have begun to put myself back together would have been *before* I opened the door. I gave him what I thought was a winning smile.

Pinto looked in the closet and nodded at Crawford. "What are you doing in there?"

"Looking for a plunger," I said, grabbing one from behind the door and proffering it as proof of my business.

"You don't have a clogged toilet again, do you?" Pinto said, grimacing.

"Sink," I said, marveling at how smoothly the lies just fell from my tongue.

He looked at me until I reminded him that he had come to see me. "Oh, right," he said, snapping out of his reverie. "About Amanda Reese. How are we on that?"

"How are we on that?" I repeated. "Not sure what you mean." I turned to Crawford, who looked as if he didn't have any plans to participate in the discussion, mesmerized by the water on my shoes.

"Oh, Amanda Reese," Crawford said, after a gentle poke to the ribs. "We've got a suspect in custody, Jay, and we're questioning him."

"Good," Pinto said.

"I'm assuming you'll give a complete
320

report to Etheridge?" I asked, after I'd listed the rest of the details on the goings-on of the weekend. Crawford, it turned out, was no help at all.

He nodded. That was very good news. A day without Etheridge, for me, was a day with sunshine and flowers and all things good and wonderful.

"Keep me posted?"

Crawford gave him a little salute not unlike the one he had given me. It came off as less sarcastic than I assumed he meant it. "Will do."

Pinto looked at the two of us for another second, curious, but walked off, his kick-boxing ass looking fine in his gabardine slacks. Crawford and I went into the hall-way.

"I'm glad you're here" I said, sliding my feet out of my shoes, once a beautiful black suede and now a soggy mess.

"You sounded down when we talked so I wanted to make sure you were doing okay," he said.

"You're a nice guy, Crawford," I said, still a little amazed that he was my nice guy. "I'm fine." I opened the door to my room and Trixie bounded out to kiss Crawford. "What are you doing later?"

"Sleeping?" he said, as if the answer were

obvious.

"I think you need to be Chad for another night."

He shook his head and began muttering. "No, no, no, no . . ."

"Well, how weird would it look for Coco to be visiting the Brookwells without Chad? Where should I say you are?"

"Working late on the Anderson account?" he said. "The Anderson account needs a lot of graphic design."

"No, you're coming with me. I want to see if the Prius is parked in the driveway."

"You can do that by yourself."

I whimpered. "But it's not as much fun without you, Chad." I looked around and, seeing no students, slid my hand into the top of his waistband. "I'll make it worth your while," I whispered in his ear.

He pulled away as if I had burned him. "Okay, that's enough. I'll come with you. Stop it," he said, taking my hand and putting it on the doorknob. "I'm going. I'll see you later."

"How about seven?" I called after him.

He didn't turn around but raised his hand in acknowledgment. The man was putty in my hands.

Or he was just so exhausted that he didn't have the energy to put up a fight.

I headed off to school after paying homage to Trixie who was obviously getting tired of hanging around the dank dorm room. She looked at me longingly as I closed the door, avoiding her snout. When I got to my office, I was surprised to find Sister Mary waiting for me. She was standing outside of my door, her back straight and her hands folded in front of her. I passed several colleagues on my way to my office who gave me sympathetic looks; if Sister Mary stopped by to "chat," it usually wasn't good.

But what they didn't know was that our relationship had changed. I no longer was intimidated by her; she had secrets just like the rest of us and now I knew what they were.

"Morning, Mary." I unlocked the office door and extended a hand. "After you?" I contemplated using the whole "age before beauty" adage, but thought better of it.

She sat on the edge of one of my guest chairs and waited until I arranged myself behind my desk before starting. "What is it that you want from me?" she asked, her face pinched.

"I want the truth," I whispered because I had left my door open.

Mary leaned over and slammed it shut. I was sure that that attracted some attention.

"You know the truth," she hissed.

I raised an eyebrow, asking, in effect, "I do?"

"Those were not Wayne's drugs."

"So Wayne says."

"They weren't his. Wayne is a very clean-living young man."

I leaned across her desk. "Yes, one who throws bottles at the heads of women who walk their dogs in cemeteries and runs at the first sign of trouble. One," I said, getting revved up, "who leaves campus despite the fact that his girlfriend was beaten and stuffed in my closet. That's the kind of young man your nephew is."

"I don't know what you're talking about," she lied.

"Yes, you do," I said, pointing at her. "Where did he go, Mary?"

She stuttered for a few minutes and surprised me by starting to cry for the second time in our relationship. Oh, Jesus. Please help me. I make nuns cry. "I don't know. He left. He cleaned out the room on the fifth floor and took the car."

I resisted the urge to chuckle. "The Prius?" Crawford was right; nobody would ever know what time he left with his quiet car. "When's the last time you saw him?" I asked.

"Lunch on Friday."

So, three days ago around noontime. He had been gone long enough to qualify as a missing person but I didn't think Mary wanted to go that route.

She continued. "I went to bring him his dinner and his room was cleaned out, so I knew that he was gone."

"Did he leave a note?"

She looked away. "No."

She was a lying mclyingpants, I knew it, and she knew that I knew it. "You're lying."

"Well, I never!" she protested.

Yes, I know, I thought. Most nuns haven't. But you're still lying.

I kept staring at her but she didn't crack. But she did offer up a little nugget. "Before he left, he said something about Spencer Williamson. About him being . . . a stoner?" She acted like she had never heard the word before. Oh, please. She's worked on a college campus since the early seventies; I was sure she had heard the word "stoner" once or twice.

"Not a crime," I said.

"Actually, it is," she reminded me, "but it may explain where those drugs came from."

"The hardest drugs Spencer Williamson does are of the organic variety. I don't get the sense that he's a full-blown junkie or that he has access to a brick of heroin." I leaned back in my chair. "Frankly, we don't even know if he is a stoner. He acts like half of the guys on this campus. Are they all stoned?"

She smiled slightly. "Good point." But any conviviality disappeared quickly. "Anyway, Wayne mentioned him before he left. I just thought you should know."

"Thanks for sharing," I said.

We stared at each other for a few minutes and she finally got the hint, taking her leave, the smell of Jean Naté staying in the air far longer than she had stayed in my office.

TWENTY-EIGHT

I offered Crawford a cup of coffee from my stash in the bag on the floor of the car.

"Just the way you like it," I said.

He was in a foul mood, not really wanting to be Chad Varick for the evening. He was still in his work clothes, though his tie was off and his shirt was unbuttoned to the third button. I could see his clean white under-shirt peeking out and I felt a swoon coming on.

"Could you button your shirt?" I asked.

He took a sip of the coffee and looked at me. "No. Chad likes to be comfortable. Come to think of it, could you unbutton *your* shirt?"

"Nice try. We're in Scarsdale. Respectable people live here."

He peered over me, attempting to see what else I had in the bag.

"Italian sub with the works or turkey on a roll?" I asked.

"What do you want?"

"I don't care," I lied.

"Yes you do."

"I don't."

"Italian sub."

I tried to hide my disappointment.

"Ha! I knew it," he said, reaching into the bag and extracting the turkey on a roll. "I didn't want it anyway. I just wanted to prove that you were lying." He opened the sandwich. "Anything on here?"

"Lettuce and tomato."

"Mayo?"

"I hate mayo," I reminded him.

He let the sandwich and its wrapper fall onto his lap. "But you were having the Italian sub."

"I couldn't take that chance."

"Mayo packets?" he asked. "Who eats dry turkey?" he muttered, taking the sandwich apart to see if I was telling the truth. I was.

I reached into the bag and pulled out two foil packets of mayonnaise. I was nothing if not prepared for food emergencies. He leaned over and gave me a kiss. "I love you," he said.

"And I you, Crawford."

" 'And I you'?" he asked. "What's with your speaking pattern lately? You either sound like a writer for *Superman* episodes or someone from Shakespearean times." He pulled open the foil packet and spread some mayo on his sandwich. "And I you!" he said gravely. "I, too, love you! And I do! Unhand her!" he added, harkening back to my encounter with Amanda and her boyfriend. The one from Princeton. They were getting hard to keep straight.

I looked out the window beyond Crawford, ignoring his performance. I saw Eben Brookwell carting a garbage can out to the curb. "Shut up!" I said. "And duck!"

Eben surveyed the street, spending an inordinate amount of time staring at our car. After a few minutes, he started across the street.

"Oh, shit. We got made," I said.

"Now you're an extra from *Boyz n the Hood*." Crawford, realizing that we weren't getting out of this without a good story, sat up straight, folded the deli paper around his sandwich, and plastered a huge smile on his face. He got out of the car and extended his hand to a very puzzled Eben.

"Well, hello, there!" Crawford said, as if running into Eben Brookwell were the most natural thing in the world.

"Chad? Coco?" Eben said.

I got out of the car and came around to where they were standing. I leaned in and gave Eben a peck on the cheek; I figured we had made it this far, why not give the old guy a thrill? After all, I was a flight attendant; friendliness was our stock in trade. "Hi, Eben. How are you?"

"I'm fine," he said warily. "What are you doing here?"

Crawford looked like a deer caught in the headlights, so I improvised. "You'll never guess! We bought a house!"

"Really? That's wonderful." His smile went from wary to jubilant at the news.

"And we came by to tell you!" I said with as much cheer as I could muster. I was going to deserve an Academy Award when this was over.

"Which house?" he asked. His kind face and his obvious elation over our move to Scarsdale made me feel really, really bad.

"Which house?" I said. "Doesn't matter. All that matters is that we'll be neighbors." I linked arms with Eben and Crawford, putting myself between them.

"No. Really. Which house?" Eben said, the smile not leaving his face.

I hadn't wanted to use this information, but it seemed like I had to. Before Crawford had picked me up for our night of subterfuge, I had gone on Realtor.com and looked at houses in our price range, finding one that might suit Coco and Chad Varick. "Twenty-seven Fairway Drive!" I exclaimed. I knew that Fairway was a few blocks away from the Brookwells and figured that that would send Eben over the moon.

Crawford looked at me like I was insane.

"Twenty-seven?" Eben asked.

"Twenty-seven? Or twenty-three?" I looked at Crawford for help. "Do you remember, honey?"

"Twenty-seven," he said in a zombielike tone, staring straight ahead.

Eben looked at me, his eyes narrowing. "Twenty-seven Fairway Drive burned down three nights ago. Boiler exploded. It *was* for sale, but obviously, it's not anymore."

I could almost hear my intestines fill with fluid at the news.

The jig was up. Eben studied my face as if the answer to his question were printed there. "Who are you, really, Ms. Varick? And why are you here?" Eben asked.

I focused on the garbage can that Eben had just brought out to the curb, hoping for some divine inspiration. When none was forthcoming, I focused on the black car driving slowly down the street, not making a sound. When I realized who it was, I threw an elbow into Crawford's side, screamed, "Gotta go!" and jumped back into the car.

But before I did, I locked eyes with Wayne, who also knew that the jig was up. Eben turned around and called to Wayne, who put pedal to the metal, and took off down the street. Crawford threw the car in drive and peeled out of the spot, sandwich fixings flying around the car.

"When this is over, I'm going to kill you," Crawford said, not unkindly. He took a corner on two wheels, following Wayne at a safe distance, the two of them slowing down to the requisite twenty-five miles an hour as a school appeared out of nowhere.

"This is like the O.J. chase," I said, my adrenaline coursing through my veins.

"If we get pulled over, you keep your mouth shut. Do you hear me?" he asked.

"I hear you," I said, bracing a hand on the dashboard and keeping one eye on Wayne while admiring the beautiful houses of Scarsdale with the other. "Look at that one," I remarked, turning my head to look at a spacious Dutch colonial with a FOR SALE sign on the front lawn.

"We're not looking at houses," Crawford reminded me. "Keep an eye on Wayne." He took his eyes off the road for a minute. "Oh, great. I have mayonnaise on my pants."

"Serves you right," I said, as I watched Wayne hang a left. "He's making a left."

"I see him."

"I thought you were looking at your pants."

He sighed. "Why don't we just be quiet for a little while?"

I agreed that that was a good idea. Since we were going so slowly, only having reached a cruising altitude of thirty-five miles an hour, I pulled my sub out of the bag and unwrapped it, taking a big bite. "Want some?" I asked Crawford, holding it in front of his mouth.

He leaned over and sank his teeth into the side I hadn't touched. Wayne made another left turn and it appeared that we were heading toward the Hutchinson River Parkway. "Where the hell is he taking us?" I asked as we merged onto the highway, finally reaching fifty-five miles an hour. Wayne puttered along in the right lane, while Crawford sped up and pulled up alongside him in the middle lane. "Tell him to pull over," Crawford said.

My hands were kind of taken up with the sub, so I rolled down the window and waved the sandwich at Wayne through my window. "Pull over!" I called.

Wayne stayed in the right lane, staring straight ahead.

"What did he say?" Crawford asked, keeping his speed at the same pace as Wayne's.

"I think he said no."

"Goddamn it," Crawford said, and took serious action. He started nosing the Passat toward Wayne in the right lane, avoiding hitting the Prius by inches. I started to get nervous.

"Have you done this before?" I asked, taking another bite of sub. I was nervous, but not that nervous. I bit into a hot pepper that made my eyes water.

"Yes," he said, and nosed toward Wayne again. Wayne drifted over to the shoulder but remained mostly in the right lane, driving the speed limit, looking straight ahead.

Crawford straddled the line on the road and finally succeeded in pushing Wayne completely onto the shoulder. Fortunately, there weren't too many people on the road at that hour, so we were able to muscle Wayne over without attracting too much attention.

Wayne got out of the car and began running along the shoulder. Crawford pulled over and put the car in park. "Stay here," he said, as he bolted from the car and began running along the shoulder, no match for Wayne and his superspeed.

"He's really fast, Crawford!" I called after him, but it was no good. The two of them were way down the shoulder, Crawford, in his tie-up dress shoes, trying to catch Wayne in his hundred-and-fifty-dollar sneakers.

The last thing I heard before I saw the state trooper's head in the sideview mirror, making his way toward Crawford's car, was Crawford screaming, "Stop! Wayne! You're under arrest!"

I put my sandwich on the dashboard, carefully wrapping it so that the oil and vinegar dressing didn't drip onto Crawford's floor mats.

The trooper arrived and tapped on the side of the car with his radio.

I smiled, hoping that there was no lettuce stuck in my teeth. "Good evening, Officer."

"License and registration, ma'am."

I then realized that I had bigger problems than lettuce stuck in my teeth.

TWENTY-NINE

I wasn't sure, but I thought I heard Crawford mutter, "I hate you," while I was thanking the state trooper for his time.

We were in the car and trying to find an exit so that we could go south and head back to St. Thomas. I started to talk.

Crawford held up a hand. "Nope. Not a word. Not yet. Too soon."

"What are you so mad about? It was your idea to run after him on the shoulder of the highway." I unwrapped my sandwich and began to eat it again now that things had calmed down.

"It was your idea to go to the Brookwells'," he said, merging into the left lane and hitting eighty miles an hour. It appeared that he couldn't drop me off fast enough.

"Interesting thing about you, Crawford: you're always 'in' when it comes to these little capers until things go a little bit wrong. Then, it's all my fault. Then, you're com-

336

pletely 'out.' "

He waited a beat. "You could have waited to tell me that when your mouth was empty." He slowed down a bit. "Is that a piece of lettuce on my dashboard?"

I wiped the lettuce off with a napkin and threw the rest of my sandwich in the bag. "I'm not even hungry anymore."

We drove to school in silence, both ruminating on the chain of events. After Crawford took off after Wayne on the shoulder, the trooper had arrived and I had had some explaining to do. When I told him that we were there to arrest one Wayne Brookwell, the trooper, initially dubious, took off after Crawford and Wayne, coming back with only Crawford. Wayne was in the weeds, a veritable Flash in a T-shirt and jeans. While Crawford discussed the situation with the trooper, I wisely kept my mouth shut, just as I had been instructed. The trooper was going to impound the Prius and put an APB on Wayne.

"What is Wayne so afraid of?" I said, not realizing I said it out loud. Crawford looked over at me. "It can't just be Costas and Brandon. And if he had explained the situation to Merrimack and Etheridge, I'm sure this whole thing could have been worked out. What is this about?"

Crawford looked at me but I could tell he was thinking. At the same time, the two us said, "They were his drugs after all."

I looked at my watch as we pulled onto campus and saw that Crawford and I had another two hours before visitation ended. Crawford was still ruminating on our conclusion. "Why don't you come in and we can talk it through?" I said. He didn't seem mad anymore and I hoped to entice him into coming in to do more than talk.

"I've got an idea," he said, and got out of the car.

We went into the dorm, which was pretty quiet. I walked to the main area, leaving Crawford in my room, and checked in with the RA on duty: Spencer Williamson.

"Hi, Spence." I perched on the edge of the desk and looked casually at the logbook. "Anything going on?" I signed Crawford into the logbook.

For a supposed stoner, Spencer's desk sitting was far superior to any of the other buffoons who supposedly kept track of things in the dorm. He flipped through the logbook. "Not really. A couple of visitors but nothing too earth-shattering."

I should hope not. "How's Amanda?"

His pale face grew paler. "She's having a tough time. She's really scared."

"If you see her, tell her that if she needs anything to come see me. Okay?"

He nodded. "Got it."

I started off down the hall, turning back when I heard Spencer call after me.

"Any sign of Wayne?" he asked.

"Not a one," I lied.

He made a little sound. "Too bad," I heard him mutter.

I didn't know what that meant and didn't feel like asking. I returned to my room, where Crawford was searching the contents of my medicine cabinet; Trixie was on my bed, a place she wasn't supposed to be. He didn't turn around when I came into the bathroom.

"You've got a lot of lipstick," he commented.

"You've got a lot of tube socks," I said. "But, unlike you, I thought it rude to say anything about it."

He jiggled the medicine cabinet, held to the wall by two flimsy screws. "Got a screwdriver?"

I left the room and opened up the nightstand drawer and went back into the bathroom. "Next best thing: a butter knife." I handed it to Crawford and watched him pull the medicine cabinet away from the wall. "What are you doing?" It finally oc-

339

curred to me to ask him what his plan was.

"Looking for drugs."

"But the police already searched the room. You were here. You saw them," I said.

"It was the end of the tour," he said and smirked, implying that a thorough job may not have been their top priority.

"Ahhh," I said. "Let me help. Where should I start?"

He turned around and pointed to the French doors. "Open them up and go into the parlor. Dig around in the dusty book-cases." He stuck his hand into the opening where the medicine cabinet had been mounted and dug around, coming up empty. "Nothing in there."

I went into the parlor and pulled down the old books that were in the bookcases, looking for secret trapdoors or fake books that might hold more drugs. When I was done with that and had discovered nothing, I sat down on the moldy settee. "Nothing there."

Crawford came into the parlor and got down on his hands and knees, searching under the settee and the one old chair, getting progressively dirtier in the process. "Hit the closet," he commanded, crawling around on the floor, feeling floorboards and pushing on the ends of the tongue-and-groove hardwood floor.

I went into the closet and took out all of my clothes, feeling along the back of it for anything out of place. I stepped into a spiderweb that coated my face with a thick mask of silk. I stumbled back out of the closet, pawing at my face and groaning. I fake-spat a few times to get the taste of it out of my mouth. I took the opportunity to wash my face and engage Crawford in conversation. This type of sleuthing was definitely not high on my list of the things I like to do; it produced more than a little dirt and definitely made us both sweaty.

"What's the word on Fred?" I asked, sitting on the parlor chair, watching Crawford carefully go over floorboards.

"He's as cranky as ever. Apparently, he and Max have been speaking to each other and are trying to figure out what they're going to do with their relationship."

"Very mature. How much of it do you buy?"

"Some of it," he said.

"You know what I think?"

He grunted in response. He knew he was going to find out regardless of whether or not he wanted to hear it.

"I think the fact that they were never really married is going to send Max straight back to him. Because she loves nothing more than a challenge."

"How so?"

"When she had him, she didn't want him. Now that she doesn't have him legally, she'll want him." I wiped my face again, sensing cobweb on the tip of my nose. "You can take that to the bank. Or OTB. Or wherever you take sure bets."

Crawford ignored me and threw back the faded Oriental rug, revealing clean and unblemished floorboards that had been covered for years. He continued his methodical crawling-pushing-prying reconnaissance, finally hitting on something. I watched as a board gave beneath his hand and came up on the other side, like a seesaw on which someone heavy had just sat. "Eureka," he said softly. He continued working on the board until it came out loose from the other boards around it and then took off another, and then another, until he had a square big enough to stick his hand into. He reached in and rooted around, his eyes on me the whole time. I could tell he had hit something when he smiled. "Gotcha."

"Whatcha got, Crawford?" I asked, almost afraid of the answer.

He pulled out a large Ziploc bag, the one

that's advertised on television as big enough to hold soccer equipment, sleeping bags, and the kitchen sink. The mother of all Ziploc bags. And inside of it was a host of smaller Ziploc bags, the ones my mother used to use to bag up a snack of pretzels or carrot sticks for me when I was in school.

But these smaller Ziploc bags didn't hold pretzels or carrot sticks.

What was inside was grainy, green, and mossy looking.

Crawford had unearthed the biggest bag of little pot bags I had ever seen.

He, however, did not look impressed.

THIRTY

Lattanzi and Marcus had already left for the day, so we got Carmen Montoya — an old colleague of Crawford's from Homicide who had recently gotten promoted to sergeant in Bronx Narcotics — and her sidekick, John Gorman. Gorman was a jovial fellow who didn't seem to be the least bit intimidated by Carmen and her gun-moll, rapid-fire speech. He looked at the pot and whistled through his teeth.

"Whaddya think, Carmen? A couple of thou in there?" Gorman opened one of the bags and took a deep sniff. "Smells like primo stuff."

"You think?" Carmen asked, her sizable backside packed into a pair of skinny jeans, the pockets almost on each hip they were spread so far apart. Her leopard-print platform shoes completed the outfit. "Whose stash, handsome?"

Carmen pretends to have a thing for

Crawford, if only to make him uncomfortable. She's got four kids and a deputy inspector husband so I didn't have any misconceptions that she was after my boyfriend.

Crawford, as usual, blushed deep red. "If I had to make a guess, I'd say this was Wayne's." He had already filled them in on the situation, starting with Wayne's disappearance and my move to campus, and ending with the hundred-meter dash alongside the Hutch. "I'm guessing that you didn't find anything else?" Carmen asked. "I'm going to get on Lattanzi and Marcus for letting this one get away the first time." She turned away and coughed the word "morons" into her hand. "You find a big brick of heroin and you don't find the trap with the pot? What a pair of losers."

Crawford shook his head. "Nothing else in here. Took the place apart. There's nothing."

"Wanna work in my squad?" Carmen asked. She was ticked. I felt sorry for Lattanzi and Marcus when she got through with them.

Trixie sat dutifully at my side, knowing something important was taking place. I leaned down and petted her head.

"Nice dog, Alison," Carmen said. "I'm

surprised they let you bring her on campus."

"It wasn't even a discussion," I said.

"What would they say if you took two of my kids? They're not as well behaved as the dog, but I sure could use a break from them," she said.

"That might be a problem," I said, smiling. I had had several encounters with Carmen over the past few months and while I had originally found her intimidating, I had grown to like her. I was still a little scared of her, but not as much as before.

"That's why we go to work. Gotta get away from the kids," Gorman said. He hefted the marijuana bag and started for the door. "Ready, Carm?"

"Whatever you say," she said. She looked at me. "Men. So bossy." She reached up and pinched Crawford's cheek. "I'll see *you* later."

Crawford bid them good-bye and went into the bathroom to put the medicine cabinet back. When he was done, he washed up in the sink. "I think those are Wayne's drugs."

"Me, too." I sat down on the toilet seat. "Who's going to break the news to Mary that her charming nephew was a dealer?"

Crawford blanched at the thought of Mary; she, and every other nun I worked with, really wigged him out. "Not me."

"No, seriously. How's this going to play out?"

He wiped his hands on the towel hanging next to the sink. "First, we find Wayne. Or Gorman does. If anyone can sniff him out, he can. He's relentless like that. Then, we question the heck out of him. Then, we probably arrest him for running a small-time drug ring out of his dorm room."

That didn't sound good. For the first time, instead of being angry at Wayne, I was scared for him. He didn't seem like the kind of kid who could handle hard time, what with his upper-class background and his seeming lack of any kind of street smarts. I then reflected on the fact that he had had more heroin in the toilet than most big-time drug dealers had at their disposal at one time and that he had been keeping most of the campus high, or so it seemed. That was a crapload of pot.

"You'll let Pinto know?" I asked. Crawford nodded, looking more tired than I had ever seen him look. The bags under his eyes seemed to have increased in size since he had picked me up and he looked like he was about to collapse. I wrapped my arms around him. "Go home."

"I wish I could lie down here and go to

sleep for two days."

"If you lie down here, I'd never let you sleep. You know that," I said, gently pushing him toward the door. I looked at the clock next to my bed. "And it's a few minutes until visitation ends. Not even enough time for you to take a catnap."

I walked him down the hall and out through the main entrance so that Spencer Williamson could log him out. I gave him a chaste kiss on the lips before sending him on his way. "Talk to you tomorrow," I said and waved as he walked across the parking lot to his car. I turned and went back to Spencer. "You okay here if I call it a night?"

Spencer looked up from his biology homework and gave me a nod. "What's going on?" he asked, hooking a thumb toward my room.

"Oh, that," I said nonchalantly. Montoya and Gorman had sneaked in through the side entrance and had been very stealthy about leaving, pot in hand, without being seen. But apparently Spencer had seen something. "Just a couple of friends who dropped by." I picked up the logbook and flipped through it casually. "I should really sign them in." I jotted down two names: Giselle St. Louis, my mother's name, and Frank Martin, the name of my first boyfriend. Nobody would be the wiser.

Before I put the logbook down, curiosity got the best of me, and as I flipped through it, I looked at it a little more closely. I saw that Mary Catherine Donnery had logged in at seven and was three minutes away from breaking visitation. I also saw that Amanda had a visitor named Brandon Tsagarakis and he, too, would be in big trouble if he didn't get his butt down the stairs and out the door before eleven. They were the only two visitors left in the building

I had a thought. I wanted to get a good look at Mr. Tsagarakis before he left the building and I wanted to make sure Mary Catherine hightailed it out of there, too. "Hey, Spencer, why don't you go ahead and take off."

He gave me a surprised look. "Really?"

"Really. I'll lock up," I said.

He gathered up his books quickly, as though if I had time to think, I would change my mind. "Good night then," he said.

I watched him go up the stairs and I walked down the hallway to turn off the lights in the TV room and the parlor room across from it. I locked the door to the patio, which Spencer had left open. I put out the overhead lights and read the paper that Spencer had left, the lamp on the desk giving off a soft glow.

Mary Catherine was the first one to descend into the lobby, giving me an overly enthusiastic "Hi!"

"Hi, Mary Catherine," I said, and pointed at my watch. "Just made it."

"Any news on Wayne?" she asked, doing a deliberate subject change.

I shook my head. "I wish I could say there was but there's nothing." I looked at her closely and could tell she knew more than she was telling. "Have you heard anything?"

She pulled a chair up to my desk and leaned across it, whispering conspiratorially. "Well, I heard that he was living in the convent. Can you believe that?"

"Really?" I said. "What else?"

"Just that he's been seen around campus."

"By whom?"

She smirked. "Professor Bergeron, I think it's 'by who.' "

Well, she had me on that one. Or so she thought. I decided not to pursue it. "By who?" I asked, cringing.

"By a lot of people. Spencer Williamson, for one."

"Yes, Spencer told me that he saw Wayne leaving before spring break. In his Prius."

"No, after that."

"Really? When?" I asked.

"He 'saw' him a few times," she said using finger quotes.

What does that even mean? Did he see him or not? "What does that mean, Mary Catherine?"

She squirmed around in her chair. "*Saw* him saw him." When it was clear I didn't understand, she put her index finger and thumb together and brought them to her lips, pretending to inhale. "Got it?"

Oh, Spencer. And I was defending you against the pothead accusations. You let me down, you crazy, anime-drawing stoner. "So Wayne was his dealer?"

"Big-time," she said. She sat back in her chair and crossed her arms, staring at me defiantly. "So what do I get?"

"What do you *get?*" I repeated.

"Yeah, do I get an A the next time I take a class with you or extra visitation?"

She was serious. "Well, I could arrange to get you a merit badge or a special mention at graduation for giving up a campus drug dealer, but that's about it. Or I could tell the cops where I got this information and they could come to your dorm room and question you further." I smiled, folding my hands on the desk. "What will it be?"

She went pale. "Forget it." She jumped up

351

and ran out the front door, adequately spooked.

As the front door slammed, I called out, "Good night!"

Once she was gone, I pulled my cell phone out of my pocket and gave Crawford a quick call, letting him know what Mary Catherine had told me. After I hung up from him, I checked to see if I had any messages, particularly from Max. A face in silhouette greeted me on the screen, the mouth open, telling me that I had three messages. That face always reminded me of Max, screaming at me for one thing or another. I prayed that one of the messages was from Max and my prayer was answered.

"I'm not mad at you, if that's what you're worried about."

I listened, not believing what I was hearing.

"I forgive you," she continued dramatically. "You were very, very mean to me but I have chosen to take the high road and forgive you for everything you said to me the other night."

I felt my face turn bright red, the heat probably visible coming out of the top of my head.

"And being not married is the best thing that ever happened to me! I'm moving back home this weekend."

"I knew it!" I screamed in the empty lobby, my voice reverberating off the tile and marble and probably traveling all the way up to Kevin's sixth-floor lair. I got up and paced around the lobby muttering, "I knew it, I knew it, I knew it . . ." until I realized that I wasn't alone. I turned around and came face-to-face with Amanda and her boyfriend, Brandon, who upon closer inspection was extremely handsome, all dark, wavy hair and brown eyes that were almost black.

"Professor Bergeron, this is my boyfriend, Brandon," Amanda said, pointing at the young man.

"Fiancé," he corrected her. He held his hand out. "Nice to meet you."

"You, too," I said. I didn't want to remind him that we had sort of met once before. The whole "Unhand her!" debacle. He didn't seem to remember so I wasn't going to bring it up. "Hey, you're a little late. Could I get you to sign out?" I asked.

Brandon walked over to the desk and signed his name in the logbook. "Sorry about that. I was worried about Amanda so I drove up here to check on her." He grabbed both of my hands in a really old-school gesture and held them tight. "Take care of her, Professor Bergeron. She means everything to me."

Oh, please, I thought. That was a little dramatic, no? But I played the part of the dutiful resident director and assured him that nothing bad would happen to her on my watch. After I got lost in his dreamy brown eyes for a few seconds. "I promise," I said, and shepherded him to the front door. Amanda followed and the two shared a cautious embrace probably because she was still tender from her beating at the hands of the two thugs. I opened the door and ushered him out. "Nice to meet you," I called after him.

"My pleasure," he said, and walked over to the same black Lincoln Town Car that I had seen him in a few days prior. Interesting car choice for a hip young guy, I thought.

Because you usually only see those kinds of cars in limousine-company fleets.

Limousine companies like the one Wayne Brookwell used to drive for before he went missing.

THIRTY-ONE

The next morning, I got up, walked the dog, got dressed, and was out of the building in record time. I wanted to get to my computer to do a search on Costas and the Tsagarakis family and I wanted to do it before things got hectic in the office area. I entered the office at six-thirty in the morning, way before anyone had any thoughts of getting to work.

I logged on to the computer and waited for it to warm up, spinning around in my chair to catch the view of the sun rising over the cemetery, seen just beyond the back courtyard of the building and across a narrow drive. Maybe most people wouldn't think that the sun coming up over the gravestones of deceased nuns was a sight to behold, and I had probably fallen into that category at one time, but this was my first time seeing it and it was truly a spectacle. It almost made me want to get up at the crack of dawn every day to witness it.

Who was I kidding? I knew that wouldn't happen. In no time, I'd be back to running down to my office five minutes before office hours or seconds before class. But it was nice to dream.

The computer came to life and I put in the name "Costas Grigoriadis." In an instant, a list of sites appeared, the first one being a company Web site for "T&G Limousine." Interesting. I paired "Costas" with "Tsagarakis" knowing that I would get more hits with a broader topic but hoping that my hunch was correct and that T&G would come up again.

Bingo.

I browsed the site and found that Costas was the founding partner of T&G and Nicholas Tsagarakis was the copartner, joining the company in 2002. So, they had been together for several years. Prior to Nicholas's joining the company, the fleet had been eight cars; now they boasted more than fifty cars. Sounded like a very successful business. And it sounded like Nicholas had brought with him an influx of cash when he signed on if the increase in the number of cars was any indication.

They were based in Newark, New Jersey, an interesting coincidence given the events of the last few days.

I didn't know if Nicholas was Brandon's father, uncle, or distant relative, but if I had to guess, I would say that he was his father, judging from the picture on the Web site and the strong family resemblance. Costas was on there, too, looking about as close to a Greek Neil Diamond as one could get, dressed in an extremely ornate smoking jacket with an ascot. Classy.

Great. Now "Cracklin' Rosie" was stuck in my head. I took a little detour to see if I could find out what a "store-bought woman" really was, searching the official Neil Diamond Web site. No dice. This was going to drive me insane.

I thought about the family business and the impending Brandon and Amanda nuptial, jumping to the conclusion that Amanda was now going to do the family proud and marry her stepfather's business partner's son, a man she wasn't sure she wanted to spend the rest of her life with. Because, I deduced, if her family was down with arranging a marriage, divorce was probably out of the question.

I typed Nicholas's name into the search engine, the same article about the joint venture coming up first, followed by a *New York Times* wedding announcement from

2003. I clicked it open, leaning in. There was a picture of Nicholas with a very young, very nubile, and extremely busty lady who was clad in the lowest-cut wedding dress I had ever seen. This was going to be good.

Athena Papadopolous, 27, of Great Neck, Long Island, wed Nicholas Tsagarakis, 48, on Saturday October 10th, at St. Spyridon Greek Orthodox Church in Manhattan. Ms. Papadopolous is in cosmetic sales for Henri Bendel and Mr. Tsagarakis is the owner of T&G Limousine. The bride was attended by sixteen attendants, including maid of honor Tiffany Caswell. Mr. Tsagarakis's best man was his son, Brandon.

That was all I needed to know. Brandon was Nicholas's son. I went back to my search on Nicholas and came up with four additional wedding announcements, the earliest dating back to 1980 and his union to Ms. Papadopolous being the most recent. What a dog. I wondered which union had produced Brandon. A couple of the weddings took place within a year of each other, making it impossible to tell.

I turned back around in my chair and stared out the window, seeing a few students walking along the little path that ran next to the cemetery and that dumped into the parking lot in front of Siena. I had a lot to digest, mentally. It was a gorgeous morning so I decided I had learned all that I needed to for the time being and that it was time to enjoy the weather. I left the computer on, but locked up my office and headed out, thinking that a trip to the river was in order.

I walked down the back staircase and through the student union and toward the exit by the commuter cafeteria, the smell of bacon distracting me and making me lose my train of thought. I veered off and headed into the cafeteria, placing an order with Marcus. I was standing by the coffee machine pouring milk into my coffee when I felt a tap on my shoulder. I turned and found myself face-to-face with Merrimack, his beady little eyes trained on me.

"I heard we've been having some excitement in Siena."

I shrugged, trying to play it off. "Nothing I can't handle."

He crossed his arms. "We're not worried about what *you* can handle, Professor."

I saw Marcus and a few of the cafeteria staff hovering behind the counter trying to eavesdrop but trying desperately not to look like they were. I focused on the spectacular view of the river behind Merrimack's head to distract myself from getting mesmerized by his rat eyes. "And I have done my best to keep the entire situation quiet," I recited dutifully.

He shot a look at the cafeteria staff and they dispersed, leaving only Marcus behind to tell me that my order was ready.

Merrimack wasn't finished. "This wasn't what we were expecting when we set up this living arrangement, Professor."

"Me, either," I agreed.

The look on his face told me that that wasn't what he wanted to hear. He seemed surprised and disappointed by my candor. "It is in the best interest of us all to find a replacement for Wayne." He uncrossed his arms and made a step toward the cafeteria door. "Nothing would please me more than to send you home." The look of disgust on his face stunned me. He exited into the hallway.

I made the rash decision to follow him. "Hey, Merrimack!" I called after him as he scurried down the marble-floored hallway toward his office.

He turned slowly, not believing that I had broken the unwritten code that he had established: he was the alpha male, I was the female who got pissed on, and I had to take it. Not so fast, buddy. I approached him, wishing I were doing anything but what I planned on. And that was setting the record straight. "Let's get one thing straight," I said.

"Please do not point at me," he said.

I dropped my hand. "I am not your problem. If the evidence proves reliable, and I think a giant bag of dime bags of pot may prove irrefutable, Mr. Brookwell was going to turn out to be a giant problem for you."

"Are you insinuating —"

"I'm not insinuating. I'm telling it as it is. Wayne was a dealer. Plain and simple. And you should thank your lucky stars that he got out of Dodge before his dealings hurt someone or he got found out and got dragged out of here in handcuffs." I was on a roll. "Because let me be perfectly clear, Dean Merrimack: if it wasn't for me and my . . ." — and here's where I lost my momentum — "boy . . . man . . . friend . . . Crawford, you were going to be in a world of hurt. It's only because of him that we have been able to keep this as quiet as we have." I stopped, flushed and out of breath from my diatribe.

"Are you finished?" he asked, regarding me with loathing and contempt.

I straightened to my full six feet in my heels. "I am." I turned and started back toward the cafeteria. "And now, I'm going to return to the cafeteria to eat my French toast."

That went well, I thought, as I sat by the window trying to cut my breakfast with shaking hands and an unstable plastic knife. I replayed the conversation in my head and determined that I had handled it precisely the way I wanted. What was Merrimack going to do? Fire me? Good. Maybe then I could go home.

I thought of Dobbs Ferry longingly and then flashed on my red bedroom and the amount of work it was going to take to fix that redecorating debacle. I took a bite of bacon, realized I wasn't hungry anymore, and pushed my plate away.

Marcus wandered over and stood next to my table, wiping his hands on his pristine white apron. Marcus is a middle-aged Jamaican man with close-cropped white hair and an extremely sexy voice and accent. I could always count on him for a smile and a great meal, despite the fact that I was buying it in a college cafeteria.

"How are you, Alison? I heard you're living on campus. Man, that's gotta stink," he said, smiling. He pulled out the chair across from me and sat down, leaning in to talk to me. "So what happened to Wayne?"

I ran my napkin across my maple-syrup-coated lips. "That's a long story."

"He coming back?" he asked, a little too interested.

"I don't know. Right now, he's in a spot of trouble," I said.

Marcus raised an eyebrow. "What kind of trouble?" he asked, looking truly concerned. I wondered if Wayne ate in the cafeteria as much as I did; I didn't recall ever having seen him there.

I put my wrists together to indicate Wayne's legal status.

Marcus whistled through his teeth. "Really?"

"Really." I took a sip of my coffee. "Did you know Wayne well?"

Marcus smiled again, this time a little sheepishly. "Let's just say that we had a business arrangement."

The realization of what he was telling me slowly dawned on me. I slumped in my chair. "You, too?" I asked, incredulous. I thought Wayne's clientele consisted mainly of the kids on campus.

He waved his hands in the air. "No, no! It's not what you think. My sister is going through chemotherapy and someone suggested that she . . ." — he struggled for the right word for the setting as students started to come into the cafeteria — "partake?" He explained to me how the antinausea meds she was supposed to take made her nauseous while the pot settled her stomach and gave her an appetite. "I saw Wayne making a little transaction in the back parking lot one day and got the idea that I could help my sister out by becoming one of his customers."

That was convenient; if Marcus was anything like me, and it seemed he was, he wouldn't have the first idea of where to buy a bag of pot. I don't know why, but I felt a little better knowing that the guy who made many of my breakfasts and more than a few of my lunches wasn't as high as a kite when he was doing so. I told him that I hoped he had a nice stash because Wayne wasn't coming back any time soon.

Marcus gave me a quick hug before he went back to the kitchen, taking my plate of half-eaten food and tossing it in the garbage can. I finished my coffee and headed back to my office. It was only eight o'clock, but I knew Crawford got to work early. I took a chance and called him at the squad.

"Fiftieth Precinct. Homicide. Detective Crawford. How can I help you?"

I stifled a laugh. If you were calling to report a murder, would you sit through that litany of phone etiquette? "Hiya, Crawford."

"Hi," he said, sounding sort of glad that I called. I remembered him muttering that he hated me as we drove off from the encounter with the state trooper the night before and I wondered if there was some lingering anger. "What's up?"

"What's not up?" I said.

He waited a few seconds. "Care to elaborate?"

"Oh, right," I said. "Here's what I found out: Costas is partners with Amanda's fiancé's father — I think — in a limousine business. His name is Nicholas Tsagarakis. If I had to guess, I would say it's the same limo company that Wayne was driving for. So Amanda's engagement seems to me to be some kind of arranged marriage between the children of business partners. Kevin told me that Wayne was moonlighting for them. Extra money, I'm guessing."

"Good work."

"And the pot is definitely Wayne's," I said, saving the best for last.

"How do you know?"

"Besides what we learned from Mary Catherine, which was hearsay at best, let me just say that someone in the building told me that he had bought pot from Wayne for his sister who is undergoing chemo." I pulled my chair up to my desk and pulled out a pad, making notes of what I had just told him. "But you can't tell anyone."

"An anonymous tip from an anonymous source who talked to someone who needs to remain anonymous? That's not going to help me," he said. "I need specifics."

"Can't give you any. It would put my friend in a precarious position."

He let out a deep sigh on the other end. "I'll tell Carmen and Gorman," he said, like it was a threat. Carmen and I were becoming closer with every case (and there had been a couple over the past year), and Gorman? Well, I'd have him eating out of the palm of my hand in no time.

"You do that," I said. "You coming over later?"

"I'll see if I can. What role am I playing tonight?"

"Well, if you get here before eleven we can play firefighter saving damsel in distress."

"Anything but a firefighter."

"Graphic designer going over the design plans with the lead contact on the Anderson account?"

"That's better. I'll call you later," he said.

Before he hung up, I wanted to know one thing. "Hey, Crawford? What's a store-bought woman?"

"What?"

"A store-bought woman. 'Cracklin' Rose, you're a store-bought woman.' What does that mean?"

"I can only guess that's it someone for hire. You know, available for dates?" he said. He let out a deep guffaw. "Where do you get this stuff?"

I didn't go into my whole "Costas looks like Neil Diamond" thing so we just hung up with him grateful that I didn't give him my elaborate explanation of why I needed to know this vital information.

I plugged away at my computer for a while, corrected a couple of papers, and played a couple of hands of solitaire, noting that I still had over an hour until my next class. I would never get up this early ever again. It gave me too much time to get into trouble.

I decided to head back up to the dorm to find Amanda. I passed my car, and checked for boots, tickets, or any other notification that I was a blatant scofflaw but there was nothing. I hoped that was the case when I returned to the dorm at the end of the day because I had big plans and I needed my car.

I found Amanda on the girls' floor; she was coming out of the bathroom, her hair wet, a towel wrapped around her body, her pink flip-flops on her feet.

"Professor Bergeron?" she said, surprised to see me on a residence floor at this hour.

"Is this a bad time?" I asked.

She smiled. "Kind of. Wait here." She went into her room and left me in the hallway to peruse my surroundings. It wasn't exactly a hotbed of activity, with every door closed and only the sound of a few showers running in the communal bathroom. She came out a few minutes later, this time in a St. Thomas sweatshirt, jeans, and the pink flip-flops. She asked me what I was doing on the floor.

When she asked me, it occurred to me I wasn't sure how this was going to play out. I decided to go for it and just tell her my plan.

She was more receptive than I ever would have imagined.

And when I saw that — the excitement on her face mixed with anticipatory glee at maybe seeing Wayne — I had a sinking feeling that perhaps my plan was just a wee bit ill-advised.

THIRTY-TWO

Amanda was as excited as I had been on my first stakeout. I played the Crawford role and told her to take it down a notch.

Amanda looked over at the Brookwells' house. "I'm just excited to see Wayne," she said.

"You may not see Wayne," I said. "I just have a hunch that this is the only place he could have gone."

"What are we going to do?" she asked.

I had to admit that I really didn't know. "I thought we'd just sit here and wait to see if there was any sign of him."

The afternoon sun turned to dusk and then night fell quickly, even though it was spring and we were getting the extra hour of daylight. I handed Amanda a PowerBar and a Gatorade and told her to eat; I knew that we could be sitting in Scarsdale for a long time, so I had packed some refreshments. I can't think if I'm hungry and I wanted to be able to make split-second decisions should the situation call for it.

I had been deliberately vague with Crawford when he had called to say that he could come for dinner, but it would be closer to nine. I let him off the hook by saying that I had a lot of papers to correct and he had a lot of sleep to get. He was just tired enough not to protest and actually sounded relieved. I wasn't happy about that, but I was glad that I wasn't subjected to his usual third degree about where I was going, what I was doing, and why. As far as he was concerned, I was safely ensconced in my room, ratty old St. Thomas sweats on my tired body, eating Trader Joe almonds and correcting bad essays.

I ripped open a PowerBar with my teeth. "How did you meet Brandon?" I asked, taking a quick look over at the Brookwells' house, every window ablaze with interior lights.

Amanda's mouth was full of gooey Power-Bar but that didn't stop her from answering. "My stepdad. He introduced us."

Just like I thought. "And love at first sight?" I asked, taking a swig from my cherry-flavored Gatorade.

"Not really," she admitted. "I thought he was hot but I wasn't sure we would get along at first."

"How come?"

"He's kind of old-fashioned."

Which to me sounded like code for bossy and possessive but I kept that to myself. "But you got beyond that?"

"Sort of. He knows that I want to have a job after I graduate and he's fine with that."

"What are you going to do?"

"I'm a communications major, so what I do is basically up to who hires me," she said ruefully. Having been an English lit major at St. Thomas, I knew what she was talking about. Had I not wanted to teach, I'm not sure what I would be doing right now.

We sat in silence for a few moments.

"Do you love him?" I asked, immediately regretting pushing the conversation when I saw Amanda turn and look out her window. Because I could see in the reflection that I had upset her.

"I guess so."

Not a ringing endorsement for this union. I didn't say anything else because, really, what could I contribute besides "run as fast as you can!"?

"Is Brandon involved in the family business?"

She shook her head. "Yes. He graduated last year and he's doing more there now.

The idea is that he takes over at some point and we'll be set for life."

"So, it's a profitable business."

She spoke softly. "It is now."

"Which means?" I pushed.

She turned toward the window again. "I've said too much."

I wondered what she meant, but I could tell I had gone too far and didn't want to press any further. It seemed like Costas and Nicholas had the whole thing figured out. I chewed on that for a minute while staring at the Brookwells' house.

"What is it that you see in Wayne, Amanda?" I left out the part where I wanted to tell her she deserved much, much better.

"He's gentle. And kind."

Probably because he's stoned all the time. Stoner boyfriends are like that. Always pleasant, but not much in the ambition department. I had made that mistake once.

"He's just a really cool guy. Different from Brandon. Less intense." She smiled. "Sure, he's got to figure a few things out but he's really cool. And he's very good to me."

A really cool guy. Try building a marriage on that character attribute and you were doomed to fail.

"You do know that he's the campus pot supplier?"

She looked at me and I could tell that she was in complete denial about that. "That's not necessarily a fact."

"Amanda, there are many clues that lead me to believe that it is a fact. Wayne may be cool but he's involved in some less than wholesome things." I tried to impress upon her, without saying it outright, that he was not as cool a guy as she thought he was. "You've got a great future ahead of you, Amanda. Sticking with Wayne may not be the best idea."

By the set of her jaw, I could tell that she wasn't on board with the idea of Wayne as the campus weed connection. We stayed silent, me not pushing it, and her considering what we had just talked about, I guessed. After a few minutes, she changed the subject.

"Professor Bergeron?"

I looked over at Amanda.

"Would you come to my wedding?" she asked. "It's in August."

"You're going to get married?" I asked. "What about Wayne?"

"I have to get married. I could never be with Wayne forever. My stepfather made that clear. I have to give up Wayne." Her eyes filled with tears behind her glasses.

I didn't often agree with Costas and his

ham-handed attempts at arranged marriage, but I was almost relieved to hear that the wedding would come off and she wouldn't have to be stuck with slacker Wayne. I prayed that Costas knew something I didn't and that the Amanda/Brandon match would be one eventually made in heaven.

I leaned over and gave her a quick hug even though I wasn't really sure she should go forward with the wedding. "I would love to."

"You can bring a date."

"Wonderful," I said, thinking that the last wedding Crawford and I had attended had been Fred and Max's. And we all know how that turned out. I hoped I wasn't some kind of wedding jinx.

I had one more thing I needed to know. "What's your relationship with Costas like?"

"I adore him," she said quickly and seemingly sincerely.

"Really?"

"Really. He's been very good to me and my mother. My father died when I was seven so he's been in my life a long time. It was his idea that I go to St. Thomas and it was the right thing for me." She sighed. "He's a very good man," she said in a way that made it sound like she had heard that from someone else. Her mother, maybe?

I sank down in my seat and rested my knee against the dashboard. I noticed a car backing down the Brookwells' driveway, its taillights twinkling in the black. It eased out onto the street, and I could see both Eben and Geraldine in the front seats, both staring straight ahead. They missed us entirely, so intent were they on looking out the windshield at the road in front of them.

I looked at Amanda. "Showtime."

"What does that mean?"

"It means that we're going to go over there and see if Wayne is in the house."

"I've already tried his cell phone like a thousand times, Professor Bergeron, and he's not answering. If he was in Scarsdale, he would have let me know."

Like he did before? I thought. And was she really this naïve? I put my hand on her arm. "Amanda, Wayne is on the run from the police department. Everyone in law enforcement in this area is looking for him and he's hiding. I'm guessing that the safest place for him to be right now is his parents' house, even though I'm sure the police went through it from top to bottom." I looked over at the house again. "Where else might he have gone?"

"I don't know," she admitted. "This is as good a start as any."

We waited a few minutes to make sure that the Brookwells had really left the area and then hurried across the street to the house. They had turned off most of the lights in the front of the house with the exception of the outdoor porch light, a light that was fancier and more ornate than the one in my dining room. I tried the front door, but it was locked. We went down the long driveway to the back of the house and saw that it, too, was black. Every light in the house was off. We stood on the patio, staring at the back of the house, me wondering if this was the worst idea I had ever had, and Amanda suddenly sobbing.

"I'll never see him again."

I didn't want to disabuse her of that notion, because that would probably be a lie. She would see Wayne again, but not as a free man. I grabbed her by the shoulders and tried to talk some sense into her.

"Those drugs were Wayne's, Amanda. So because of Wayne, you were beat up and left in my closet. That's not a man that you want to see again," I said, but realizing that I wasn't really getting through to her. She was shaking her head back and forth, not wanting to hear me. I didn't want to raise my voice to make sure she got the point, so I continued whispering. "He's no catch,

Amanda." I wasn't sure she was better off with Brandon, but if the choice was between him and Wayne, I knew where my vote was going to be cast. I took her hand. "Let's get out of here."

We started down the driveway, making it only a few steps when we heard someone whispering Amanda's name behind us. I turned just as she did, and saw the shadow of a tall, thin man standing at the edge of the property by the fence that separated the house from the one behind it. I'd recognize that slack-jawed pot dealer anywhere.

"Amanda!"

She started off down the driveway before I could stop her, throwing herself into Wayne's arms and kissing him. Me, I wasn't so excited to see him.

"Hey, Wayne!" I called. "Every cop in New York State is looking for you. What are you doing? Hiding in plain sight?"

Wayne got closer and I could see the sallow complexion and the bags under his eyes. "Funny," he said. He threw a thumb over his shoulder to a very elaborately decorated shed, one that looked like a miniature house. In fact, it was nicer than my house. "I live there. My parents don't even know that I'm here."

I looked at the barn/shed, suitable for

Snow White and her seven little people and looked at Wayne, six foot three if he was an inch, most of it made up of leg. "You live in there?" I asked incredulously. "What do you do for food? For bathroom needs?" I asked as daintily as possible. I didn't really want to know . . . or yes, maybe I did.

"I wait until my parents leave in the morning and then I use the house. My father still works downtown and my mother substitute-teaches most days. I go in, shower, eat, and get what I need. They have no idea."

I wasn't so sure about that. I bet they did have an idea and they were keeping their mouths shut until they could come up with a better plan. Eben and Geraldine were lovely but they weren't stupid. Anyone with half a brain could tell when someone else was eating their Cheerios.

"Weren't the police swarming this place?" I asked.

"For a few hours," he said, "but I hid."

"You're a regular MacGyver, Wayne," I said, a bit awed.

"A what?"

"Forget it." Just the most famous Canadian action hero this side of Montreal. Kids today. No respect. "You've got to turn yourself in, Wayne."

He shook his head defiantly. "Not going

378

to happen."

I ticked off the details that I had. "First of all, we know about the pot. We found it. The police have it. Add that to the heroin and you're looking at some serious time. Then, you ran away from a police officer and a state trooper, so that's some kind of crime," I said, nonspecifically. I'd fallen behind on my *Law & Order* watching and couldn't remember what violation category that fell under. Resisting arrest, perhaps? "Third, because of your nefarious activities, this girl that you profess to love" — I threw my arm around Amanda protectively — "has been beaten and left stuffed in a closet." I paused. "I don't know what she sees in you, Wayne. You're a real gem."

Wayne stared at the two of us, his mouth agape. I thought that he knew about Amanda's brush with the thugs already, so maybe he was stunned at my recitation of all his crimes and misdemeanors. When he recovered from the shock, he asked softly, "Are you okay?"

Amanda shrugged dismissively. "I'm okay." It seemed like even though I had doled out the information that I had about Wayne in little snippets so as not to overwhelm her, Wayne was obviously losing his romantic luster for her.

"Come with us, Wayne," I said. "Give yourself up. It will be better for you if you do."

He turned and walked back toward the shed. "Not happening."

I went after him and grabbed his arm. "It's happening. You can't hang out here forever." And then I went in for the kill. "And what if these thugs go after your parents? What then, Wayne?"

I felt him go tense. "Don't say that."

"They took your girlfriend, beat her, and stuffed her in my closet, where she could have suffocated. Suffocated, Wayne. As in died." He slumped a bit and I could tell I was getting to him. "Why did they come after her, Wayne? Do you owe them money for the heroin?" That's the part that I couldn't figure out.

"That wasn't my heroin!" he protested again.

I switched tack. "What about your parents? What if they come after them? Do they deserve this?"

"This is not all my fault!" he cried. "That wasn't my heroin. I don't do that stuff. I don't sell it. I'm just trying to make a living and get out of St. Thomas once and for all." He wiped a shaky hand across his face. "How would you feel if you were me and living in a dorm with a bunch of rich kids with nothing better to do than party and get high?"

I didn't want to remind him that I taught those same kids and that not all of them were rich and/or constantly stoned.

"I'm twenty-six. I should have a life by now."

"And why don't you, Wayne? Why are you driving a car leased to your mother and doing a job that your aunt got for you? Why aren't you on your own?" I turned and looked at Amanda, who looked as if she were hearing a lot of this stuff for the first time. She didn't appear happy. What she appeared was disappointed.

He continued walking toward the shed. "Leave me alone."

I let him go, watching him head back to the shed. I sneaked a look at a very depressed-looking Amanda, who was staring up into the black sky, lost in thought. It was very quiet because the thing about rich neighborhoods like this is that they usually are, cars traversing their streets only if necessary. Because of the dead quiet, the sound of the footsteps advancing on me from behind, fast and determined, sounded much louder than they should have.

I turned and came face-to-face with Brandon.

Yes, this plan was definitely ill-advised and about to take a turn for the worse.

Brandon raced past me, nearly knocking me over as he cruised by. He got to Wayne in a split second, or so it seemed, and grabbed the much taller, yet thinner, man by the collar and threw him to the driveway.

Amanda let out a bloodcurdling scream that I was sure alerted every neighbor in a half-mile radius that trouble was afoot. I was pretty sure that nobody ever screams in Scarsdale so I knew the call to the police was being made right now.

"What are you doing here?" I asked, and ran over to try to pry the two of them apart, getting tangled up in arms and legs and ending up on my ass on the driveway. I was shorter than Wayne but his excessive running left him probably only twenty pounds more than me; Brandon was stockier and a little harder to contain. Amanda was no help at all, screaming at the top of her lungs while standing to the side. "Amanda! Enough!" I called. The last thing we needed were the cops showing up and I was sure they were already on the way with the commotion on the driveway.

I don't know how I was able to do it —

maybe the two of them realized it wasn't really all that decorous to wrestle with a middle-aged college professor — but I managed to pull Brandon off Wayne, who jumped up and stood in front of the two of us, Brandon trying desperately to shake me off. He was strong, but I had three inches on him and held on tight, my arms laced through his; he struggled for a few seconds and then relaxed a little. "Calm down," I said. "Now, what are you doing here?"

"I followed the two of you here," he said, panting. He made one more halfhearted lunge toward Wayne, but I held him back.

I looked at Amanda. "And how did he know we were on our way to Scarsdale?" I think I already knew the answer but wanted confirmation.

Even in the dark, I could tell that she had flushed a deep red. "I told him that we were coming here and I was going to break up with Wayne."

Wayne looked like he had been punched in the stomach. He bent over at the waist and tried to regain his composure.

Brandon looked triumphant, and when I felt him relax even more in my arms, I released my grip. "See?" he said to Wayne. "She doesn't want anything to do with you. Leave her alone." He pointed at the middle of Wayne's chest.

Wayne approached Brandon and got in his face again. "I will not leave her alone. She doesn't love you."

She looked at Wayne, her eyes filled with tears, her whole body slumped in sadness. "It's true. I'm marrying Brandon. Just like I said I would."

That was a ringing endorsement for the union. " 'Just like you said you would'?" I asked incredulously. "How about 'because I love him with every fiber of my being?' Or 'because he's the love of my life'?" I asked.

She looked at Brandon. "I'm sorry, Brandon. I never should have cheated on you." She looked at Wayne. "I'm sorry, Wayne. I got confused."

" 'Confused'?" he asked. "Confused by what? Confused by him?" he asked, pointing at Brandon who crossed his arms, a smug look on his face. Clearly, he felt that he had won. "Why don't you ask him about the business?" Wayne said.

I looked over at Brandon, who looked more than a little confused. Whatever the bait was — and if indeed there was any — he didn't take it.

Amanda looked at Brandon. "What's he talking about?"

Brandon shrugged, looking genuinely

puzzled. Either he was an incredibly gifted actor or he didn't know what Wayne was talking about. "No idea." He gave Wayne a confused look. "What are you talking about?"

Wayne didn't have a chance to respond because after hearing the wail of sirens in the distance, it wasn't long before we all caught sight of two police officers, hands on their guns, sauntering down the driveway. I instinctively put my hands up. When I noticed that the trio of love-struck young adults didn't and were looking at me like I had lost my mind, I dropped them slowly. "Good evening, Officers," I said cheerfully. "If I were you, I'd cuff him now," I said, throwing my head in Wayne's direction.

The two cops — both of the handsome, suburban variety — looked at me quizzically. The taller one asked me for more information.

I explained further. "There's a warrant out for his arrest. And he runs like the dickens so don't let him get a head start."

Tall cop cuffed Wayne while the other got on the radio and called back to the station to check on my story. I suggested that he save some time and call Crawford, giving the cop his cell phone number. Wayne was vehemently protesting his innocence.

"Do you want to tell her, or should I?" he said to Brandon.

"I don't know what you're talking about," Brandon said evenly.

The cop talking to Crawford told Wayne to shut up so he could finish his conversation. I looked at Wayne, who had turned into something like a caged animal, one of the officers holding one of his arms.

"I think you do," Wayne said cryptically. The shorter cop, a buff, body-builder type, finished his conversation with Crawford, hung up, and read Wayne his rights. Wayne responded by bursting into tears. "It's a mistake!"

I decided that the best course of action would be to keep my mouth shut. I didn't want to remind Wayne of the giant Ziploc bag of pot we'd found in his room; regardless of whether the heroin was his or not, the pot was enough to lock him up for the time being. That, my dear Wayne, was not a mistake.

The cops dragged him off, assuring him that he would get his one phone call as soon as they got to the station. I hoped his parents hadn't gone too far, because their plans for the evening were going to be cut short by having to bail their youngest out of jail.

Amanda was weeping softly next to me, taking in the whole scene. She looked at Brandon. "You should go home," she said.

I watched as Wayne was put in the back of the police car. He looked at the three of us beseechingly as the car drove away and I had another one of those moments where I felt sorry for him. Why did that keep happening?

Brandon took Amanda in his arms and she started to cry loudly. I moved away from the scene, catching one last glimpse of him holding her at arm's length and pushing her hair away from her face. He pulled a tissue from his pocket and wiped her tears.

I continued down the driveway and crossed the street. Before I got in the car, Amanda called to me that she and Brandon were going somewhere together to talk. That seemed like a very good idea to me.

I drove back to campus wondering why, now that we had found Wayne, I felt worse than I had before.

Thirty-Three

I tossed and turned most of the night, still saddened by the turn of events but relieved that Wayne was now in custody. I thought about him protesting his innocence about the heroin; he never said that the pot wasn't his but he was adamant about the more serious drugs being in his possession. I'd have to ask Crawford about that. Was it normal to lie about something like that or did he think Wayne was telling the truth?

I felt relief that this mess was coming to an end until it dawned on me that Merrimack and the rest of the housing office were going to have to find a brand-new resident director to replace me since Wayne was never returning. And I knew the wheels around here turned very slowly, and right now they had an RD — me — who wasn't getting paid to do the job, something that would appeal to Etheridge and his penny-pinching minions. Surely they weren't going to leave me here? Or were they?

That was a wrinkle I hadn't ironed out.

I finally got up around six, my eyes dry from lack of sleep and from living in a dusty, most likely mold-filled environment. I leaned on the cracked sink in the bathroom and stared at myself in the mirror, wondering how, for the third time, I had come to be involved in such a complicated situation. I decided that that was not somewhere I wanted to go that early in the morning, and without coffee, and that I would table that internal monologue for a time when I was feeling and acting more coherent. I took one last look at myself. "I'm sick of this," I said to my haggard reflection. Trixie padded in, her nails clicking on the old black-and-white tile on the bathroom floor. She jumped up and put her paws on the sink, her eyes imploring me to do something, anything, that would get her outside. I went back into the bedroom and pulled a sweatshirt over my head, slipping my feet into my clogs.

I took Trixie down to the river, a mist rolling off it and soaking the two of us. I took a seat on a flat rock and watched her play in the water, chasing a couple of brave ducks who were waddling along the shoreline. The sun was tucked away behind a few clouds and it was chillier than I thought it would be. I crossed my arms on my chest and put my head to my knees, all the better to consider everything that had happened the night before, not to mention since I had moved onto campus.

I thought of my conversation with Amanda and wondered how I would attend her wedding knowing that she was ambivalent, at best, about Brandon. I also thought of her stepfather, his father, and the business, and her response to my question about whether or not the limo company was profitable. "It is now," she had said. I thought about that and surmised Nicholas's coming to the company and Amanda's marriage were surely related in some way. Now that Wayne was out of the way, I decided that I would turn my attention to the mystery of Amanda's impending loveless nuptial.

And immediately came to the conclusion that a ride to Newark was in order. And that I needed Max and her patented feminine wiles to seal the deal.

I put Trixie back on the leash and ran up the hill to the dorm, breathless when I entered the side door. I went into my room, hastily showered, dressed, and was back out the door and on my way to my office within a half hour.

I immediately turned on my computer,

tapping my foot impatiently while I waited for it to warm up. I decided to put all my feelings about Max, my red bedroom, her self-absorption, and her sham marriage aside, deciding that I needed her help. I e-mailed Max: *"What's your day looking like?"*

Max, the original BlackBerry addict, responded immediately. She was probably still in bed, able to sleep and text at the same time. *"Why?"*

"I need you to come with me to Newark." I was banking on Max's patented approach to life — act now, think later — to get her to commit to coming with me. And I figured that this was as good a way as any to move past the rift between us. Because if there was anything I knew about Max, it was that she would rather pretend things didn't happen than talk about and resolve them in a mature fashion.

She seemed to have to take a minute or two to think about my request because her reply was delayed. *"What's in Newark?"*

I typed quickly, my response cryptic. *"The answer to all my questions. What are you wearing?"*

"I don't do text sex with my friends."

"That's not what I meant. Do you look sexy?"

"I always look sexy. You?"

I ignored that; I've known Max long

391

enough to recognize a one-word dig. *"You in or out?"*

"IN." She put a smiley face next to her response. *"I'll be at STU by 5."*

I clapped my hands together and immediately set about figuring out where T&G Limousine was and how we would get there. I found them again on the Web and jotted down their telephone number. I rehearsed my spiel a few times before picking up the phone, my heart racing as I dialed the number. Someone picked up on the second ring.

"T&G. For all of your car service needs. How can I help you?"

"Oh, hi," I said. "My name is Martha Raymore . . ." — I stuck with something close to Max's name because anything else would confuse her — "and I'm with the law firm of . . ." I forgot what the fake law firm was called, so I scanned my bookshelves for inspiration. "Plath, Dickinson, Shakespeare, and Austen." I smacked my head with the phone. Shakespeare? It didn't seem to register with the person who answered the phone because she asked politely what she could do for me. "Oh, right. Well, I'm the office manager here and I was told by Mr. Plath that I should look for a different limousine company for our attorneys."

"Great. I'll need to put you in touch with one of our partners, Mr. Grigoriadis or Mr. Tsagarakis."

"It would be great if I could meet with both. Tonight? Say seven-thirty?" Newark was farther away than I had anticipated.

The operator hesitated. "I don't know if I can arrange that but I'll ask them when they come in."

Right. It was barely after seven in the morning. I let my excitement get the better of me. "Thank you."

"Can I call you back?" she asked.

Absolutely not, I thought. I didn't want to leave any kind of trail regarding who was making the call. "I'm going to have a very busy day. Can I call you back?"

"Of course. How about some time between eleven and noon? My name is Adriana. Just ask for me."

"Thank you, Adriana. I'll call you later." I hung up and wiped my palms on my skirt. I was definitely going to hell, and there, I would most definitely have sweaty palms for all eternity. Before I forgot, I jotted the name of the fake law firm and the name "Martha Rayburn" onto a sheet of paper, not realizing that it wasn't the name I had given the lovely Adriana until I called her back, from my cell, between classes, at eleven-twenty. I stood in an alcove on the fourth floor, having just come out of my ten-thirty class.

"T&G Limousine. For all of your car service needs. How can I help you?"

"Can I speak with Adriana, please?"

"Speaking. Who's calling?"

"Hi, this is Martha Rayburn."

"How can I help you?"

I got a little impatient. "You said to call you back between eleven and twelve? To see if I could get an appointment with Mr. Grigoriadis and Mr. Tsagarakis?" I smiled as one of my students walked by and waved in my direction.

She hesitated. "Oh, yes. Ms. Rayburn. I had written 'Martha Raymore' on my pad. My apologies."

Stupid, stupid, stupid. "That's an easy mistake to make!" I said gaily. "Everyone does it!" Even me! I neglected to add.

"I have an appointment set up for seven-thirty. Does that work for you?"

"That's perfect!" I said, whoever I was. "I'll see you at seven-thirty." I hung up and crept out of the alcove, attempting to blend into the flow of students changing classes. I don't know why I felt compelled to act as if I weren't doing anything wrong — I wasn't — but I have the most finely honed sense of guilt ever. I made my way to my next class, repeating the name "Rayburn" over and over until I had it right.

I called Crawford at the precinct, but he was out. I left a message with one of the cops to tell him I had called, knowing that if he had a busy day in front of him, I was unlikely to hear from him for a long time, if even today. This made me happy; I hated talking to Crawford after I've lied excessively. I feel like he can read my mind, and even if that's not the case, I feel like he could get the truth out of me very easily.

The day seemed endless. I finally got back to my room at four-thirty, washed up, and changed into jeans and a T-shirt. I walked Trixie, seeing Max's cab in the parking lot on my way back from the cemetery, which had become Trixie's official spot for her evening walk.

Max got out of the cab, looking extremely vixenlike in a black cashmere sweater that accentuated her stupendous rack, and tight black pants. She had a red pashmina shawl thrown over her shoulders, which matched the red of the soles of her thousand-dollar boots. She threw her arms out. "Good enough?"

"Good enough," I said. I resisted going over and giving her a hug because just the sight of her reignited my feelings over the guerrilla redecorating.

"What? No hug?" she asked.

I gave her a loose, quick hug. "Let me get my car keys," I said, breaking away from her and the cloud of Opium that enveloped me when I got close to her. "Go wait by the car."

Once we were in the car, I outlined my plan. I also filled her in on the latest goings-on with Amanda, Wayne, and Brandon. "Nicholas is a hound dog and likes the ladies. At least that's what I'm guessing by the five marriages."

"So, I'm supposed to charm the pants off of him?" she asked, pulling down the visor to check her makeup.

"Not literally."

"Duh. I'm a married woman," she said.

No you're not, I thought. I let it go. "Your name is Margaret Raymore." At least I hoped that was the name; I couldn't remember what name I had given Adriana and I couldn't find the piece of paper I had written the original name down on. All I knew was that it was close to Max's name and that was it.

"Why?" she asked. "That's a sucky name."

"But you can't use your name or my name," I said. "You're an office manager at

Plath, Dickinson, Shakespeare, and Austen."

She turned. "How the hell am I supposed to remember that?"

I looked into the sideview mirror and attempted to merge into the rush-hour traffic on the George Washington Bridge. "Sylvia Plath, Emily Dickinson, William Shakespeare, Jane Austen." I thought that would help.

She rooted through her giant purse. "Wait. I need to write that down." She found a pen and a piece of paper. "Say it again."

I repeated the name of the fake law firm. "So I want you to meet Nicholas, look around the office, and tell me if anything looks hinky."

" 'Hinky'?"

"Yeah. Hinky. Out of the ordinary. See if he hits on you. See if he's weird in any way."

"What's that going to tell us?"

I swerved to avoid being hit by a Pepperidge Farm truck. "I don't know. But those thugs who beat up Amanda are from Newark. This company's in Newark. She's marrying the son of her father's business partner. I think he put a lot of money into the company. I have all of the puzzle pieces but I just don't know how to put them together."

"Well, when you put it that way," she said, pausing, "that tells me nothing."

"Can you just play along, Max?" I pleaded, hitting the Jersey Turnpike and feeling better about being off the bridge even if the view was far less scenic.

"I'll play along," she said, exasperated. "This is quite a caper."

We drove to Newark in near silence, avoiding the conversational elephants in the room. Ah, Jersey. Bergen County was lovely, as was the shore. I love the shore. But this stretch of turnpike was dreary, dotted with factories and the occasional strip mall. It was pretty depressing.

Max finally broke the silence. "So, this Margaret Raymore."

"Right," I said, my voice wavering a bit. I tried to think back to my original conversation with Adriana or imagine in my mind's eye what I had written on the piece of paper after I had spoken to her but I couldn't remember either. I hoped "Raymore" was right.

"That's it, right?" Max said. I could tell by her tone that she knew I was unsure.

"Margaret Raymore," I said, trying to sound as definitive as I could. I still wasn't sure, though.

"We know she's hot. But does she have a

boyfriend?"

"I don't know. Does it matter?"

"I just want her to have some game. Does she have game?"

"She has loads of game. She runs one of the biggest law firms in Jersey. She's an excellent office manager."

The GPS, my dear friend Lola, told me to exit and I obeyed her command, getting into the right lane and making my way to the exit. I followed her directions through Newark — again, not the most scenic vista I've ever seen — and found T&G. I parked across the street in a strip mall and pointed to a one-story building with a fleet of Town Cars, stretch limousines, Suburbans, and a host of other vehicles parked on either side and, presumably, behind the building. The building was nondescript with a small sign indicating that we were at the right place. I guess you didn't need a flashy setup to operate a limousine company; as long as the cars were new and clean and worked, nobody cared where they came from.

"So what am I supposed to do again?" Max said, looking a little nervous, and obsessively running her hands through her cropped hair. She's usually a gamer; I wondered what was making her so tense.

"Just tell them that you're thinking about

changing limo companies and that you heard that T&G was the best."

"And why can't you do it?"

I sighed. We had been over this. "Because Costas knows me."

She nodded. "Right."

"Just get a sense of things. Does Nicholas act weird? Is there anybody else around? Is there anything to indicate that things may not be on the up-and-up?"

She looked at me, panic in her eyes.

"I know it's a long shot, Max, and believe me, I wouldn't ask you if I didn't have to, but I need to find out what's going on for Amanda's sake."

She took a few deep breaths and finally put her hand on the door handle. "Wish me luck."

"Godspeed."

"What? Godspell? What does that have to do with this?" she asked.

"Good luck, Max."

"Thanks. I'm gonna need it." She opened the car door. "Does Margaret Raymore flirt?"

"If she has to," I said.

Max got out of the car and, after looking both ways, crossed the busy street that separated the strip mall from the T&G building. I dug into my pocketbook for my cell phone, which had begun to chirp half-way to Newark, indicating that I had a voice mail message. I had turned the phone to vibrate so that I wouldn't have to be disturbed while driving.

I pulled out the directions that I had downloaded from the Internet that morning — although I had Lola I still liked to have something printed — and looked at what I had written across the top: Martha Raymore. Then I remembered my conversation with Adriana and our discussion about my fake name. The second time Adriana and I had spoken. I had played along and gone with Martha Rayburn. Max was supposed to be Martha Rayburn not Margaret Raymore. My stomach did a little flip when I realized I had given Max the wrong name.

I leaned down and looked out the passenger side window of the car, watching as Martha/Margaret made her way to the front door of T&G.

I said a silent prayer that Max was still able to think on her feet. Obviously, thinking on my feet wasn't my strong suit, nor was memorizing an alias that I myself had created.

Max was gone for far longer than I ever would have imagined, and when we hit the one-hour mark, I nearly lost consciousness from the stress. My thumbnails were bitten down to the quick, and in an amazing display of hindsight being twenty-twenty, I came to the realization that this was a very bad idea. What did I hope to find out? That yes, Nicholas Tsagarakis was a ladies' man? Who cares? That he had flooded the company in cash and, as a reward, wanted his son to marry Costas's daughter? That maybe — and this was clearly a long shot — one of the guys who attacked Amanda was associated with the company? I didn't know what I was hoping to find out and wasn't sure why I even cared. If Amanda didn't have the guts to tell her stepfather that she didn't love Brandon, that was none of my business. She was a big girl and I had known her a week. Didn't concern me.

But it did, in a way. I had married a guy once who didn't love me and things had turned out very badly. I didn't want to see anyone go down that road, and if I could stop Amanda, I guess I could move beyond my failed marriage and realize none of it had been my fault. Or could I?

This had started as a way for me to find Wayne and get my life back. Well, we had found Wayne, he was behind bars, and hopefully, at some point, I would be free of the Siena dorm.

I looked in the rearview mirror and spoke to myself. "Time to move on, Alison."

About five minutes later, I finally saw Max exit the building and run across the street, this time barely looking to see if a car was coming down either side of the boulevard. As she approached the car, I could see the flush in her cheeks.

She got in and immediately starting beating me with her purse. "My name was *Martha Rayburn* not *Margaret Raymore!*" she yelled, the blows to my head coming fast and furious. "What the hell is wrong with you?"

I covered my head with my hands. "I know! I know! I remembered after you got out of the car."

She eased up with the beating after a few more blows to my midsection. "I had to blame it on some girl named Adriana who I don't even know!"

I rubbed my head. "Wait. Who blamed it on Adriana?"

"They figured out that she had written the wrong name down . . . or the right name," she said, giving me a dark look, "and said that she's pretty scatterbrained so I had to agree with them."

Poor Adriana. So now my lying was going to involve getting an innocent receptionist

403

in trouble. Great. I took a deep breath. "Did you get anything? Did you learn anything new?" I looked over at T&G. "Why were you in there so long?"

"They've got a whole marketing spiel that I had to sit through." She dropped the timbre of her voice and intoned, "Welcome to T&G. The best in limousine service and more." She closed her eyes as if wanting to forget the whole thing. "There's PowerPoint slides, a slide show, music, Nicholas and Costas, the kid . . ."

"Wait. Which kid?"

"Nicholas's son. The hot one. Brian or Bryce or . . ."

"Brandon."

"That's it."

"Really? He's part of the presentation?"

"He *was* the presentation," Max said. "He did the whole thing while Daddy sat at the conference table across from me, making bedroom eyes at me the whole time." She grimaced. "Then Daddy gave me the double-handed handshake at the end. I swear if I had given him an inch, he would have given me a hug with the ass grab."

I put my hands on the steering wheel, lost in thought. "Anything else?"

"That's it." She dug into her purse and pulled out a lipstick, which she reapplied perfectly without looking in the mirror. "Oh, there was one more thing."

I waited but she seemed to have lost her train of thought. "Yes?"

"The kid had a cut on his head. He had those Band-Aids that you put over stitches. I don't know what they're called."

"Steri-strips?" Teaching in a college with a large nursing program had its advantages. One of them was being able to name every Band-Aid appropriately.

"I guess. He said he was in a minor fender bender."

"Did you believe him?"

She shrugged. "Do I care? No," she said emphatically. "Can we get the hell out of here before I get diarrhea from the stress? I'm getting too old for this."

I started the car and began to pull out of the parking lot. I stopped at the exit, looking for an opportunity to merge into the flow of traffic, but since we had arrived, the number of cars had picked up and I didn't see a safe way to get in. I sat and stared at T&G. "Is Nicholas handsome?" I asked, more out of curiosity than anything else. I was fascinated by serial wedders and anyone who had more than three marriages certainly fit the bill.

"Sure, if you like muscley, swarthy, Don

Juan types with a roving eye."

That didn't tell me anything but I didn't push it because my attention was diverted by the front door of the limo company opening and Brandon exiting with his father. "That him?" I asked. Brandon was chatting amiably with his father, whom Max had described to a T. She had left out the best part of the description, though, and that was what appeared to be the extremely dapper pin-striped suit he was wearing. I could see the high gloss of his Italian leather shoes from where I sat, too. "You didn't mention the metrosexual quality," I said, pointing across the street. I drove into the intersection and managed to find an opening in which to insert the car. I took one last glance across the street, and found myself staring back at Brandon, who did a quick double take as I drove by.

"Shit," I muttered.

"What?"

"I think we were made," I said, looking in the rearview mirror.

"Made what?"

Brandon was staring after the car as I inched forward toward a light that seemed to change from red to green and back again in the space of ten seconds. After about a minute, plenty of time for him to memorize my plate number, I drove through the intersection and into the night, hoping that the sight of my car — with its New York license plate — didn't arouse his suspicion and that in the dark, he couldn't tell that it was me driving the car.

These sorts of capers always left me extremely paranoid.

Max snorted, knowing exactly what I was thinking. "There is no way he could tell that that was you."

"A narrow, two-lane road separated us from the building. There is definitely a way he could see us."

Max considered this but changed the subject, as she is wont to do when she doesn't want to deal with reality. "We should eat," she said. "I'm starving." She looked out the window. "There! There's a diner."

I made a quick right turn into a diner not a mile from T&G. It occurred to me that we should go farther out of town if we were going to eat, but my growling stomach said otherwise. Hunger always trumped caution in situations like this. I unfortunately had to park right in front as all of the other spots were taken; I had wanted to put the car in the back so that it wouldn't be visible from the street.

We entered the diner and got a booth in the back. Max opened the menu even though she probably could have recited the entire culinary repertoire to me by heart; Max is a diner aficionado, having eaten at the one by school every Friday (fish night in the dining hall) and Sunday morning (they didn't serve her favorite breakfast food — hamburgers) the entire time we were at St. Thomas.

"Why do you even have to look at the menu?" I asked, taking a sip of warm water from the short glass in front of me, still hot from the dishwasher.

"I have to see if something speaks to me," she said dramatically. "And right now, the meat-loaf dinner is telling me that I need to eat it right now."

Our waitress approached the table and asked for our order. Max did order the meat loaf and a glass of cabernet; I was interested to hear her reaction to the diner's house wine. I ordered a cheeseburger and a chocolate shake. Max gave me a look after the waitress walked away.

"A chocolate shake?"

"Yes," I said. "And your point is?"

She looked away. "Nothing. No point."

This wasn't about a cheeseburger and the tension between us had ratcheted up a notch now that we weren't trying to convince ourselves that our sleuthing was a great idea and would yield crystal clear results. Or a rapprochement. I leaned across the table. "Listen. I eat every meal in the commuter cafeteria. I've eaten more salads and Salisbury steak dinners than I care to count in the past week and a half. If I want to have a friggin' chocolate shake and a cheeseburger, that is my right." I pulled a napkin out of the holder on the table and wiped my brow, which had become quite sweaty during our drive. "So where are you living right now?" I asked, my tone still testy. I wasn't going to bring up the red bedroom but I wanted to find out if she had permanently vacated my home.

"I told you already. I'm back home."

"What are you going to do? Are you going to get married for real or just live together?"

"We are married," she said in the same voice she would use to speak to a kindergarten student.

"No you're not."

"We're just not married in the church," she said. "But we're married."

I didn't know how a woman so smart — she runs a cable television station, for criminy's sake — could be so stupid. "Did Fred tell you that?" It sounded like something he would say just to appease her.

She put her hand over her heart. "We're married here, in our hearts, and that's all that matters."

"No it doesn't. You can't be married in your hearts. There's no such thing as being married in your hearts. You have to be married by the state of New York or by the Catholic Church. Or wherever else you worship. You need to be married by someone who can actually marry you," I explained. I must have raised my voice, because the elderly couple at the next table shot daggers my way. "Sorry," I said to them, baring my teeth in an unsuccessful attempt at a smile. "You haven't even been together long enough to have a common-law marriage," I added dismissively. And that's when I knew I had gone too far. Her face became a mask of hurt and betrayal.

"Why can't you just be happy for us?" she asked, welling up. "Why can't you be happy that I'm happy?"

I was saved from having to come up with an immediate response by the delivery of my shake and Max's cabernet. I took a big draw from the straw in my shake, the cold seeping up my nasal passages and giving me a tremendous pain between my eyes. Serves you right, I thought. First, I had made a nun cry and now I had made my best friend cry. It had been a wonderful week. "I am happy for you, Max. I couldn't be happier," I said, which was the truth even if my tone or my body language didn't convey it properly. I was exhausted, and hungry, tired of living on campus, and afraid to go home to a red bedroom. But really and truly, I was happy if Max and Fred had decided to put their relationship back together. If it made them happy, it made me happy.

Right?

We ate our dinners in silence, her not responding when I asked if the house cabernet tasted like old shoe or was actually palatable. I was too hungry to lose my appetite for what turned out to be a giant, juicy, and extremely greasy burger, and I inhaled the whole thing in record time.

My back was to the door and the height of the booth obscured Max's line of sight. So, when Brandon slid onto the Naugahyde bench next to me, the two of us were caught completely by surprise.

I tried to pretend that running into one of my students' boyfriends in a town far, far away from where I taught and lived was the most natural thing in the world. I swallowed the hunk of greasy burger that got stuck in my throat and greeted him warmly.

"Hi, Brandon!" I said, with way too much cheer.

He kept his eyes on Max. "Good to see you again, Ms. Rayburn? Or is it Ms. Raymore?"

Max studied her meat loaf for a few seconds, shoving a huge piece into her mouth and pointing at her bulging cheeks with her fork.

"She doesn't want to talk with her mouth full," I explained.

Brandon folded his hands on the table. In profile, I could see the strong resemblance between him and his father. "Shall we cut the crap, ladies?"

I pushed my plate to the side and turned to face him. "Fine. Her name is Max Rayfield, she's my best friend, and I just want to know what's going on at your company, why two thugs beat up Amanda, and what, if anything, anyone there has to do with that. Especially you." I took in his shocked expression. "Your turn. Go."

Brandon blanched a bit at the mention of the beating that Amanda had withstood.

"Oh, and why you have those stitches," Max chimed in.

I looked over at her. "Thanks, Max. I forgot about that."

Brandon looked down at his hands. "For

starters, there is nothing going on at T&G besides car service, nobody at our company had anything to do with what happened to Amanda, and I don't know who those guys were. I'm offended that you would even suggest that I knew something about that," he said evenly, but I could hear the anger simmering beneath the surface of his tone. And I hadn't suggested that he himself had anything to do with it — at least not outright. I took note of the fact that he had taken my suggestion so personally. "Secondly, I hit my head on a doorjamb at the office. Seven stitches. Nothing to write home about. You can ask my father, the doctor at Newark General who stitched me up, or look at the door, which still has blood on it." He paused. "Or you can ask my sister, Adriana, who was there when it happened."

None of that would be necessary. Just the thought of opening your head on a doorjamb made me weak in the knees. I was happy, though, that Adriana would still have a job the next day, despite the tough time she'd had coming up with Max's proper alias. It was a family business, and she was in the family.

"I don't think I need to follow up on that," I said, pointing at his head.

"Fine. We run a very successful, financially

viable business, Professor. We pay our taxes, pay our staff well, and keep things on the up-and-up. There is nothing going on at T&G that would concern you or that has anything to do with what happened to my fiancée." He put his head in his hands. "If you think I had anything to do with what happened to Amanda, you're crazy. I would never hurt her," he said, his words muffled because his hands were over his face. "Ever."

He was pretty forceful about his declaration of honesty when it came to his company and apparent love for his fiancée. I responded with a weak, "Okay."

He picked his head back up and looked at me. The anguish on his face convinced me that he had nothing to do with what happened to Amanda. "Go back to the Bronx, Professor Bergeron. And if you have any questions in the future," he said, reaching into his back pocket and pulling out two twenties, throwing them on the table, "please feel free to call me directly. I don't enjoy being lied to." He got up. "I hope you enjoy your dinner. My uncle Christos owns this place."

I had one more thing I wanted to ask him and it didn't concern nefarious activity at T&G or anywhere else. "Are you and Amanda going to get married?" I asked.

He smiled sadly. "I hope so." He put his hands in his pockets, and all of a sudden, he looked more like a lovelorn kid than the slick criminal for which I had had him pegged. "Do *you* think we're going to get married? Amanda said she talked to you about this . . ." He didn't seem to know what to call the situation.

"Love triangle?" Max offered helpfully.

Again, the sad smile. "I guess. I'm hoping —"

Max interrupted him. "Fight for her. If you love her, fight for her." I kept quiet and wondered if I should let her advise him. Having left her husband for the flimsiest of reasons, I wasn't sure if she was the right person to offer her uninformed opinions on relationships. "You seem like a nice kid. You've got a good job. And you're easy on the eyes. You can win her back."

Brandon was staring at Max, a little glassy-eyed, apparently not knowing whether he should take her counsel to heart. In the space of a half hour, she had gone from being a lying accomplice in my wacky caper to Dear Abby. "Well, thanks," he said. "Maybe I'll do that."

"Do it!" she said. "I'm telling you, you're meant to be with that girl." She had no way of knowing that but she was on a roll and there was no stopping her. "Finding true love these days isn't easy so you need to be sure you make it work." She returned to eating her meat loaf and it was clear that this portion of the night's festivities were over.

Brandon beat a hasty exit. I leaned around the booth and watched him leave. When I was sure he was gone, I leaned back in and watched Max continue to fill her face with meat loaf and mashed potatoes.

"Those stitches almost made me lose my appetite," she said, downing her half glass of house cabernet in one swig. "Wanna go?"

I looked at the two twenties on the table and decided that we would allow Brandon to pick up our dinners. Because if T&G was doing as well as Brandon claimed it was, he was in a better position to pay for dinner than I was. I got up. This night had been weirder than any I had ever experienced and I had a lot of crazy experiences on which to draw. "I'll feel better once I'm back in my dorm room," I said. "And I'm loath to admit that."

THIRTY-FOUR

We weren't going right past her house but it was close enough so I dropped Max off in Tribeca. I pulled up in front of her luxury condominium and turned the car off.

"I'd love to say that I had a great time, but I didn't," she said, putting her hand on the door handle.

"Sorry."

"That was a really stupid idea."

"I know."

"And we accomplished nothing."

"Okay," I protested. "I get it. Bad idea. Goals not accomplished."

She got out of the car and was ready to end our adventure when she changed her mind. She leaned back in. "Something's off between us."

I feigned ignorance, not wanting to get into a whole thing right before leaving her. "What do you mean?"

"You were kind of mean to me the last

time I saw you." She pouted. "The only reason I came with you today was to try and fix things. Between us," she added, in case I didn't know what she was talking about.

We had journeyed back to the alternate universe that Max seemed to be inhabiting lately. My hands tightened around the steering wheel and I rested my head between them. "I don't think we should do this right now," I muttered to the dashboard.

She sighed. "We should do it soon."

I nodded. "Okay. Just not right now. Not in my car while I'm parked in front of a fire hydrant." We had a lot to talk about but my energy was flagging, and if history was any indication, that meant that I would end up crying uncontrollably, agreeing that I had been "kind of mean" to her, and asking for forgiveness. And I wasn't going to let that happen. "Thanks for your help. Say hi to Fred."

She made a sad face. "He's kind of mad at you, too," she said, putting her hand on her hip. She made a face to convey her approval at his anger. A few seconds later her expression changed and she was smiling. "Oh, by the way, how did you like your bedroom?"

"That's another thing I really don't want

to talk about."

"You didn't like it?" she asked, genuinely surprised.

I looked out my window for a second, trying to figure out how to break it to her that I liked my bedroom the way it was before: dull, boring, bland, and beige. "Remember when I told you that you should do the opposite of whatever it is that you're thinking?"

She let out a huge sigh. "Of course."

"You should have done that before you had my bedroom painted."

"Your room was dull. Boring. Bland." She let out another sigh. "And beige. You've got to spice things up a bit."

I banged my hands on the steering wheel. "No I don't. I like things the way they are. I'm dull. I'm boring. I'm kind of beige. Why are you always trying to change me and everything about me? You've been doing that since we first became friends and I've put up with it."

"You don't have to be dull and boring, you know," she said. "And you don't give yourself enough credit."

"You think that if people aren't exactly like you and living life on the edge every single minute, their lives aren't worth anything." This was exactly why I didn't

419

want to have this conversation; the minute the words were out of my mouth, I could see her face crumble. Obviously I had gone too far. "I don't want to live like that, Max. I don't want a red bedroom. I just want to live my boring life."

She was silent for a few minutes and I thought the conversation was over. Apparently, it wasn't. "Well, if you want to live like that, then I guess I have to let you."

I could feel my temperature rising. Her own life had been a mess and she had turned to me, Miss Bland and Boring. Now she wanted to spice things up for me. It wasn't her place to do that and I told her so. "Close the door, Max." She started talking again and I held my hand up. "Close. The. Door." I repeated this slowly so that there wouldn't be any doubt as to what I wanted to do or what my mood was.

She gave me one last sad look before slamming the door and hurrying across the street to her building. A uniformed doorman came out and held the door for her. Just like St. Thomas, I thought. Except that the only people who wore uniforms were . . .

. . . students who drove limousines.

It hit me like a ton of bricks. I hadn't needed to go to Newark. All I'd had to do was grab that slacker Michael Columbo and ask him what was going on at T&G. I remember having seen him in a uniform and knew that he was working to make extra money. I also remembered the little T&G embroidered on his shirt pocket. Why hadn't it occurred to me earlier? Oh, right. The black mold in my bathroom in the dorm was eating away at my brain cells. And I hardly ever slept because of the lumpy mattress on the twin bed. As a result of the mold and the exhaustion, I could barely remember my own name.

When I saw that Max was safely inside the building, I maneuvered my way through the downtown traffic, light at this hour, and headed back toward St. Thomas, a ride that would take about twenty minutes if the West Side Highway wasn't too backed up.

Fortunately, the traffic gods were on my side and I sailed up the highway, getting back to school in record time. I attempted to angle into my usual parking spot, noticing too late that an orange cone had been placed where my car would normally go, obviously the work of the security department. I ran over the cone, dragging it underneath the car and wedging it between the undercarriage and the blacktop. Hearing the cone drag along the ground, and smelling the burned rubber when I got out of the car only increased my agitation. I got into a crouch and assessed the damage. There wasn't any smoke, and nothing seemed to be smoldering, so I made the executive decision to leave the cone there until the morning when I could properly deal with the situation. It was dark, cold, and starting to drizzle. My best friend had seriously offended my sensibilities, yet had turned the situation around to make it seem like it was my fault. My other best friend, a man of the cloth, was a stupid, lying, Roman-collar-wearing dumbbell. I had many problems. The orange cone would have to wait.

I stood up, Michael Columbo's handsome face at eye level when I straightened out, scaring the dickens out of me. I grabbed my chest. "Oh, God!"

He looked as startled as I did and he was the one who approached me. I could see where he was headed: the black Lincoln Town Car that I had pulled in beside and hadn't noticed. "Sorry." He was in a T&G uniform: black jacket, black pants, a uniform hat in his hands.

I grabbed his arm. "C'mere. I want to talk to you." I frog-marched him in through the side door of the dorm, him protesting the entire time that he had to go to work. I checked my watch; it was eleven o'clock. "Why are you going to work so late?" I asked.

"I have an airport run." He shifted from one foot to the other. "They're late."

"Kinda late to be going out, don't you think?" I didn't mean to sound judgmental but seeing the look on his face, obviously that's the way it came out.

He looked at me, his baby face out of sync with his muscular man body. "It's my job," he said. "I have to work. Otherwise, I can't go here."

I put my hand on his arm. "I didn't mean —"

He looked down at his feet. "I know. I would rather be in bed right now but this job pays well."

"Did you get the job through Wayne?" I asked.

He nodded.

"When did you start?"

"Right before spring break." He twisted his hat between his hands. "I drive businessmen to the airport and they tip big." His eyes got wide. "Really big. If I didn't have this job, I wouldn't be able to stay in school," he reiterated. "My parents lost most of my college fund when the market tanked. I had to get a job."

"Where do you drive them? Kennedy? La-Guardia?"

"Kennedy or Newark. Most of the people I drive are flying internationally. Mostly Mexico and Latin America."

"Do you only do runs for Mexican and Latin American trips?"

He shrugged. "Mostly. Sometimes my fares go to Europe. But those guys going south of the border make up most of their clientele."

"Those guys?"

"Yeah, the businessmen that I drive. That's most of the business. At least that's what Wayne told me."

That was odd. Why did the business cater to men going back and forth to Mexico and Latin America? I wished I had had this information before I had sent Max/Martha/Margaret on a wild-goose chase to find out information in Newark.

"Do you do anything else?"

"Sometimes I drop packages off at T&G."

"Packages?"

"Yeah. I'll meet someone at the airport, they'll give me a package, and I'll drop it off at T&G."

I looked at him, the whole thing sounding kind of fishy. "Package? What kind of pack-ages?"

He shrugged. "I don't know," he said, getting indignant. "I just go where I'm told."

"And where is it that you're told to go?" I asked, getting equally indignant.

"I usually meet someone somewhere, give them the package, and drive off. It takes about ten seconds and I get fifty bucks."

I stared at him intently, trying to discern whether he was as dumb as he sounded, completely naïve, or a slick operator. When he looked at me, his eyes suddenly wide, I had my answer. He was a little dumb, a lot naïve, and had been used by someone at T&G.

His shaking voice conveyed his panic. "Oh, wait . . . ," he said, grabbing his head. He crouched down, putting everything together and not liking the way the puzzle was beginning to look. "Oh, no . . . I didn't think . . . you don't think . . ."

I knelt next to him and put my arms around his shoulders.

"I needed the money," he said again, his voice sounding small and like a boy's rather than a man's. I heard a hitch in his throat as he stifled a sob. "I really needed the money. I didn't think."

There was nothing for me to say as he worked the whole thing out in his mind. He dropped his hat on the floor. "Should I go to work?" he asked.

I thought for a moment. "Call in sick," I recommended. "I'll call the detectives working the case. They'll want to talk to you."

His face went white. "I can't talk to them. They'll arrest me."

"No they won't," I assured him, helping him stand up. "I'll tell them what we talked about and that you didn't know what was going on." I gave him a quick hug. "Don't worry." Something occurred to me while I was looking at him. "You didn't put one of those packages in Wayne's room right before spring break, did you?"

I thought I was going to have to revive him when the reality of what he had done hit him. "Yes," he croaked.

"Who gave you the package and told you to put it in Wayne's room?"

"Mr. Grigoriadis. He said I would be doing him a big favor." He grabbed his head again. "I used my master key because I thought I was doing the right thing. Mr. G. told me that Wayne needed what was in the package." He closed his eyes. "I think I'm going to be sick."

"It'll be okay," I reassured him. "Did Mr. Grigoriadis give you all of your jobs?"

He nodded.

"Did you talk to anyone else at T&G

about your schedule?"

"No." He shook his head. "Oh, God, I am in such big trouble. How could I be so stupid?" He started talking to himself, as if I weren't there. "I wondered why the money was good but I didn't think about it. I should have known better."

I gave him another hug but could tell that he was in for a sleepless night, particularly if the cops decided to question him tonight rather than in the morning. I watched him walk down the hall toward the stairs, his shoulders slumped, still muttering to himself about how he should have known that what he was doing wasn't on the up-and-up.

He was a good kid and he had been taken advantage of by Amanda's father. I thought of the two times Costas had dropped by and wondered why he had come to see Wayne. Hadn't he known that planting the drugs in Wayne's room — for whatever reason — would either scare him off or get him in trouble with the school? Or had he stopped by to find out if Wayne was truly in the weeds, away from school and, more importantly, Amanda? I decided that I would work this all out with Crawford, who was my first phone call when I got back to my room. But, first, I had to do my job, which was to find out if all was well in Siena Hall.

Bart Johannsen and his lacrosse stick were on duty as usual, but the dorm was quiet as it normally was at this hour. Bart was dead asleep, his head on the desk, one hand still holding the lacrosse stick upright. Neat trick. My limbs usually go slack when I fall asleep but I don't have a possession as valuable as the mighty lacrosse stick. I ignored him for the time being, choosing instead to make sure the front door was locked before I called it a night. I went to the outer door and saw that someone had wedged a piece of wood under the bottom of the door, keeping it slightly ajar and making sure that anyone who entered wouldn't have to ring the bell and wake up our fair prince sitting desk. I pulled the wood out, disgusted by the laziness of the staff, and walked back to the desk, knocking the wood lightly on Bart's head.

"Hello?" I kept tapping until he woke up.

He finally jolted awake, the lacrosse stick clattering to the floor. He bent down and picked it up, the safety of the stick being his main concern. "What?" he asked, a little annoyed that he had been awakened.

I held out the piece of wood. "Did you know that someone propped open the door?" I asked. I dropped it on the desk for effect.

He rubbed his eyes. "No."

"Well, you would have if you had stayed awake."

He twirled the lacrosse stick. "Hey, get off my back. It's late. I'm exhausted."

"Something tells me you wouldn't have trouble staying awake if you were on your way to a party," I said. Gee — when had I turned into Sister Mary? I heard my voice and how I was talking to him and immediately toned it down. "Why don't you take off?" I asked. "You do look a little tired."

He looked at me like I was going to turn back into Mr. Hyde, but when he saw the concern on my face and my smile, he started collecting his books and his lacrosse gear.

"Thanks," he said before heading up the stairs, taking them two at a time.

I flipped through the logbook to see if there were any wayward visitors whom I needed to see off when eleven hit. No Mary Catherine, which made sense because Michael was working. None of our other usual suspects — girls or guys dating someone in the building. But there was one interesting entry: Costas Grigoriadis. He had signed in at nine-thirty and hadn't signed out. Had he come in and wanted to take Amanda to dinner, he wouldn't have needed to sign in, he would have just waited in the lobby until she had come down. So, that meant he was somewhere in the building. Was he in her room? I called Amanda's room and got her roommate, Shari.

"Hi, Shari, it's Dr. Bergeron."

She yawned. "Oh, hi, Dr. Bergeron."

"I hope I didn't wake you."

Clearly, I had, but she was kind enough to pretend otherwise. "No, that's okay," she said.

"Is Amanda there?"

She yawned again. Got it. You were sleeping, I thought. "No, she's out," she said. "She's sitting desk at Emanuelle tonight. One of the RAs needed coverage."

So where was Costas? That didn't make any sense. Shari yawned a third time, reminding me that I hadn't responded. "Thanks, Shari. Go back to bed."

Bart was long gone but I tried to call his room as well. There was no answer, leading me to believe that either Bart had immediately conked out upon arriving at his room or he had stopped somewhere along the way. I was too tired to try to find him. Instead, I went about locking up the building for the night. I looked into the TV room and saw that it was empty, despite the fact that the television was on. I wandered down the other end of the hall, away from my room, and checked the various rooms — the old dining room, another common room, and the room with an old piano in the corner — and saw that they were all empty.

I headed back to my room, and as I listened to my shoes make a clicking sound on the marble, I realized that Trixie wasn't making a sound as she usually did when she heard me approaching. I put my hand on the knob, curious about the silence that greeted me. I had my keys in hand but it turned out I didn't need them; the door was unlocked. I couldn't remember if I had left it like that or not. When I opened the door to my room and entered, seeing Costas sitting in a chair in my parlor room, I only had one question.

"What did you do with my dog?"

When he didn't respond, I repeated my question. "What did you do with my dog?"

Costas beckoned me to come into the parlor, but I stood in the doorway to the dorm, looking around to see if Trixie was anywhere in the suite. A quick look told me she wasn't in the bathroom, and if she was in the parlor, she was drugged because there was no way she would have allowed Costas to come into the room without setting up a howl. A howl that even the comatose Bart Johannsen would have heard in the midst of his snore-filled slumber.

"I'm not coming in, and I'm not leaving until you tell me where the dog is," I said, my panic increasing with the realization that she wasn't in the room.

"The dog's fine," he said. "Come in. I want to have a little chat with you." He remained in the chair. Had I had warmer feelings toward Costas, I would have warned him of the black mold that was probably eating away at the decades-old Styrofoam cushions inside the chintz upholstery.

"I can hear you just fine from here," I said. "Talk."

"There seems to have been some misunderstanding," he said.

The strains of "Cracklin' Rosie" filled my head and I attempted to stay with the conversation. After getting up as early as I had, and after what I had done all day, including the trip to Newark, I was exhausted.

When I didn't answer, he continued. "You see, my daughter loves Brandon. She's going to marry him in August, despite your attempts to break the two of them up."

"She's not sure if she loves him." And I knew a thing or two about being married to a spouse who doesn't love you. I was something of an authority on the subject.

"She does. She loves him very much. They've been together for four years and she's going to be very happy. She's going to have a very happy, very secure life," he said. "Just like her mother."

"She was in love with Wayne until recently. She's a young girl and she's very confused." I leaned against the doorjamb. "Did you come all the way here to admonish me about listening to your daughter talk about love? Because that's all that's happened."

He shook his head sadly. "If only that were the truth. You sent that woman to see us tonight. You want to know something. I'm just not sure what it is."

"I want to know why you are forcing Amanda to marry Brandon. I want to know why two thugs from Newark, where your company is located, beat her up. I want to know why the bulk of your business comes from men going back and forth to Mexico and Latin America. And I want to know why," I said, going out on a limb, "I found a brick of heroin in Wayne's room when the strongest thing he's ever had in his possession is pot." I left out the fact that they were multiple bags of pot, but that didn't seem to be a necessary detail. I crossed my arms over my chest. "Does that answer your question?"

"Those are just questions, not answers." Costas leaned forward in the chair, his weight making it tip toward me slightly. I resisted the urge to tell him to be careful; if he fell flat on his face and busted his nose, it would give me a chance to hightail it out of the building and over to the security booth at the entrance to campus, not that the guys in there would be much help. Not when there were doughnuts to be consumed. Costas stood. "Let's take a ride."

I ran out into the hallway and headed to the side door. But Costas was faster than his stocky, Neil Diamond body would suggest and he was on me before I had a chance to get the door open, the old knob its usual cranky self, barely budging when I tried to turn it. He grabbed my shoulder and dragged me back into my suite, throwing me onto the bed and slamming the door behind us.

I sat up straight and watched him as he paced the room. "How did you get in here?" I asked, gesturing around the room.

He smiled. "Easy. After that kid at the

desk fell asleep, I went into his knapsack and took the master keys."

I would have to have a word with Bart when this was over. If I was still alive. "What do you want?"

"I want you to stop interfering in my family's life."

"That would have taken a phone call, Costas. This is a little extreme," I said, chuckling, but not feeling amused. I moved to the edge of the bed so that if I had to, I would be able to get off the sagging mattress quickly. Sitting in the middle of the bed would keep me entombed on the depressed, springless mattress.

He pointed at my face. "You're very nosy."

"So I've heard."

"And you've stuck your nose in where it doesn't belong."

"Like where? Like where you had a young kid who needed money for school take drug dealers back and forth to the airport? Or how you had him act as an unwitting drug mule for you?" My voice was shaking, more from anger than fear. "Or like where you planted drugs in Wayne's room to scare him off campus and away from your daughter? Is that where I've been sticking my nose?"

His face changed a few times, and it looked like he was deciding whether to go with indignant, denial, or straight to confession. But if he confessed, he was going to paint himself into a corner, because then he would have to make sure that I went away. Forever. I didn't entertain that possibility as I pushed him on the details. "So, did you start with Wayne and then ask him for a recommendation for a patsy? Michael Columbo is a nice kid. You could have ruined his life."

"Better his life ruined than my business go bankrupt," he said, although that was no excuse for what he had done.

"You have Nicholas. You don't need anything else," I said, assuming that Nicholas had infused T&G with the cash it needed to stay afloat.

Costas did a double take. "Nicholas?"

I didn't say anything.

"Nicholas?" he asked again, this time letting out a belly laugh. "Are you kidding me?" He leaned in close to me and I got a whiff of pungent aftershave. "Nicholas is so busy paying alimony and paying off Brandon's college expenses that he doesn't have a pot to piss in."

"He didn't give you any money toward the company?" It wasn't the first time one of my theories was out of left field and proven wrong but I had been pretty dead certain that this one was right.

"At first, but that's gone," he said, leaning against my dresser and folding his arms across his chest. I took this as a sign that he was letting down his guard and peppered him with more questions.

"So you decided to start a 'side business,' " I said, "to make a little extra cash? I bet that's lucrative. That oughta keep you afloat for a while, huh?"

His guard wasn't completely down; he didn't answer the question.

"So, Wayne. You planted the drugs in his room. Why?"

He didn't mind telling me the answer to that one. "I wanted him away from Amanda. And he was going to expose the whole plan." He smiled at a recollection. "Moron was trying to blackmail me."

So there it was. He did want Wayne away from Amanda, but more than that, he wanted Wayne to go away for good, not exposing the illegal doings at T&G.

"What was to stop Wayne from exposing you once the police picked him up? What made you so confident that he was going to run?"

He laughed. "Because I had a little dirt on him, too."

Right, I thought. That made sense.

"And he's a loser. I made a bet that he would try to disappear and I was right." He laced his fingers together. "That's why I stopped by. I wanted to make sure he was gone."

He had tried to disappear all right. But the first rule of trying to disappear is to leave the premises completely. Going to the convent was a bad move all around.

"And if he stayed, and tried to implicate me, there was nothing that would reveal me. I'm a respected businessman in Newark. Nobody would have believed a cockamamie story coming from a two-bit pot dealer." His smile got wider when he thought of his plan and how flawlessly it had been executed. The only snafu was when I moved in and starting nosing around.

I wanted to know something else. "Why are you so hell-bent on Amanda marrying Brandon?"

"He's Greek, he's smart, and I know his family. He loves my stepdaughter . . . no, he adores her. What could be better?" he asked. "I met my wife two times before I got married," he said, putting up two fingers. "We were married twenty-five years before she died. She was the best thing that ever happened to me," he said, his eyes misty at the remembrance of the first Mrs. Grigoriadis.

"With the exception of Victoria," he said, quickly amending his original contention. "And, of course, my stepdaughter." He straightened up suddenly. "Okay, trip down memory lane is over. Let's go."

"Let's go?" I asked, a knot growing in my stomach. "Where?"

He looked at me sadly. "You don't need to know that."

I don't know why I had thought this man — an obviously loving husband and father — would tell me all of this and then just leave. Of course he had planned on killing me all along. A tear ran down my face. "Just go and none of this will ever leave this room. I won't tell a soul."

"You already have," he reminded me. "Don't you have a boyfriend who's a cop?"

I nodded. That revelation usually gets me in trouble in situations like this.

Costas continued with his train of thought. "He'll figure it out. But if you're gone, he'll be focused on other things. This whole thing," he said, throwing his arms wide, "will go away. The kid's not going to say anything, right?"

I thought about Michael Columbo and his terrified face when we figured out exactly what he was doing to put himself through school, and I realized that he would be just as happy quitting his job and never speaking of his employment at T&G ever again. "They'll know it's you."

Costas shook his head. "No. They won't." He reached into a small bag on my dresser — one that I hadn't noticed previously — and pulled out a syringe filled with some kind of liquid.

I didn't know what it could be, but I let my mind wander into some very depressing territory. "What's that?" I asked.

He turned. "Heroin. Grade A stuff. You'll have a nice trip and then" — he snapped his fingers — "nothing."

All of a sudden, "Cracklin' Rosie" sounded very sinister to me; I wouldn't ever listen to it the same way again. "Hey," I said, trying to throw him off while I concocted a way out of the situation, "has anyone ever told you that you look like Neil Diamond?"

Costas let a small smile play on his lips. "You're a very strange woman." He held the syringe up and tapped it with his finger.

"And do you know what a 'store-bought woman' is?" I asked, a sob escaping from my throat as he grabbed me and pulled me up. Outside my door, I heard the familiar sound of nails tapping on marble, and I managed to let out a scream before he

440

lunged toward me and put a meaty hand over my mouth. Trixie set up a howl on the other side of the door and I heard Bart Johannsen's voice.

"Professor Bergeron?" he called. "Are you okay?"

I looked at Costas, my eyes wide. His grip tightened. He looked from me to the door several times.

Bart began banging on the door. "Professor Bergeron?"

I started to squirm and thrash, succeeding in knocking the syringe from Costas's hand, and giving him a big, hard kick in the shins. When his hand slipped a little I let out another garbled scream.

Bart stopped knocking and I prayed that he was smart enough to do what I thought he would do, rather than run for help. As I heard his body make contact with the old door for the first time, I said a silent prayer of thanks that good, old, lazy, sleeping Bart had a better head on his shoulders than I would have thought. I imagined his giant Scandinavian body — broad shoulders and tree-trunk legs — being hurled against the door and hoped that the door would cave in before Costas broke my neck or choked me to death.

Costas let me go and scrambled after the

syringe. I jumped on his back and began to hit him around the head; he used the hand not holding the syringe to swat at me. He stood and shook me off, and I fell against the dresser, which hit me in the small of the back. I started for the door, but he blocked my path, knocking me sideways onto the bed. He stood and pulled his arm back, ready to stab me anywhere he could. On my back, I had one last chance, and I used it; I pulled my legs back and, with all my might, kicked him in the crown jewels.

Bart crashed through the door at exactly the same moment as Costas crumbled to the floor, grabbing his crotch and writhing in pain. Trixie was right behind him and she circled Costas, knowing instinctively that he wasn't a nice man. She took a chunk out of his calf for good measure and the sound that Costas let out was something I hoped I would never hear again. Bart took in the scene and looked at me.

"I can't find my master key," he said, as if he had come into the room in the conventional way.

I was out of breath and I gasped for air. "It's okay," I said, bending over and putting my hands on my knees. I looked up at him. "Thanks."

"Is that Amanda's dad?" he asked, pointing at Costas.

"Doesn't matter," I gasped, reaching for the phone. I dialed 9 for an outside line and called 911. "You watch him, and if he makes a move to get up, bust his head open."

I knew that lacrosse stick would come in handy eventually.

Thirty-Five

I had to sit on my suitcase to close it, pulling the zipper around the side while jumping up and down to see if I could squash the contents down any more than I had originally. Trixie was staring at me. I guess I did look kind of odd: I was dressed in my graduation outfit of black robe and goofy velvet doctoral tam.

"I know. It's ridiculous looking," I said, finally getting the zipper all the way around. I hadn't realized how much I had brought over to the dorm in the last several weeks, but I certainly had more to bring home than I had come with when I moved in. I dragged the suitcase off the bed and took a look around the room. "Say good-bye to hell, Trix."

She responded by giving me a halfhearted woof.

"I know. You're going to miss the cemetery and the river." I bent down and kissed the top of her head. "I promise. We'll come back and visit."

Things had settled down considerably since the "Costas affair," as I had taken to calling it and everyone who had had some involvement seemed to be getting on with their lives.

Costas had sung like a bird once he was in police custody, and had given up the other thug who had beaten up Amanda and who was still on the loose as well as everyone who had ever used T&G for anything other than car service. Turned out Costas wasn't quite as slick as he thought he was; he owed someone very high up in a drug cartel a lot of money for the heroin brick he had planted in Wayne's room and those people don't play around. Unbeknownst to me, they had set his wife's car on fire when she was shopping at Target in addition to beating the hell out of Amanda. It didn't do him too much good to give the guy up, but maybe it made him feel better. I didn't know. And I certainly didn't care.

He was going to jail for a long time, that was for sure.

I knew that the business was still going, though now that its main source of income had been cut off, and the papers had written about the story in detail, it was hanging on by a thread. Brandon and Amanda's chance for having a financially secure future were certainly impacted by Costas's decision to turn to the dark side in order to save his business, one that he had started with a thousand bucks and a dream after emigrating from Greece back in the seventies.

As for the rest of the players: Michael Columbo eventually lost the thousand-mile stare that he adopted after being subjected to a police interrogation and living with the knowledge that he had been an unwitting player in a drug operation. He had one more year to go at St. Thomas and I was helping him figure out how he was going to stay, looking at financial aid packages and loans that would give him a financial hand.

Bart Johannsen reveled in his role as my savior and seemed to be getting more booty calls than he had before he saved my life. Fortunately, when Costas had decided to pay a visit to Siena dorm, Bart had actually been awake and had forced him to sign in, even though Costas had said he was "just staying for a minute." If I hadn't seen Costas's name in the logbook, I never would have expected to see him. I don't know that that had helped me in any way, but at least I hadn't been totally surprised. Bart told me that after he had left the desk, he had decided to do some laundry, completely refreshed after his nap during working hours. When he went to the basement, he had found Trixie tied to a dryer and extremely agitated. He knew that I wouldn't leave my dog in the laundry room and had decided to investigate. And I thank God that he did.

My last few weeks at school were spent hunting young women down and urging them to leave Siena, and Bart's warm embrace, before visitation ended. Bart still fell asleep every time he sat desk but I decided that I really was in no position to take him to task for it. The lacrosse team had had a great season and went to sectionals, losing in the first round.

Mary Catherine Donnery, in a move that shocked even me, stayed with Michael Columbo during his dark hour, helping to coax him out of the depression into which he had fallen. She still tried to break curfew every chance she got, but I always caught her. I think. She was pretty slippery.

Wayne was out on bail pending his trial, living with his very disappointed parents. I got little information from Sister Mary, who was still angry at me for some reason, despite the fact that her darling nephew had been keeping half of St. Thomas high. I don't know who Pinto or Etheridge paid off, but the story was kept pretty quiet so there wasn't much to see in the paper. Wayne had been arrested in Scarsdale and that's where the story stayed. Wayne's former employment was mentioned in the news stories but the giant bag of pot and where it had been found was mysteriously missing information. Crawford told me what he knew, but since he really wasn't all that interested in what had become of Wayne Brookwell, I didn't get too many details.

For obvious reasons, the Brookwells and the Varicks were no longer on speaking terms.

Amanda hadn't mentioned Wayne since that night on the driveway.

I felt kind of bad that I had suspected Brandon of wrongdoing in the whole T&G/Wayne thing but I had been grasping at straws at that point. If I ever had a chance to see Brandon again — and I suspected that graduation day might provide that opportunity — I would apologize to him. It wouldn't be the first time I had mistakenly accused someone and, if my track record proved anything, it wouldn't be the last.

As for me, I decided to move out of the dorm on graduation day and return home. I chose to put the red bedroom behind me and had hired an old friend to repaint it; I never discussed it with Max and she never brought it up. Merrimack had warned me that if they hadn't found a suitable candidate for the resident director position by the beginning of August, I would be moving back in.

I told him to stick it.

There was a soft knock on the door; it was Kevin, someone I hadn't spent a lot of time with in the past few weeks. He took in my getup and chuckled. "Nice hat."

"You say that every year," I said. "And people in Roman collars shouldn't throw stones."

"A mixed metaphor coming from our esteemed literature professor?" he asked.

I took his arm and pulled him into the room, leaving the door open. The last thing I needed was someone seeing our campus chaplain emerging from the previously closed door to my suite. "What's up, Kevin?" I asked, returning to my packing.

"Going somewhere?"

I thought that was obvious. "Hopefully, I'm going home."

"Really?"

"Yes. Really." I got worried; did Kevin know something about my situation that I didn't? I thought I had been pretty clear with Merrimack about my plans to leave.

"I don't think they've found Wayne's replacement yet."

I threw my toiletry kit on top of my suitcase. "Not my problem."

Kevin clapped his hands together. "Okay. Subject change. I just want to say, for the very last time hopefully, that I'm very, very sorry about what happened with Max and Fred. And I'm asking for your forgiveness."

I stared at Kevin for a few minutes. "Come here," I said, holding out my arms to give him a hug.

"I think I'll stay here," he said, pointing to the ground. "But thank you. I wanted to make sure everything was okay between us."

"It's fine, Kev," I said. We had seen each other a few times since everything had happened but we hadn't cleared the air officially. He was embarrassed and I was angry. But time heals, as they say. I have two best friends — and he's one of them. I didn't want to waste any more time being angry at a situation that would eventually resolve itself.

He was on an even shorter leash than usual when it came to the archdiocese and had stepped up his efforts around campus to become the best chaplain St. Thomas had ever seen. When he started a Tuesday night Scripture study group for the students, I knew that he was trying to stay out of trouble and get back in the bishop's good graces.

"See you at graduation?" he asked, smiling.

"You will. I'll be the one in the velvet tam," I said, doffing my hat.

After he left, I did one more sweep of the bathroom, making sure that everything I had brought in with me was removed. When I came out, Amanda was in the doorway, looking less like the funky communications student she had been during her time at St. Thomas and more like a young woman. Her hair in a loose bun, she was wearing a pretty black and white dress with an empire waist and patent leather T-strap pumps. "Hi, Professor Bergeron." She only met my eyes for an instant before looking down.

"Amanda! I hardly recognized you," I said. "Come in, come in." She sat on the edge of my bed and watched while I pulled some books off the shelf in the parlor room. "Are you excited about graduation?"

She nodded but not before her eyes filled with tears. "I am."

I knew why she was crying but I didn't press it. Costas was in jail, awaiting a trial for drug trafficking, assault and battery (me), money laundering, and a host of other transgressions. Amanda and I had spoken a few times since my final encounter with her stepfather but we had never talked in detail about that night. But I could only imagine what she felt: betrayal, hurt, shock. Costas, the man she thought she could trust and could count on — the man who had changed her life as well as her mother's — was nothing more than a criminal. I sat down on the bed next to her and attempted a pep talk, something I'm not great at giving.

"You've got your whole life in front of you, Amanda. What Costas did has nothing to do with you or where you're headed."

"I know," she said softly. "I really do."

I put my hand over hers and even Trixie came over and rested her head on the bed next to Amanda. "Are you going through with the wedding?" I asked.

She shrugged. "I'm not sure. Brandon really does love me but I'm not sure what I want to do right now."

It was out of my mouth before I could think. "Then wait." I realized that it was none of my business but I couldn't help myself. She had to wait. Her mental health depended on it. Her whole life depended on it.

"I won the Communications Award," she said, changing the subject, a little embarrassed at the revelation.

"So I heard!" I said. "Sister Donna spilled the beans." Give the head of the communications department a glass of chardonnay and she would reveal every secret she had. I smiled, thinking of her confiding in me during our final faculty cocktail party of the year. "I can't imagine anyone who deserves it more."

She got up from the bed. "I'll see you at graduation?"

"You'll see me at graduation," I confirmed and wrapped her in a big bear hug.

"Professor Bergeron?" she said from her muffled place between my chest and my underarm.

"Yes, Amanda?"

"I can't breathe."

I let go. "Sorry." I dropped my arms. Over her head, I spied Brandon in the doorway.

"You're still here?" he asked Amanda, a big smile on his face. He held his hand out and we shook. "Hi, Professor Bergeron. Amanda told me she was coming by to say good-bye to you."

"Hi, Brandon. It's good to see you again."

He was unbelievably gracious to me, despite the fact that I had accused him of a number of activities that he obviously had never been involved in.

Amanda reached out for Brandon's hand. "I'm ready."

I followed the two of them into the hallway, bustling with activity as students packed to leave for the summer, greeted their families for the graduation ceremony, and said good-bye to friends. I reached out and touched Brandon's shoulder. "Wait."

He turned. "I'll catch up with you, Amanda," he said, and she started down the hallway.

I crossed my arms over my chest, not sure where to begin. I decided to start with an apology. "I'm sorry, Brandon. I really am."

He stopped me before I could go any further with an explanation. "You were looking out for her. That's all that really matters."

I was amazed by his maturity. "Well, thanks, then."

"No. Thank you," he said and shook my hand again. "Hopefully, we'll see you soon."

I knew what he meant — the wedding — but I also knew that Amanda was going to take her time in making her decision on their relationship. "Good luck, Brandon."

He nodded. I had to admit, he had grown on me. Whereas I had once thought him old-fashioned and possibly controlling, I now could see how much he cared about Amanda.

"Go. Go meet up with Amanda and her family. I'll see you in a little while."

My bags were packed and sitting by the door when Crawford showed up a few minutes later. "You look sexy," he said, taking in my robe and tam.

"That's because I am sexy," I said. "I'm not wearing anything under this robe."

"You're kidding."

"Yes, I am," I said, unzipping my robe to expose my very boring dress.

He snapped his fingers. "Too bad." He walked into the room and greeted Trixie. "After graduation, I'm buying you the biggest martini known to mankind, some kind of red meat, and then I'm taking you back to my place for some —"

"Gymnastics?"

He smiled. "Good enough." He ran a finger over the top of the dresser, coming up with a fingerful of dust. "Promise me you'll wear that hat."

"You know it."

He leaned against the dresser, just like

Costas had a few weeks before as he prepared to kill me with an overdose of heroin. "Pick the place and the martinis are on me."

"You do know that graduation is over by one? It's a little early to start pounding martinis."

He pushed forward off the dresser and came toward me. "You've been living in this dump for over a month." He put his arms around me and the past five weeks of celibate hell came flooding back at once. I got a little weak. "We need to celebrate."

"You're right," I whispered, having lost my voice.

"We've got to get you out of here," he said. "The sooner, the better."

I looked out of the corner of my eye at the clock on the nightstand and saw that I had to go. "You coming with me?" I asked, still enjoying being in his embrace.

"I'm not letting you out of my sight," he said.

And I believe he meant it.

THIRTY-SIX

Crawford and I went down to the office of the City Clerk on a balmy day in early June for a wedding.

School was over and things, for me, had slowed down considerably. Amanda graduated, with honors as well as the Communications Award, and had secured herself a job at Crime TV, thanks to a few pulled strings from Max. But even though she had gotten into the company through a connection, Max told me that everyone at the network was impressed with Amanda; she came in early, stayed late, and worked as hard as anyone they had ever seen. She was living at home with her mother and seemed happy, according to Max who saw her on a daily basis. Although she was a bit embarrassed about doing postproduction on the Hooters waitress show, Max promised her it was a stepping stone to bigger and better things.

I hoped she was right.

Max and I had reached détente, although she kept calling it "deterrence." She had suggested that we meet for dinner at her favorite restaurant in Manhattan, and I had agreed, thinking that meeting in a public place was a far better idea than either my house (the red bedroom would have certainly come up) or her apartment (her Neanderthal not-her-husband lurking around). We went through pretty much everything, and ultimately, agreed to disagree about the events that had led to our falling-out.

I looked down from my perch on the steps to see if I could see Crawford; he was ambling down the street, the tallest guy in the midst of a throng of Asian tourists, as if we had all the time in the world. We didn't. We were actually cutting it kind of close. I had gotten a new dress for the occasion, a backless halter number that felt like it would slide off at any moment, but which I had been talked into by the salesgirl at Neiman Marcus. I had on my most expensive pair of shoes, a pair of Jimmy Choos that Max had given me when she had tired of seeing me in my Dansko clogs for an extended period of time. They were beaded sandals that I loved though I got a little nauseous every time I thought of how much they cost. I had to admit, though, I looked like a million bucks. Even Crawford, who isn't prone to declarations of love or lust, gave me a wolf whistle when I approached him on the steps of City Hall. I could feel my cheeks go red.

"Wow. Coco, you've outdone yourself," he said, making me do a little twirl to get the full effect. He leaned in and gave me a long kiss. "Seriously. You look gorgeous."

"Thanks," I said, rolling my eyes. I'm not good at taking compliments. "Let's just remember that you've only had sex a few times in the past three months, so you may not be the best judge of 'gorgeous.' "

"Good point," he said, grabbing me around the waist. "Ready?"

We ran up the stairs and went through the metal detectors, Crawford taking a little longer because of the firepower he was carrying in his holster and on his ankle. Once through, we made our way to the City Clerk's office, where civil marriages in the state of New York took place. When I had heard that we would be standing up as the witnesses at the wedding, I didn't think it would be very romantic, having only attended religious services. But when we got to the City Clerk's office and saw all of the couples standing there, in business attire to full-blown wedding wear, and how happy they were, I changed my mind. A bride was a bride, and if she was happy, it didn't matter where or how she got married to the love of her life.

Kevin was waiting for us when we got to the office. I was glad that we had settled our differences over the Max and Fred affair, and I know he was, too. He waved enthusiastically as he saw us coming down the hall.

"Great day, huh?" he said, beaming. I didn't think he'd be this excited to be at a wedding that he wasn't officiating at, but he was clearly thrilled. "Where's the happy couple?" he asked.

Crawford looked around, able to see over the heads of the diverse grouping of couples in the hallway. "I don't see them."

I surveyed the crowd. "Me, either."

"I hope they're not late," Kevin said. "They've already started calling names."

And just as he said that, the clerk's assistant came out of the office. "Ms. Maxine Rayfield and Mr. Charlemagne Wyatt? Ms. Rayfield and Mr. Wyatt?"

I looked at Crawford. "Charlemagne?"

He shrugged. "I had no idea." He wasn't as shocked as I was, but after working with

Fred for as long as he had, nothing shocked him anymore.

I turned to Kevin. "Charlemagne?"

Kevin went pale. "I was to take it to my grave."

"You knew?"

Kevin nodded. We looked around some more. Kevin leaned in and whispered in my ear, trying to change the subject. "You may just go to hell for wearing that dress."

"I'm willing to take that chance," I said.

The clerk was getting impatient. "Ms. Rayfield and Mr. Wyatt!"

I heard Max's voice come from behind us. "We're coming! We're here!" She ran down the hallway, a little pixie in a tight, short red dress, and the highest heels I had ever seen. I didn't know how she could walk, never mind run, in them, but there she was, sprinting like a champ in five-inch heels. Fred was lumbering along behind her, still a foot and half taller than her in spite of the high heels. He looked sort of hand-some, I guess, in a sport coat and khaki pants, an outfit that he would wear to the coroner's office or to a homicide. And now, to his wedding.

I mentioned my interest in Fred's sarto-rial choice to Crawford. "He went to an autopsy right before this," he said, as if that answered the question.

"Huh," I said, nodding, as if I found this to be the most normal thing in the world to do before your wedding.

Max and Fred made it to our little group and the five of us walked to the clerk. We were led into the small room where the judge presided over the marriages. Max and Fred faced each other and I thought about how different this was from their St. Thomas wedding: three hundred people; Max in a big, white dress, Fred in a tuxedo; Max's father crying as he walked down the aisle. Here, we stood in front of a man in a suit in a nondescript courtroom in a city building. Boy, how things had changed.

But Max still cried when she said "I do," and Fred still looked like he was going to the guillotine, which, given the events of the past couple of months, was probably appropriate. But he cracked a little smile when the judge pronounced them "husband and wife" and Max jumped in his arms, showering me with petals from the bouquet that she was holding.

I spat out a couple of the petals and looked around the happy couple at Crawford, who was looking back at me, a bemused smile on his face. We exited the room and went out into the hallway where the other couples, guessing that Max and Fred were now married, broke out into applause.

Because the day was so beautiful, we all decided to walk to the restaurant that Max had chosen for us to have lunch. We were the only guests; Max had decided, in a display of remarkable restraint and judgment, not to tell her parents about her fake marriage, deciding instead to go ahead and get married civilly without anyone being the wiser. There was no reason for her devoutly Catholic parents to know that Kevin had screwed up, she had left her husband for a couple of weeks, and that they had decided to remarry at City Hall. It was just much too complicated, messy, and tawdry for the Rayfields. I was glad that they would never know anything of what had transpired in their daughter's life during the spring of this year.

Crawford and I trailed behind the two of them, holding hands. Kevin was chatting with Max about her dress and completely taken up with that.

"That was nicer than I would have expected," Crawford said, giving my hand a little squeeze. We weaved in and out of the throngs of people in downtown Manhattan, keeping an eye on Fred's bald dome, which bobbed up and down like a buoy in a sea of tourists.

"Yeah, who knew that City Hall weddings could be so romantic?" I asked, choking up. This wasn't how I expected the story of Max and Fred to end, but as I had learned after being friends with Max for as long as I had, nothing was ever what it seemed. Her life followed a different trajectory from mine and who was to say that that was wrong?

My feet were starting to hurt and I looked down at my gorgeous sandals thinking that a hike on city streets really wasn't what I had had in mind when I had gotten dressed that morning.

"So, what do you think?" Crawford asked.

I examined my toes as I walked, looking for signs of blisters. "What do I think of what?"

He hooked a thumb back toward City Hall. "That. Weddings."

"I just told you," I said, feeling a blister start on the back of my right heel. "It was more romantic than I thought it would be."

"You think so?"

I stopped at a lamppost and pulled my leg up behind me to examine my heel. "Oh, great. Now I have a blister."

Crawford grabbed my hand. "What do you think?"

I was completely preoccupied by my

blistered feet and I grabbed on to the pole to steady myself now that Crawford had claimed my other hand. "What do I think of what?" I asked, losing patience with a conversation that seemingly had no subject.

He shrugged. "You know."

I sighed. "I really don't, Crawford." I looked down the block and could see Max, Fred, and Kevin crossing the street in front of a Duane Reade drugstore. "There's a drugstore. Would you go and buy me a box of Band-Aids?"

Crawford had a weird look on his face; it was a cross between exasperated and unnerved. He started down the street and went into the drugstore, coming out ten minutes later with a small bag. I had given up all hope of following Max and Fred and they didn't seem to wonder where we were; in my small purse was the name and number of the restaurant and I knew that it was only a few blocks away. But still . . . I would wonder where we were. I guess the giddy lovestruck couple was only interested in each other. And the priest tagging alongside the bride.

He came back and took the box of Band-Aids out of the bag. When I had finished bandaging up my foot — it took three Band-Aids to take care of the damage and that really compromised the look of the sandals — I thanked him for the first-aid run.

He reached back into the bag. "I have one more thing." He pulled out a cherry ring pop, which was essentially a giant, diamond-shaped piece of hard candy on a ring.

I clapped my hands together gleefully. "I love ring pops!" I said. "I haven't had one of these in years!" I held out my hand and Crawford slid it onto my ring finger. "You know that means we're engaged, right?" I sucked on the candy. "I take my ring-pop proposals very seriously."

He looked at me and smiled. "That's what I was hoping."

ABOUT THE AUTHOR

Maggie Barbieri's father was a member of the NYPD, and his stories provide much of the background for her novels. This is her fourth *Murder 101* mystery; Kristin Davis of *Sex in the City* has optioned the series for television. Maggie lives in Westchester County, New York.

We hope you have enjoyed this Large Print book. Other Thorndike, Wheeler, Kennebec, and Chivers Press Large Print books are available at your library or directly from the publishers.

For information about current and upcoming titles, please call or write, without obligation, to:

Publisher
Thorndike Press
295 Kennedy Memorial Drive
Waterville, ME 04901
Tel. (800) 223-1244

or visit our Web site at:

http://gale.cengage.com/thorndike

OR

Chivers Large Print
published by BBC Audiobooks Ltd
St James House, The Square
Lower Bristol Road
Bath BA2 3SB
England
Tel. +44(0) 800 136919
email: bbcaudiobooks@bbc.co.uk
www.bbcaudiobooks.co.uk

All our Large Print titles are designed for easy reading, and all our books are made to last.